LAST NEW
BEGINNING

By the Author

Something Between Us

Last New Beginning

Visit us at www.boldstrokesbooks.com

LAST NEW BEGINNING

by

Krystina Rivers

2023

ISBN 13: 978-1-63679-261-3

THIS TRADE PAPERBACK ORIGINAL IS PUBLISHED BY
BOLD STROKES BOOKS, INC.
P.O. BOX 249
VALLEY FALLS, NY 12185

FIRST EDITION: JANUARY 2023

CREDITS
EDITOR: BARBARA ANN WRIGHT
PRODUCTION DESIGN: STACIA SEAMAN
COVER DESIGN BY JEANINE HENNING

Acknowledgments

I think for a lot of people, 2020 is a year that will go down as one of the worst years experienced by those alive today. And while, with no end in sight, I watched the news in horror with climbing death tolls and was terrified for the people I love, for me personally, 2020 wasn't terrible. I was incredibly lucky to not have been touched personally by any COVID deaths or serious illnesses, and I thoroughly enjoyed working from home. It was fun to spend so much time with my wife, actually eat meals together, and sexually harass each other at the "water cooler." Although it was very hard not seeing the rest of my family for a year any place other than on a screen, it was nice to not be on the road for work all the time. I used quite a bit of this newly acquired free time to tap into my creative side and write my first book, *Something Between Us*.

When 2021 came along, the world started to open back up. I went back in the office and on the road but with a changed view of life and how lucky I am to have the life I have with my wife, our fur babies, our house, and our extended families. I also started writing this book… But then 2022 arrived. The year that I hate with a passion. I lost my grandfather, whom I lived next door to for my entire childhood and who was like a second father to me, only a couple of weeks into the year. I had a breast cancer scare, and I lost my best writing buddy, Citrus, our twenty-pound floofy orange cat. I also did all of this without my wife sitting next to me and holding my hand as she has done for every difficult thing we've endured in the last twenty-one years because she had to report for a deployment with the National Guard the day after my grandfather passed away. So to say I loathe 2022 doesn't come close to expressing how I feel.

And yet the bright spot of it, what has gotten me through most of it, is what you are holding in your hands now: this book and everything that goes along with being a new author. Writing, editing, creating, attending events where I have been privileged to meet other authors and readers…all of this became my therapy this year.

So firstly, thank you to all of the readers in the world who choose to pick up one of my books. Without you, none of this happens, so you have my deepest gratitude.

Thank you to everyone at Bold Strokes Books who has taken a chance on me, supported me, and rooted for me. Rad and Sandy, thank you for continuing to allow me to chase my dream with you. A special thank you to my favorite editor, Barbara Ann Wright. I see so many writers online who dread getting their edits back and going through them. I love every moment that I edit with you. Your commentary makes me laugh until I cry (especially about Jennifer), and all of the work we do together makes my books a thousand times better.

Thank you to my wife, Kerri. You are my biggest fan, my constant source of confidence, my best friend, and not a day goes by that I don't give thanks for you. By the time anyone reads this, we will be together again, but as I write this, we still have about a month and a half to go, and I could not wish these days to go by any faster than I already do. Thank you for helping me with ideas, plot points, homophones (looking at you, complement/compliment), and for always being my first and only beta reader. I'm grateful that you love me despite my numerous faults including but not limited to: how much time I spend writing, how much time I spend on the road or at the office, and how much I love wine. I love you with all of my heart, and although I love our video dates, I cannot wait until you are back in my arms. You are the reason I can write about love. It's always for you.

To Citrus, the best writing buddy there ever was. You always tried to give me carpal tunnel, but your snuggles helped get me through my most difficult plot points. You were the goodest, sweetest boy, and your mommies love you so much.

Thank you to my entire family. Your support of both me and *Something Between Us* is nothing short of amazing to me, and I am so lucky to have all of you. Mom, your never-wavering belief in me since birth has always made me know I can do anything I set my mind to. Mom Angel, your hugs give me life, as does your steady support and love. Cheryl, it's been so fun to be on writing journeys at the same time, but I've said this before, and I really mean it this time: You're next. Dad, Catey, Mindy, you all are amazing, and I love you. Pop Fain, you were always the steady one, helping to guide us and reminding us that our family was special and to be treasured. You were right, and I am so grateful to have had you for thirty-nine years of my life. You are in my heart now and always.

To all of my new author friends who are too many to call out individually…I am so glad I found you. Or maybe I'm so glad you decided to adopt me. Kris, Ana, Morgan…my nugs. You have been rocks for me of late and I love you for it. I can't imagine this writing world, or any world, without you.

To everyone I'm friends with on the interwebs…although we may not have met in person, your community and support mean more to me than you know. For those of you still working on your first stories, I know you can do it. For those of you who are strictly readers, thank you for being you and interacting. For those of you who provide mentorship and support, thank you for your generosity. I love this sapphic community, and I am so grateful to be a part of it.

Finally, to all the strong, badass women out there; all the women who have probably been called unsavory names behind their backs and behind closed doors; all the women who came before us to pave the way, the women I walk beside today and aspire to be like, and the women who will carry the torch into the future…thank you. I see you and we've got this. Kerri, Mom (Michele), Mom Angel, Mom Josie, Cheryl, Catherine, Malinda, Aunt Joanne, Deb, Beth, Heather, Karen, Jill, Kim, Teresa, Melanie, Karen, Allison, Julia, Adrienne, every author I know, and everyone else I'm running out of room to name, but you know who you are…Following your path and being badasses. I love you. I appreciate your confidence, your strength, your heart, and your willingness to persevere and overcome.

To Mom Angel and Pop Fain,
whose lifetime of love has inspired generations
and without which none of this would be possible.

CHAPTER ONE

Skye Kohl stood under a borrowed black umbrella, her irritation increasing with each breath as taxi after taxi sped by despite her outstretched hand. Hopefulness blossomed as every car approached and was dashed as each one sped past. Hell. She should've known better than to think she could run downstairs at the last minute in the pouring rain and immediately grab a taxi. Normally, it wasn't an issue, as her office was on Wacker Drive, and cabs regularly whizzed by. However, in an early spring downpour, she was just as likely to find a hundred-dollar bill sitting on the sidewalk as an empty taxi.

Skye checked her watch again, jaw clenched. If there was one thing she hated, it was being late. Technically, she wasn't going to be late—yet—but as a commercial real estate broker, anything less than thirty minutes early was late, and even that was pushing it. Forty-five minutes early was better. An hour, ideal. She needed time to get to the building, pretend to be friendly with the security guard, get all the lights turned on, and open the blinds to make sure the empty space would show as well as possible. And she needed time to verify that she was still presentable and have a cushion in case the prospective tenants were ahead of schedule on their tours.

And this taxi situation was getting dire. She probably should have called a Lyft, given the weather, but she really hated taking rideshares. Unfortunately, she'd mistakenly thought she'd be able to grab a cab before the rain really picked up since it had barely been a drizzle when she'd left her desk. By the time she got downstairs, however, it was a full-fledged downpour.

Unfortunately, the entire city of Chicago had apparently known it was coming and had taken every single taxi. At least she was able to snag an umbrella from lobby security, so she wasn't getting drenched.

It seemed much too early in the spring for this heavy a thunderstorm. A bolt of lightning flashed, and a clap of thunder immediately followed. Skye ducked on reflex and hoped it was farther away than it sounded since she was standing outside holding a lightning rod. But there was no way she was ditching it and getting drenched. She tightened the belt around her trench coat and was just about to give in and try calling a Lyft when, incredibly, a taxi pulled up right in front of her, and a man in his forties jumped out. Skye thanked the heavens for this small miracle and darted into the cab before someone else could snatch it. "The Maxwell Building, please," she said, not even looking at the driver, and they were off.

Skye appreciated that cabbies weren't generally chatty by nature. She much preferred the luxury of driving herself, but when she couldn't, she tried to take a taxi over a talkative rideshare driver. She liked her private time to think on the way to a meeting or showing to rehearse in her head what she was going to say. Who the hell had time for chitchat? Also, they were almost always from the suburbs and didn't know the city all that well, so they rarely took the most efficient route and actually stopped for yellow lights rather than speeding up. Unbelievable.

This driver, however, was the exception. He must have recently switched to one of the taxi companies. "So what are you heading to the Maxwell Building for? Business meeting? Visiting a boyfriend?"

She was looking in her briefcase to make sure she had her keys and her listing brochures. "Business," she said in a clipped tone. A boyfriend? Really? Ass. As if it wasn't bad enough that she was going to have to fix her drowned-rat appearance when she arrived with a scant twenty-eight minutes to spare—make that twenty-six unless this guy started driving a little faster—but now he was also trying to horn in on her preparation time?

"I just moved to Chicago. I'm from Rhinelander. Ya know, Wisconsin?"

Skye tried to tune him out as she went over the particulars of the space she would be showing, but the way he said Wis-*cahn*-sin was jarring. She was having a hard time concentrating.

There are a lot of great office buildings in this city. There's no denying that some of the best buildings in the world are here, but getting to have your own floor with only thirty-thousand square feet in a building of this caliber is rare. By choosing a boutique—

"I'd lived my whole life in Rhinelander, thirty-nine years, if you can believe it."

Damn this guy for interrupting again. Skye tried to get back into the groove. *By choosing a boutique building like this, you control your full floor and have your own private bathrooms, rather than being on a quarter of a floor in another building,* she mouthed. This was almost routine, but she still liked to go through every word and tailor it for each prospect. *At this property, you—*

"But I just couldn't do it anymore. I wasn't cut out for all that small-time living, so I moved here and decided to learn the city by driving a cab."

Jesus. She refocused. *You still have new-building amenities such as a tenant lounge, fitness center, and rooftop deck, but—*

Wait. This guy doesn't know the city? She peered out the window and realized they were about six blocks in the wrong direction. "Do you realize you're going the wrong way?" She huffed, trying to quell the anger simmering below the surface.

"Oh, sorry, ma'am. Do I need to turn around?" he slowly said in his thick Wisconsin accent, craning his head to the left.

"Yes. Immediately." How could this jackass have whatever certifications are required to drive a cab in this city? Skye tried not to growl. She *needed* to be at the Maxwell twenty minutes ago.

By the time she arrived, she only had twenty-three minutes before her tour was supposed to start, so she jogged into the building without taking the time to put her umbrella up and waved at security as she sprinted to the elevators as quickly as she could in her heels. She prepped the space and then popped into the ladies' room to primp and make herself look more presentable. Her nose was red from standing in the cold for so long, but there wasn't much she could do about that other than dab a little powder on. She smoothed her hair, put on a little textured cream to tame the flyaways, and touched up her mascara and lipstick.

She shook her head at herself in the mirror and tried to will away her frustration at the rain, at the cabdriver, and at being late. She did a few slow inhales and forceful exhales that normally did the trick. When she felt like she'd gotten control of her emotions, she left the restroom. Unfortunately, as she turned the corner, her irritation ticked back up again.

Rob, the prospective tenant's broker, stood in the corridor in front of the glass door to the vacant suite. She was late after all. Dammit.

"Hey, Skye." He smiled the charming smile of perfect teeth and white privilege that came from having a family that called itself "upper middle class" but was actually a *little* higher on the socioeconomic scale. He'd grown up on the right side of town and had spent every summer at his family's Michigan cabin—which some would probably call a mansion—that was right on Lake Michigan itself. Not middle class at all. "I was about to text you and see where you'd gotten to since the space was open."

The problem was, she wanted to dislike him but couldn't. Despite his classically handsome face and impeccably trimmed beard, identical to every model on the cover of *GQ* in the last decade, and having had every advantage in life handed to him on a silver platter, he was a genuinely good guy and straight shooter. Though he looked like and had the same background as ninety percent of the commercial real estate brokers she'd worked with, Rob had never stabbed her in the back, unlike some.

She smiled and pushed her annoyance down. "Hey, Rob. Sorry to keep you waiting. Getting a taxi in this town in the rain is murder."

"Don't I know it. I'm driving today, thankfully, since we're on a tour, though I have to double-park everywhere, so I'm hoping I don't get a ticket. The group is already inside checking it out." He gestured through the glass door where three men and two women wandered around the space and pointed out the large windows in front of them.

"Looks like they like it?" she asked.

"They love the location and that they can get a full floor."

"Any objections I should be aware of?" she said, trying to get a slight edge in case there was anything she should focus on downplaying or spinning. Or emphasizing why something seemed like a drawback but was actually an advantage.

"Truthfully, no. If your client isn't too stingy, I could easily see this one coming your way."

"Great to hear, Rob. Thanks for the intel. Though I bet you've said that to all the landlord reps you've met with today." She winked to let him know she was kidding. Mostly.

He brought his hand to his chest and feigned being shot. "Definitely not, Skye. I only speak the truth, and you wound me with your cynicism."

She didn't actually think he said that to everyone but liked to give him a hard time. Rob was one of the few brokers who knew for certain that she was a lesbian, and she saw him almost like a brother. But a brother she would fight to the death in order to get the best deal for her client. They didn't compete for business generally—as he normally

represented tenants and she normally represented building owners—
but when they were negotiating a deal, things could get heated.
"Don't be so sensitive, or everyone is going to start thinking you
have a vagina, Rob." He barked a laugh at her vulgarity while she hated
herself for saying it. But it was one of the reasons she was always seen
as "one of the guys" in the brokerage community. It was advantageous
for her professionally, despite how queasy she felt disrespecting her
gender and demeaning herself. Regardless, it contributed to her success,
so she played the role she needed to play.

"Well, if that rumor grows legs, I'll know who started it, and I'll
definitely steer my clients away from this building, even if it is perfect
for them." Skye laughed at that. Unlike some brokers, she felt confident
Rob wouldn't really do it. "Shall we head in, and you can give them
your best pitch?" he asked, angling his head toward the door.

He opened the door and gestured for her to walk in first but quickly
followed and introduced her to the group. They were a medium-size
law firm, but they were looking to grow in their new space, and this
building was perfect for them. It was close to the train, there was a
public parking garage right across the street, and since the Geffen
Family Trust, one of Skye's best clients, had purchased the property a
little less than a year ago, the building amenities were stunning.

They had installed a state-of-the-art fitness center, conference
room facilities, and to top it off—literally—they had one of the best
rooftop decks in the city. Normally, it was open for any employees
looking for a little fresh air or a nice place to have lunch, but it could
also be rented out for private events in the evenings and on weekends.
They even had a wedding booked in a few weeks.

The only drawback was the restrooms on the floor. They were
dated and simply didn't feel clean, even though they absolutely were.
When one of the partners in the firm, Mr. Braud—pronounced "bro"
because why wouldn't it be—exclaimed at how old they looked and
how no one in the firm would sign off on a building with such old
restrooms, Skye was quick to say, "I can assure you, Mr. Braud, the
owners of this building will happily redo the restrooms if you lease this
full floor. New lights, new flooring, new wall coverings, new fixtures.
I promise, you won't even be able to recognize this restroom, and all
the finishes can be handpicked so you don't have to settle for someone
else's tastes."

"Well, that's a relief," he grumbled. "What about additional private
restrooms? If, say, we wanted a private restroom for the managing

partner and a couple of restrooms for the senior partners to share?" He seemed to be the only person on the tour not completely enamored with the building. And of course, the higher-ups wouldn't want to share restrooms with the peons at the firm.

"Absolutely, Mr. Braud." That could be a costly add, and Skye wasn't one hundred percent certain how or *if* they could accommodate all of those restrooms, but no need to get into that now. For this first tour, there wasn't anything that they couldn't make happen to get this deal done. The answers were always yes on the first tour. Hell, the answers were almost always yes until the actual lease negotiations began. Then, once they were committed, the owner's attorneys could be the ones to say no.

The law firm spent nearly an hour walking the space and checking out the building's amenities. Skye was starting to get nervous that she was going to be late to her next showing, which was on the other side of the city, when Rob finally said, "Okay everyone, if we want to make it to our next tour, we're going to have to head out, but from the looks of it, we'll be back for a second tour and can spend as much time as we need."

Skye let out an internal sigh of relief as Rob herded the group out. Normally, first tours lasted half as long, and Skye was going to have to hurry to make it to her next. She'd text Rob later and verify that they'd made the tenant's short list, but she was confident that they would after that showing.

After locking up, Skye headed downstairs. She was checking her phone for any new emails or voice mails and barely registered the group of people standing to her left in the lobby until she heard her name being yelled by a familiar voice.

"Hey, Skye! Do you have a sec?"

Skye looked up and saw her old friend and mentor, Ellie Efron—who happened to be the head of acquisitions for the Geffen Family Trust and was thus also her client—standing in the group calling out to her. The timing was dicey, but she was simply going to have to make it work. She smiled broadly as she walked over. Despite the worry of another delay, she was happy to see her old friend and favorite client.

"Hey, Ellie. Great to see you," she said as she approached the group and hugged Ellie. She'd known her since her sophomore year of high school at Walter Payton Prep. Ellie had been fresh out of college and had been assigned as her mentor. She'd always been Skye's greatest cheerleader throughout her career, and running into her unexpectedly—

despite the stress about her timeline—warmed Skye's chest. "I didn't know you were going to be at the building today. I just finished a tour. You look amazing, by the way. I love this suit."

"Always charming, Skye. I've already hired you to lease the building for us. No need to suck up now," Ellie teased.

"It would be sucking up if it wasn't true, my dear, but this red jacket looks amazing on you, and you should try harder to take a compliment with aplomb rather than deflection." Ellie might be trying to deflect, but everything Skye had said was true. The red, double-breasted jacket looked stunning with slim-fitting black pants. She looked like she'd just walked out of a Neiman Marcus catalog.

"Well, then, thank you for the compliment. It's new. Alexander McQueen." Ellie beamed.

Skye's attention was drawn to a woman in the small group who looked about Skye's age but was standing in the lobby like she owned it, which was ironic since she actually *was* standing next to the owner. Skye had never seen her before, and even though her demeanor rubbed Skye the wrong way, there was something alluring about her presence. She had delicate facial features and a short, undercut hairstyle that accented them perfectly. Her dark blond hair was short on the sides but had a windswept and whimsical style on top that defied gravity and was decidedly feminine. As was her makeup. Her dark plaid blazer over a white blouse and jeans all looked like they had been tailored for her and only enhanced her appeal.

Skye tried to hide the fact that she'd been checking out the stranger and brought her focus back to Ellie. She didn't think she'd missed anything. She was quite certain. Pretty certain, anyway.

"We just toured the newly finished roof-deck and were talking about additional projects," Ellie explained.

"I must've just missed you up there, but I've had incredible feedback on tours when we popped up there to look. I think it might be what closes the deal on the tour I had this afternoon." The deck was one of the best amenities and had been money well spent.

"That is great to hear. You can thank Bailey here. It was her crew who built it, among other projects in the building." Ellie gestured to the woman who had captivated Skye on her approach.

Skye extended her hand. "Hi, Skye Kohl."

Bailey smiled, and though Skye wouldn't have thought it possible, she became even more attractive. "Nice to meet you, Skye. Bailey Kaczmarek, City Beautiful Construction."

Skye idly wondered how the hell Kaczmarek was spelled until the moment their hands touched, and her gaze jumped and connected with Bailey's. Did she feel the same little jolt? Skye had to remind herself of the appropriate grip for a business handshake. Not so soft as to feel wishy-washy and not so firm that it seemed like she was trying to intimidate. It was normally second nature, but Bailey's green eyes had uncharacteristically bewitched her for an instant.

"So sorry, where are my manners? I forgot that you two haven't met," Ellie said.

Skye realized she was still holding Bailey's hand and released it. "What happened to Greg?" she asked, her face warming slightly as she *tried* to mentally step back into the moment.

"Unfortunately for me," Bailey said, "he decided to retire a few weeks ago. It was well-deserved, but we miss him."

Skye was happy for him too but felt the loss for the building and projects still to come. He had always been her go-to estimator when a prospect was looking to price a floor plan, and he was so familiar with the property and their normal subcontractors that he could flip a number back to her quickly. She wasn't sure how someone new would stack up. "That's too bad. He was a great guy."

"He still is. He's retired, not dead." Bailey laughed, but Skye didn't appreciate being made fun of. She chuckled along half-heartedly as her face warmed again for a whole different reason. Who did this newbie think she was?

Ellie, apparently sensing the quick change in emotion, said, "And you remember our building architect, Ryan Tayler, don't you?"

Skye turned away from Bailey, extended her hand, and reminded herself to smile as she said, "Of course, Ryan. Great to see you again."

"Likewise." He had a professorial aura with his tweed jacket, little goatee, and round spectacles. The round shape of his eyewear made it difficult to think of them as glasses. He wasn't the chattiest person, but his eye for design was unrivaled. Ellie was lucky to have him on this team.

Bailey again grabbed Skye's attention. "This is Jennifer Meyers. She's a senior at Purdue and is interning with us. She's been invaluable since Greg retired."

Great, Skye thought, a newbie *and* an intern. Not exactly a dream team for the building. Skye mustered a smile and shook Jennifer's hand as well.

"It's rather fortunate that we ran into you today, Skye," Ellie said. "We were here to check out the roof-deck, but we ended up talking about the spec suite you've been bugging me for as well. Do you have ten minutes so we can run you through our ideas?"

Ellie was referring to an existing "raw" space that was just four walls, a concrete floor, and the exposed ceiling, which would be converted into a leasable space on a speculative basis without a tenant in line to lease it. Skye had been reminding Ellie regularly that there were a lot of tenants in the market who waited until the last minute to search for new space and were forced to either renew in place or lease a spec suite because they didn't have time to wait months while a space was built out for them.

Owners were often reluctant to commit because they had to make a lot of assumptions about what a prospective tenant might want, but at the end of the day, Skye had seen time and again that spec suites leased faster than raw spaces. They also allowed the building to showcase higher-end finishes that could help close a deal even if it wasn't for the spec suite itself, so Skye had been pitching for weeks to get Ellie on board with a spec suite at the Maxwell.

She really, really didn't have time, but Ellie was one of her largest and most lucrative clients, so she didn't want to disappoint. She was elated that Ellie was considering moving forward with the spec suite and also wanted to make sure she had a hand in the layout and design. She loved Ellie and Ryan, but she'd seen a lot more finished spaces than either of them.

"Of course," Skye said with genuine excitement. "I'd love to discuss your thoughts and provide a little input. I do have something across town shortly, but I can carve out a few minutes. It looks like the rain stopped, so hopefully, getting a cab will be less of an ordeal."

As they walked to the elevator, Skye fired off a quick text to one of her junior brokers to cover her next tour since she would almost certainly be late. She sighed in relief when he texted back that he would leave right away. As long as she didn't spend too much time here, she'd be fine to meet up with the showing after that.

She loved the sixteenth floor of this building. The views were stellar, the bathrooms had already been renovated, and the space available was ideally sized, key for spec suites. The goal of a spec suite was to lease it at a premium because the hard work was already complete, and they could move in as soon as they needed.

When they walked into the space, Ellie said, "Bailey, do you or Ryan want to outline what we discussed earlier as far as a layout is concerned?" Skye already had the space laid out in her mind, so she frowned and wondered whether their thoughts would match her own. She was unsurprised that Ryan didn't start the conversation, though he would be the one actually drawing the plan. He was an introvert and always seemed to prefer letting others do the talking.

However, she was surprised when Bailey said, "Jennifer, you were here for our walk-through. Why don't you take Skye through it?"

Ugh, the newbie didn't want to do it so she was making the intern, who was barely more than a child, take the lead. This should be... *interesting.*

"Of course," Jennifer mumbled. Though once she got going, she found her confidence. Skye was oddly proud of her, even if the ideas were all wrong. Maybe not *all* wrong but definitely not all right. "You have two window walls, so we thought it would make sense to put private offices along this wall"—she indicated the shorter wall—"and leave this wall open for a cube area."

"Oh no, that doesn't make sense at all," Skye said before she could continue. "There are so few firms these days that want perimeter offices that I wouldn't do that on spec. Can we put five or six offices along this wall?" She gestured to an interior wall. She didn't understand why everyone still always went to perimeter offices by default. Those had gone out of style three or four years ago. Probably longer.

Jennifer was clearly nervous again as she fumbled in her bag. "Uh, I'm not sure, let me get my tape measure and see what we're working with. That might work. I...I'm not sure."

Bailey mercifully jumped in and eyeballed the length of wall they had to work with. "Six offices would be pushing it. You probably have space for four moderately sized offices or five small ones, max. But that isn't the primary issue." She turned. "Jennifer, do you want to go through the real issue?"

Skye didn't understand why Bailey wanted the intern to do all the work, but whatever. She really didn't have time for this, but good God, Bailey worrying her lower lip as she contemplated the wall did something to Skye's lower half that she was not comfortable with. At all.

Jennifer nodded and swallowed before she said, "The plumbing chase is along this wall." She indicated pipes midway down the wall in question. "If you want to put a kitchen in this space, the most cost-effective location is going to be right here because this is where the plumbing already is. If you put offices here, you won't be able to fit a kitchen."

General contractors, and their interns who barely knew what a tape measure was, sometimes had so little imagination. "A kitchen is nonnegotiable for a space this size, but that isn't the right spot for it. It might be a little more work, but you *could* put the kitchen here, couldn't you?" Skye asked, staring sweetly at Bailey. If anyone had the answer, it was going to be Bailey and not the intern. God, she missed Greg.

Doe-eyed Jennifer started to stutter. "Uh, yes, maybe, I think, maybe."

Bailey finally put her out of her misery. A little muscle twitched in her right temple, the only tell that she might be annoyed as she said, "Yes, we *probably* could put it here. We'll have to core into the ceiling below after-hours to run the plumbing, and the plumbing subcontractor will have to measure to make sure we have enough room to get the pitch. If that checks out, yes, we can do it. It's not going to be cheap, though. Ellie, are you okay with that?"

"Look," Ellie said. "I can't spend a ton of money on this space, but Ryan, can you draw up plans for each scenario, and Bailey can price them both?"

"Of course," they said simultaneously and then laughed. Skye waited for Jennifer to yell "Jinx," but, despite how young she looked, she apparently wasn't in grade school.

Skye, however, was pleased everyone was coming around to her way of thinking. She surreptitiously stared at Bailey's ass as she spun in a semicircle and looked at the space in contemplation, and though Skye really didn't have time to enjoy the view, the way Bailey's jeans cupped her bottom was nothing short of delicious.

Skye quickly outlined her remaining thoughts before finally saying, "Okay, I'm really sorry, but I've got to run so I'm not late for my next showing, but thank you. Bailey, Jennifer, nice meeting you. Ryan, Ellie, always a pleasure." She shook everyone's hands, hugged Ellie again, and ran out, praying she still had time to meet up with her final showing.

❖

After Skye jetted out like her trench coat was on fire, Bailey took a long breath through her teeth and silently applauded herself for remaining calm despite Skye's complete and utter self-involvement and disregard for others.

"Whew," Ellie said, seemingly echoing Bailey's thoughts.

"I know you've known her for a long time, Ellie," Bailey said, pausing to get her thoughts together so she could express herself without being insulting. "But is she always that…opinionated?"

"Opinionated," Ellie said, tilting her head side to side as if weighing the word. "I like that as a description, and yes, she absolutely is. Though, she was a little extra abrupt today."

Abrupt wasn't quite the way Bailey would put it. Bitchy came to mind—though self-absorbed, icy, or aloof would also do the trick—but Bailey definitely wasn't going to say that about one of Ellie's friends and the broker she'd hired to lease this building. Her company had worked with Ellie and the Geffen Family Trust for a long time, but for the last four years or so, Bailey had been out of the estimating game, and Greg had run Ellie's account. However, since Greg had retired and Ellie was one of her longest-standing and most valuable clients, Bailey wasn't going to give her another estimator until she'd handpicked the right one and had a chance to work with them on the account.

Bailey shook her head as she looked around and noticed that Jennifer still looked a little pale. "Jennifer, don't worry, you did fine." She was embarrassed about how Skye had treated Jennifer, as if she was insignificant and "just" an intern. Her jaw tightened just thinking about it.

Ellie put a hand on Jennifer's shoulder. "You did great. Skye is a tenacious broker and has amazing vision, but sometimes, she gets caught up and doesn't realize how she comes off. I've known her since she was in high school, if you can believe it, and she's always been… headstrong, I'd say." Ellie laughed. "And with more confidence than is probably healthy. To put it mildly."

They laughed at that apt description. "Well, this was a productive day. Thanks, everyone," Ellie continued. "I want to keep Skye looped in on all discussions for this buildout. She really does have her hand on the pulse of the market, and I value her input. I understand that her vision may be more expensive, but she's right. Her layout, if we can swing it price-wise, *will* show better."

"I'll draw up two plans for you to price, Bailey," Ryan said. "It should be a pretty quick turnaround. Probably a few days, if you want to get your subs teed up for a walk-through next week."

"Perfect." Bailey was not looking forward to working with the frosty Ms. Kohl on this project, but hopefully, she wouldn't have to spend much time with her. With any luck, she would occasionally give design inputs and leave Bailey and her team to do their jobs.

CHAPTER TWO

When Bailey backed her crew-cab Ford Ranger into her garage after work that evening, she still hadn't gotten over how rude Skye had been that afternoon. Brokers. She was self-centered, impolite, vain, and controlling, but Bailey was proud of herself for holding her shit together and not letting Skye's abrasive personality bring out an unattractive side of herself. She had her siblings to thank for her ability to control her temper, she supposed.

Growing up the youngest of four in a three-bedroom, one-bathroom, typical Chicago bungalow, it had only been natural for them to rub one another the wrong way often, and one thing her mother hadn't tolerated was fighting in the house. They had gotten good at keeping their frustration suppressed until they were somewhere appropriate to let it all out. And most of the time, by then, they'd all forgotten why they were upset in the first place.

When Skye had so patronizingly said, "It might be a little more work, but you could put the kitchen here, couldn't you?" Bailey had thought she might crack a molar in her effort to not lose her temper. She'd had such a condescending tone. Clearly, enough time hadn't passed for Bailey to forget why she was so annoyed. And yet, with chagrin, she remembered her quickening pulse when she'd seen Skye walking toward them in the lobby.

Bailey slammed the truck door with a little more force than necessary. Skye hadn't been wearing anything revealing; in fact, she'd worn a long black trench coat that hadn't even revealed her silhouette, other than a trim waist beneath the tightly cinched belt. Truthfully, what had first grabbed Bailey's attention had been a peek of ankles in designer pumps—that couldn't be less practical in the rain—after hearing the click-clack of heels across the terrazzo floor.

From there, she'd noticed a perfect blond lob—that didn't have a strand out of place despite the humidity—and deep blue eyes. So blue they were almost gray. When they had shaken hands and made real eye contact for the first time…Bailey's stomach had done a somersault into her throat. Skye holding her hand for an instant too long had made sweat break out on her lower back, and Bailey had prayed her palm hadn't also gone noticeably damp.

But then Skye had opened her mouth, and any flutter of attraction had evaporated in an instant. Typical, self-important broker. Bailey tried to tell herself she no longer had even an iota of attraction toward Skye and focused on the slight physical resemblance to her ex-fiancée, Mary, in hair color and height. She certainly acted as self-important and manipulative as Mary had been.

Bailey shook her head in disgust and walked across her backyard to her brownstone. She'd bought this house four years ago, shortly after the company had really started to get traction in the commercial side of the business. In this neighborhood, she wouldn't have been able to afford it if it hadn't been run-down and in need of serious work, but she had lovingly restored every detail she could—the original woodwork, the crown molding, the cornices along the roofline—even though it had taken her the better part of two years.

She opened the back door and walked into the kitchen, one of the two areas where she'd modernized instead of simply restoring. She loved to cook and had spared no expense.

Her admiration of her kitchen broke when her blue nose pocket pittie, Patsy, came running to welcome her home. As Patsy rounded the corner, her poor legs went much faster than her stocky body, and she struggled to find traction on the hardwood. When she finally found purchase, she ran sideways into Bailey's legs, a regular occurrence, unfortunately. Bailey had already bent her knees to brace for impact. Patsy's exuberance always got the better of her.

"Did you miss me today, sweetums? Mommy missed you *so* much," Bailey said and squatted to be on her level. She stopped spinning and switched to licking Bailey's chin. "You're such a sweet girl. You want to go outside?"

Patsy started to jump and spin again, and Bailey winced when she bounced into her legs. "Okay, let's go." She grabbed a 312 beer from the fridge and let Patsy out. Patsy took the stairs two at a time before jumping over the bottom three to flounce into the grass. Bailey took a moment to wonder at the small joys of a dog's life. Patsy bounded into the yard as if there was a platter of T-bones in the corner, innocent glee propelling her until she stopped to smell whatever caught her attention.

Patsy kept Bailey sane in a world of Skyes, unreasonable subcontractors, and too few hours in the day. She accompanied Bailey to work whenever possible as City Beautiful Construction's unofficial mascot but not while in the field. Most building owners had a no-dog policy. Luckily, she owned CBC's converted warehouse in the far West Loop and would never implement such a policy.

Patsy sniffed at the fence dividing Bailey's garden from the rest of her yard. Her rectangular cedar planter boxes looked so barren in March against the sea of brown grass after the brutal winter. However, in a few short weeks, she would have the beginning of some plants, and in a few months, those boxes would be overgrown with Jurassic Park–sized kale, arugula, tomato plants, and squash vines.

Watching the transformation of her garden over the growing season and being able to cook directly from her harvest were Bailey's favorite parts of the spring, summer, and early fall. There was something about walking into the garden and picking her own tomatoes and basil to make a caprese salad that was entirely satisfying, and she couldn't wait.

Her phone ringing in her back pocket brought her out of musing. Her mom. She put it on speaker. "Hey, Mom."

"Hi, Bailey. What's cooking?" Her mom's melodic voice sounded tinny through the speaker.

"Nothing yet. I just got home. I'm watching Patsy frolic and having a 312." Bailey took a sip of beer and relished the slightly citrus flavor, though she should've taken the time to pour it into a glass with an orange slice.

"Eating this late isn't healthy, Bailey." She was such a worrier, but Bailey couldn't help smiling. That night, her mom would no doubt say a prayer for her to get out of work earlier so she could eat dinner at a *normal* time.

If there was a God, Bailey was confident they didn't have time to worry about what time she ate dinner, but her mom needed a feeling of control, a way to look after her children even though they were grown. Bailey thought it a little crazy but appreciated that she cared.

"It's only seven fifteen, Mom." She didn't want to admit how often she was at the office at a quarter after seven, especially now that Greg had retired. She really needed to find a replacement. "I'm not going to turn into an evil gremlin if I eat after eight, I promise."

"As long as you're taking care of yourself." She let out a long-suffering sigh, and Bailey couldn't help but chuckle. "Anyway, can you come over for dinner tomorrow?"

"Why, what's tomorrow?" The deck was going to need another coat of stain this summer. She looked forward to that as much as she looked forward to working with Skye on this spec suite. She shuddered at the thought. No, actually, staining the deck would be preferable.

"There has to be a reason I want to see my youngest daughter? Maybe I just want the joy of your company. Maybe your uncles are coming, and it'd be nice for you to give Uncle Chester an update. You know he misses being in the action."

There was no way that was true. Uncle Chester had let her buy him out five years ago because he was tired of working. She'd love to see him, but he loved spending every morning in the neighborhood coffeeshop with his "coffeeshop five," gossiping about neighborhood goings-on, playing golf four days a week, and meeting new women online as he continued his quest for "the one."

Her mom was probably trying to set her up with the niece of her hairdresser's cousin or something. Whatever random single lesbian she'd heard of that week. She didn't seem to understand that Bailey was happy unattached. She needed to focus on the business. She'd seen from Uncle Chester's four failed marriages—as well as her own failed near marriage—that relationships didn't mesh with running a busy construction business. She simply didn't have the time and didn't want to go through the pain. Driving Mary away was enough pain to last a lifetime.

It wasn't until after their breakup that she'd realized how manipulative Mary was, but if she hadn't been so absorbed with work, maybe Mary wouldn't have gotten so bad. Regardless, what could she say that would get her out of dinner?

"Bailey? Hello? Are you still there?" Her mother probably knew she was trying to come up with an excuse.

"Yes," she sighed.

"I'm making your favorite Polish meatballs. I don't expect to have leftovers, so if you want some, you'd better come over."

"With homemade mashed potatoes?" She wasn't fighting fair.

"Is there any other way to eat them?"

"Fine, I'll be there." She was tired of being set up, but there were few things she wouldn't do for Polish meatballs. And maybe she was reading too much into things, and her mom wasn't trying to set her up. Again. She could only hope. And if she was, Bailey would figure out some way to put her off. Polish meatballs were worth the effort. "I'll see you tomorrow, Mom. I love you."

"See you tomorrow. Five thirty sharp. I mean it. And bring Patsy. I love my grandpuppy."

After she hung up, Bailey whistled and yelled, "Come on, my crazy blue girl."

Patsy immediately ran toward the stairs. Bailey had rescued her a few years ago, though who had rescued whom was up for debate, as it was Patsy who had gotten her through her rough breakup. She didn't know what she'd do without that blocky-headed dog. Her muscled chest and big jaws looked scary at first glance, but no one could ever mistake Patsy for aggressive. Her face was always set in a goofy grin that melted Bailey's heart.

"You're the only woman I need, Patsy. Grandma will get that eventually." Bailey squatted and ruffled Patsy's floppy ears in exchange for a kiss. "You ready for dinner?"

❖

Skye stood on her mother's doorstep and wondered why her mother and grandmother wouldn't let her and her sister, Natasha, buy them a nicer place to live. Her mother insisted she wanted to keep living in an apartment in the same neighborhood she'd loved since childhood rather than move to a nicer neighborhood or a larger place. Not that there was anything wrong with Ukrainian Village—it had gotten a lot nicer since she was a kid—but it was annoyingly far from Skye's place and Natasha's. And despite the decreasing crime rate, she still worried about parking her black Audi TT coupe on the street.

When her mother opened the door she said, "Why do you insist on knocking, Svyatoslava? I tell you again and again, the door is going to be unlocked, just come in." She grabbed Skye with a force that belied her small stature and pulled her inside.

"Maybe I keep hoping you'll stop leaving the door unlocked, Mama." She kissed her cheek, enjoying the smell of the Olay moisturizing cream.

"Nobody messes with the old ladies in this neighborhood, Slava. Stop worrying."

"Criminals don't care who you are or how old you are. And please, please call me Skye. That's my name and has been for a long time." It drove her crazy to be called Svyatoslava or Slava. She'd changed her name more than a decade ago. Not that there was anything wrong with Svyatoslava.

It simply wasn't her name anymore.

"Hotsy-Totsy, 'Skye Kohl,'" her mom said patronizingly. "Tell me, what was wrong with Svyatoslava Kuchytska? Your sister doesn't have any problems being a famous writer with her given name, Natasha Kuchytska."

"It's damn near impossible to say, no less spell. It's hard in business to have a name like that. I'm proud of my Ukrainian heritage, I'm proud to be your daughter, but this is who I need to be to be successful. Could you imagine me trying to spell that over the phone? It's twenty letters long."

Her mom huffed. "Let's go, *Skye*." The name rolled off her tongue like it was synonymous with child abuse, but at least she'd said it. That was progress.

"Hey, Babulya, Natasha." Skye leaned down to give her grandmother and sister hugs and settled around her mother's small table that barely had enough surface for four plates and four glasses, but there wasn't room for a larger piece. "Something smells amazing."

"Since you were coming over for dinner, your Babulya decided to make holubtsi."

Skye's mouth started to water at the thought of delectable cabbage rolls with spiced ground pork and rice filling. If there was a heaven, it would be a place where she could eat holubtsi every day and not gain a pound. "Mmm, thank you, Babulya. My favorite. But I come over at least two or three nights a week. What's the special occasion today?"

"Your mama just tries to make you feel guilty," Babulya said, her accent dripping heavily despite having lived in the US for decades. "Don't let her. I wanted holubtsi, and you get to reap the benefits." She winked at Skye as her mom swatted her arm.

"If you and Babulya would be willing to move to the North Side, I could see you every day. Natasha and I would love it if you lived closer." If only her mother would be open to that idea.

"Seeing you every day is too often. How would I keep any secrets?" They all laughed as Skye slid onto her seat.

Natasha choked on a sip of water. "She told you, Skye."

Tears brimmed around Skye's eyes. "I would like to point out, however, that you *live with* your mother. You already don't have secrets."

"Babulya knows not to pry or snoop. Unlike you, my dear."

Skye choked on her sip of water. "Mother!" But before she could truly respond, the kitchen timer went off.

"Help your babulya," Mama said and gestured to the oven.

"Of course." Skye jumped up from her seat. She tried to pitch in however she could at Mama and Babulya's house. Babulya's knees weren't what they used to be. She grabbed potholders and pulled the pan out of the oven. "Do you want it on the table?" she asked before she realized there was no room.

"Just put it on the stove," Babulya said.

Skye grabbed plates and started spooning a couple of the rolls on each. "Even if you stay in this neighborhood, we could get you a larger place. Have a larger dining room tab—"

"Enough," her mom screeched. "Why do you insist on trying to change where we live? Your grandmother and I are happy here. On this block, we know everyone, we know the mailwoman, we know the grocer on the corner. We have everything we need. We don't need some big fancy apartment in Lincoln Park. If we have a bigger place, it's more to clean."

"If it's only that, we could hire you a cleaning person. Natasha and I both have one." Their mom had spent her entire working life cleaning for other people, and Skye would happily hire someone so she never had to clean again.

"Skye." Natasha placed a hand on her arm. "They're happy here. Stop pushing."

Sheesh, now even Natasha wasn't on her side? She didn't understand why her mom and grandmother wouldn't let her take care of them. She knew this method of attack wasn't the way to win, but she couldn't help herself, even though she'd put their backs up again.

"Look, I'm sorry. I know I get…" She paused, looking for the right word. "Aggressive. I just want you to be happy. The two of you always took care of Natasha and me when we were kids and through college. I want us to be able to return a bit of the love and care you gave us now that we've made something of ourselves, which is all to your credit. I want to…say thank you."

After her father had passed when she and Natasha were little more than babies, Mama and Babulya had both worked two jobs to keep them afloat and had made sure they studied so they could get into the best public high school. The Chicago Public School system had a handful of nationally ranked magnet high schools that had a competitive admission process, and as poor kids, if they hadn't gotten into one, their chances at getting into a good college—or affording any college—would have been bleak.

Babulya patted her cheek with fingers swollen and crooked from arthritis. Skye relished the cool feel, her slightly papery but still soft skin, so familiar from her childhood. Probably due to the decades of using Olay. "Your heart in right place, bunny. But don't be so pushy." She kissed her pliant cheek. "I love you. I'm sorry." She reached across the table and grabbed her mom's hand as well. "I'll drop it."

"I doubt it'll last forever, but we'll enjoy the peace for now." Her mom smiled, but the glint in her eye said she would appreciate it if Skye let it go forever.

She would for now. Forever was a different story. She just needed to figure out the right approach next time. "Either way, let's enjoy these holubtsi." She moaned as the first bite landed on her tongue. They were a lot of work to make, but oh God, were they good.

Later, after they said their good-byes and were walking down the stairs, Natasha asked, "Can I bum a ride?" Only eleven months younger, Natasha had a charming smile, a near match to Skye's own, which they both used whenever they needed something. And right now, Natasha's was turned up to a thousand.

"You didn't drive?"

Natasha barked a laugh. "Do I *ever*?"

"I don't know why you even have a car."

"No one does, and yet I pay every single month for it and the garage space for a car with about a thousand miles on it after three years." She shook her head as she walked. "Come on, don't make me call a Lyft. Please." Again with the charming smile that was almost like looking in a mirror.

How could she resist? She rolled her eyes. "Okay, fine, get in. But you're out of my way, so you owe me."

"Since I never drive, you could say anything, and I wouldn't know if you were being truthful. You're probably lying right now." She giggled and poked Skye in the ribs like she used to do when they were little kids lying under the covers after Mama and Babulya went to bed, whispering about their grandiose futures and hopes and dreams.

"You wish," Skye said before zipping out into traffic.

Natasha grabbed the oh-shit handle. "Jesus, you almost hit that guy!"

"Beggars can't be choosers when they beg for a ride." How did she think she had room to criticize when Skye was going out of her way?

"I did not beg."

Skye laughed. "Fine, but I have a strict bedtime to stick to, and I need to make up the time to take you home."

"Oh my God, if it's that much of an imposition, just pull over and let me out. You don't have to be an ass about it. It's not like I can't afford a Lyft. I just wanted to spend a little time with you. Like the old days."

Shit, she'd really hurt Natasha's feelings. She honestly didn't know why she was being such a bitch. Especially to her sister, the woman who knew her best in the world. She reached over and grabbed Natasha's hand. "I'm sorry. I don't mean to be such a jerk. You're not an imposition." She squeezed and was encouraged when Natasha squeezed back. "It's late, so there's no traffic, and it would be fine even if there was. I miss spending time with you too."

"Sometimes you're just so hard-charging. You have a goal, and you don't care who you hurt to get there."

That was too bright a light on her in that moment, and it stung a little. She breathed in through her nose and sighed before speaking. "I know, I'm sorry. I…I like things the way I like them and have a hard time pivoting to accommodate others. I don't mean to be a bitch. Well, at least not all the time."

Natasha punched her arm, ostensibly at the "not all the time" comment. "Just an idea, but you could try not being a bitch *all* the time." She laughed.

"Yeah, but it's so fun." It was also a part of her professional persona. Though she could *probably* do a better job turning it off when it wasn't needed.

Natasha shook her head.

They drove for a few minutes in comfortable silence until Skye surprised herself and said, "I met a woman today."

"Oh?" she asked, excitement bringing her voice an octave above normal.

"Yeah." Skye would never admit it, but she got a little dreamy thinking of Bailey. "She was beautiful. It's not like it'll go anywhere, but the more I annoyed her, the more attractive she became. She's got this sexy little angry twitch in her temple that gives away her irritation and—"

"You're like a teenage boy. Not that I'm the master of relationship advice—"

"That's putting it mildly," Skye said and laughed. Natasha had an unfortunately long string of not-so-great ex-boyfriends.

Natasha continued as if Skye hadn't tried to cut her off. "But if you didn't treat every woman like that, maybe something would go somewhere. For example, be kind, compliment her, take her somewhere nice, treat her like she's intelligent, and not look down on her?"

She might have a point, but the thing was, Skye wasn't looking to date. She really *couldn't* have a relationship. They weren't compatible with her life. She wasn't ready to out herself at work and refused to hide someone. Besides, she didn't need a relationship to make her happy. She was very happy on her own, living by her rules, and had no intention of changing.

"Speaking of being a teenage boy," Natasha continued. "You've got to stop trying to beat Mama and Babulya over the head with the idea of moving. That approach is never going to work. I'd love them to live closer and in a nicer place and a safer neighborhood too, but harassing them is only going to make Mama dig her heels in even more."

"I know, I just don't know why they have to be so stubborn."

"They're happy. They like that apartment and don't want to leave the neighborhood. You can't force them."

"I want to take care of them. Like they took care of us." It was so frustrating when she obviously knew better. "And it would be nice not to have to drive so far to see them."

"They're proud, and they made their own way in a foreign country. They don't need our help, though they will take it in small ways. That might be all we can do for them. They're living their lives, not ours."

"Ugh, I know." And she did. She didn't want to accept it, but she would leave it alone. For now, anyway.

"It's the long game, sister of mine. You've got to be patient. And lucky for you and me, here we are at my apartment. See, that didn't take so long, did it?"

"Thirty minutes to go five miles, not long at all, sister of mine." Skye smiled to take any hint of heat out of her words. "Thanks for keeping me company. I love you." She pulled Natasha into a hug.

"I love you too. And you're only like ten minutes from that monstrosity you call a condo, so don't be a baby. I'll see you soon?" Her tone was questioning, and it pulled at Skye's guilt. Luckily, she'd already made plans for them.

"Of course. Want to take a SoulCycle class and grab brunch on Saturday? I already reserved our bikes." Spinning was Skye's preferred method of keeping in shape. There was something about pedaling like her life depended on it in a candlelit room that helped her get in the zone.

"Ugh, did you put us in the front row again?" Skye was well aware that Natasha didn't like being the center of attention, but the front row in SoulCycle was the best place to be. She wasn't going to admit that now, however.

"You'll have to wait and see."

"You suck." Natasha smirked. "But I love you. I'll see you Saturday. Sister shake?" she asked before getting out.

"Why're you such a nerd, Tash?" They'd had their secret "sister shake" since childhood, and sometimes Natasha still pulled it out.

"Excuse me, you're the one who came up with it, so who's the real nerd?"

"I was eleven!"

"No excuse. It was still your idea." Natasha stared expectantly.

"Fine, it's dark out here anyway." They bumped elbows twice, tapped the back of their hands together once, shimmied their shoulders with a hum, and kissed the other's thumb and whispered, "Sisters for life," together.

"Love you, now get the hell out of here. My bed is calling." Skye blew a kiss. The sister shake might be nerdy as hell, but it always made her feel swaddled in warmth and love.

CHAPTER THREE

The following Thursday started off amazing for Bailey. She was in a groove. She got in a nice run that morning before work and saw her first cardinal of the season, a good harbinger for a great day ahead. That was affirmed when she found out she had been awarded two major, multi-floor tenant construction projects for different office buildings in the Loop, which meant her crews would stay very busy well into the summer.

However, she was vaulted out of that groove when Skye invaded her subcontractor walk-through at the Maxwell Building that afternoon. Subcontractors from every trade were walking around the space so they could price out Ryan's two drawings, which the group would use to help Ellie narrow down which improvements were musts, which were "nice to have," and which were candidates to be cut.

But Skye came whirling in like a microburst set on the destruction of Bailey's orderly bidding process. "Oh good, glad you're here, Bailey. I was upstairs for a second showing and thought I'd swing by to see if anything was going on. Are you bidding out the drawings we reviewed on Monday?" she asked with a visage of innocence, as if she couldn't tell that was exactly what Bailey was doing and was hell-bent on complicating it.

Bailey channeled the inner cheerleader she'd never been as she looked at Skye. With more cheer than she had expected to find, she said, "Oh hi, Skye. I didn't know you were going to be in the building today, or I would have invited you to stop by." A complete and total lie. If she had known Skye was going to be in the building, she would have rescheduled her walk-through. Something about Skye's bulldozing style continued to rub her the wrong way, even when she was being nice.

"This space is going to be stunning once it's built out. Don't you think?" Skye looked back at her.

"Yeah, definitely," Bailey said when she realized it wasn't a rhetorical question. What did Skye actually want?

Skye grinned, and Bailey was transfixed by how white and straight her teeth were. *Focus. You've got a job to do.* She was irritated at herself that a smile from a pretty—but annoying—woman had her heart rate ratcheting up.

"Do you mind if I walk around for a few minutes? I promise, I won't get in the way. I just want to…" Skye paused as she seemed to think things over. "Sit with the space for a bit," she said with a nod.

Shit. The last thing Bailey wanted was Skye talking to any of the subcontractors, but she couldn't come up with a plausible reason to turn her down. "Oh, go ahead," she said before the exchange became awkward. She waved toward the space invitingly and prayed Skye stayed out of trouble, though she didn't feel optimistic.

Bailey huffed once Skye was out of earshot. The way Skye wore her clothes was entirely unfair. Today she was in a wide-leg, cream-colored pantsuit with a burgundy camisole providing a splash of color. Bailey wouldn't have expected cream to be a color Skye could pull off with her very light hair, but somehow, she looked stunning. Cream also wasn't a color that normally flattered one's back end, but the way those pants hugged Skye's hips and butt before widening into her legs was nothing short of divine.

Bailey shook her head, appalled at how quickly she was distracted by a pretty face and a nice ass, and pulled out her tablet in an attempt to get some type of work done. She was three emails in and already frustrated because she'd only just remembered that she had a lunch she couldn't miss the next day when she heard exactly what she'd feared— Skye confusing her subs—from one of the two possible kitchen locations. The more expensive one.

"Do you think you could price this wall in glass?" Skye said.

Jason, the drywall sub said, "Well, yes, ma'am, but that isn't on the plans."

Skye laughed, and Bailey could imagine her placing a hand on Jason's arm as she leaned in. "But I think it could really add to the space. This skyline is gorgeous, and shouldn't anyone walking by be able to see it? If the wall was glass, it would create an airy feel."

With remarkable diplomacy, Jason said, "I think it would look nice either way, ma'am, but it isn't my place to decide what to build. I price what's on the drawings. If I price something that isn't on the drawings, my competition is guaranteed to have better pricing, and I'd like to win this job."

Bailey had been trying to stay out of it for fear that she might wrap her fingers around Skye's slender neck, but she couldn't take it anymore and walked around the corner in time to see Skye lean in with a flirty smile and say, "What if you put it as a little alternate at the bottom?" Her hand was definitely on his arm, and Bailey's steps faltered as Skye almost caressed him.

Bailey cleared her throat. Skye took a subtle step back, and poor Jason's face was as pink as a sunrise. He probably didn't often have women flirt with him at work to get their way. It wasn't really how construction worked. *It* shouldn't *be how the world works.*

Bailey grimaced, wondering if this was Skye's normal MO and part of the reason she was such a successful broker. She hated herself for the thought—she knew from experience that it was hard being a woman in business without other women assuming you'd slept your way to the top—yet she couldn't deny what she had just seen. Her jaw clenched as the scene brought back unpleasant memories of another attractive blonde who used sex as a tool.

She forced her jaw to relax. "Skye, what are you trying to get Jason to change in the pricing?" she said with more calmness than she felt.

Skye grinned again. "I just asked if he could price out making this wall glass. So it would feel more open but still provide a noise barrier so people in the office won't be disturbed by those taking breaks." It sounded so rational, but Skye didn't seem to understand how this process worked.

Bailey nodded and again reminded herself to relax her jaw before she fractured it. "Jason, if you don't mind, please go ahead and price it as an alternate. I'll let Bobby know so it's in both proposals."

"Of course," he said and tipped an imaginary hat at her.

"Skye," she said, turning her focus back. "A word, please?" Her clenched jaw was back, so it came out as more of a growl than she'd intended.

She stepped all the way out into the hallway so they could have some privacy. She had to tread lightly here; Ellie relied heavily on Skye and her opinions. Also, since Skye was one of the top office brokers in downtown, Bailey wanted to stay on her good side so if another owner or tenant asked her for a contractor recommendation, City Beautiful Construction would be at the top of the list. But she also couldn't let Skye go around confusing her crews and subcontractors.

Once in the hallway, Bailey spun and reminded herself not to glare. She could have a rational conversation with Skye. "Look," Bailey started. Skye had the good sense to look a little discomfited with her lips pressed into a thin line while she smoothed nonexistent wrinkles from her suit. "I know you're opinionated, and honestly, you have good ideas."

"Well, yeah. This is what I do for a living. I show people what they want and convince them it's what they need."

Great, her arrogant side was back. Bailey wasn't too small to admit that she had a good eye, but any appreciation for it disappeared in the shadow of her overinflated ego. "As I was saying, you have good ideas, but if you come crashing my bid walk-through and start changing the plans midstream, you confuse the subs, and you jeopardize my ability to get consistent bids." Bailey exhaled sharply. "Our goal here is to keep Ellie happy, and secondly, create a gorgeous space that is cost-effective and leases fast. Agreed?"

"Agreed."

"To do that, I need to get the pricing back quickly. If the subs are confused, that delays the pricing. If you want to make changes, let me know. If they're minor, I'll issue them, and if they're major, we can discuss them with Ellie together. I will never go behind your back to Ellie or a tenant or another broker. I simply ask that you show me the same respect." She prayed the irritation coursing through her wasn't entirely apparent on her face.

"That sounds reasonable. I'm sorry if I was stepping on your toes. I hate it when people do that to me." She actually looked at her feet, and Bailey contemplated whether it was in shame or because admitting she wasn't perfect was a Herculean task. Bailey held in a chuckle at the thought.

"Also, if you want to flirt while on the clock, that's your business." Skye's face went a little white as her mouth opened. "But when you're on a jobsite of mine, please have a little discretion. I'm friends with Jason's very pregnant wife, and she would not appreciate you trying to throw yourself at him for a favor." Shit, Bailey hadn't meant to say that. It went against the entire "making peace" point of the conversation.

Yet, she hadn't been able to stop herself. Even the hint of cheating infuriated Bailey after the demise of her near marriage to Mary.

Skye recoiled as though she'd been slapped, and her face went from pale to red in an instant. Bailey's chest constricted. Had she misinterpreted Skye's body language? She didn't know how she could have with the way Skye had been leaning into him, fingers trailing on his arm. It didn't seem like there was much room for interpretation. Skye's eyes narrowed as she glared. Bailey lifted her chin defiantly and tried not to squirm, certain she was right.

❖

Skye could not believe—Could. Not. Believe—the audacity of this woman. "You are way out of line," she nearly spat. "You completely misread the situation if *that's* what you think was going on, and I don't have anything else to say to you."

She stalked to the elevator lobby, not letting Bailey get in another word. She would have to lie in the hole she'd already dug for herself. Skye jammed her finger into the elevator button so hard, her fingertip turned white. Just to be sure the elevator registered the call and hurried to her floor, she pressed it another five times.

Did she sometimes engage in a little harmless flirting in order to get what she wanted? Maybe. But that was all it was. She wasn't promising anything. She absolutely never *threw* herself at anyone. She didn't sleep around, and she didn't have time for dating. The last time she'd actually had sex was an embarrassingly long time ago. And if she was going to *throw* herself at someone, it wouldn't be a six-foot-five bearded bear of a man in flannel. He was like a youthful Grizzly Adams. Gross.

Good God, *if* she was going to throw herself at someone, which she wasn't even close to doing, it would have been someone who looked more like Bailey: long and lean and a little androgynous with her short haircut, yet still quite feminine with her lightly applied makeup and clothes that enhanced her elegant figure.

Skye had watched Bailey for a moment or two through the glass door before she'd walked in. Wearing jeans and a deep navy blazer over a pale blue button-up with the sleeves rolled to mid-forearm, Bailey gave a tantalizing glimpse of surprisingly delicate wrists and the barest hint of cleavage. Skye hadn't meant to stare, but Bailey ordering the men around and then focusing on her tablet with her reading glasses was much more intriguing than Skye had expected. Those sexy reading glasses did something to Skye's stomach that she was unwilling to examine too closely. She wouldn't mind being ordered around by Bailey for a bit. She doubted she would listen, but take-charge Bailey held a shocking appeal.

Bailey's implication that Skye was little better than a prostitute had yanked her harshly out of that little daydream. It was a common refrain in a male-heavy industry: the only reason she—or any successful female—was successful in commercial real estate was because they'd spent a lot of time on their backs. Or their knees. But hearing that implication in Bailey's voice stung more than it should have. The desire to break down that misperception was one of the reasons she belonged to Professional Women of Real Estate or POWRE. Ironically, she thought she might have a POWRE luncheon tomorrow. She'd have to check her calendar.

Regardless, Skye had worked her ass off for almost ten years to get where she was. Hell, more than ten, as she'd been working harder than her peers since middle school. She knew what had made her one of the top brokers in the city: she'd made more cold calls, attended more events, networked more, and straight up outhustled all her colleagues. As a result, she'd just been named one of the business journal's "Thirty Under Thirty," for fuck's sake. She'd *earned* that. Nothing had ever been given to her, and she'd never done anything even close to what Bailey had accused her of. It left a sour taste in her mouth.

She waved a quick good-bye at security as she stormed out the revolving door. The rush of chilly air helped cool her indignation, and she reminded herself that she was a professional. She wasn't a schoolgirl, and she didn't answer to Bailey Whatever-the-hell-her-last-name-was-ski. Some underling newbie at her favorite construction company. What Bailey thought didn't matter one bit. Not one iota.

After stalking a block away, Skye finally got her emotions back in check, and she decided to give Ellie a call. Not to talk about her interaction with Bailey but to give her the good news about the tour she'd had that afternoon. Her tour from last week was back today, and Rob, their broker, had told her that after their other tours, he was ninety-nine percent sure they were going to select Maxwell for their new office. He wasn't even expecting them to want to counter the most recent offer, and Skye was elated.

The Maxwell Building was perfect for them. Even if she'd likely have to work with Bailey on at least the initial pricing for their construction, which was unfortunate. But she'd worked with bigger assholes. She could handle it.

CHAPTER FOUR

Bailey was running late. She hated running late. Hated it. But it was becoming more of a habit than she would like. This morning, an estimate walk-through had run over when one of the other general contractors bidding the job wouldn't stop asking dumb questions, the answers to which were already in the request for proposal sent out by the property manager. They didn't all need to be standing there for it, but Bailey hadn't wanted to be the one to pipe up and say she had to run. That wouldn't look professional. But it was great that the property manager had kept telling the GC that "As stated in the Request for Proposal…" or "Included with the RFP was…"

Bailey suppressed a laugh thinking about it again, knowing that the GC had pissed off the property manager; no way was he getting awarded the work unless he came in significantly below everyone else. And even then, Bailey was pretty sure the property manager was so annoyed that she would fight the selection of this GC even if he was the lowest. She was feisty and actually one of Bailey's favorite clients.

When she hurried into the lobby of the downtown JW Marriott, Bailey scanned the cavernous space, looking for the A-frame sign that would point her in the direction of the ballroom for the POWRE event. She didn't see one at first and panicked that it wasn't even at the JW, then saw a coat check at the top of the escalators and decided to check up there. Happily, her intuition was correct. She was taken aback, however, to see a seating chart assigning the attendees to particular tables for the lunch program.

The desk attendant called, "If you want to come check in with me, your table number is on your badge, and I can direct you so you don't have to waste your time there."

"Oh great," Bailey said with relief. "I didn't realize how busy this event was going to be. I didn't mean to run this late, but my last meeting ran over."

"You're at table twenty-two," she told Bailey. "Go in those doors on the far right, and then walk up that side. You're at the table three rows from the back on the end. I think everyone else at your table has checked in, so there should be one empty seat. The formal program hasn't started yet."

Bailey felt a surge of relief knowing she wouldn't be interrupting a speaker. She *really* would've hated that. "Thank you so much, Liesel," she said after checking the woman's badge.

She snuck into the back of the ballroom. Liesel was right. They were serving salads but the formal program hadn't started. She counted tables up the side of the room, finding hers easily. As she headed that way, she saw the back of a very familiar blond lob that, if she was correct, would not be happy to see her. And, of course, the only empty seat was directly to the blonde's left. When someone at the table said something funny, she laughed and turned just far enough to confirm Bailey's suspicions. Skye Kohl.

Hell. This was going to be an indigestion-inducing lunch.

Which would make two meals in the last twenty-four hours where her digestion had been affected by Skye. As yesterday had worn on, the look in Skye's eyes before she'd walked away had continued to unsettle Bailey. She'd been so confident after seeing the way Skye had run her hand over Jason's arm, but her horrified expression when Bailey had called her out had her second-guessing her assumptions. And had perhaps exposed underlying biases that she wasn't proud of.

By last night, Bailey had come to the conclusion that, although she didn't condone flirting with subcontractors to get her way or going around Bailey to make requests of her subs directly, she'd been in the wrong with her last barb. Bailey was embarrassed to admit that her experience with Mary and resultant sensitivity to cheating had likely played a part in her reaction.

Even more than she hated being late, she hated being wrong. And she hated apologizing. Unfortunately, she needed to do it now. She'd been hateful, and that wasn't who she was at her core. She just thought she'd have a little more time before running into Skye and having to do it.

Alas, that was not to be, so Bailey put one foot in front of the other, dodging the occasional server carrying trays of salads, and headed to her seat. Perhaps it would be better this way so there wouldn't be any lingering awkwardness the next time they saw Ellie together.

"Is this seat taken?" Bailey asked, placing a shaky hand on Skye's shoulder and leaning so she could be heard over the noise.

Several emotions flashed across Skye's face, startlement to irritation to resignation. "No, if the assignments were correct, I do believe it belongs to you. I'd been hoping you'd decided to sit somewhere else. Or skip the event altogether," she said with a grimace, disdain prevalent in her tone.

Bailey felt nauseous and knew she deserved the ire but still didn't like it. She liked to be the one grimacing at their interactions, not the one causing a grimace. No, that train of thought didn't make sense. She should prefer that they get along or at a minimum, not want to strangle each other.

Skye turned back to the woman on her other side, but Bailey stopped her with a hand on her arm. "I owe you an apology. I'm truly sorry for—"

"Can we *not* do this now?" Skye snapped. "I'm in the middle of something." She gestured to the rest of the table with a subtle tilt of her head.

"Of course," Bailey said, chastened. "But perhaps I could buy you a coffee or a glass of wine after this?" She felt compelled to clear the air as soon as possible. They did have to work together, and Bailey felt like a shit.

"Fine," Skye conceded. "But you'd better watch where you place your hand. What might people think?" She looked pointedly at Bailey's hand—the one Bailey had forgotten she'd placed there—and then back up.

Shame flooded Bailey at the deserved jab. She yanked her hand away as if the temperature of Skye's jacket was seven hundred degrees and jerked into her chair. "Of course. Sorry." Her skin prickled with embarrassment.

Well, that probably couldn't have gone much worse. Bailey reached for her water with a sweaty hand. Though she couldn't pinpoint what she could've done to make it better, other than not have been an ass yesterday, of course.

Luckily, the current president of POWRE stepped to the microphone. Bailey let out a sigh of relief that she didn't have to make small talk and focused on the center of the room.

By the end of the program, Bailey had made several connections around the table and was even scheduled to send one of her guys to bid a project for a property manager she'd just met. All in all, a productive afternoon. With the exception of the frostbite along the right side of her body from her tablemate.

Before the applause for the speaker ended, Skye leaned toward her and said, "I haven't forgotten that I agreed to talk to you, but there are a few people I need to see to before I head out. Are you okay mingling before we grab that drink?"

Bailey resisted the urge to shake her head at Skye's blatant eagerness to get away. "Of course. I would be remiss if I didn't do a little networking myself. I blocked out the rest of this afternoon for this, so let me know when you're ready."

"Will do," Skye said and walked away, her hair swaying behind her.

Bailey headed toward the bar that had been set up during lunch in the back of the room. It might only be two thirty, but it was happy hour for her and anyone else lucky enough not to have to head back to their offices.

"Bailey!"

She turned, searching the crowd. When her eyes landed on a petite brunette with an adorable pixie cut, Bailey smiled automatically.

Bailey had briefly dated a friend of Kirby Davis. Things with the friend had been short once Bailey had realized the friend was looking for Ms. Right rather than Ms. Right Now, but she and Kirby had hit it off and were often each other's wing women at these events.

"Hey, you," Bailey said, pulling Kirby into a hug. "I didn't realize you were going to be here. I thought you were out of town or something."

"At the last minute, I ended up pushing the trip. This is a good event, and I didn't want to miss it."

"One of the best of the year," Bailey agreed. Even with being the boss, she sometimes appreciated an excuse to go to a nice lunch and spend the afternoon drinking and chatting up potential clients on company time. And old friends, of course.

"I wanted to thank you for your insights last month on that little issue with my condo board."

"Of course, what are friends for? Hopefully, you never need me for an issue like that again, but I'm always at your disposal for any questions regarding construction." She still couldn't believe that two management company employees and several board members at

Kirby's condo had created a fake company and passed invoices for work never completed in order to embezzle money. "How much did they end up embezzling? Have you gotten to the bottom of it all?"

"Ugh. It's crazy." Kirby dropped her voice to a whisper. "Over one-point-five million dollars."

"Oh my God. That is *in*sane," she whispered back. "I can't believe no one realized it."

"I know. Thankfully, the condo management company made us whole, and we pressed charges against the board members. Everything got cleaned up, but how outrageous." Kirby faced the bartender as they made it to the front of the line. "Old-fashioned with Maker's Mark, please, half the normal sweetener. Bailey, what can I get you?"

"I can get my own drink, Kirby."

"I know you can, but you single-handedly saved my condo a ridiculous sum of money, so the least I can do is buy you a drink." She laughed as she good-naturedly punched Bailey on the shoulder.

"Good point." Bailey laughed as well. "I think you actually owe me a lot of drinks."

"Don't push your luck, friend."

"How quickly your loyalties turn." To the bartender she said, "Grey Goose and tonic with a lime, please."

"Coming right up." Bailey really appreciated when these events hosted a top-shelf bar.

The bar was open, but Kirby gave the bartender a generous tip. As they walked away, Bailey said, "I hear cheers are in order for you."

"What do you mean?" Kirby tilted her head to the side.

"I heard through the grapevine that Ms. Perpetually Single is off the market."

A hint of red made its way into Kirby's cheeks. "There are no secrets in this industry, are there?" She shook her head and clicked her tongue.

"So my source was correct, then?" Bailey teased.

"Yes. I…" Kirby bit her lip and stared into her drink. Very uncharacteristic for her. Bailey had decided to let her off the hook, but Kirby finally said, "It was quite unexpected, but someone from my past was suddenly back in my life. I tried to fight it, but it turns out that the Fates had other ideas. Quinn refilled a hole I didn't realize was there."

Bailey could see the love in her eyes. She gagged a little on the inside but supposed it was sweet. "I'm happy for you. Though it will be harder being one of the last ones not on the hunt for my soulmate.

Regardless, cheers to you and Quinn and your happiness." She lifted her glass.

"Thank you," Kirby said with a look of true contentment plastered across her face as they clinked glasses.

Bailey worked the room with Kirby for more than an hour and a half before she caught sight of Skye slowly making her way toward where Bailey was chatting with a small group of women. She felt a mix of regret and relief; she'd begun to wonder if Skye had forgotten about her.

When she arrived, Bailey politely introduced her around the circle and was quite surprised when Kirby said, "Skye Kohl…did you just get named to the 'Thirty Under Thirty' list?"

Skye's face pinked slightly. "Yes, first and only time. I won't qualify after this year, but how did you hear that? The list hasn't been released yet."

Bailey was surprised she was twenty-nine. Judging by her youthful face and level of self-absorption, she could've been much younger. Though given her professional accomplishments, Bailey should have known she wasn't as young as she seemed.

"There are no secrets in this industry," Kirby said and laughed. "Just ask Bailey here." She lightly shoved Bailey in the arm and turned back to the larger group.

As Kirby shifted her attention away, Skye quietly but sharply said, "I've talked to everyone I want to. Do you want to get that drink?" Her lips were drawn back slightly, as though she smelled something unpleasant and was trying to hide her reaction.

Bailey chose to ignore her displeasure. "Sure." She made her excuses to the larger group and to Kirby, said, "It was great catching up with you. Let's do a happy hour soon. Maybe you can bring Quinn. I'd love to meet the woman who got *you* to settle down." She sniggered.

Kirby rolled her eyes but mimed texting. "Sounds great. Text me." When Skye took a step back to leave as well, Kirby congratulated her again and said good-bye.

Bailey didn't miss Kirby's raised eyebrows and questioning stare as she walked away with Skye but shook her head. She certainly wasn't going to get into anything with Kirby right then. It wasn't something she wanted to explain, anyway.

Bailey and Skye decided to head to Once Upon a Wine, the best wine bar in downtown, to grab a glass rather than stay at the hotel lobby bar. Better selection and decent pricing. Bailey also appreciated that there was less of a chance of a colleague eavesdropping or interrupting them.

They managed polite chitchat on the two-block walk over, and Bailey impressed herself with her ability to carry a conversation about the weather without it devolving into a major disagreement, given that she and Skye seemed like oil and vinegar.

They grabbed a table, and Skye picked up the wine-by-the-glass list and perused it. Lost in contemplation, she thankfully didn't seem to notice Bailey's attention. Bailey was hypnotized watching her absentmindedly toy with her earring. Her fingernails, surprisingly short given the terrifying trend of stiletto nails currently in vogue, were delicately manicured and traced the edge of the diamond accented swirl at her left ear. Skye sighed a "hmm" as she released her earring and ran her index finger around the outside of her earlobe. Bailey's mind wandered as she had a flash of what it would feel like if that finger was hers, or better yet, her tongue. She swallowed. Hard.

Hell. She had to get her hormones in check. She really did not like this woman at all. And yet she could not pull her gaze away as Skye's finger moved from her ear down to her neck.

When Skye said, "They have such a great selection. I don't know what to choose," Bailey finally ripped her eyes away from Skye's ear. With relief, she saw that Skye still hadn't looked up and seemed, thankfully, entirely oblivious to Bailey's ogling.

"I know, so good," Bailey said, even though she hadn't yet looked at the list. She realized with horror that she wasn't talking about wine. Shit. She mentally chastised herself. What was it about this infuriating woman that brought her lust-eyes out to play? She did finally look at the list right before the server came to take their orders.

Skye asked for a glass of cabernet, and since Bailey hadn't really looked, she quickly said, "Make that two, please." As she said it, however, she skimmed the list and realized Skye had ordered the most expensive wine on the menu. Bailey shook her head, wondering if she'd done that on purpose since Bailey was buying. Probably. Well played, she silently admitted, and she couldn't even be irritated. If their positions had been reversed, she suspected she would've done the same.

There wasn't an easy way to do this, so she jumped right in once the server walked away. "I'm incredibly sorry for what I implied yesterday. I didn't really mean it."

"Oh?" Skye arched a perfect eyebrow, and her voice dripped with incredulity. With that one word, Bailey knew this was going to be more difficult than she'd hoped. Not that she should have been surprised.

"Honestly? In the moment that I walked around the corner and saw your hand on Jason's arm and the way you were leaning in? Yes, that is what I thought, but that says more about me than you." That was embarrassingly true. "I was being an idiot. I don't know you, but I do know your reputation. I know Ellie thinks very highly of you. I'm sorry that I thought it, even for a moment, and I'm sorry I said it. Truly. I have a little baggage when it comes to cheating, and I unfairly jumped to a vile conclusion." Bailey placed a hand on Skye's wrist, hoping she could see the sincerity on her face, even though Bailey hadn't meant to share that much about herself.

"You already know that it's hard to be a woman in this field. There aren't many of us. We're making gains, but we aren't there yet. Anytime I close a huge deal, there are always the little men who say things like, the only reason the client picked me was affirmative action, or more offensively, I only won the assignment because I was sleeping with the client. Your implication sounded a lot like them, and it was even worse because it came from another woman."

The hurt in her eyes affected Bailey more deeply than she would have expected. She had never seen Skye so vulnerable. Hell, until that moment, she hadn't really believed Skye could *be* vulnerable, and that made her feel even worse than she had before. "I know. I was irritated that it felt like you were trying to undermine me, and I was a bitch. I'm sorry. Truly." She looked at the table in embarrassment at her behavior and then back at Skye.

Skye studied her for a drawn-out breath before finally emitting a long-suffering sigh. "Fine, you're forgiven. Please stop with the sad puppy dog eyes. I can't take it anymore."

Bailey scoffed but lifted her glass. "I do not—emphasis on the not—have puppy dog eyes. But…" She smiled and waited until Skye met her gaze again. "Here's to fresh starts. Maybe with less assumptions and a little more mutual respect?" She hoped Skye didn't take that toast poorly. Bailey was completely in the wrong, but for them to be able to work together effectively, Skye needed to try a little bit too. Bailey hoped that, after they got to know each other a bit more, interacting might be easier for them both.

Skye squinted with pursed lips. "You're really pushing it here, aren't you?"

Bailey chucked but didn't say anything.

"Fine. I will admit that we could find a little more respect on both sides. To a new beginning." She clinked her glass against Bailey's, and they both took a sip.

It was Bailey's first taste of the wine Skye had chosen, and she couldn't stop the moan that escaped her lips as it delighted her palate. It was a bold California cabernet, and Bailey couldn't have picked something better had she scoured the list herself. With her eyes still closed, she swirled the wine and took another sip. "Wow."

When she slowly opened her eyes, still appreciating the flavors on her tongue, Skye was a little flushed and was watching her intently.

"Sorry, did you say something?" Bailey asked. "I was a little enamored. If it was legal to marry a wine, we'd be heading to the courthouse right now." She must have missed something important with the way Skye was staring.

"No, no. I'm glad you like it."

"I might regret saying this." She smiled so Skye would know she was kidding. Mostly. "But you have impeccable taste. This wine is amazing."

"Oh, you can't take that one back." Skye clicked her tongue and nodded. "Bailey Kaczmarek thinks Skye Kohl has impeccable taste. Could you say that again? I'm going to open the recorder app on my phone." She threw her head back and laughed, and Bailey stared at the delicate line of her throat. She wondered what Skye's pulse point would taste like.

Jesus, where had that come from? She shook her head and hoped again that Skye didn't notice the extra attention. She cleared her throat, trying to relieve the sudden dryness, and took another sip of wine. Neither were particularly effective. "I didn't say you had impeccable taste in everything. I was only talking about the wine."

Skye, still laughing, managed, "Oh no, you don't. You said, and I quote"—she mimed opening a notepad and flipping to the correct page—"'you have impeccable taste.' You did *not* say, 'you have impeccable taste *in wine*.' I heard you and took note. Right here." She flashed the imaginary notebook in her palm. It would be annoyingly cocky, except that Skye letting go and relaxing enough to laugh so hard her eyes were tearing up connected to Bailey on a deeper, more basic level. She thought for what felt like the seventy-fifth time that afternoon that she really needed to get herself under control.

She scoffed while suppressing her own laughter. She wasn't going to give in. "I am amending my previous statement to apply to wine only. You have impeccable taste *in wine*."

"You can lie to yourself all you want, Bailey, but you and I both know the truth. This one," she pointed her finger toward herself and tapped it lightly on the bare skin exposed in the vee opening of her blouse, "has impeccable taste. Maybe I'll add that to my business card. I can see it now, 'Skye Kohl, licensed real estate broker and woman of impeccable taste.'" She gazed at a far corner of the room with a dreamy expression.

Bailey couldn't hold her laughter back at that image. "Oh, please send the first card to me. I'll post it on the bulletin board in my office." Who knew Skye actually had a sense of humor? Bailey had, up until this conversation, imagined her living in an isolated ice palace, like Elsa in *Frozen*. No real warmth or personality. This was going to complicate things.

"So she does have a sense of humor." Skye beamed at her, and Bailey again noticed how perfectly straight and white her teeth were. "I was beginning to wonder if you had a stick…" Bailey cocked her head and wondered if Skye was really going to say that. Happily, Skye toned down the rest of her phrasing. "Uh…someplace uncomfortable."

Bailey chucked. "Right back at ya. Word for word. No offense, since you just said the same about me."

"None taken." Skye winked.

Bailey didn't think anyone outside of romance novels and creepy dudes in bars actually winked. More surprising than the wink itself was her reaction to it. The bees flitting about in her lower belly were too much in that moment, so she stood quickly—but hopefully, casually—and said, "On that happy note, I…I'll be right back." She headed to the restroom as rapidly as she dared without taking out a billboard to advertise her nervousness, praying Skye hadn't seen the blush she could feel creeping up her chest.

CHAPTER FIVE

Skye couldn't believe she was legitimately enjoying herself with Bailey. She'd been admittedly pissed after their last meeting and, as a result, had given her a hard time when they'd first sat down, but since then, Bailey had relaxed, and Skye was…having a good time. Though it was bizarre how Bailey had jumped up from the table and nearly run to the restroom.

When Skye had agreed to this drink, she'd been certain she'd try to drain it while she let Bailey make an insincere apology, then make her excuses because she couldn't imagine something worse than spending time with Bailey of her own volition. However, as the end of her glass was nearing, she was actually thinking about asking if Bailey wanted to get another. And maybe a cheese plate. Bailey was funny and certainly wasn't hard to look at, either.

Not that she would let her mind go there. Yes, Bailey was beautiful with her high cheekbones and green eyes, darker near the pupil and vibrant around the edges. Her hair was different today as well. Rather than windswept like the first two times, today, it had soft loose waves floating above her head like a choppy ocean of hair that was begging for fingers to run through it. And, God, the look on her face when she'd taken her first sip of wine…

Whoa. Where had that come from? Skye needed to keep her hands and her thoughts to herself. It was probably the one glass she'd had at the event and the second she'd had there. That had to be it. Therefore, as soon as Bailey got back, she would say she had another engagement and get out of there before any other inhibitions were dulled. Yes, that was the safe choice. And luckily, Bailey was on her way back.

However, when Bailey sat down, those were not the words that found their way out of Skye's mouth. Instead, she said, "Looks like we're nearing the end of our glasses. Want to have one more before we call it a night?" *Shit,* she thought as a small voice inside her chanted, *say yes, say yes.*

Bailey checked her watch, and Skye could see her chewing the inside of her cheek. "Sure. Let me text my neighbor and ask if she can let my dog out."

Skye really didn't like dogs. At all. They were drooly and smelly and dumb. And got hair all over your clothes. But she certainly wasn't going to say that after the look that came over Bailey's face when she spoke of her dog. Instead, she asked, "Oh, what kind of a dog do you have?" She thought that was what someone was supposed to ask when someone else said they had a dog. Even though she couldn't care less.

Bailey looked up from her phone, her face a little dreamy. "I've got a pocket pittie. A pocket pit bull," she clarified when Skye narrowed her eyes. "She's basically a smaller version of a traditional pit bull. She still has that stocky frame and a head that is way too large for her body, but she only weighs about thirty pounds. Do you want to see a picture?"

Skye was surprised that she had asked rather than pulling out a picture of her dog, but Skye was trying to be polite. New beginnings and all that. "Yeah, I'd love to see her." An exaggeration, especially since pit bulls were known for being vicious. Maybe she *should* make an excuse that she'd forgotten she had something else this evening.

Bailey scrolled a few times before grinning and selecting a photo. "Sorry, I have a lot of work photos on my phone, and I wanted to find a good one of her." She flipped the phone around, and Skye smiled at the expression on her face before she even looked at the photo.

The image surprisingly softened her a little bit. The dog was probably still smelly and dumb, but she was almost cute, with a gorgeous gray coat and an enormous head that made her look a little like a bobblehead. That huge head was cocked to the left, and one of her ears stood up while the other one flopped toward her jaw. If dogs could smile, Skye would have sworn this little girl was smiling at the camera. She grabbed the phone, zooming in on her face before she realized she was doing it.

"What's her name?" she finally asked.

"Patsy."

"She's adorable. I honestly am not a *huge* dog person." That was putting it mildly. "But she has a sweet face. Aren't pit bulls supposed to be vicious?" She watched Bailey's face fall. "I don't mean anything by that. I just thought they were mean dogs with those big jowls and muscular chests? I'm sorry, I don't really know much about them other than the gangs in my neighborhood had them growing up, and they seemed really mean." Shit. She hadn't meant to share anything about her childhood, much less that she'd grown up in an area with gangs.

Luckily, Bailey seemed to be focused on Skye's perception of the dog and not about her childhood secrets. "They are as mean or nice as any other dog. It's all about how they're raised and how they're loved. If they're loved. Pit bulls are sometimes known as nanny dogs because they're loving and loyal. Unfortunately, those traits can be exploited, but Patsy wouldn't hurt a fly. Well, that isn't entirely true. She's a terrier and loves to chase squirrels and bunnies, and I'm not sure what she would do if she caught one, but luckily, they know better than to camp out in my yard." Bailey laughed, and Skye's chest went tight.

The server walked up, and Bailey ordered another round. "Is another glass of the same good for you?"

Skye was a little surprised because she'd intentionally ordered the most expensive glass on the menu. So maybe Bailey had money despite being the company's newbie. Or she was expensing the cocktail hour. Either way, Skye was happy for another glass. "Sure. What about a cheese platter? They have a pecorino that is the best I've had in the city. It's perfectly nutty and sharp but not overly so."

Bailey seemed to school her face as she shrugged one shoulder, and Skye didn't know what to make of it. However, Bailey said, "Sounds good to me. A little cheese to soak up some of this wine wouldn't go amiss, even though I'm not driving." Apparently, Bailey also wanted to stay, even though she seemed nonchalant.

Skye wasn't going to overanalyze it. "If you aren't driving, can you walk home from here?" she asked, curiosity getting the better of her. And she was eager to change the subject before Bailey remembered the gang comment.

Bailey cackled. "Technically, I could, but it would be an awfully long walk. I live in Andersonville."

Skye laughed since it was about ten miles from where they were. "An especially long walk after a few glasses of wine."

"Happily, we have taxis and Lyfts and Ubers to save us."

"You said it. I wouldn't even walk home from here, and I live in Lincoln Park, which is much closer." Andersonville was an interesting development, however, and Skye's heart fluttered as she wondered if it confirmed her suspicion about Bailey's sexuality. "Andersonville, huh? Where the ladies are?" Andersonville had a reputation for being where lesbians lived and played. Though she knew she was playing with fire with that question and shouldn't have asked it, she couldn't keep it in.

Bailey seemed to have a hard time not choking on her wine, which brought a smile to Skye's lips. She attempted to hide it by taking another sip of her own wine.

Once Bailey managed to stop coughing and was able to take a drink, she said, "Not as many as there used to be, and a lot of the old bars have closed, but yes, I suppose." She paused and stared into her glass as though trying to decide if she wanted to say something else.

If there was one thing Skye had learned in business and closing deals, it was that it was always better to remain silent for a couple of beats longer than felt comfortable. If there was an awkward pause, most people would try to fill it with something, and oftentimes, they would be much more candid than they had intended. Skye wasn't disappointed today, either. She rarely was with this negotiation tactic.

"I would be lying if I said that reputation didn't influence my decision to look there." Bailey shook her head. "My mother would be much happier if I'd chosen to live closer to the family enclave out in Jefferson Park." Her cheeks flushed, and Skye wondered if she'd also said a little more than she'd meant to. Was Bailey feeling enough of an effect from the wine that her tongue was that loose?

However, it was a nice confirmation that Skye's gaydar still worked well, even though she would never do anything about it.

She was going to ask about Jefferson Park when Bailey surprised her further by asking, "Are you, you know, a…fan…of Andersonville?" Her eyes grew wide and panicked at her own question, as if she'd surprised herself and was perhaps a little embarrassed, but she didn't try to take it back, and another awkward silence descended upon the table. Bailey swirled the wine in her glass without lifting it from the table and seemed mesmerized by the small whirlpool she created.

If Skye didn't answer, would Bailey start talking more? Reveal more? But after a few beats with nothing but silence, against her better judgment, Skye confirmed the roundabout question. "I am. A fan…of Andersonville, that is. I have a lot of fun memories there." Oh God. Why did she say that? It was dangerous on so many levels.

Skye focused on Bailey's collarbones and throat and watched as she swallowed forcefully and then took a sip of wine. Skye bit the corner of her lip as her effect on Bailey caused an unexpected flare of heat within her. She wasn't ready to explore any of that mess. She also wished she could rewind the last two minutes and not make that comment about Andersonville to start all of this.

"Um." Skye paused. "If you could keep that little Andersonville nugget to yourself, I would appreciate it. I'm not *entirely* out in our little professional community." She didn't like the flash of disappointment on Bailey's face, so she placed a hand on Bailey's arm and clarified: "It's not that I'm not out at all. I don't hide who I am. I'm out to my family, my friends, my actual friends in the industry. I go to Pride. But at work, I don't talk about who I'm dating. I mean, I don't really date seriously anyway, so there's never been someone whose photo I wanted to have on my desk."

Bailey nodded slightly, so Skye continued, "I know there are some rumors about me, but I've never confirmed nor denied. I'm already 'that aggressive female broker.' I don't want to be 'that aggressive dyke broker.'" She had no guilt over who she chose to be open with, but for some reason, the look on Bailey's face made her feel sad deep down. Entirely ridiculous.

"I get it," Bailey said. "It's unfortunate that we live in a world where that has to be a thing."

And there was that soulful stare again. Things had gotten a little heavy, and that little flare was threatening to awaken inside her once more, so Skye tried to steer them back to a safe subject. She cleared her throat more robustly than was probably necessary. "So you grew up in Jefferson Park?" It was quite a ways northwest of downtown and was generally seen as a working-class neighborhood, though it was quickly gentrifying.

Bailey leaned to the side and coughed softly. She rubbed her fingers through the short hair on the left side of her head before facing Skye again. "Yeah, Dad's retired Chicago PD, and Mom stayed at home with us until I went to kindergarten, then went to work in the front office at the school so she could stay close. Blue-collar through and through."

"There's no shame in that," Skye said without much thought. She wanted to share more about herself and her very blue-collar background, but that would make her so…vulnerable.

Before she came to a decision on how much to share, Bailey said testily, "Why would there be any shame? I'm in the construction business. Still pretty blue-collar." Her eyes flashed, and Skye realized she needed to tread lightly to not ruin what they had shared this afternoon.

"I didn't…" But unfortunately, she was having a hard time deciding what she could say that would make things better and not worse. She rarely struggled with what to say but finally settled on a simple, "I'm sorry. I didn't mean that the way it sounded. Look, I'm the daughter of a janitor and the granddaughter of an immigrant from Ukraine who became a janitor when she moved to the States. It doesn't get much more blue-collar than that. I grew up in Ukrainian Village. It was important to my mom that my sister and I had better lives than she'd had."

"So that 'better' meant making the magical transition from blue-collar to white? Because you can't be considered successful if you *work* for a living?" Bailey's pitch was as sharp as the blade of a knife.

Since when was wanting to have a white-collar job a crime? She needed to be able to work with Bailey, and things were rapidly spinning out of hand. "That's not what I said. I'm sorry if my intent was twisted. I didn't mean that there was anything wrong with a blue-collar job."

"Didn't you? That perception that everyone needs to have a college degree to succeed is one of our country's greatest lies. Are you aware that a union carpenter with a few years' experience can make six figures and have essentially zero in student loan debt? And they generally make more than half that less than a year out of high school? But we place so much emphasis on going to school and taking on crippling student loans so we can wear suits and feel superior about ourselves. And that viewpoint just reinforces the stigma that that's the only path. Not that it's easy for everyone—getting into unions can be tough, especially for women and minorities—but no one even talks about it as an option. There are a lot of different ways to succeed, and there is never any shame in being blue-collar or not going to college."

Skye was taken aback by such a passionate reaction. She certainly hadn't meant to offend and wondered if Bailey hadn't gone to college, if that was why she was so prickly. That didn't make sense because she wasn't in a trade. She worked in construction, but she was on the estimating and business development side versus the getting her hands dirty side.

"I'm really sorry, Bailey. I truly didn't mean to offend." She placed a hand on Bailey's forearm in an attempt to get her to make eye contact again.

When Bailey looked up, the corners of her mouth were turned down. Skye didn't like this sad version of her. "I know you didn't. I don't think that you get it, though. Just because we went to college and wear business clothes or suits doesn't make us better than anyone else."

Well, that answered the college question but still didn't explain why she was so passionate about it. Skye tried a different tactic. "I don't think I'm better than anyone."

Bailey cut that train short with a quick tilt of her head, disbelief written all across her. "Don't you?"

The undertones of condescension got her back up. "No!"

"Maybe I'm making too many assumptions." Bailey sighed and looked at her watch. "I'm sorry, but I didn't realize how late it was getting. I promised my parents I would trek out there for dinner, so I have to run." Before Skye had a chance to process her words, Bailey signaled for the check.

Skye should feel relieved, but she didn't. She also didn't want Bailey to know she was disappointed, so she made a subtle show of looking at her own watch and gasping before she said, "Oh, goodness. How is it already six thirty? Me too."

When the server walked over, Bailey handed him her credit card without even looking at the bill.

"I was going to see if we could split that, but you didn't even give me the chance to ask. Are you planning to expense it?" Skye said.

Bailey scoffed and stared for a beat before shaking her head. "No, but thanks. You can get the next one." Her tone wasn't warm, and Skye wondered if she was as certain as Skye was that there wouldn't be a next time after the train wreck this one had become.

"Okay, well, thank you for the drinks. The wine was delicious."

"You're welcome."

Skye tried to be civil again. "So I guess I'll see you on-site next week when we go through the budget pricing with Ellie?"

Bailey let out a long breath with her eyes closed, and Skye tried to keep her temper in check, but it was becoming more challenging with every passing moment. What *was* this weird-ass mood swing? Skye hoped the server came back with the credit card quickly.

Bailey opened her eyes. "Yep. Friday morning."

"I'll see you then, I guess."

"Yep." Bailey seemed to stuff her credit card into her wallet while simultaneously putting her coat on. A feat of physics. "See you then," she said and walked away, leaving Skye with an unpleasant emptiness and the feeling that a tornado had slammed into their table and kept moving.

Skye resigned herself to the fact that she and Bailey wouldn't ever be friendly colleagues. Even cordial acquaintances might be too much to hope for. Which was unfortunate because up until she'd somehow pissed Bailey off beyond the point of recovery, Skye had been having a great time. A really great time. The best time she'd had with someone she wasn't related to in as long as she could remember.

As she got into her taxi a few minutes later, she realized they had forgotten about the cheese platter they had ordered that had never arrived. She idly wondered if Bailey had been charged for it and hoped not, despite the uneasy end to their evening.

CHAPTER SIX

As Bailey parallel-parked her truck a few houses down from her childhood home, Patsy went on high alert, looking out the window as though, if she let her guard down for a moment, someone might try to carjack them. "Settle down, Patsy girl. No bad guys are out there. I promise. We're just at Grandma's house."

Patsy was an odd dog. She was fine while they drove forward, but the second Bailey put her truck into reverse, Patsy became certain that death was imminent. Unfortunately, her crazy barking and jumping around like a lunatic made it much harder to see where Bailey was aiming the back end of her truck. She managed it without hitting anything. It just took longer than necessary.

When Bailey walked in the front door, she yelled, "Hey, Mom, hey, Dad. Watch out, the little tank is on the loose." She released Patsy from the leash. As always, Patsy darted straight toward the kitchen. It was amazing she could run in anything resembling a straight line with how wildly her butt was wiggling in excitement.

Bailey had barely slipped her shoes off when her mom moved into the doorway to the kitchen and squatted to receive Patsy's excited kisses. "Patsy Cline, Grandma's best girl," her mom said as she pulled Patsy into her arms. "There's my baby."

"Don't worry about me, Mother, it's only your actual baby at the door," Bailey muttered under her breath.

But Bailey's mom still had bionic hearing. "You have given me the perfect grand-puppy. You should take that as a compliment. I love you just as much as I love your baby, sweetheart."

"Thanks, Mom," Bailey said, walking into the small kitchen of her youth. Granted, it had seen a few updates since then. The old plywood cabinets had been upgraded to oak, the old laminate countertops exchanged for granite. The ancient appliances had been swapped out for stainless steel. The sole exception was the gorgeous, copper-plated Chambers stove that was still in as perfect condition as it was back in the 50s when Bailey's grandparents had bought it. It shined like a harvest moon in a country night sky. Although Bailey had a gorgeous, modern, professional stove and range in her own home, she still had a little stove envy because her mother's was so beautiful, even though it had half the features of her own.

"It smells amazing in here, Mom. What are you making?" When her mom finally stopped kissing Patsy and stood, Bailey pulled her into a hug, leaning back a little to avoid the remnants of wet dog kisses on her face. "I don't really understand why you let her kiss you that much, Mom."

"*Pfft,*" her mom said and playfully slapped her shoulder. "She's your dog. Maybe you should teach her not to lick like it's going out of style."

"Mother," Bailey said, exasperated. "I do, but when you lean down and let her have her way with you, you tell her that it's okay to do that."

"*Pfft,*" she said again and went back over to the stove. "I know that's not true. And we're having golumpki." Cabbage rolls. One of Bailey's favorites. Uh-oh, that probably meant eligible bachelorette number thirty-seven would be coming by this evening, so her mom had made her favorite to get her in a good mood.

"Yummy," Bailey said despite her mild irritation. "Who else is coming to dinner?"

"Oh, the usual. Your siblings, Gammy…" She trailed off suspiciously and busied herself with the pan on the stovetop.

"Who else, Mother?" Bailey pushed.

"Well, I was at the hairdresser with Gammy this week." Oh boy, exactly as Bailey had suspected. "And they have a new shampoo girl."

Great, a shampoo girl from the salon who happened to be gay. Shit. Bailey realized her inner monologue was starting to sound a lot like the snobby Skye Kohl. She redoubled her efforts to not be judgmental.

"Shampoo girl is a misnomer, as she wasn't exactly a young girl, and apparently, used to drive trucks. She took the shampoo job as an intermediate step to retirement. Anyway, she also goes to our church, and her youngest is thirty-one or something and also happens to be gay, so I invited them over for dinner. They're nice women."

And there it was. "Mother." Bailey huffed. "Didn't I ask you to please stop setting me up with strangers? I don't have time to date. And I don't have the inclination. Things didn't work out with Mary. Uncle Chester was divorced too many times to keep track of. This job doesn't lend itself to a relationship, and I'm completely okay with that. Please believe me and stop trying so hard."

Her mother simply said, "Hmm," and kept bustling around the kitchen.

Before she could press the point, Gammy came downstairs. "Bailey," she exclaimed. "I'm so happy to see you."

Bailey walked over to the stairs to scoop her petite grandmother into a hug, mindful not to squeeze her too hard. "Gammy, it's so good to see you."

"Why the surprise? I live here." Gammy's brows furrowed. "Are you drunk?"

Bailey barked a laugh. Gammy had moved in with her parents about a year after her grandfather, Pop KZ, had passed away while Bailey was at college. "Not surprise, Gammy. Just excitement. I've missed your face." She was probably Bailey's favorite person on the planet. When Bailey was a kid and her siblings had been off doing fun, older-kid things, Bailey had stayed at Gammy and Pop KZ's house, and they'd always made the sleepovers seem more fun than whatever her older siblings had been up to. They'd been like a second set of parents.

"Missed me? It's been three days, kid. But it's flattering. It's good to see you too, my dear." Gammy pulled her into a hug again, and Bailey let out a contented sigh. It had been a long week, and the disastrous drinks with Skye the night before had been the icing on the cake. Wrapped in her grandmother's arms, Bailey could feel the stress of the week slide from her shoulders into a benign pool at her feet.

Bailey whispered so her mom hopefully couldn't hear. "Also, I'm hopeful that you can protect me from Mom's matchmaking. Don't you ever want to have a family dinner where you don't have to worry about some interloper that Mom's trying to set me up with hanging about?"

"She only does it because she loves you, my dear." Gammy patted her on the back. "But I'll do what I can." Gammy gave her a discreet thumbs-up and wrapped an arm around her hips as they headed back toward the kitchen.

Pandemonium broke out as her brother, Brian, his wife, Melissa, and their toddler twins, Jacob and Jeremy, burst through the front door. Jacob and Jeremy were both crying and trying to punch each other.

"Please, someone, save us from these terrorists," Brian shouted as he closed the door.

Melissa laughed. "Brian, stop. Though if anyone wants to distract these two, we would happily entertain offers."

Bailey chuckled in relief that she didn't have kids of her own but had nephews she could play with at any time. She called for Patsy, knowing that she was sitting dutifully next to her mother while waiting for "accidental treats," as her mom liked to call them. And she would be elated once she realized that little people were here to love on her.

"Jeremy, Jacob, who wants to see their favorite cousin, Patsy?" They immediately stopped trying to hit each other and looked at Bailey. "But you have to stop crying and be gentle. Your yelling and swinging arms will scare her." That would be true for most dogs, though not Patsy. However, Bailey needed the lower decibel level for her own sanity and was pretty sure the rest of the family would thank her for the tiny white lie.

They ran to the dining room where Patsy sat vibrating with excitement at seeing the boys. "Okay, give them a little love," Bailey said. Patsy jumped from the sit she was barely holding and ran over, her little body wiggling like crazy. Within thirty seconds and after bathing both boys' faces in wet kisses, she lay on her back, in heaven as the twins rubbed her belly and nuzzled her face.

"Thank you," Brian and Melissa whispered, pulling Bailey into a hug.

Brian continued, "I have no idea what actually started their little tiff, but they've been going at it off and on since Melissa picked them up at daycare."

"Happy Patsy can be of assistance. Really, she's in her element, and they'll tire her out so much that she probably won't even need an evening walk tonight." Bailey trusted Patsy with the boys but still kept an eye on them, just to make sure they all played safely, and the boys didn't do anything to scare Patsy.

Shortly after Brian and company took over the house, Bailey's sisters, Roxanne and Jessica, arrived with their husbands, Dave and Ed. All her siblings lived within a few minutes of their childhood home, so they'd walked over together. About five minutes before dinner was ready, Bailey was unsurprised to see "the setup" arrive.

Elena was attractive, with long wavy brown hair and a beautiful complexion. Bailey liked her well enough, but there wasn't a spark, despite her mom's efforts to push them together. During one of the more obvious attempts to get them to spend time alone, her mom asked Bailey and Elena to get the cake out of the refrigerator and serve it.

They never served dessert—normally, everyone lined up and grabbed dessert like they did dinner—and asking Bailey and Elena to serve dessert to thirteen people, plus the twins, seemed ridiculous, but Bailey wasn't in the mood to fight. It would give her a few minutes to make sure Elena didn't have unrealistic expectations.

As soon as they were in the kitchen alone, Bailey faced Elena and said, "You seem really great, and I could totally see being friends with you. I don't want this to be awkward, but my meddlesome mother refuses to take no for an answer when I ask her to stop doing this. I'm not on the market right now." She squeezed Elena's arm to soften the blow.

"Oh, thank God. That's so much less awkward." Elena laughed. "I'm not on the market, either."

"And yet you came here on a blind date to meet a woman and her *entire* family?" Bailey laughed at the ridiculousness. "Could you please grab the dessert plates?" She pointed to a cabinet as she reached into the refrigerator to pull out the two cake containers. Her mother had been on a baking kick and was trying out new recipes every few days for family dinners. They were all delicious, but Bailey had had to increase her running mileage to offset it.

Elena shook her head. "It's only to get my mother off my back. This will buy me a few weeks before she tries to hook me up with someone else."

Bailey chuckled. "Glad to hear I'm not the only one with a mother intent on marrying me off. Although…" She took the lid off the first cake container, the delicious smell giving her a sugar high before she even took a bite. "Some aggravation is acceptable to be able to eat this cake. It looks like pistachio today and smells amazing."

"That does smell delicious," Elena said, grabbing a knife out of the block and handing it over. "The really stupid thing is, I have a girlfriend."

"You what?" Bailey stopped slicing and glanced at Elena. She couldn't understand why Elena's girlfriend would let her go on random blind dates.

"Yeah." Elena sighed sadly. "But I'm afraid to tell my parents about her."

"I don't mean to pry, but you're obviously out, or your parents wouldn't be trying to set you up with me, so what are you afraid of?" She went back to slicing and plating.

"I'm afraid they won't accept her because she's not white, and she's not Catholic. So I'm afraid to tell them."

It saddened Bailey that this was still a worry. "I'm sorry, that sucks. How long have you been together?"

"Five months," Elena answered after a moment.

Bailey gasped. Had she heard her right? "Five months?" At Elena's nod, she said, "Five months is a long time to hide something like this, especially if your mom keeps setting you up every few weeks."

"I know. I'm a coward." Elena dropped her forehead onto the counter.

"I don't know your parents, but if, as staunch Catholics, they were able to get comfortable with you being gay, I'm betting they'll be able to get past the other issues. I know it's scary, but you can't keep this a secret forever."

"Ugh, I know." She groaned. "But I don't know if I'm ready."

"You're probably never going to be. But you should do it before it's too late." Bailey smiled, feeling sorry for Elena and also thankful her family had never made her fear bringing someone home—after the initial coming-out panic, anyway. "Not that I'm an expert, but if you want, we can exchange numbers, and you can text me anytime you need cheerleading or encouragement or someone to vent to."

"Cool. That'd be great. Thank you."

After dessert, Brian and Melissa packed up their sleeping boys and headed out, followed by Elena. It seemed she didn't want to be rude but was ready to get home to her girlfriend. Not that Bailey could blame her.

However, her mom must have seen Bailey give Elena her phone number. As soon as Elena drove off, her mom said, "See? I knew if I introduced you to enough women, you'd find one that you like."

Roxanne and Jessica said, "Ooh, Bailey's got a girlfriend," and giggled. Sometimes, they were so creepy.

"Sorry to disappoint you, Mom, but it wasn't like that at all. She's going through something, and I told her I'd be her cheerleader. That's it." Bailey wouldn't break Elena's confidence, but she also didn't want her mother to have any false illusions. "And you two." She pointed at her sisters. "What are you, twelve?"

Roxanne and Jessica made faces, but Bailey watched her mom's face fall before she said, "Well, hell. Back to the drawing board, I guess."

Why was she always subjected to a guilt trip because she wasn't interested in another random setup? "No, Mom. Not back to the drawing board. Please, I implore you, stop. I'm thirty-three years old—an adult by all standards—and I do not need my mother to find me a mate. You have three other married children and two grandchildren, plus a grand-puppy, so you aren't missing out on *anything* by me not being married."

"It's not me who's missing out, sweetheart, it's you." Her mom patted her cheek lovingly. "And anyway, how am I going to get you to move back home unless you get married?"

Bailey tipped her head back against the couch. "Mother, it's not like I moved to the other side of the country. I live, like, seven miles from here. In the same city. It takes me twenty minutes to get here."

"Yeah, but you can't walk."

"Leave the poor girl alone, Loll." Gammy thankfully came to Bailey's rescue. "She can live wherever she wants, and she's still here for dinner several nights a week."

Her mom good-naturedly scoffed. "*You* can say that. All your kids live within a mile of here."

"That's true, but seven miles is still very close. I bet I could still walk it," Gammy the spitfire said.

"You got it, Gammy," Bailey said and gave her a high five. "And on that happy note, I've got to head home and get that one"—she pointed at a snoring Patsy—"and this one"—she pointed at herself—"into bed. We're beat." Of all the setups her mother had sprung on her, Elena was the most normal, but Bailey truly had no use for any of it. She and Patsy were very content and had no intention of changing that. She didn't need a relationship to be happy.

On the ride home, however, with vehement denials of wanting a relationship still at the top of her mind, Bailey flashed back to drinks with Skye the other evening. It wasn't a date, but it had almost felt like one. Bailey had been completely surprised at how much she'd been enjoying herself until the end. When Skye dislodged the stick up her ass, she was funny. It had been fun to flirt with her. Just a little. Until Skye's snobbery had made an appearance again. Had she overreacted? Maybe.

Knowing Skye was completely self-made altered Bailey's view of her a little, yet she'd still reacted in anger without giving Skye a chance to explain herself. Shit. Why did the picturesque woman rub her the wrong way so often? And why did she continuously force her way into Bailey's thoughts? It was probably best to just let frustration and irritation sit between them; it was easier than fighting the pull between them when they were both relaxed and enjoying themselves.

CHAPTER SEVEN

Other than the certainty of awkwardness with Bailey, Skye had been looking forward to the meeting to go through the exact scope of work and pricing on the spec suite this week with Ellie. One of her favorite things about real estate was watching a raw space, a complete blank slate, be transformed into something tangible and beautiful and getting to be a part of the process. She knew that, sometimes, she could come on a little strong, but she had such a clear vision of what a space could look like—and in turn, how much she could lease it for—that she wanted to make sure she laid everything out for Ellie. That was part of her duty as the owner's agent for leasing.

But, God, it was going to be uncomfortable with Bailey. Skye still wasn't really sure what had happened last week. Bailey's reaction had been so bizarre. It wasn't like Skye had insulted blue-collar workers. It wasn't like she had anything against them, but regardless, she didn't want Ellie to notice any tension, so she was determined to keep things friendly and light during the walk-through.

As if summoned from her subconscious, Bailey walked through the front doors into the lobby with the intern in tow. Shit, what was the intern's name? Skye was normally excellent with names, but for some reason, she was having a hard time coming up with this one, and she couldn't admit it. Especially not after the faux pas last week that she still didn't understand.

Skye implored her subconscious to kick in. What words might she have thought about this girl? She closed her eyes for a brief moment and pictured herself two weeks ago, standing in front of her. Young, inexperienced, curly hair, college, amateur…wait that was is. *Jennifa the amateua.* It didn't matter that it didn't exactly rhyme or that neither word was an actual word. Her name was Jennifer. The tension slid from Skye's shoulders.

She opened her eyes and grinned as they walked up. Bailey's ability to rock the dressier-than-business-casual but not-quite-business-formal look was quite charming. Today she was in dark jeans with a white blouse and a pinstriped charcoal blazer, the sleeves rolled up her forearms again. It seemed almost too casual for their world, but the way Bailey carried herself and the way her clothes fit made them perfect for the occasion.

Before Skye could spend too much time staring, she forced herself to say, "Bailey, Jennifer, great to see you again." They both looked surprised, though Bailey hid hers a little better, and Skye gave herself a mental high five on the name recollection.

It didn't last long, however, as awkwardness set in when no one said anything other than hello. Luckily, Skye was an accomplished small talker. "The sunshine today is gorgeous, isn't it? So much nicer than a couple weeks ago. I'd wished I'd decided to wear galoshes instead of heels in that freezing torrential downpour." She laughed at the memory of her poor wardrobe choices that day, but neither Bailey nor Jennifer even cracked a smile. Tough crowd.

Finally, Bailey said, "Yeah, I wish our office was closer so we could've walked today."

"Where's your office?" Skye asked, trying to keep the conversation going while praying that Ellie and Ryan would hurry the hell up; this was bordering on physically painful.

"West Loop," Bailey answered curtly.

"Oh, nice. In one of the new office buildings that have gone up or been renovated in the last few years?"

"No, we're in an older warehouse a little farther west. A little outside the 'trendy' area." She actually made air quotes.

"Oh," Skye said. Given their reputation as one of the premier interior construction companies in the city, she had been expecting City Beautiful Construction to be in a newer loft. Skye was a little disappointed. Thinking of CBC in an old building tarnished their image, as it seemed in contrast to what they stood for as an interiors construction company.

The tension was still palpable, Jennifer still looked like a nervous puppy, and Bailey's eyes were shooting daggers her way, almost as if she could feel Skye's judgment. Skye wondered if she should offer to buy lunch or something to clear the air but dismissed it because Jennifer being there would certainly make a candid discussion all but impossible.

Skye was preparing to talk about the Cubs' opening day in another attempt to make small talk, but thankfully, Ellie and Ryan finally walked into the lobby, putting an end to the painful moments—that felt like hours—of stilted conversation. Even better, Bailey smiled when she looked toward them, and her face finally lit up. Skye wished she'd been the one to put that expression on Bailey's face, but her heart still tripped.

She sighed as they approached. She hugged Ellie and shook Ryan's hand. "Shall we head up and see what Bailey and Jennifer have for us today?"

"Perfect," Ellie said.

When they all stepped off the elevator, Skye was pleasantly surprised to see Maureen Browning and Bradley Schrock, the property manager and chief engineer, standing just inside the vacant suite. Bradley was a pain in the ass whose primary word was no, but Maureen was nice and did a good job steering things from no to maybe with Bradley. Maureen was also efficient and didn't believe in making things harder than they needed to be.

Before Skye had a chance to speak, Ellie said, "Oh, I forgot to mention that I also invited Maureen and Bradley. I thought they might be helpful in talking feasibility of construction, possible tenant impacts, etc."

"Great idea," Bailey said and walked in the suite door. "Maureen, Bradley, great to see you both again." Her face lit up again as she smiled. She hugged them, and Skye wondered how she had time to get to know them so well since she'd only been working on this assignment for a few weeks. And she really didn't seem all that friendly. Apparently, she just wasn't that friendly to Skye.

Bailey pulled several folders from her leather messenger bag and handed them to Jennifer to pass around, pulling Skye from her thoughts before she could contemplate Bailey's relationship with the building staff further. "Per our meeting on-site several weeks ago, Ryan drew up two separate plans on the most cost-effective location for the kitchen and the logical location for it if price were no option. If you open the folders Jennifer is passing around, you'll see both drawings on either side of the folder and their respective bids."

"Thank you," Ellie said and tucked a lock of curly hair behind her ear.

Skye watched the group review the drawings. She didn't need to review either as they were both crystal clear in her head, so she flipped to the important pages detailing how much each option would cost. She quietly inhaled through her teeth at the difference between the cost-effective plan and the one that she knew made more sense in the space. It was going to be a tough number to convince Ellie to take on.

Bailey said, "I wanted to meet on-site today to look at the bids and decide which layout makes more sense and see if there are areas to bring the price down by cutting nonessential elements."

Skye suppressed her scoff. The "nonessential elements" had to be her additions to the plans.

Ellie whistled and said, "That's a pretty large difference between both plans. Bailey, why is the number so much higher, and are there any places we could save?"

Skye wasn't surprised to hear Ellie's shock, but she hoped she could find a way to still convince Ellie to go with the costlier option.

Skye didn't listen much to what Bailey said. She knew why it was more expensive. It wasn't on the existing plumbing stack, and bringing plumbing to the other side of the space was costly. However, she was confident it was the right layout, so as soon as Bailey stopped talking, Skye said, "Ellie, I know the cost difference is more than what we'd like to see, but the kitchen makes so much more sense on this other wall. Envision, if you will, walking into the space and having an open reception area with room for a few guest chairs and artwork on this wall." She gestured to her left. "Imagine the first impression of a bright, airy reception versus a closed reception with no room for seating."

Skye hoped her words were making an impact. Ellie was nodding and seemed to be chewing on the inside of her cheek, which meant she was processing. Skye also chanced a glance at Bailey to see if the daggers were still coming her way and was pleased to see that they had been put away. For the moment, at least.

"Let's keep walking and talking about tour impressions, Skye," Ellie said.

Victory. Though Skye had a long way to go before she closed this deal, the fact that Ellie was entertaining this possibility despite the cost was a very good sign.

❖

Bailey wasn't sure why Skye kept glancing over as though trying to challenge her to disagree on the vision she was laying out. Bailey agreed that the more expensive layout would flow better in the space. That also worked out very well for Bailey, as a higher-cost buildout would mean more profit, both for her in-house crews and as the admin fee she tacked on each of her subcontractors' contracts. She just wasn't confident that, if she held the purse strings, she would be comfortable spending that much more on the space.

Skye was a marvel to watch. She had the entire group wound around her little finger with her vivid descriptions as she glided through the space, pointing and gesturing, creating a clear picture of what the space could look like. It really was no wonder that she was one of the top brokers in the city. Hell, Bailey was ready to lease the office before she was done, and she already owned her own building.

It also didn't hurt that she had gorgeous blue-gray eyes that filled with delight as she talked about the views. Bailey could feel the excitement radiating from Skye's lithe body as she moved gracefully and spoke about finishes. Watching her created a pleasant hum low in Bailey's belly. Her palms grew damp. Everything about Skye in those moments was hypnotic.

Bailey realized she was zoning out, and the meeting was pretty much over as Ellie acquiesced, and Skye got everything she was asking for, even the glass wall she'd requested when she'd crashed Bailey's subcontractor walk-through. Bailey really needed to focus. "Maureen, will you be drawing up the contract to get rolling on this?" she asked, eager to get the paperwork completed so she could start buying materials and contracting with her subs. She did a little internal cheer at the tidier profit, thanks to Skye's persuasiveness.

"You'll have it tomorrow," she answered in her typical bouncy manner.

Bailey was gathering her things to leave as Skye asked, "Before we all head out, does everyone have a few minutes to run up to the seventeenth floor and look at the floor plan for the law firm that we're getting close to terms with? Ryan has a tentative space plan, and it'd be great to get some feedback on feasibility and a ballpark estimate from you, Bailey. And Jennifer." It sounded like she'd added Jennifer as an afterthought, but that was still progress as far as Bailey was concerned. And she'd remembered Jennifer's name rather than referring to her as the intern as Bailey would've expected. Score one for Skye.

The detour only took about fifteen minutes, which was a relief as

Bailey had a busy afternoon ahead. She had to get back to wrap up a few things at the office and then get home to get ready for the annual children's hospital fundraising gala. It was a cause that she and her family strongly believed in, so City Beautiful Construction was always a sponsor. It was a little annoying because of the effort that went into getting ready, but it was also fun to get all glammed up. It wasn't like she often had the occasion to wear a ball gown.

Working with Skye after their awkward wine date hadn't been as bad as she'd thought. Wait. Not a date. Why had she called it that? Jesus. *Definitely* not a date. Skye seemed determined to put on a good show and pretend like nothing had happened, which was fine with Bailey and good for optics with Ellie. And Skye couldn't really be expected to understand why Bailey was so sensitive on the blue-collar topic. It was possible that she *might* have overreacted. A little bit. But she really didn't want to talk about it. And she still thought a little distance between them was better. They'd gotten entirely too comfortable over that wine.

CHAPTER EIGHT

Skye had always enjoyed dressing up. As a little girl, she'd begged her mom for all of the princess dresses in the store. For Halloween, she'd always been a fairy princess, Cinderella, Tinker Bell, Sleeping Beauty, Anastasia, the list went on and on. There was something about putting on a beautiful dress, impractical shoes, and jewelry that always lifted her spirits, and she'd never outgrown that love.

In her chosen profession, she had numerous events every year that allowed her to wear formal attire, but the children's hospital gala was her absolute favorite. It was a great cause, they hired great bands, and some of the top movers and shakers in the city were always in attendance, so the networking was outstanding.

Skye had spent weeks searching for the perfect gown and knew she'd nailed it again this year. She'd found a gorgeous, deep-red, one-shoulder gown that cascaded down her body. The dress was floor-length and flowed around her legs, but it was asymmetrical, and on the left, it opened to mid-thigh, depending on how she sat or walked. She could drape the fabric over her leg while sitting so no one could see how high it was cut, but when she walked, it would draw attention to her favorite attribute: her legs.

She was confident she would turn at least a few heads this evening with her wardrobe choice. She just hoped it was the right heads and that she could avoid the lecherous old-school brokers. The few who remained were all seventy-plus and had been in the business since it was acceptable to smoke in the office and still acted as if they thought sexually harassing women was a reward for doing a good job. She couldn't quell her shudder. Most of them had retired at this point, but she really couldn't wait for the rest of them to.

She turned her head in the mirror to ensure that the knotted updo she had paid a small fortune for that afternoon was still perfect and that her infinity teardrop diamond earrings were still securely fastened before walking out the door to the town car she had ordered for the evening. She certainly couldn't drive in her heels.

The ballroom at the end of Navy Pier was marvelous for so many reasons, but since it was literally at the tip of the pier—which was more than a half mile from end to end—it could be a very long walk. Skye had made that mistake the first year she'd attended this event and had sworn to never repeat it. It was bad enough standing in impractical heels all night but quite another to walk half a mile, then stand for hours, and then walk another half a mile back to the car on blistered feet. She *could* have looked at that as a lesson in shoe selection, but she'd chosen to take it as a lesson in situational awareness and ordered a town car every year instead.

Walking into the grand ballroom always took her breath away. The gorgeous domed ceiling covered in fairy lights was resplendent and never ceased to make her feel like she'd stepped back in time to an era of elegance. She imagined it was similar to how attending a ball at the Chicago World's Fair in the thirties or an event out of Fitzgerald's *The Great Gatsby* would have been. If only she was in a flapper dress.

Skye made a beeline to the bar before she went to find people she knew. It was always easier to work a room with a glass. It gave her something to do with her hands and was also an excuse to get out of any uncomfortable groups. She found the "I just finished my glass and need to get another" excuse basic but effective; the "this wine has gotten too warm, and I need to exchange it for another" excuse was a bit prima donna-ish but still worked; and in desperate times, there was the *accidentally* bumping into someone and dropping her glass excuse. That last one was quite embarrassing and only for dire situations. It also required drinking something that wouldn't stain anyone's clothing if there was an unintended splash and was the reason Skye normally stuck to white wine at these events, despite her preference for reds. She'd only had to use it once, but she always left her options open.

As she neared the front of the bar line, she felt a hand on her elbow. "Please get two of whatever you're going to order," Ellie whispered.

She smiled. "Anything for you, dear. How long have you been here with no drink?"

Ellie rolled her eyes. "Forty minutes of pain. First one of our attorneys got to me. Then, Alderman Brooker, who oversees the ward for a property we're looking to redevelop, wanted to talk about the rezoning and what type of building signage we wanted to put up. Then an old friend from college. I've been trying to sidestep to the bar since I walked in the door."

"That's your problem. You can't sidestep. You've got to make a beeline and make no eye contact. If you look at anyone, they're going to stop you. I'm pretty sure *you* taught me that trick, though, so why weren't you using it?" She nudged Ellie in the ribs and wondered why she had let herself get hijacked.

"I tried, but our attorney, Barry, practically yelled to me from halfway across the room, and I couldn't ignore it. It was embarrassing, really. That guy has no social skills. And I've been trying to be less conspicuous, but it is what it is. It can be hard to get across a room." She shook her head in frustration, but her face lit up when Skye handed her a glass of wine. "Oh, you do know the way to my heart." She sighed.

"If only," Skye said as she winked. It was true that she'd had a major crush on Ellie in high school, but she'd thankfully gotten over it as she'd matured. Ellie had been larger than life to a young and underprivileged Skye, and she'd seemed to have everything Skye wanted for herself. A good education, stability, fashion sense, and a comfort with her sexuality that Skye could only envy at that point. She'd also taken Skye under her wing and had helped her with her college essays and interview prep. It was really no surprise that Skye had had a little hero worship for years.

Skye was pulled out of her internal monologue when Ellie breathed contentedly as she sipped her wine. "I don't know if it's because I've been parched for an hour or if this wine is actually decent, but this is delectable."

Ellie's penchant toward exaggeration when they weren't around anyone she was trying to impress always struck Skye as humorous. "I don't know if I'd say delectable, but it's good. It's very good. I'm happy it's an oaky chardonnay rather than a buttery one."

"Me too. Speaking of very good," Ellie said, "I'm in love with your design for our spec suite at the Maxwell. I don't want to spend the extra money, but it is going to be worth it. I'm so happy you pushed for the kitchen on the perimeter."

"Thank you, Ellie. I'm glad you like it." Her chest swelled. She knew the space was going to be perfect, and she was elated that Ellie was fully on board and wasn't having second thoughts.

"What do you think our chances are with your attorneys?" Ellie asked.

"Very good. They seem to love everything about the building, and if the off-the-cuff pricing Bailey gave us is accurate, we're going to have some room to move on the rate if needed and still meet your investment objectives." She'd felt good about the lawyers from their first tour on that fateful—or was it unfortunate—day she'd met Bailey. Whether fateful or unfortunate, she was starting to trust Bailey in a professional capacity, even if she was new to CBC, and even if they couldn't find footing on a personal level.

"Now that's what I want to hear," Ellie said. "Speaking of Bailey, are things okay between you? I noticed some tension."

Shit. Skye was certain they'd done a better job of hiding their animosity. She didn't want a friend but also a colleague and client like Ellie to think she couldn't play well with others. "Nothing to worry about. We've had a professional difference of opinion or two, but I think we're through it. Nothing to worry about at all." Even if they hadn't fully resolved their issues, Skye was pretty sure she was being truthful regarding their professional conflicts.

"Good. Her firm does amazing work, which you obviously know. You've seen the roof-deck and the lobby."

"Those were Greg's jobs, weren't they? Isn't Bailey new?" She had never seen Bailey before their meeting a few weeks prior.

"Skye, you really don't know who owns City Beautiful? I'm a little surprised."

"What do you mean?" She felt a sinking feeling that her very uncharitable thoughts about Bailey might have been unwarranted.

"For a woman in commercial real estate, Skye, I'm really surprised at you. Bailey owns CBC. She's owned it for about five years. So *their* work in the building is ultimately *her* work. Honestly, she's only working on the Maxwell as a favor to me. When Greg retired, she knew I was nervous about an untested estimator and superintendent coming on board because it's such a high-profile building, and she stepped right in."

Skye was embarrassed. Thankfully, she'd never called Bailey a newbie to her face, but still. It was mortifying that she hadn't realized one of the best interiors construction companies in the city was woman-owned. And by a woman she knew. "Oh wow. No, I'm ashamed to say I had no idea."

"You need to be a little less self-absorbed, my friend." Ellie said it playfully, but Skye acknowledged there was an underlying truth to the words. "She does some of the best work in the city. You should've known who she was."

"You're right." Skye stared into her glass and felt rightfully chastened, embarrassed at her obliviousness.

"Also, she's not too hard on the eyes, is she? Entirely too young for me and not my type, but I can appreciate her aesthetics." Ellie smirked.

Skye's eyes snapped up to Ellie's, trying to close her mouth fast enough that Ellie wouldn't see the shock plastered across her face. "I, uh, hadn't noticed," she stammered unconvincingly.

Ellie, her lips pursed, head tilted in incredulity, said nothing.

"Okay, fine I noticed," Skye admitted. "But, God, is she infuriating."

"Infuriating? How?"

"I…" Skye trailed off, no longer certain why she'd found Bailey so infuriating. "She just is," she finished weakly.

"She just is, huh?" Ellie said as she nodded knowingly. "Have you seen her tonight?"

"She's here?" Skye inhaled sharply. She feared this evening was going to take an unexpected turn, and Skye hated—*hated*—the unexpected.

"Yes, and looking dazzling. Though, I haven't had a chance to say hello yet. Why don't we go find her?"

Of course, at that moment, Bailey walked up. "Find who?" She looked at Ellie without even acknowledging Skye's presence.

Skye wondered if Bailey really hadn't recognized her or if she was blatantly ignoring her. She was hoping it was the first, though it might be a little sexy if she was so pissed that it was the latter. Wait, why did her mind go there? It must be Ellie planting ideas. And why would that be sexy? Anyone ignoring her intentionally was not sexy. Not at all.

What *was* sexy was the expanse of Bailey's chest that was visible above her gown. Her black dress was strapless and deceptively simple. It enhanced her broad shoulders and perfect collarbones, and Skye could just imagine grazing her teeth across that flawless—

"Skye?" At the sound of Ellie's voice, she pulled her eyes from those collarbones and prayed no one had seen where she'd been staring.

"Sorry, what? I was thinking about the attorneys we're wooing." A total lie, but no one had to know. Only Ellie's knowing expression said she wasn't getting away with anything. Shit. She hoped Bailey, at least, hadn't noticed.

"I asked if you needed another drink, as I have found the bottom of my glass." Ellie said.

"Oh no, thank you. I'm fine." Skye still had a half of a glass but wished she'd finished it so she could have an excuse to go to the bar. Hell.

Before Skye could say anything else, Ellie had glided away.

"That was abrupt," Bailey said, finally acknowledging her presence as Ellie walked away. "Hi, by the way." A hint of a smile crossed her lips. Even that was a little sexy. She was utterly screwed.

"Hi back. And well, she is pretty thirsty." Skye laughed. "She'd been here for forty minutes before she could break away to the bar. She had an almost feral look in her eyes when she came up behind me in line earlier."

"Feral?" Bailey's hint of a smile growing into a nearly full one sent Skye's pulse stuttering.

"Even you would look a little feral if an alderman grabbed you and wouldn't stop talking for half an hour." Skye winced as she imagined it.

Bailey rolled her lips in, shook her head. "Good point. I won't judge. I mean, I wouldn't judge anyway, but if I was her, I'd have probably taken the whole bottle from the bar rather than a glass. Wait, which alderman?"

"Brooker. Ellie has a redevelopment she's working on in his ward, and he wanted to 'talk about the rezoning.'" She used air quotes. It was almost certain that Brooker just wanted to stare at her chest. He was smarmy, and Skye didn't understand why he kept getting elected, but Ellie didn't have a choice but to humor him since aldermen had a ridiculous amount of power in those types of decisions within their wards.

Bailey gagged. "Shit, I wouldn't have tried to take one bottle, I'd have swiped two to deal with the PTSD of his leery eyes molesting me for a half hour. Ugh."

"So you've worked with him, then?" Skye said.

Bailey laughed silently and shook her head. "Unfortunately. The perv even ogles my chest, which isn't particularly impressive and is generally not on display."

They'd have to agree to disagree about the impressiveness of Bailey's chest. In her current gown, Skye was having a hard time focusing elsewhere. "You really are funnier than I'd given you credit for."

Bailey's eyes went wide at Skye's words. She hoped she hadn't offended her again. At least, not too much.

Bailey smirked and said, "Right back at ya. I thought you were a dry snob when we met the first time."

Skye laughed. "A snob? Maybe on occasion but never dry." She lifted her glass and grinned.

"You said it, not me." Bailey wiggled her eyebrows playfully as she clinked her glass against Skye's. However, when they stopped laughing, neither of them looked away. Even as Bailey lifted her glass and took another sip, her eyes remained locked on Skye's. Skye's breath caught. She took a sip of her own wine and swallowed with more force than was necessary.

What was this moment? Why couldn't she stop it? Someone finally bumped Bailey from behind, severing their uncomfortably intense connection. Skye looked into her glass in an attempt to recenter herself and ended up obsessing about how she'd upset Bailey the other night.

She didn't think she'd done anything wrong, but there was something about Bailey that made Skye care about what she thought. And hate that she'd upset her. Why did she feel the need to apologize for a crime that she didn't even understand that she'd committed? But she did and needed to address it. "Look, I'm not sure what I said the other night at the wine bar that offended you, but I'm really sorry. I don't look down on people who aren't white-collar. At all. My mother and grandmother couldn't have been more blue-collar, and I love them more than anyone on this planet."

Bailey's eyes went a little cloudy before she said, "It's okay, and I'm sorry. It probably didn't make much sense how angry I got, but that's a sore spot for me. I had a cousin who was a few years younger than me and he…" She trailed off without finishing her thought.

It wasn't lost on Skye that Bailey used the words "had" and "was" when she talked about him, and she didn't want Bailey to feel like she had to get into a painful topic in the middle of a gala. She squeezed Bailey's free hand. "We don't have to talk about this now. You don't owe me an explanation."

"I know, but I want you to be able to understand my overreaction a little. My cousin…traditional school wasn't his forte other than classes where he got to work with his hands, like shop. Unfortunately, he felt like everyone had to go to college in order to succeed, but he didn't do well in his classes, took out a ton of debt trying to impress his horrible girlfriend who still broke up with him when she saw he wasn't going to be an ace stockbroker. Anyway, he didn't see any way out...and..." Bailey shrugged and waved her hand.

"Oh my God, Bailey, I'm so sorry for what you and your family must have gone through." She squeezed her forearm. "It's unfathomable." Her heart broke for all of them, and Bailey's outsized reaction the other evening made so much more sense.

"I know this really isn't the time or place, but I just...feel like I probably seemed crazy. Regardless, I'm sorry about the other day, and I hope we're good? Can we try another one of those new beginnings?" Her forehead wrinkled.

"Sounds good to me." Skye smiled, and when Bailey returned it, her face glowing, Skye's heart fluttered, and warmth spread through her center.

She was grateful when Bailey changed the subject to a safer topic, away from revelations that were far too personal to share. She hoped that the heat in her belly would begin to cool.

"I'm surprised to see you drinking white wine. I would have expected you to be a loyalist to the bold reds through and through," Bailey stated.

Skye tilted her head, curious. "That's an interesting statement. Why would you assume that?"

Bailey nervously chuckled. "Oh God. This is probably going to come out wrong, so I'm going to need you to promise to take it lightly." She took a sip, as if fortifying herself for whatever she was going to say next.

Skye laughed. "Well, that's ominous, but sure. Whatever you say will be taken lightly." She held up three fingers. "Scout's honor."

"Okay, then. I envision red wine drinkers to be serious, dedicated. But white wine drinkers are a little more lighthearted. Leaving work early in the afternoon to go enjoy happy hour on a patio. Free-spirited, even. And you are definitely not free-spirited. I don't think." She flashed a half-playful smile that was also half a grimace.

"You don't think I'm playful? What about my new business cards: Skye Kohl, woman of impeccable taste?"

After taking a sip, Bailey flicked her tongue along her top lip, and in an instant, the feel in the air changed. Rather than cooling, the heat growing between Skye's legs flared as wetness surged, and her heart was starting to feel like she'd just done an all-out sprint in SoulCycle. She took a half step forward, her feet moving of their own accord before she realized. She certainly hadn't authorized them to do that. She wanted to chastise them but feared giving anything away. And she couldn't look away even if she wanted to.

Bailey's gaze flicked toward her mouth and back up, and Skye noticed the little pulse in Bailey's temple again. She'd seen it the first time they'd met, but standing this close, she couldn't resist lifting her hand, even knowing it was a bad idea. "You have a little tell in your temple." She grazed two unsteady fingers along Bailey's hairline, barely touching her skin, but she still watched Bailey's breath hitch, felt her own catch in response. "I can always tell when you're irritated by this little twitch. You probably don't even realize it. Tell me," she whispered, "what have I done to irritate you now? I can't think of anything." She paused. "Nothing at all." Her pulse was hammering so hard, she could actually hear it.

Bailey leaned into Skye's touch, her pupils contracting. Skye lingered along her temple, turning into a caress. Bailey's lids became heavy. Was that desire? Skye shivered as she tried to resist this pull but struggled to find any willpower.

"I…" Bailey began, but a clatter came from the bar on the other side of the room, breaking them from their trance.

Skye realized just how close she'd been to kissing Bailey. Someone she didn't even like and someone who, as a colleague, she absolutely couldn't get involved with. And especially not right there in the middle of one of the biggest events of the year. Surrounded by colleagues. She stepped back and shook her head.

With a little distance, she took a long deep breath and was able to recenter herself. She cleared her throat once. Twice. "Well, to be honest, I'd rather have a red, but at a packed event like this, with people jostling everywhere, I'm too afraid to spill. Also, you have to watch out for purple lips and teeth while drinking red, and that is too hard to do here."

Bailey blinked rapidly, her pupils dilating back to their normal size. "Very logical."

"That doesn't mean that I can't be playful." She tried to smile but no longer felt playful as she struggled to process the kiss they'd almost shared.

"You're right. I'm sure you can be very playful," Bailey said, the pulse in her temple throbbing again.

"Exactly."

"I also don't generally drink red wine at events. Mostly for the same reasons that you outlined," Bailey said, her voice wavering even though her back was suddenly rod straight.

God, when had they gotten so formal again? Skye knew it was better to have some distance between them, but it still made her sad, almost longing for something that would never—could never—be. She gestured to Bailey's glass, which was still three-quarters full with a clear liquid and a lime trapped in the ice. "Gin and tonic?"

"Vodka tonic, actually. With a lime, clearly." Bailey swirled her glass and took another sip.

"Solid choice." The awkwardness had become too much for Skye, so she took one last long sip of wine so she could invoke one of her go-to excuses. "Well, on that note, it would appear that I need another drink. Perhaps I'll catch up with you later?" Not that she really meant that. She'd try to stay away from Bailey if she could, since her willpower apparently couldn't be trusted that evening.

"Sounds good."

As Skye turned, Bailey reached out and lightly touched her arm, causing goose bumps to break out along her skin.

"And Skye? I'm glad we cleared the air. I enjoy talking to you."

"Likewise," Skye said with a smile she was sure looked brittle and headed to the bar before she could do anything else she would regret. Because she also enjoyed talking to Bailey, but she liked it a *bit* too much and as such, needed to steer clear.

CHAPTER NINE

Bailey spent the next two hours networking with local politicians and business owners. She chatted with Ellie again when they came across one another at the silent auction table, and Bailey bid too much on several baskets. She won an all-inclusive, long-weekend getaway at a Michigan bed-and-breakfast, as well as a Cubs club-seat package. She hadn't expected to win more than one thing, but she didn't mind spending the extra money. It was all for a good cause.

And through it all, her mind kept replaying those moments with Skye, when they'd moved closer and closer to one another. Bailey heated at the thought; she'd really wanted to kiss her. With Skye's abrupt departure, Bailey wasn't sure if she should be upset or relieved that the bartender had dropped his tray and shattered the moment as surely as he'd shattered every single glass he'd been carrying.

She certainly wasn't looking for a relationship, and getting involved with Skye was undoubtedly ill-advised. They had to work together, and until she found a replacement for Gary, they would likely be working together a lot. And carving out time for a healthy relationship simply wasn't in the cards, not with all the demands of Bailey's company. A recipe for total disaster.

There was something undeniable between them, though. A heat that Bailey had a hard time denying now that she knew Skye wasn't a total fire-breathing monster. Why couldn't they have stayed there, hating each other, where it was easy to deny that attraction?

Bailey pushed out one of the doors and onto the end of Navy Pier. She hoped getting a little air would help clear Skye out of her head. She'd always loved this part of the city at night. She could look out on the abyss of the lake, the darkness only broken by the twinkling lights of pleasure cruisers. She almost felt alone in the city. But in the opposite direction, the beautiful skyline reminded her that she lived in one of the busiest cities in the nation. Even so, other than the muted music coming from the ballroom, Bailey couldn't hear any of the hustle and bustle of the city. It was a nice reprieve.

She began to walk along the outside of the building, appreciating the chilly air and the sounds of the lake, but she caught the silhouette of someone standing at the very end of the pier and leaning against the rail overlooking the lake. The woman's outline was enthralling as the wind teased several whisps of hair that had come out of her updo and swirled her dress around her ankles. She looked lonely by herself, and it conjured the image of a widow waiting for her sailor to return to port after an ill-fated trip.

Bailey took a few steps toward the woman, drawn by her body's very visceral reaction, before she realized it was Skye out there all alone. Her steps faltered.

The way they'd left things earlier, Bailey wasn't sure if her presence would be welcome. And, good God, if their conversation became as uncomfortable as their last few exchanges, she'd rather go back inside. She tried to convince herself to do just that before Skye saw her waiting there like a stalker. But despite the tightness in her chest, Bailey found herself compelled forward by an unseen force.

When she was a few steps away, she said, "It's gorgeous out here, isn't it?"

Skye jumped nearly a foot in the air. An impressive feat in the heels she was wearing. Bailey appreciated the flash of leg as Skye's dress blew behind her, the shorter side showing an expanse of thigh before Skye had a chance to readjust it. "Jesus, you scared the shit out of me, Bailey!"

"Sorry." Bailey chuckled and put her hands up to show she meant no harm. She felt a little guilty, but even with her eyes flashing in alarm, Skye was still beautiful, hauntingly so with her pale hair in the moonlight.

Skye rolled her eyes and nodded as she gazed back toward the water. "It truly is. I love the peace of the lake at night."

Bailey leaned against the railing. "You could almost think you're the only person in the world. If not for the music coming from the ballroom, of course. It was just getting so hot in there. I had expected the crowd to dissipate a little by now."

"It was really stuffy, and everyone was starting to talk so loud as the collective inebriation level increased."

"Oh God, yes. Honestly, I'm not sure why I'm even still here." Bailey could have left a while ago—should have left a while ago—but something had kept her there. She'd wanted to see Skye one more time in that phenomenal dress and maybe not leave things on such a weird note. Not that she had admitted that to herself as she'd continued to circle the ballroom while pretending she didn't know who she was looking for. Given the impossibility of a future for them, she didn't *want* to admit it now.

"Me too, truthfully. Some handsy old broker kept putting his hand on my shoulder...I came out here to get some fresh air for a few minutes, but now I really don't want to go back in." Skye chuckled and shivered, nearly imperceptibly. She'd barely moved, but Bailey had felt the slight shift.

She stepped closer until their arms were touching to give Skye some of her body heat and was shocked at the icy feel of Skye's bare arm. "You're freezing. How long have you been out here?" Bailey rubbed Skye's arm, then stepped behind her and started running her hands up and down both arms to warm them. She knew she was playing with fire by touching Skye's silky skin, but she didn't want her to freeze. And now that she was touching her, Bailey couldn't pull away. She was drawn to Skye like iron filings to a magnet. She wondered if Skye could feel it too.

"I don't know. Twenty minutes or so?" Her voice was hollow, and Bailey rubbed faster. "Hmm, that feels nice." Bailey's stomach tightened at the softness in her voice.

"Are you okay? You seem...I don't know. Sadder than earlier." Bailey wanted to pull her into a hug but worried it wouldn't be welcome.

Skye chuckled mirthlessly, "I love this stuff, but sometimes it's just so..." She sighed as she trailed off and fluttered a hand in the air. "Exhausting. You might think that as a broker, I'm an extrovert, but really, I'm an extroverted introvert. I love to be around people, but to recharge, I need some downtime. After this much networking for so many hours, I needed a little quiet."

"Sorry if I'm interrupting," Bailey said quietly.

"No, no, you're fine. There's something about you that makes me feel at ease. At least right now." Her shoulders bounced in nearly silent laughter before she mumbled, "God, why did I just say that? I must've had more to drink than I thought."

Bailey was going to pretend she hadn't heard the last bit when, without warning, Skye faced her.

"I didn't even finish my second glass of wine, so that's not it. What is it about you that makes me say all these things I don't mean to?"

Bailey stilled her hands, fighting the urge to pull her in. "I don't know, but I'm right there with you. Every time I'm with you, I find myself oversharing in one way or another." Bailey stared, captivated, as Skye's lips curled into a half-smile.

However, that smile dimmed as another shiver ran through her.

Bailey didn't want her to be cold, but she also wasn't ready to give up this alone time. "I know where we can go to get warm but not be subjected to handsy old guys, if you're up for it."

Skye nodded, and Bailey ran her hands down to Skye's wrists, then pulled her back toward the ballroom. The irony of trying to help her avoid handsy men while simultaneously stroking her arms wasn't lost on Bailey, so as soon as Skye pushed off the railing, Bailey released her. She missed the feel of her skin but was already walking such a tightrope that she didn't dare reach back out.

As they walked back toward the building, Bailey caught Skye staring at her, and she couldn't breathe. When she opened one of the ballroom doors, Skye pursed her lips. "I thought we weren't going back into the gala."

"We aren't, exactly. Have a little faith." Bailey tilted her chin toward a staircase off to her right. "It should be warm but a little more peaceful up there." She hoped this plan didn't backfire. She knew their relationship could never evolve into anything more than professional colleagues—she wasn't in a position to think about anything more—but Bailey couldn't help indulging herself that evening, bathing in whatever magic had a hold on them both. She only hoped that magic didn't pull her in too deep and make her do something she would inevitably regret.

"Lead the way, Captain," Skye said and bit her lip.

"Captain, huh? I might have to put that on *my* business cards. 'Bailey Kaczmarek, owner and captain of whatever ship we're on.' It has a certain ring to it, doesn't it?"

"Maybe." Skye snickered, and Bailey squeezed the door handle harder to hide the tremor in her hand.

The balcony was blissfully empty. Bailey had known it was open for this gala but suspected it stood empty because there wasn't a bar up there. The band and the ambient noise of hundreds of conversations were markedly quieter. Bailey leaned against the balcony rail next to Skye and looked down at everyone.

"So many people," Skye said.

"Yeah, but don't you just love this room?" Bailey's gaze was riveted upward and out rather than at the mob milling below.

"Of course. It's a great venue."

"Yes, but it's so much more. The eighty-foot domed ceiling, all of the lights. It's gorgeous. And yet those twinkly lights are on steel beams. The walls were built with reclaimed Chicago common brick. Doesn't it help keep you grounded in the fact that Chicago may be a city of glitz and glamour, but it's also a city of the working people? It's undoubtedly champagne and flowers, but you can also feel that it's grounded in steel and brick, can't you?" She made a fist. Squeezed it. "It's gritty and tough and built on the shoulders of the blue-collar worker and yet still calls to opulence." She waved toward the throng of people. She loved the contrasts that defined this city. It was her favorite city in the world.

"I've never thought about it, but you're right. It's a city of dichotomies."

"It's got its problems, some much worse than in other cities, but the history…it's a city that said, go ahead, you can burn me down, but I'm going to build myself back better than ever. If you tear me down, I'll rise from the ashes with feats of engineering and architecture never seen before. There's a life lesson in there too."

When Skye didn't say anything, Bailey looked over to find her staring with a crooked grin.

"What?" Bailey asked.

Skye shook her head. Chuckled. "I had no idea you were so passionate about this city, Bailey Kaczmarek. The dreamy look on your face…It's…" She bit the side of her lip, and one hundred percent of Bailey's attention focused there. "Well, it's cute, is all."

"Cute, huh?" She didn't know what to make of that.

"Yep," Skye said, a faint stain of pink appearing in her cheeks.

Bailey was at a loss for words, so she looked back out over the crowd and watched the couples dancing together. "I love this music. When I was a kid, my dad used to listen to it when he was working in his shop, and I'd be looking over his shoulder and handing him tools like he was a surgeon in the OR. Glenn Miller, Benny Goodman, Billie Holiday, Frank Sinatra. It always makes me nostalgic for those afternoons, just me and my dad."

"I love to watch the dancing," Skye said wistfully. "To be carefree and dance at such a stuffy event…I've never danced with a woman outside of a gay club."

That admission cracked Bailey's heart. Was Skye so afraid of being outed that she'd never taken a woman to a wedding or something? Or was it simply a lack of opportunity? They both stared into the crowd for a few more minutes.

When the band began to play the Sinatra version of "I've Got You Under My Skin," Bailey chuckled at how those lyrics embodied her feelings toward Skye. Then she had a thought. "Do you want to dance?" she asked quietly, nervous but wanting to share a first with Skye.

Skye's eyes widened. "I can't. Not here."

Bailey's heart fell. "Not down there in the crowd. Up here. If we take a few steps back, no one will be able to see us. I promise. A friendly dance. Between friends. Nothing more." Skye looked unsure, but Bailey took a step away from the rail and held out her hand, silently asking.

Skye stared, eyes unreadable, then placed her hand in Bailey's. Butterflies on speed took off in Bailey's stomach at even that little bit of contact. She was worried how her body would react when a lot more of Skye's skin was touching hers, but she couldn't stop this freight train now. She had neither the willpower to stop nor the desire to muster it.

Bailey led her to a window facing the city skyline and pulled Skye to her, leaving mere inches between their bodies as they began to sway to the music. The smooth skin of Skye's back beneath her fingertips, the soft puff of Skye's breath against her cheek, the way they were both dressed to the nines, and the unadulterated romance of dancing to a live band with the entire city as their private backdrop was making it difficult to breathe. She stopped trying to regulate her breath and finally let it come as it might. She didn't think she'd pass out. And even if she did, Skye would catch her.

Bailey wasn't sure how long they danced, but Sinatra blended into "Cheek to Cheek," which then became "The Very Thought of You," and then countless songs until Bailey couldn't keep track. Skye kept getting closer until their bodies were pressed as tightly as their dresses would allow. Bailey's mind quieted, and she just experienced the moment.

Her forearm was against the bare skin of Skye's back, and Skye's head rested on her shoulder. Skye's chest pressed firmly into her own as she inhaled and released slightly as she exhaled, the damp heat of her breath across Bailey's chest made Bailey's entire body tingle. Every few steps, Skye's bare leg brushed hers as that asymmetrical hem lined up with the slit in her own dress and intensified the pressure between her legs, which had been at a low buzz since they'd started dancing. She knew she should put a little space between them to stop it from happening, but she didn't have the willpower for that, either. At least the butterflies had quieted down and gone to sleep.

After what could have been an hour or five, Bailey noticed that the conversations from below had quieted. She reluctantly decided to bring them back to reality. She leaned her head back slightly, and Skye lifted hers in response. "I hate to say it, but I think this thing is winding down, so we should probably head out before a staff member comes up here to sweep and catches us."

"Yeah," Skye whispered. But she didn't move. She just stared at Bailey with stormy eyes.

Bailey ran her thumb tenderly along the edge of Skye's jaw. Caught up in the moment, in the romance of their secret dance and ensconced away in plain sight, if someone had offered Bailey a key to the city, she wouldn't have been able to stop herself from leaning in. She watched for any flicker of indecision in Skye's expression, but there was none. She paused, not wanting to force Skye into something, waiting for her to travel the last millimeter.

When Skye did, her lips were as smooth as Bailey had envisioned and felt perfect against Bailey's. She tightened her arms, pulling Skye infinitesimally closer as her brain stopped functioning, and she moved entirely by sensation: the feel of Skye's skin, her lips, her body flush against Bailey's, the scent of her hair, the tingles along the nape of her neck where Skye's fingertips toyed with the fine hairs.

Skye opened her mouth, and Bailey followed, their tongues intertwining as if they had done this a thousand times. Bailey slid a hand down Skye's back to cup her bottom, and the feel of Skye tilting her hips into Bailey's weakened her knees. Someone moaned softly. Bailey didn't particularly care who. She only cared about how kissing Skye felt in this moment. She could have stayed there for an eternity.

A loud click echoed throughout the empty ballroom, and all of the lights went out, leaving only a few emergency fixtures. Bailey pulled away and looked around. "Oh shit," she whispered. "We'd better get out of here before they lock us in."

"Oh my God, let's go." Skye kissed her, just a brief brush of their lips, but the jolt knocked Bailey's world off-kilter again. She grabbed her hand, and they ran toward the stairs and out into the night. As soon as the door clicked closed behind them Skye said, "Shit, I forgot my wrap at the coat check."

"Son of a…mine is there too." Bailey couldn't believe she'd forgotten. "Well, let's check some of the doors closer to the front of the ballroom."

They walked around the perimeter and checked several doors. All were locked. Of course. "Well," Bailey said, resigned to probably never seeing her wrap again. "I guess we'll have to call tomorrow and try not to freeze tonight."

Skye giggled. Bailey couldn't believe she had emitted an honest-to-goodness giggle and was forced to call her out. "Was that a giggle, Skye Kohl, licensed real estate broker and woman of impeccable taste?"

"It's ridiculous, isn't it? We end up locked outside of the largest charity event of the year in Chicago, in April, wrap-less, with temperatures quickly dropping, and all I want to do is take off my shoes because my feet are killing me." She giggled again. "The real question is, why don't *you* find this funny?"

Bailey found her giggles contagious, and one bubbled out of her as well. "You're right. I want to take off my shoes too. It's been a really long night in these bastards. I make a motion that since we closed the ballroom down, we're entitled to walk around barefoot. It's probably not *that* disgusting out here."

"I second that motion, but it's probably best to not think about how dirty the ground is," Skye said and gripped Bailey's biceps as she bent and slipped off her high heels. Bailey instinctively flexed as Skye gripped her arm. She didn't want to examine whether she flexed so Skye wouldn't slip or so her arm would feel ripped under Skye's fingers. When Skye stood back up, Bailey slipped her shoes off as well.

"The ground is cold, but my toes are so sore, it feels nice. It's like an icepack." Bailey sighed.

"Oh my God, yes. Stretching out my Achilles is like heaven right now. How did you get here this evening?" Skye asked, tucking her arm into Bailey's as they walked to the pick-up circle. Skye lightly ran her thumb up and down the inside of Bailey's arm, and Bailey's clit twitched in response. She had to fight the instinct to swoon, it felt so good.

"Lyft."

"Oh, I hate Lyft," Skye said with a groan.

Bailey was confused. "You prefer Uber?"

"No, no, no." Skye laughed. "I hate them both in the city. The drivers never know where the hell they're going."

"Well, that's true, but out to Andersonville, a Lyft is about half the cost of a taxi. Not that I'm cheap, but it seems foolish to overpay when Google Maps is as good as the map in a taxi driver's brain, and, let's be serious, the back of a Lyft is always cleaner and more comfortable than a taxi. Especially at this time of night."

Skye laughed, and it quickened Bailey's pulse. She was in deep. Too deep? Probably. She had enjoyed this evening so much more than she'd expected. She wasn't ready to pull the plug and dreaded the moment they had to say good night.

"I ordered a car for the evening. I honestly thought I would have more to drink than I did, but someone distracted me for half the evening, so…" Skye gave her a side-eye.

"You can't blame that on me," Bailey retorted.

"Oh really?" Skye slowed to a stop and looked at Bailey with pursed lips. "Who followed me out to the pier? Who suggested we go up to the balcony? Who suggested that we dance? Who leaned in afterward?" Her voice was barely a whisper as she walked her fingertips up to Bailey's shoulder. A chill unrelated to the cool April air ripped through Bailey, and she covered Skye's hand with her own to quell it.

"When you put it that way, it sounds like you were an unwilling participant." Bailey said it lightly but felt anxious for Skye's reply. She knew she'd gotten caught up in the moment, but Skye had surely felt like a willing participant. There was no way Bailey was the only one who'd felt their connection.

"Not unwilling at all," Skye said, squeezing her shoulder, and Bailey sighed in relief.

"But?" Bailey drew that single word out into three syllables. She could sense Skye was holding something back, and although she didn't want Skye to express her doubts about what this was or could be, it would be easier if she did.

"Where do we go from here?" Skye looked at their bare feet peeking out from beneath their dresses.

Bailey swallowed the lump in her throat. "I…I don't know." She wasn't sure what to say. Everything in her was screaming to not let this be it, but… "I don't really do relationships. Running a business takes a lot of time. I'm married to CBC." Every word grated on her skin, even though she knew they were true, and nipping whatever this was in the bud before it could develop was the right choice. But for the first time in a long time, a tiny piece of her wanted to take a chance.

Skye let out a long sigh. "I'm not a relationship person, either. Nor do I sleep around, and definitely not with professional acquaintances."

"Me either. So. What do we do now?" Sadness settled around her body, dampening the entire evening.

"I don't know." Skye shook her head sadly. "I mean, we normally can't spend more than two minutes together without someone blowing up. We're like bleach and ammonia. It'd be crazy to consider something so unprofessional just for...Just crazy."

"True." She and Skye had off-the-charts chemistry, but before this evening, every time they'd talked for more than ten minutes, they'd ended up pissing each other off. It would be foolish to think about breaking rules that she'd put in place to protect herself. She shouldn't. She couldn't. Especially not with Skye, a colleague.

"I think maybe we go back to how we were before. But, uh... nicer." Skye chuckled dismally.

"Never again speak of this little..." She swallowed trying to think of the right word. "Interlude?" The words tasted bitter on her tongue, but she was confident they were making the right decision. It was only her libido that disagreed, and that certainly couldn't be trusted to make the right decision. "Never think of it again, even."

"I think that's for the best, don't you?" Skye asked.

"Yeah. Unfortunately, I do." They took a step away from each other in silent agreement. "Obviously, we simply got caught up in the romance of the evening, but it was a mistake and doesn't mean anything. A one-time indiscretion."

"Yeah," Skye said.

"I guess I'll see you around the Maxwell, then?"

"Guess so," Skye said with finality.

Bailey wanted to take Skye home with her more than she'd wanted anything in her entire life, but they'd just agreed it was a terrible idea. And it was. There was no way she could sleep with Skye once and then pretend like nothing had happened when they had to keep working together. But given the evening they'd just shared, the kisses they'd shared, would she still be able to work with Skye and not continually think of kissing her? This wasn't going to be awkward. Not at all.

❖

At nearly two a.m., Skye finally let herself into her penthouse condo and dropped the shoes she'd been carrying on the marble floor of her foyer. She knew she should put them in her closet, given the price she'd paid, but she was exhausted. So far beyond exhausted, she probably wasn't even in the same zip code anymore. Why the hell was this gala on a Friday night after a long day at the end of a long week of work? That had to be why the rational, responsible side of her brain had been on the fritz all night.

They'd waited for Bailey's Lyft in awkward silence for about fifteen minutes while her own town car sat idling nearby. They could have gotten into her car to wait, or better yet, she could have just given Bailey a ride home, but that felt too intimate. Skye was afraid that if they were locked together in a warm space, they might end up locked together in another way, one they'd both agreed was not appropriate. As if *anything* this evening had been appropriate.

When Bailey's car had finally pulled up, Skye had reached out to pull Bailey into a friendly hug as Bailey had stuck a hand out as if to shake, thrusting it directly into Skye's midsection and hitting the bottom of her breast. They'd both stumbled over words of apology before stepping away and waving farewell. After a magical evening, the final twenty minutes felt like falling through the ice on Lake Michigan in January.

With the way Skye's head was spinning, she knew that she'd never sleep, so she unzipped her dress as she walked through her living room and laid it across the back of the couch. She knew she should hang it up, but that seemed like too much effort. Making her way through the dark in her underwear to the bar tucked into the corner of her library, Skye pulled out a lowball glass and poured two fingers of Johnnie Walker Blue into it, wrapped a robe around herself, and stepped out onto her balcony.

She could see down into the barely illuminated Lincoln Park Zoo, though most animals were probably sleeping at this hour. In the reflection of the full moon, she could see the subtle ripple of waves on Lake Michigan, and it took her back to standing at the end of Navy Pier, watching the shimmering waves earlier that evening. She took a sip of her Johnnie Walker, appreciating the hints of vanilla and smoke on her palate, the barest of burns in the back of her throat, and thought back on the night.

She'd only intended to step outside for a few minutes for some fresh air and to cool off, but then, as now, she'd stared into the dark water and had gotten lost in her thoughts. When Ellie had first said that Bailey was at the gala, Skye had imagined her looking stunning in a fancy black pantsuit. As she'd only ever seen Bailey in pants and jackets, she'd assumed that Bailey didn't wear dresses. Boy, had she been wrong.

The deceptively simple floor-length black gown had accentuated Bailey's every curve. It had knocked Skye off-balance and had to have been the reason Bailey had gotten caught going round and round in Skye's thoughts like the Ferris wheel on the pier. Skye had been wondering what Bailey's lips would have felt like before that bartender had dropped a tray of glasses; maybe Bailey materializing out of nowhere wouldn't have been so terrifying if Skye hadn't been fantasizing about Bailey when she'd shown up.

When Skye went outside, she had wanted to be alone to brood about the social acceptability, which apparently still remained, of men putting their hands on women in the general course of conversation and how unfair it was. But she'd enjoyed talking to Bailey—a lot—and it had distracted her from the unfairness of it all.

And when Bailey had tried to warm Skye up by rubbing her arms…Skye wondered if Bailey had realized exactly how much she'd turned Skye on between their proximity and the feel of hands running up and down. A pleasurable shudder raced through her chest as she thought back to it.

When they'd gone back inside, it had still been so pleasant and comfortable. It hadn't felt like Skye was talking to someone she disliked, someone she'd been butting heads with for weeks. When Bailey had asked her to dance, Skye had known she should have said no. Her defenses against Bailey were already on life support, and nothing good could come from having their bodies so close together while her guard was down in a starry ballroom. And she could *not* afford to date someone in the industry and risk it getting out that she was a lesbian. Real estate was still such a small, conservative community. She didn't know any other brokers in the industry who were gay. Being outed would be a career killer.

But she hadn't been able to resist. Bailey had looked so gorgeous with her arm outstretched, and because everything was already off-kilter that evening, Skye had gotten lost in Bailey's arms for what felt like seconds and hours at the same time. It had been the most romantic evening Skye had ever had. And once they'd started dancing, things had gone from pleasant and comfortable to incendiary, and the longer they'd danced, the harder it was to resist her.

Kissing Bailey had started to feel inevitable, and Skye had never wanted it to end. Bailey's mouth had fit so perfectly upon hers that it felt as though their lips had been sculpted as a pair. Designed to fit together, two halves of a whole.

However, when they were walking outside, she'd felt the weight of everything that had happened pressing down on her. They had to work together, and she couldn't jeopardize their professional relationship more than she already had. And she wasn't looking to date or find something serious. She'd made the right decision, even though her heart felt otherwise.

Even if she wanted to date someone, Bailey was the last person she'd consider. Too much was at stake. Yet as Skye continued to sip her scotch on the balcony, she'd never felt so alone. Her condo seemed cavernous, and she was reluctant to return inside and go to sleep knowing that all four bedrooms and bathrooms would be devoid of life other than Skye herself. No plant, animal, or human companionship awaited her. Maybe she should text Natasha and see if she wanted to hit up Soul Cycle together in the morning.

No, it was way too late. She'd wake Natasha up, and they'd never get good bikes booking this late on a Friday night.

She'd go to bed alone and wake up alone. Just like every night. Just as she wanted.

CHAPTER TEN

Today was the day, and Bailey was excited. It was—cue the music—planting day! She was expecting her sisters Roxy and Jessica any minute. She was looking forward to the planting, spending time with her sisters, and hopefully, keeping her mind off "The Incident" with Skye that they had both sworn to never even think about again. It had been a week, and Bailey was still failing miserably to live up to that promise.

She'd had meetings at the Maxwell twice this week, and Skye had been in attendance each time. They'd both held on to their professional demeanors, and Bailey was certain no one was the wiser. However, her body hadn't quite gotten the message that "The Incident" had never actually happened.

As she exited her garage, juggling several trowels, cultivators, and shears in her arms, she saw her neighbor struggling with the trash. She deposited the tools on top of one of the planter boxes and quickly ran to the fence. "Mrs. Martin, can I help you with that?"

"Oh, thanks, dear." Mrs. Martin's perfectly coiffed short hair blew in the slight breeze, and her large smile always filled Bailey with joy. She was about seventy-five and was one of Bailey's favorite people in the world.

Bailey took the trash bag from across the fence and ran it out into the alley to toss it into her garbage can.

"Big day for you, huh?" Mrs. Martin pointed to the garden when Bailey came back.

"I love planting day. It's one of my favorite days of the year as it's full of so much promise. My sisters should be here soon."

"It's so nice that you girls all help each other with the gardening."

Mrs. Martin was the best neighbor. She always let Patsy out if Bailey was going to be late, and she often made an extra plate of food and left it in Bailey's refrigerator on those nights, giving Bailey much-needed sustenance when she was far too tired to cook. She also kept an eye on things if Bailey had to go out of town for a few days, including watering the garden. In exchange, Bailey tried to help out with whatever she needed and kept her in fresh vegetables all summer. Mrs. Martin always said she would have done those things regardless, and that was what made her such a treasure.

"Well, Roxy is the primary help with the gardening." She laughed. "Jessica doesn't like to get her hands dirty, so she keeps us in refreshments more than anything. But you do need someone with clean hands to open the wine and prepare snacks, so it all works out." Her sisters, despite being twins, were opposites in personality. But even with their quirks, she wouldn't trade them for anything.

Mrs. Martin patted her on the arm. "Good for you three that you've got a system. And I love that I get to reap the benefits of all your hard labor." She chuckled melodically. "Your tomatoes are the best I've ever had." She brought her hand to her heart in a fake swoon.

"Careful there. Don't get yourself too excited. It's still going to be a couple of months before I have any to harvest, but I'll keep you supplied all summer and fall." She always grew more vegetables than she could ever eat and loved being able to share them with her friends and family.

At the sound of the front gate swinging into the fence, Bailey looked over in time to see Roxy and Jessica, both carrying trays of sprouted plants, come into the yard. Patsy ran to investigate and "help," but Bailey yelled, "Patsy, come!" just before she collided with Roxy's legs. "Sorry, that was a close call. Anything else to grab in the car?"

"Hell, yes. Get out there and grab an armful," Roxy yelled.

Once they'd gotten the car unloaded, Roxy and Bailey started preparing the garden, and Jessica went inside to make drinks. "I love planting," Bailey said. "It's weird, but there's something so soothing about cultivating the soil, fertilizing, transplanting the little sprouts, spreading some compost. It's calming."

Roxy squinted one eye. "Hmm. Something you need to be calmed down from?"

Was she really that transparent? She normally did a pretty good job keeping her feelings in check. "No, nothing. I'm great. It's a relaxing process, and it's nice that it's something we can do together."

Roxy continued to stare with what seemed like mild disbelief. "Great, huh? Interesting."

Bailey was saved from trying to change the subject when Jessica came out carrying a tray with three plastic glasses of wine and a plate with cheese and crackers. Leave it to her to bring a serving platter to a planting party. "Refreshments are served. Let the drunk gardening season commence!"

Once their snack interlude finished, they went back to gardening. However, as soon as they finished planting and sat at the table on the deck for dinner, Roxy was back on her. "So earlier," she said. "What were you needing to get out of your head about, Bailey?"

"I never said anything about being in my head." She hoped the denial would work. She'd only commented about how calming gardening was.

"Yeah, but you implied it."

Jessica jumped in. "Yeah, you were really quiet today, Bailey. That's not like you. What's going on?"

"You wouldn't even know, Jessica, as you didn't spend a lot of time outside." Putting her on the defensive seemed the most likely way to deflect them. She really didn't want to get into her blunderous evening with one Skye Kohl.

"Don't start with me. I'm the queen of refreshments. It's a title I hold proudly. And don't try to change the subject. We want to know why you're all broody."

No such luck changing the subject, then. "Seriously, it's nothing. Just a weird evening last Friday."

"That is awfully vague. What was so weird about it?" Roxy asked, pointing her fork.

"It's not even worth going into," Bailey said, knowing that they weren't going to give up but still pretending she could get them off the scent.

"Hmm." Roxy looked at Jessica. "I think the only time she says that is when there absolutely is something to talk about. And it *is* worth going into."

"I agree with that entirely, Roxy. Methinks the lady doth protest too much."

Using their twin psychic powers, they looked toward Bailey and said at the same time, "So stop trying to deflect and spill."

"You two are really fucking creepy when you do that. Like those twins in *The Shining*."

They both continued to stare without saying another word, and then in tandem, arched one eyebrow and tilted their heads to the right.

"I say it again, creepy. But fine. There's this woman at work—"

"Someone who works for you? Oh no, that's no good," Roxy said, taking the lead in the interrogation.

"No, no," Bailey said, exasperated. "She doesn't work *for* me. I would never cross that line. She's a broker, the leasing agent for one of my best clients, and I've been working with her on a construction project."

They both nodded.

"Seriously, can you please get out of sync? You're really freaking me out."

"Sorry," they said at the same time. Bailey rolled her eyes.

"But we'll stop," Jessica said. "If we can help it."

They giggled, and Bailey shook her head. Lost cause.

"Look, there isn't anything to tell. At all. We've been butting heads at the Maxwell Building for the last couple of months or so, but last Friday, we found some common ground and got a little caught up in the moment. But we decided it was a mistake, and as far as we're concerned, it never happened."

Jessica gasped as her jaw dropped an inch. "Did you sleep with her?"

"No!" Bailey couldn't believe Jessica would think she would casually sleep with a colleague. Someone she had to work with regularly. Someone who ran in the same social circles as she did. "We just kissed." And as Jessica and Roxy smirked, Bailey realized she'd been played. She hadn't had any intention of saying that, but Jessica had manipulated her perfectly.

"Look," she continued, "we kissed. It was a one-time thing. Neither of us has time to date, and I have no inclination. Mary and Uncle Chester proved that there's no way to have both romance and a thriving business, and I have no desire to break my own heart again. Or anyone else's."

"Bailey, Bailey, Bailey." Roxy always said her name three times in a singsong when she was patronizing. "Uncle Chester has been divorced four times because he spent too much time taking his clients to strip clubs. *Not* because he was trying to build a business. Don't get me wrong, I know he really expanded Pop K's business when he took over, and I love him to death, but if he'd spent a little more time going home to his wife at five and a little less time going out, he wouldn't have been so inept at being married."

Uncle Chester wasn't a model husband, but inside, he was a good man, and he always put City Beautiful first, which was necessary to keep the business flourishing. And Bailey was grateful for the work he'd put into CBC and the condition the business had been in when she'd bought him out. "You don't know that, and running a small business is a lot of pressure. You're responsible for the livelihoods of a hundred or more people. Employees, their spouses, their kids. One wrong deal, one big mistake, and it can all evaporate. It's the third generation of family-owned businesses that is the most vulnerable and the most likely to fail. By giving it the time it needs, I had to neglect Mary and our relationship, and look what happened." Clearly, neither Jessica nor Roxy could truly understand the pressures sitting on her from that responsibility.

"What a crock." Jessica laughed. "Mary was a self-absorbed bitch that none of us liked."

"What?" Bailey felt blindsided. She knew her family wasn't Mary's biggest fan, and they hadn't been heartbroken when she'd left. Was Mary self-absorbed? Definitely. A bitch? Sometimes. Her self-centeredness was one of the reasons they'd worked for so long. Mary had been so focused on herself that she hadn't gotten upset when Bailey had regularly worked too late. But for Jessica to throw it out there so coldly was surprising.

Jessica didn't miss a beat. "And businesses are most likely to fail before their fifth year. A business and a home life are not mutually exclusive. Millions of business owners are also dealing with spouses, kids, families and are just as busy if not busier than you."

"I have a kid." Bailey gestured to Patsy, who was rolling around in the grass. "I have a family." She gestured at Jessica and Roxy and then in the general direction of Jefferson Park where the rest of their family lived.

A smile ghosted across Roxy's lips but didn't reach her eyes. "Bailey, Bailey, Bailey. It breaks my heart that you don't understand that there is more to life than work, your dog, and our extended family."

Bailey wished she could come up with a witty retort, but her words were on hiatus. She was content with her life, wasn't she? And content or not, even if she was going to break her own rules, she'd be a complete and utter fool to do it with Skye Kohl, Ice Princess of real estate. Woman of impeccable taste. Woman with a few too many similarities to her ex. She didn't even like her. But if that was true, why couldn't she stop *thinking* about her?

CHAPTER ELEVEN

Skye tried not to be too smug when she said, "Uno." She was answered by a collective groan from Natasha, Mama, and Babulya. She'd failed at not being smug, but she liked to win. Even more than she liked to win, she hated to lose. She could see in the looks they were giving each other that they were trying to conspire against her and figure out what her last card might be.

But she'd known this was coming. They had to be getting tired of her winning nearly every hand, and as their aggravation grew, they became more cutthroat, even allying against her. So on this, the last hand of the evening, she had a little trick up her sleeve so they couldn't thwart her.

Natasha sighed exasperatedly. "Don't you ever get tired of winning?" She shook her head before placing a red four down with enough force that their wineglasses sloshed on the tiny kitchen table.

"The thing about winning..." Skye pursed her lips, paused for effect. "Is that it really never gets old." Okay, that definitely sounded smug. So much for trying to be on her best behavior.

The notion made her think of Bailey; she certainly wasn't winning anything there. She hadn't been able to get Bailey or that dance or *that kiss* out of her mind in the weeks since and had been wondering if they'd made a mistake in nipping anything between them in the bud. Dating a colleague wasn't ideal, but Skye had been suffering from a severe lack of focus lately because of Bailey. She brought her fingers to her lips and could still feel Bailey's against them.

Mama's cackle brought her out of her reminiscence. "So full of herself, my little hotsy-totsy Skye." She placed a green four, changing the suit. Her eyes drilled into Skye as she set the card down, a sly smile bordering on a sneer across her mouth.

Green definitely wouldn't stop Skye from winning. Only one more card between her and her victorious Wild card. One she'd drawn several cards in order to protect a few turns ago while looking for a green or a seven. She would have drawn up to four in an effort to preserve her Wild card, but that third one had been green.

She watched Babulya's face as she selected a card from her hand and could feel the evil plan unwinding from the glint in Babulya's eye before she even threw down her Wild Draw Four.

"Shit." Skye hated being outmaneuvered. She prided herself on playing the long game and reached for the draw pile, disgusted, when a thought dawned. "Wait a second, you still have quite a few cards there, Babulya. I don't believe there's not another card that you could play." She prided herself on knowing every rule. If she was right, Babulya would be the one drawing four.

"Are you sure you want to do that, bunny?"

"Absolutely."

Skye was so certain that when Babulya flipped her hand around to show no green cards or fours, her jaw nearly hit the table. "Fine," she said through clenched teeth as she now drew six cards rather than four, more cards than anyone at the table. She also noticed the secret smiles between all three of them. She had been played. Mama knew Babulya didn't have anything green, which was why she'd changed the suit.

For frick's sake.

Frustration burned hot in Skye's veins. However, she wasn't going to take this one lying down. She ordered and then reordered her cards.

"Skye, are you still free Friday night?" Mama asked, distracting her from her plotting.

"We're having dinner, right?"

"Yes, but a slight change of location. Babulya and I made plans with a new friend, and we're hoping you could drive us and have dinner out in Jefferson Park."

"Jefferson Park? Why? That's almost the suburbs." Skye suppressed a frustrated sigh and smoothed two fingers between her brows in an attempt to iron away the wrinkle that always appeared when she was annoyed.

"Your snobbery is showing, Skye." Natasha laughed, her eyes daring her to disagree.

Skye gritted her teeth more.

"We have friends. They invite us to dinner party. We go together," Babulya said, effectively closing the matter.

"Well, okay, then. What time should I pick you up? And don't think you're getting out of this, Tash. Number one, we're being dragged to a dinner with strangers, and number two, my car only seats two, so I'll have to drive yours."

❖

Bailey was running late. Again. Even though it was just a family dinner, she still didn't like it. Unfortunately, she ran late more often than she liked to these days as it seemed like there was always something that held her up at work. This afternoon, it was a minor injury on a construction site late in the day due to a distracted carpenter.

He had apparently been texting while walking and had tripped over an extension cord, landing on an open toolbox. He'd needed six stitches in his right leg and wouldn't have any true lost time, so it wasn't major, but Bailey was irritated because it could have been much worse. There was no room for distraction on an active construction site. Period.

Despite her irritation, she still ran to the urgent care clinic so she could see the carpenter for herself and have a chat with the site supervisor to make sure he would run a tighter ship in the future.

And she still had to stop to pick up Patsy before heading to her parents' house.

To make matters worse, there was an unfamiliar car sitting in the little driveway next to her parents' garage. Shit. That almost certainly meant her mom had some new setup waiting for her. That was not what she needed, but she clipped the leash on Patsy's collar, and they walked in the back door to face the music.

They were greeted by a blast of heat, delicious smells, and her mother's booming voice. "Where the hell is that girl?"

"Who, Mom?" Bailey asked, knowing that she was the girl in question. "And why are you yelling?"

Before Bailey had a chance to let Patsy off her leash, her mom pulled her into a tight hug. "You're so late. I thought we might have to send out a search party. You get later and later every week. You're working too hard." Her mom grabbed her chin and shook her head.

"Sorry, Mom. It really wasn't my fault today. Where's Dad and Gammy? Who else is here?"

"They're in the living room with Roxy and a few friends. Everyone else was busy tonight. Brian is in the Dells with the kids. Jessica and Ed are out to dinner, and Dave is working late."

Shit. The caginess with "friends" and slipping that in before she detailed where everyone else was? It was definitely another setup. But did her mom really think she was going to ignore it?

"What *friends*, Mom?"

"Oh, just some women I met at the market a day or two ago. Mine was out of ground pork, so I went to one closer into the city. I met a mother and daughter who were also getting pork, so we talked about what we were both making, and apparently, we make very similar dishes. I make Polish golumpki, and they make Ukrainian holubtsi, so we decided to try each other's. I'm cooking today, and then Anastasia and her daughter Yulia are going to cook their holubtsi next time for us."

Yulia was a pretty uncommon name. Though Bailey wondered how old she was if she could be at the market in the middle of the day when other people were at work. Her mom grabbed her by the hand and pulled her into the living room.

As Bailey stepped into the room, she was taken aback at the number of people. The small area was standing room only. Gammy and a petite, gray-haired woman who had to be the matriarch of the guests sat in the wingback chairs in front of the window, laughing as they chatted.

Her dad was sitting on the love seat across from a young blonde with a large smile who looked vaguely familiar and another woman who had to be her mother, the resemblance was so keen. Bailey's attention, however, was drawn to the final blonde standing in the corner next to Roxy.

By the small shakes of her shoulders, she was laughing quietly at something Roxy had said. Her hair was twisted up and secured with a clip. The line of her neck was regal in its length, ending at the top of a lithe torso that was comfortably clad in a flowing, long-sleeved cream-colored blouse and tight, dark jeans.

Bailey's body had a visceral reaction to the woman's silhouette, and she was pulled toward her. She mentally chastised herself for objectifying this woman. It had to be her lingering confusion from the gala a few weeks ago that had her stomach stirring in response to a woman whose face she hadn't yet seen. And who was another setup by her mother. Or was it the woman on the couch that was supposed to be her "date"?

Bailey reluctantly looked back to her mother, who softly cleared her throat to get everyone's attention and started the introductions.

First, the petite matriarch, Anastasia Melnyk, who preferred Ana to Mrs. Melnyk or Anastasia. Then Ana's daughter, Yulia, and Yulia's younger daughter, Natasha.

When Bailey shifted her gaze back to the remaining stranger, Yulia's other daughter, her brain finally registered who it was, and her mouth fell open. Standing next to Roxy with an expression that was a mix of chagrin and suppressed smirk was none other than Skye Kohl.

And, dear God, no, she appeared to be holding the much-hated picture of Bailey from middle school. Her hair was in frizzy pigtails, and she was wearing her Sally Jessy Raphael glasses. She had gigantic braces and was holding her first-place Mathletes trophy. Could she look any nerdier?

And now, Skye, the woman who had been bouncing in her thoughts for weeks—especially since the night of the gala—was standing in front of her, in her childhood living room, in front of half her family, holding a photo that, in vivid color, showed exactly what a dork Bailey had been as a child.

Jesus.

Skye placed the photo back on the shelf and broke the awkward standoff when she walked over with her hand outstretched. "It's nice to see you again, Bailey," she said softer than Bailey had ever heard her speak. That sexy smirk was still there, but her ears had a tinge of pink that said she was a little embarrassed as well. Bailey wondered how long she had known that she'd been standing in Bailey's family's living room.

Bailey wrapped her fingers around Skye's smooth hand—that lacked even the hint of a callous—and flashed back to holding Skye in her arms. Kissing her in the hidden alcove above the ballroom. *Fuck.* "Good to see you again too." She congratulated herself on her ability to string that many words together.

"You two know each other?" Bailey's mom asked.

Bailey stammered, "Uh, yes." *Dammit, brain, get your act together.*

Luckily, Skye saved them. "We're colleagues. Sort of. I lease one of the buildings that City Beautiful Construction is doing some work in, so our paths have been crossing quite a bit lately." She rubbed at her neck, and Bailey had a hard time looking away from those long fingers brushing against the elegant column. She vividly remembered the feel of those fingers against her own neck, playing with her hair near the end of the gala.

"Oh, how nice. Is it the Maxwell Building? Bailey showed us pictures of the rooftop deck. Isn't it gorgeous?"

"It absolutely is. I get wonderful feedback from every group I take up there." Skye looked between them, and her smile turned devilish, sending another jolt of heat between Bailey's thighs. *Uh-oh.* "Are you a workaholic, Bailey? Do you talk so much work with your family that you even pull photos out at family dinners?"

Bailey rolled her eyes, irritated at how sexy Skye was even when she was teasing. "The company has been in my family for three generations. Everyone gets curious about what's going on, and that deck is a showpiece." She shrugged.

Patsy, who was still attached to her left wrist, distracted everyone by barking. "Of course, my little Patsy girl, how could we forget to introduce you?" Bailey reached down and unclipped the leash.

"Patsy, this is everyone. Everyone, this is Patsy. She's my sidekick and Mom's favorite grandchild."

Bailey's mom swatted her arm. "Don't say that. Everyone will believe you."

"I believe it, so whatever." Everyone laughed, but Bailey was confident that Patsy was, in fact, her mom's favorite.

Patsy was sitting next to Bailey's leg, quivering with excitement at so many new people to greet. "I hope everyone is okay with dogs," Bailey said. "She'll be unbearable if I keep her leashed up all night, but she doesn't jump and will just sniff at your shoes unless you pet her."

The corners of Skye's lips turned down, and she stuck her hands into her pockets, but even she nodded. Typical snooty Skye. *Probably doesn't want a stray dog hair on her perfect pumps.*

Everyone went back to chatting as Patsy made the rounds. Bailey was surprised that Ana, Yulia, and Natasha all seemed to be dog people and couldn't help but wonder where Skye had developed her aversion.

To avoid any stilted conversations with Skye, and to give herself a few minutes to process the turn the evening had taken, Bailey went into the kitchen to help her mom finish the last bits of dinner.

"Isn't she a looker?" her mom asked as soon as the kitchen door swung closed behind her.

"Jesus, Mother." Bailey huffed and ran her fingers through her hair. "Haven't I asked you to stop doing this? You never listen, and now you've brought in someone I already know. Can you say awkward? Or was it the other daughter you're trying to pimp me out to?"

"Don't be crass, Bailey." Her mom threw two oven mitts at her. "Take the potatoes out of the oven."

Bailey rolled her eyes. What was that? Twice in the last ten minutes? She didn't think she'd rolled her eyes that many times since she'd been a teenager. However, she acquiesced.

"To your other point, yes, the one you've been making lust eyes at since the moment you saw her is the one. The other daughter, Natasha, is also single but straight."

"How does that even come up in a casual conversation at the market?"

"A mother never reveals her secrets. Chalk it up to gay parent radar. Like gaydar, but I can sense the parents of gays. Get it?" Her mom chuckled, and Bailey rolled her eyes for the third time that evening. The muscles behind them were starting to ache.

"Yes, Mom, I get it." Bailey laughed at the absurdity of this entire evening that was a long way from being over.

CHAPTER TWELVE

Dinner had not been nearly as bizarre as Skye had predicted. She had wondered when she'd first agreed to go to some random stranger's house for dinner if they were all going to be murdered, Jeffrey Dahmer–style. To be safe, she brought her pepper spray.

But when they'd arrived, and everyone had seemed so warm and friendly, she'd wondered if her mom had just made a new friend. But when everyone had started asking about where the other daughter was, Skye had known it was as ridiculous a setup as it seemed. Though just not a murderous one.

Her mother had never tried that before. She understood that work always came first, and Skye wasn't ready to settle down. She had wondered if this was payback for Skye nagging her about moving to the North Side so often.

She'd never imagined in her wildest dreams that the wayward daughter would be the woman whose touch she hadn't been able to clear from her mind since the gala.

That was, until she was chatting with Roxy and looked at the pictures on the bookshelf and everything had clicked into place. Bailey couldn't have been more than twelve or thirteen while holding that Mathletes trophy, wearing a proud, goofy grin with braces larger than her mouth. It gave Skye a glimpse of a side of Bailey that she hadn't known existed. The gangly dweeb. *Very* similar to Skye herself at that age.

Bailey's family was also endearing. It was clear she hadn't expected a setup, either, although her family had apparently been in on it. The way they maneuvered around the table, switching seats until Skye was next to Bailey, where neither of them had room to move away, was nothing short of masterful. As a long-term strategist, she could appreciate the work, even if it was uncomfortable to experience. Sitting next to Bailey hadn't been a hardship, though. They'd settled into comfortable conversation despite their previous questionable encounters. But Skye had kept catching herself staring at Bailey's hand. She'd watched her thumb trace the top of her wineglass and had flashed back to that thumb running along her jaw right before Bailey had kissed her. The way Bailey had held her knife, gentle but with authority, had reminded her of those fingers gently but firmly pulling her closer as they were dancing and later kissing. Her heart rate had quickened again remembering that kiss.

What had happened to never thinking about it again?

Lost in her thoughts after dinner, Skye didn't hear anyone approach her at the kitchen sink and jumped when she heard, "What are you doing out here?"

"Jesus, Bailey. What the fuck?"

Bailey was standing two feet behind her with her hands on her hips, looking good enough to eat. "You're awfully jumpy, aren't you?" Her cheeky grin created an unwelcome flutter in Skye's chest. "This is the second time I've made you jump like that."

"Well, when you sneak up on someone like a fucking ax murderer, what do you expect? Were you a ninja in another life?" Skye smiled at the pot she was washing, not daring to actually look at Bailey for fear she couldn't keep a straight face. "Or were those the classes you took on your nights off from being a Mathlete?" She laughed and looked at Bailey from the side of her eye to see that telltale temple twitch. She had the impulse to touch it again, the way she had at the gala before the crashing dishes had broken the spell, but her hands were all soapy.

Bailey huffed through her nose. "I knew you weren't going to let that damn picture go."

Skye chuckled and continued scrubbing. "How could I? Little geeky Bailey was so adorable. I wanted to pinch her cheek."

"Jesus." Bailey shook her head, yet all Skye could think about was leaning toward her and kissing her, to hell with her soapy hands. "Anyway, what are you doing? You snuck off to the bathroom and never came back."

"Isn't it obvious? I'm washing the dishes. I didn't want your mom to have to do it after we all left. But I knew that if I said what I was going to do, she would have objected." Skye certainly didn't want

Gammy or Loll to have to do them after they'd cooked for hours. She knew from experience that cabbage rolls took a long time to prepare. "That's uncharacteristically thoughtful of you."

Skye's back stiffened. Ouch. Bailey didn't even look guilty after lobbing that grenade. Back to not being able to spend more than two minutes together without someone saying something shitty. She scrubbed the pot harder until her knuckles banged the lip of another dish, and she yelped. "That was harsh," she finally said. "Am I really that much of a bitch that you don't think I can do anything nice? Or hell, mildly considerate?" She tried unsuccessfully to keep it light, but the hurt and shame made her skin prickle, so she stared into the sink, scrubbing the pot ferociously while ignoring the sharp pain in her knuckles and pointedly not looking up.

"God, I'm sorry. I didn't mean it like that. Shit." Bailey placed a hand on Skye's shoulder. "Let me help you, at least. I was being an ass. I'm sorry. Really." She grabbed the pot Skye had been scrubbing like Lady Macbeth trying to get out the spots and rinsed it on the other side of the sink. "I don't know why I said that. I really don't think you're a bitch. Not anymore, anyway." She let out a breath, and Skye could feel the tension radiating from her when their arms brushed. "Despite our differences, I've found myself quite liking you. Despite our promises to forget that kiss the other night ever happened, I can't stop thinking about you. I can't stop fantasizing about doing it again. So to combat all of that, I've been trying to focus on the things you've done that have irritated me, and thus, I'm the bitch here." Her hands stilled under the stream of water, and she looked at Skye.

Into Skye.

Her mouth went dry at the desire she saw there. Her hands rested on the edge of the sink, but she realized she'd started leaning toward Bailey even as she whispered, "This is a really bad idea."

"I know." Bailey's eyes flicked to Skye's mouth as she shut off the water without looking.

"I haven't been able to stop thinking about you." Skye chuckled mirthlessly and squeezed the counter. "After that first week, I started avoiding the Maxwell. I've been sending one of the junior brokers because I was afraid to run into you. Not the best behavior for someone who only makes money when she leases a space."

"I actually haven't been to the Maxwell in two weeks for the same reason. Who knew we were so alike?" Bailey's lips curled into a smile, but her voice was so quiet, Skye could barely hear it. "See? We do have some things in common." Bailey ran a thumb along Skye's jaw as she had before their kiss at the gala, and Skye's knees weakened. Her eyes fluttered closed, and she closed the gap between them, lightly brushing Bailey's mouth.

Bailey moaned and pulled her closer. Skye ran her fingers up Bailey's back, soapiness be damned as she deepened their kiss. Bailey's tongue nudged her bottom lip, and Skye's legs went wobbly at the delicate rasp. She leaned back against the counter for support and pulled Bailey in, seeing stars and stifling a moan when one of Bailey's knees slid between her thighs. Had her body reacted this quickly to anyone before? From a simple kiss? Not that there was anything simple about this kiss, but she curled her fingers into Bailey's lower back, hoping she could somehow get Bailey closer. Bailey pressed into her until she tilted her head back on a gasp as Bailey began kissing the sensitive spot on her neck, right below her ear.

The sounds of a low grumble preceded Bailey pulling away. She rested her forehead against Skye's, breathing heavily. "Shit. Someone wants her evening walk."

Skye's head was still cloudy. "What?"

"Patsy. She wants her evening walk and is only going to get more annoying if I ignore her."

"Maybe it's for the best. We agreed this is a bad idea." Skye suppressed a growl of her own. She'd never wanted to throw caution to the wind more in her life. The feel of Bailey pressed against her, her fingertips tracing shapes along Skye's back through the silky material of her blouse, made her forget everything she'd thought she knew.

Another grumble had Bailey lifting her head to glare at her dog. "Patsy, can you give me one damn minute? Mommy is busy right now!"

Patsy answered with a grumble, but this time, it bordered on a bark.

Did people really refer to themselves as moms to their dogs? Was it just Bailey? It was almost cute. Perhaps everything about her would be cute while Skye was entirely too turned on to be standing in her crush's parents' kitchen.

"Fine, dog. You win," Bailey said. "If I let her go on like this, someone is going to come in to investigate why I'm ignoring their favorite grandchild when she clearly needs attention. I'd better take her out. You aren't going to sneak out while I'm away, are you?"

Skye took a breath to collect her thoughts. The rational choice *would* be to get the hell out of there before she fell farther down this rabbit hole. But she didn't think she had the strength to do it again. To pull away. Bailey was looking at her as if she could see the gears turning in her head. The right choice was to make an exit.

But Skye couldn't get that through her head, so she said, "No, I'm not ready to go yet. I'll be here when you get back. Unless..." Was she really going to suggest this? Apparently, yes, she was. "Unless you wouldn't mind company. I could stretch my legs after all that rich food."

Before the words were even fully out, Bailey said, "That'd be cool."

Bailey's eyes got wide as she spoke, which was freaking adorable as well. How was Skye supposed to have any self-control when Bailey was vulnerable enough to say something as relaxed as "that'd be cool" and reveal how much she really wanted Skye to go? She tried to hide her smile.

Bailey cleared her throat. "I mean, Patsy would really think it's cool. She desperately needs everyone's love and approval."

Skye wasn't sure how she felt about Patsy, but everything inside her was pushing her toward Bailey, and she couldn't ignore it. "Well, if it's for Patsy, how can I deny her?" Jesus, where had those words even come from? However, the brightness of Bailey's grin could rival the lights on Broadway, and Skye would have promised her anything in the universe to keep it there. Even pretending to like a smelly, drooly, blocky-headed dog.

She squeezed Bailey's arm and said, "I'm not done with you today, either."

After Bailey yelled to the family that they'd be right back, she clipped Patsy on her leash, and they went out the kitchen door. It was an unseasonably warm late-April evening, but a shiver ran through Skye at the coolness of the evening air.

Apparently, Bailey noticed as well. "I'm sorry, I wasn't even thinking of the temperature tonight. Do you need to go grab a jacket or something?"

Skye was too embarrassed to admit it, but she hadn't brought one. She'd thought her silk blouse would be sufficient for an evening indoors. She certainly hadn't planned on a stroll outside. "I'm fine. Thank you, though." Yet another chill ran through her, and she wasn't able to subdue it.

"Come here for a sec." Bailey grabbed her hand and pulled her toward a dark red truck. She opened the passenger door and pulled out a gray zippered hoodie with City Beautiful Construction's logo embroidered on it. "Here. I know you're fine but just in case it gets a little cooler. Patsy would hate for you to be uncomfortable because of her."

Skye wasn't sure what to say. The women she normally "dated," in the most casual sense possible, were typically too concerned about fashion to care all that much about her comfort. And if they did, they certainly didn't frame it in a way that wouldn't make Skye feel weak. "Thank you." She pushed her arms into the sleeves, and Bailey's fingers brushed hers when they both reached for the zipper. Skye put her hands into her borrowed pockets and let Bailey zip her up.

"I like the way you look in my clothes," Bailey said. A half-smile appeared as the zipper neared the top of its track, and she looked at Skye. Her concern had an easy warmth spreading through Skye's chest and landing in an unfamiliar tangle of flutters in her stomach.

"Thank you." Unable and unwilling to resist, she grabbed a handful of Bailey's shirt and pulled her in for another gentle kiss. "Thank you," she whispered again.

"Well, if that's all it takes to get your appreciation, I'll stop trying so hard."

Skye pushed her away. "Just stop." Had her knuckles just brushed the inside of Bailey's breast? Maybe. Was she sorry about it? Not so much. That was certainly inappropriate, but again, she had lost her ability to really care. And as long as she didn't examine that realization, it didn't scare the shit out of her.

Skye wiggled her arms inside the sweatshirt, appreciating the softness against her skin. It also had the most delicious scent, one hundred percent Bailey. Lavender and vanilla and pure yumminess. "I didn't want to admit to being cool, but this is lovely." The warmth surrounding her skin was nothing short of decadent.

Bailey simply smiled and let Patsy pull them down the street.

"So where did the name Patsy come from? It's so old-fashioned."

"It is, but it's her coloring. In pit bulls, that gray coat is actually called blue or a blue nose. Blue made me think of the song, 'Crazy.' You know, for feeling so—"

"Blue. Patsy Cline," they both finished.

Bailey's eyes twinkled in the light of the full moon blazing on the clear evening.

"You're a Patsy Cline fan in addition to being a big band and jazz fan?" Skye asked.

"Are you surprised?"

"Not really." She couldn't pinpoint why, but it seemed to fit Bailey. "I love old music. Sometimes, it seems like we complicate the shit out of things in this day and age, technology and connectedness, and it's a lot. Things were simpler back then. Though I doubt I would've enjoyed being a lesbian in those days."

"You're a woman of many layers, Bailey Kaczmarek."

They smiled at each other for a long moment when Bailey's crazy-ass dog sprinted toward the deserted street, jerking the leash. The force knocked Bailey squarely into Skye. They stumbled for a few steps before Skye slammed into a tree and kept them from toppling. The air whooshed from her lungs. She tried to catch her breath as she found herself pressed tightly between the tree and Bailey's muscled torso. Instinctively, she wrapped her arms around Bailey, anchoring her in place.

"Patsy! Get over here," Bailey yelled, the leash straining against her wrist. Patsy came trotting back as if she hadn't just tried to kill them all, and Bailey leaned back as far as Skye's embrace would allow. "I'm so sorry. I should have warned you that she can be erratic. She probably saw a bunny or something."

"Hmm," Skye said, not particularly concerned with how they got there as she appreciated the unexpected closeness. She dug her fingers into Bailey's back, and Bailey's hips answered, curling into her, causing the flutters in her stomach to flit even faster.

"Sorry," Bailey whispered again.

"I'm not," Skye said.

"You're not?"

"You really can't tell?"

Bailey shook her head weakly.

Skye didn't believe the half-hearted denial. "I haven't been able to get the memory of your body against mine out of my head for days, and now, here you are. Perhaps a little rougher than last time, but I can't say I'm disappointed at all."

"It is something, isn't it?" Bailey dipped her head, and Skye hungrily took her mouth. It was uncanny how Bailey could generate an erratic heartbeat with a simple kiss. Though in all honesty, none of Bailey's kisses could be described as simple.

When Bailey's tongue slipped into her mouth, she slid her hands down Bailey's back, stopping at the swell of her hips and pulling her even closer.

"Oh God. I need…" Bailey moaned.

Skye was pretty sure she could fill in the blanks. She bit Bailey's lower lip, loving the feel of it between her teeth. Bailey moaned again, clearly loving it too, and her hips began to subtly move against Skye's center. Pleasure coursed through her veins at this new pressure between her thighs. She tipped her head against the tree, offering her neck, and Bailey blazed a path along her skin, alternating between light flicks of her tongue and little nips of her teeth. She began to move her hips against Bailey's on instinct.

Skye blinked at a quiet grumble from Patsy, their self-appointed chaperone that evening, and she remembered where they were. She loosened and pushed a little space between them, allowing the fog in her brain to begin to clear. "Jesus, we're in the middle of the street." It took every ounce of her self-control to get the words out when all she wanted to do was pull Bailey back in and kiss that sexy grin off her face, despite being on a public road.

Bailey swallowed as she stared. Skye squeezed her hands into fists on Bailey's hips, as if she could physically hold on to her self-control "Yeah. Right. Sorry, I lost my head for a moment. This is where I grew up. I know all the neighbors. Jesus." She stood up straight, removing her weight from Skye, and looked at Patsy, who was benignly sniffing at a dandelion that looked very out of place in the otherwise neatly trimmed lawn. Skye shivered, missing Bailey's warmth.

"Well, that was…" Skye trailed off as Bailey assisted her off the tree and started walking back.

"Nice?" Bailey didn't release her hand, and Skye's wrist tingled where her thumb lightly brushed back and forth.

"Yes. And no."

The corners of Bailey's mouth fell.

Not wanting to hurt her, Skye quickly said, "I mean, yes, it was nice—very nice—but…" What the hell was she trying to say? She knew intellectually that they shouldn't get involved for all the reasons she'd been agonizing over for weeks, but she couldn't deny that it also felt so right. "Fuck."

"What are we going to do about this? About us?" Bailey asked, releasing Skye's hand to wag a finger between them.

It was a valid question. One Skye didn't have a damn clue how to answer. "I have no—" She was distracted by the house in front of them. "Isn't that your parents' house?"

"Yeah," Bailey said so slowly that it lasted nearly the length of a sentence.

"Where…is my sister's car?" Where could she have gone? To the convenience store or something? "Tasha hates to drive. I actually drove her car here this evening. I can't imagine where…" She didn't realize she had stopped walking until Bailey looked back at her from a few paces away.

"Are you coming?"

"Yeah, sorry, it's just weird." Skye gestured toward the empty driveway.

"Why didn't you drive your own car if you were the driver?"

"Oh, mine doesn't seat four. No real back seat."

"Ah. Why am I not surprised that you have an impractical car?" Bailey laughed, and Skye was surprised to find herself not taking offense at the implications behind that question.

"I cannot deny that I'm not always the most practical person." She shrugged at her own insouciance. "I like pretty things, and my black Audi is nothing if not pretty." She ran her finger over Bailey's lapel.

Bailey shook her head and laughed. "Now, *that* I can see."

"Maybe if you're lucky, I'll take you for a ride one day, and you can see exactly how pretty she is." She bit the inside of her lip, surprised again at her blatant flirting. She couldn't seem to help herself. Something about Bailey put her internal filter to sleep so deeply that whatever popped into her head popped out of her mouth almost in the same instant. This was dangerous.

"A ride, huh?" Bailey's lips rolled in as she inhaled. An odd face on most people, but even that looked good on her. "I might be interested in going for a ride with you. I imagine you like to be in control." She trailed one finger down Skye's sweatshirt-covered arm, and Skye would have sworn she could feel her skin through the two layers of fabric. "I like to be as well, but I think letting you drive could be fun. Every once in a while."

"We should check our schedules. Get something on the calendar," Skye said. As though she was meeting an old colleague for a drink rather than talking about going for a *ride* together. As though the thought of that *ride* didn't cause a shiver to ripple down her spine.

They stared, Bailey's index finger hooked in Skye's pinkie, finally finding skin beyond the end of her borrowed sleeve. Skye didn't make a move toward the house or toward Bailey. She was afraid to break the spell. Afraid to voice how much she wanted to take Bailey for a ride in every sense of the word.

Skye had no concept of how long they stood there. She wondered what was going through Bailey's mind. Wondered if Bailey was just as conflicted as she was. Wondered what was going to happen next. The last time they'd shared such an intimate moment, they'd both pulled away. She didn't think *she* had the strength to do it again tonight. Not after spending time together with both their guards down.

"Where on earth do we go from here?" Bailey finally said on a long sigh.

Skye smirked. "Probably inside to see where the hell my sister is." She didn't want to break the tentative connection they seemed to be forming, but she also wanted to solve the mystery of where her sister was.

"That isn't exactly what I meant, but it's a place to start." Bailey shrugged, released Skye's finger, and gestured for her to lead the way. She tried to repress the feeling of loss at that break in connection.

Boisterous laughter struck Skye when she walked back into the Kaczmareks' living room, followed immediately by the lack of people. Her entire family was gone. She stopped so suddenly that Bailey ran into her, though Patsy weaved her way past.

"What's…Oh." Bailey must have just noticed that it wasn't only Natasha who'd left.

Skye used her public speaking voice to get the room's attention. "Excuse me, where did my family go? Is everything okay?"

After a pause, Bailey's mom said, "Your sister texted you."

Skye reached into her back pocket to grab her phone and came up empty. She always had her phone. Had she lost it? Had it fallen out of her pocket against the tree? No. She'd put it on the counter before she'd started washing the dishes. "Excuse me for a sec."

She darted into the kitchen, and there was her phone, right beside the sink. She grabbed it off the counter and saw two missed calls and four text messages.

Where'd you go? Babulya forgot to take her stomach pill, so she wants to head out so she can get home before her stomach starts to act up.

Loll says Bailey would be happy to take you home. Is that okay?

Even Mom is pushing us to leave now. Text me back ASAP, or I have to assume you are okay with us leaving you.

K, sorry, going. Text me later when you get this. Love you.

Seriously? They'd stranded her in Jefferson Park? Skye was flabbergasted. She clenched her right fist and restrained herself from banging her phone on the counter. She needed to stay calm. She certainly didn't want to embarrass herself by making a scene in front of the Kaczmareks, who, as a whole, were some of the nicest people she'd ever met.

It wasn't like she couldn't call a Lyft. It would be expensive, but she could handle it. When she walked back into the living room, Bailey was sitting next to Loll, whispering something that looked heated.

Loll shook her head vehemently and shrugged. Skye could see Bailey's temple twitching from across the room, so she must have really been clenching her jaw. Loll nodded toward Skye, and their discussion came to a halt as Bailey stood.

The irritation slid off Bailey's face as she walked toward Skye, and her lips bowed into a smirk. "Looks like I'm going to be taking you for a ride first. Apparently, Patsy and I are your Lyft drivers this evening. Hopefully, you don't mind riding in a little less luxury than you're used to."

"It's a little early for me to be giving up control, but it would appear as though my family has forced my hand," she whispered softly. Bailey's eyes grew wide, and her final step faltered. Teasing mission accomplished. "But I don't want to put you out. I'm rather out of the way, aren't I?" Although she wasn't yet ready for her evening to be over, she also didn't want to be in Bailey's debt.

"Eh, at this time of night, traffic won't be bad. And Patsy loves car rides." Bailey's eyes gleamed with humor, and Skye decided to lean into the flutter in her chest rather than run from it.

"Okay then, Lyft driver. I'm ready when you are." Skye was looking forward to spending more time with her, even if it was just going to be to talk since they would be driving. Skye found herself eager to discover the boundaries of what could be.

CHAPTER THIRTEEN

Bailey still couldn't believe the audacity of her mother—and Skye's, for that matter—as she neared Skye's condo building. She would have never believed her mother scheming enough to actually strand one of her setups at the house so Bailey would be forced to drive her home. Not that it was a hardship. Sure, Skye was out of the way, but traffic wasn't bad, Bailey had nowhere else pressing to be, and she really wasn't ready to say good night. They had shared easy conversation the entire ride to Lincoln Park.

"This is me on the left. You can pull up under the canopy there." Skye pointed to where a valet was still on duty, even though it was nearing midnight. Jesus, how much were her association fees to cover that?

The valet moved toward Skye's door, but she gestured for him to give her a minute and looked over, the corner of her lip caught between her teeth. Bailey wished for a moment that it was her own lip between Skye's teeth, and a persistent hum started low in her belly.

"Thank you for the ride," Skye said, her voice subdued and a little gravelly, as though she'd just woken up and they hadn't been speaking almost nonstop on the ride over. That voice alone sent a rush of heat surging between Bailey's legs.

"Of course. Any time." Bailey smiled and tucked a loose lock of Skye's hair behind her ear. It was gorgeous in this more relaxed, wavy style, only barely contained. Bailey enjoyed her straight lob as well, but the soft waves made her seem loosened up, like a real person and not an ice princess out to conquer the world. It was sexy.

Bailey wanted to kiss her, but she wasn't sure of the protocol. They had already decided that anything unprofessional between them would be a mistake. And yet they'd kissed in her parents' kitchen. And on their walk. And she still yearned to feel Skye's skin beneath her fingertips and her lips beneath her own.

Bailey moistened her dry lips with the tip of her tongue as she watched Skye, looking for some sign or clue that would tell her what she wanted. Did she want Bailey to kiss her? Did she want to invite her up? Did *Bailey* want her to invite her up?

The questions bounced around her head like the ball in *Super Breakout*, stuck between the wall and the ceiling. She looked at their hands, Bailey's resting lightly on top, both on Bailey's knee. When had that happened?

"Do you…" Skye paused, bit the inside of her cheek. "Want to come up for a drink or something?" The words came out rushed. Like she wasn't sure she would get them out if she didn't push them all out in a single mouthful.

Yes! her libido screamed, and it took everything in her not to answer exactly like that. "I would, but I've got Sleeping Beauty back there." Bailey angled her head toward where Patsy was snoring quietly on the back seat. "This building doesn't seem like the type of place that allows dogs."

"I'm pretty sure they do. I've seen other dogs around the building. Mostly, they're tiny things, but I don't think there's a rule against any of them." She then proved that Bailey didn't know her at all when she rolled down the window and yelled, "Charlie, we allow dogs in this building, don't we?"

He tipped his hat. "Yes, ma'am. Do you want me to park your car now?"

Skye looked at Bailey expectantly. She desperately wanted to say yes, but was this the right choice? Should she still use Patsy to try to get out of it? "Are you sure that, even if your building allows dogs, you want one in your apartment?"

"I'm sure she'll behave. We bonded a little bit earlier. I don't think she'll pee on my area rugs. Do you?"

"No, it's past her bedtime. She's just going to sleep, probably."

"Well?"

"Sure, a drink would be nice." Skye's wide smile was the most genuine one Bailey had seen and made her feel a little gooey inside.

The elevator ride to the top floor was uneventful but for a few lusty glances. Bailey resolved that no matter what, she wasn't going to stay over. She'd have her drink, they'd talk about what they were going to do about this undeniable attraction, and then she and Patsy would head home.

It was a solid plan. One she prayed she'd have the strength to stick to. Maybe Skye wasn't even offering sex that evening, and it was pretty presumptuous to assume that she was. And yet every time Bailey looked at Skye, that pull hit her, and she was fairly confident she knew what was on the table.

The grandeur of Skye's condo shouldn't have been surprising. It fit with her personality, though the more Bailey got to know her, the less pretentious she seemed to be.

"What can I get you to drink?" Skye asked.

"Whatever you're having is fine."

"Macallan Twenty-Five?" Skye looked at her with an arched brow.

"Isn't that older than you are?" Bailey laughed, not sure why she was ribbing Skye about her age but unable to help herself. She was only a few years older, but it seemed like giving Skye a hard time was half the fun in all their interactions. And she *had* thought Skye was much younger when they'd first met.

"Not quite. It's not like you're that much older than me, old and wise, yet not funny, one. And I am a few years older than this scotch." Skye rolled her eyes, which made Bailey laugh.

"Well, as long as you were born when it went into the bottle...but isn't that a little extravagant for a random Friday night?" Bailey couldn't break the eye contact and took a shallow breath before continuing. "Are you trying to impress me with your expensive bottle of scotch?" Bailey had never had Macallan Twenty-Five, but she thought the bottle was well over two thousand dollars.

"What can I say? I'm feeling a little indulgent this evening." Skye looked confident, but Bailey could see her nibbling on the inside of her cheek, belying that confident facade. "You *can* let her off that leash, if you want. I didn't invite you up here expecting her to be tethered to you." She pointed to Patsy.

Patsy was sniffing around as far as she could, but with only six feet to work with, that wasn't far. "Are you sure? She'd love to be able to explore, but I'm afraid she might get into something."

Skye shook her head slowly. Almost sadly, Bailey thought, but what sense would that make? "Nothing to get into, really. She'll be fine. She seems like a good girl."

"Okay." Bailey bent to unclip Patsy's leash. She wandered around the room, sniffing at the base of the furniture before walking to Skye's ankle boots and lying down.

"See, good girl. Now about that drink?" Skye circled back to the original topic.

Bailey shrugged and tried not think about the effect Skye's gaze had on her. "If you want to waste your good scotch on me, I'm not going to argue."

Skye cocked her head, seemingly lost for words, perhaps for the first time in her life. "Why would you say wasting it? Good scotch is meant to be shared with good company."

Bailey opened her mouth, but no words would come out, so she examined Skye's expression. Was she good company? And did Skye really think she was worth two hundred dollars an ounce? "Good point. Fine spirits, fine company, let's do this."

Skye pulled out two crystal lowball glasses and set them on the bar before pulling out a Macallan bottle that looked like she'd had maybe one drink out of. She poured them a very generous two fingers that was probably three hundred dollars in each glass.

Why was Bailey's mind so hell-bent on calculating how much her drink was? The next thing she knew, she'd be calculating each sip. Jesus. *Get out of your head.* She forced herself out of her musings and walked to the bar where Skye still stood.

Bailey took the glass, and one of Skye's fingertips grazed hers. Her hand trembled at the contact, and for a brief moment, she feared she might drop the glass. Wouldn't that be great?

"Careful there," Skye said, but Bailey knew she'd felt the crackle too. She could see it in her wide eyes.

They stared for a beat before Skye raised her glass and said, "Here's to new beginnings."

Bailey mirrored her. "Another one, hmm? Maybe let's try to make this the last new beginning for us? I'm tired of starting over."

"Me too." Skye brought their glasses together with a little pling.

Bailey inhaled the amber liquor and was surprised at how fruity the aroma was. Her mouth watered as she brought the glass to her lips. She took her first sip and decided in that moment it was worth every penny. "This is the best scotch I've ever had. In my entire life. It's unbelievably smooth."

The corner of Skye's mouth curled up again, and Bailey's stomach did strange things when the tip of Skye's tongue captured a drop of the scotch clinging to her upper lip. "I'm glad you like it. I've only had it once, and I can promise, this time is more enjoyable."

"Why?" Bailey took another small sip, confirmed it was still amazing.

"You," Skye said simply.

Bailey's breath caught. What could she say to that? She cleared her throat but still couldn't chase down any words, so she took another sip.

"Why don't we take these out on the balcony. It's a beautiful night," Skye said while Bailey stood charmed. She opened what appeared to be an entire wall of glass that, when open, allowed her living room to extend almost seamlessly into the balcony. It was much more private than Bailey had been expecting and had a cute seating area with a blue love seat and ottoman and two matching chairs opposite.

Skye streamed a big band station, sat on the far side of the love seat, and propped her feet on the ottoman, her legs crossed at the ankles. She'd left more than half the couch vacant.

Bailey wasn't sure where she should sit. She ended up next to Skye as that seat had a better view of the lake than the chairs. She let out a long sigh. "This is deceptively comfortable."

"I know, right?" Skye said. "Do you mind if I slip my shoes off? My toes are tired of being cramped."

"Of course not. It's your place, and it's not like I haven't seen your feet before, if you recall walking around Navy Pier with no shoes on."

Skye sighed, released her hair from its clip, and used her fingers to fluff it. "When I got home that night, I ended up out here in my robe and sipped a little scotch while I tried to process everything."

"The Macallan?" Bailey wasn't sure why she'd asked. Maybe to stop herself from thinking of Skye naked under a robe. Unfortunately, as soon as that image popped into her mind, she couldn't dispel it.

Skye chuckled. "No, Johnnie Blue." She slipped off her boots and massaged her Achilles for a moment before propping her bare feet back up on the ottoman.

Bailey was transfixed by Skye's fingers on her ankles and tried to focus on the conversation despite the electricity thrumming through her body. "Still a solid scotch."

"Yes, but not nearly as good as this one," Skye said silkily. She twisted her hair back up into the clip, and Bailey couldn't decide if she preferred it up or down.

"True. Did you have any epiphanies about us while in your robe out here?" Bailey still couldn't get that vision out of her mind. She wondered if Skye had been standing against the rail of her balcony, arms dangling over as she held her glass or if she'd sat on the couch. Had the robe slipped open to her knees when she'd propped up her feet? Did it slip all the way up to her thighs? Was it silk like her blouse tonight?

Skye chuckled softly, seemingly to herself. "Not a one about us."

"Did you have one about something else?" Bailey was still spellbound by Skye's feet. While she generally wasn't a foot person, Skye with bare feet made her seem more human. Open and vulnerable. And her bare feet also made Bailey think of bare...other things.

Skye sighed and took another sip. Bailey appreciated how the muscles in her neck worked reflexively yet delicately as she swallowed. She tightened her fingers into a fist to resist the urge to trace those lines.

"Damn, this is amazing." Skye stared into her drink for what felt like an eternity. "I started wondering why I have this huge place for just me. I've got four bedrooms, four bathrooms, and a gigantic outdoor living area upstairs. I never entertain because I don't really like people in my personal space."

"And yet you invited me here?" The budding intimacy between them was scary but also felt right at the same time.

"How about that, huh?" Skye pursed her lips. Let out a little huff. "I've also never been a dog person, and here I am, inviting you *and* your dog up here. I don't know what it is about you, but it feels easy to be candid. I don't think I've ever been so unfiltered with anyone. I open my mouth, and what I'm thinking falls out. See? Here I go again." She finished her drink and set the glass on a small table beside the love seat. She took the clip out of her hair that wasn't holding much back anymore anyway and ran her fingers through, shaking it out again. But rather than putting her hair back up, she set the clip on the side table.

Bailey wanted to slide down next to her. Instead, she looked out at the lake and squeezed her glass harder. "I like it. It's endearing." When Skye didn't respond, Bailey turned back to find Skye watching her. "What? Do I have something on my face?" God, wouldn't that be her luck?

Skye sank her teeth into her lip, and Bailey's mouth felt like the Sahara. She took her last sip but held on to the glass as though it was the only thing tethering her to this moment. "No," Skye whispered. She ran a finger around the shell of Bailey's ear, and Bailey's blood rushed to that point. "What are we going to do about this thing between us?" That finger moved down to Bailey's neck, and Skye started to knead the knots from a long week.

"I don't know," Bailey breathed. "I don't have time to date, and we work together, but I haven't been able to get you out of my mind since the gala. No matter how hard I try." As Skye continued to massage her, Bailey started to drift forward. "That feels amazing."

Her eyes glided closed, and when she opened them, Skye had also drifted toward the middle of the love seat. Their mouths were mere centimeters apart. Bailey's gaze flicked to Skye's mouth, and that was all it took to close the gap.

Their kiss started slow and soft. Skye's lips barely grazed Bailey's, and she still tasted sweet from the Macallan. Skye's hand at the back of her neck urged her closer, and electricity arced behind her ribs every time their tongues brushed. She pushed Skye back on the love seat until she was lying on top of her—as much as the short love seat would allow—and placed her glass next to Skye's on the table.

Skye's fingers moved from her neck and were running through her hair while the other hand moved to her waist, pulling her hips into the space between Skye's thighs. The soft give of breasts beneath her own drove Bailey nearly mad with need, and she ground her pelvis into Skye.

Bailey cupped Skye's breast and dragged her thumb across the nipple until it hardened into a peak through her shirt and bra. The feel of that erect nipple through the silk of her shirt had Bailey's vision clouding over. Their hips began to move together ever so slowly.

Skye's foot slipped off the ottoman. "Bailey," she moaned. "We should take this to the bedroom."

Bailey levered herself up. Skye had never looked more beautiful than she did in that moment, with swollen lips and rosy cheeks. Bailey wanted to sweep her up in her arms and lock her away from the rest of the world until Monday morning. Instead, remembering why this was all a terrible idea and feeling like a tease, she sighed and pushed back into a seated position and looked out at the lake again.

"You have no idea just how badly I want to do that." Bailey dropped her head onto the back of the love seat.

"But?"

"I hate myself for saying this and I'm going to hate it even more when I get home tonight, but I don't want to move too fast." Bailey rolled her head to the side. "I want you so badly right now, I ache, but I don't know if we should do this. I don't want either of us to look back and regret doing something we can't undo."

"Goddamn you. But you're right. And I hate you for it." Skye's chest was heaving as she leaned back. She was so attractive in that moment as she struggled to regain control of her emotions. Bailey loved and hated that their connection did that to her. "Fuck," Skye groaned as she pushed herself up and scooted back into the corner of the couch. "So what's next?"

Bailey wasn't ready to end their touching, so she grabbed Skye's hand. "Fuck if I know." Skye squeezed. "Maybe we take a day or two to think everything through?"

"You're a tease." Skye closed her eyes and shook her head. When she opened them, she said, "Can I see you tomorrow?"

Tomorrow would at least give them a night to sleep on it, but that didn't seem like quite enough time. Bailey didn't think the need for Skye that she was drowning in could possibly subside within twenty-four hours. "How about if you come over to my place on Sunday afternoon, and I'll cook you dinner? That gives us a couple of days to think."

"I'm supposed to be one of the best negotiators in the city, but you drive a hard bargain." Skye blew out a long-suffering sigh. "I guess that works." Skye stood and pulled Bailey up. "While I would love for you to stay, I won't be able to keep my hands off you if you do, so…" She trailed off. Patsy jumped to her feet too.

"Same. I'll text my address." Bailey really didn't want to leave, but if she stayed, she knew she didn't have the strength to keep her hands to herself either.

"Okay," Skye said.

Bailey clipped Patsy's leash on beside the door, and Skye pulled her into a hug, pressing a soft kiss to her cheek. She leaned toward Bailey's ear rather than releasing her and whispered, "I'll be thinking of you in the shower shortly with my favorite handheld showerhead."

Bailey's jaw dropped. She pressed a hand to her chest and said, "An arrow to the heart."

With a devilish grin on her face, Skye pressed another quick kiss to Bailey's lips and shoved her out the door.

CHAPTER FOURTEEN

When Bailey awoke on Saturday spooning Patsy rather than Skye, regret at having walked away from Skye and all she'd offered stabbed sharp in her stomach. She rolled out of bed and prepared to go for a run, hoping that would help clear her head so she could figure out what she wanted to do. Unfortunately, she spent forty minutes vacillating between how much she wanted Skye and how bad an idea it was, so her mind was more jumbled when she got back than when she'd left.

She tried to work in the garden, but even while pulling weeds, her mind traveled to the feel of Skye's lips, her silk-covered nipple, and then she imagined Skye taking care of herself in the shower after she'd left.

In her mind's eye, Skye stood in a large, walk-in shower with a glass door. She was leaning against the back wall, watching herself in the mirror through the glass as she ran one hand over her breast and squeezed her nipple while using a handheld showerhead creatively with the other. Bailey had given herself one hell of an orgasm the night before with that image and might need to do it again later today. Perhaps that would clear her mind. She stifled a groan as she imagined Skye pinching her nipple again and bringing herself to another orgasm.

Jesus.

"Good morning, Bailey!"

Bailey jolted at the sound. "Good morning, Mrs. Martin. How are you?" She knew she wasn't on her A game if Mrs. Martin could sneak up on her.

"Oh, I'm fine, dear. I was checking in. You looked like you were attacking those weeds with actual malice. Is something wrong?"

She was the sweetest woman around. "Thank you, but I'm fine, I promise. Did you see we're starting to get a few tomatoes here?" She deftly changed the subject as she gently lifted a portion of the vine so Mrs. Martin could see. "They're small, but it's a great start. We're going to be in produce soon."

"I can't wait, dear. Well, you enjoy your Saturday. I'm off to bingo happy hour."

"Happy hour? It's not even noon."

"When it's bingo for senior citizens, it should always be happy hour. When you go to bed at seven, you've got to start early." She laughed, shimmying her shoulders. "Plus, who knows how much time we have left? Why waste it being boring at home. You've gotta live your life the way you want to, Bailey. Having fun during the day isn't just for old people, either." She winked and walked into her garage.

Feeling like a whirlwind had blown through her yard, Bailey tried to get back to weeding, but Mrs. Martin's words stuck with her. *You've gotta live your life.* That was what she was doing. Wasn't it? She had a thriving business. She had Patsy. She had her family. She really didn't feel like she was missing anything. At least, she hadn't until she'd met Skye. Now she didn't know which way was up.

But she'd tried the forever commitment thing before, and it had blown up. Exactly as it always had for Uncle Chester. It was damn near impossible to pay enough attention to a significant other while busting one's ass to keep the business successful. Even billionaires often couldn't make their marriages work.

So where did that leave her with Skye? While she hadn't had sex since she'd broken her engagement with Mary, she didn't plan to be celibate for life. And the pull she had with Skye was getting harder to ignore. Maybe they could do casual? More than friends with benefits but less than full-on dating? They could just hang out. See where the world took them. Exclusive but not serious. No expectation of a future.

Bailey finished pulling all the weeds in the beds and switched to pruning the yellowing leaves from the tomato vines. It was so beautiful to watch how well they did after a good pruning. It should spur lots of new flower activity.

Would Skye be open to something casual but also exclusive? Bailey had no intention of ever getting married, but she didn't like to share. That was really important, a point driven home by Mary's infidelity. She didn't sleep around, and she expected the same thing from anyone she brought home.

She finally felt like she was starting to get a handle on this crazy situation. It didn't have to be all or nothing. Their relationship didn't need to be the sort that required diligent tending the way she tended her garden. Weeds and pruning wouldn't matter in their relationship garden if they were just hanging out. They could harvest the fruit when it was ripe with no hurt feelings if nothing was ready. And they could keep things professional when working together. Plus, she was pretty close to hiring an estimator and project manager to take over the day-to-day for Ellie's buildings.

"Okay, Patsy girl, are you ready for your favorite part? It's time to fertilize."

Patsy jumped up at the word. She loved the smell of the different fertilizers and went a little crazy while Bailey was sprinkling them. Bailey held her breath, thinking about how disgusting dogs were as she grabbed three bags of fertilizer and her hand cultivator to help spread it around.

She didn't have to wait until tomorrow to see Skye. If she had things sorted out in her mind, what was the use in waiting? Seemed like unnecessary patience. Before she could second-guess herself, she set the fertilizer bags and hand cultivator next to the nearest bed and pulled out her phone to fire off a quick text to Skye.

What are you up to today?

Immediately, the three response dots began to bounce. Then they stopped. Then they bounced again. Then stopped. What the hell did that mean? Anxiety roiled in Bailey's belly. Instead of fertilizing, she stared at her phone until finally Skye responded.

Curled up on my new favorite love seat, watching a little TV and reading a book. You?

Her new favorite? Bailey felt her smile grow at the thought of that love seat newly becoming Skye's favorite. She certainly had a soft spot for it after last night.

Bailey: *Gardening. It's my Zen, thinking space.* Well, that was very true. She really did do her best thinking in the garden.

Skye: *What kind of a garden is that Zen? Do you have one of those big sandboxes with the rake and the rocks and stuff? Like a sand trap on the golf course?*

Bailey: *Ha! No, just a vegetable garden. But I find the repetition of weeding and pruning very relaxing. Any interest in a tour?*

Skye: *You mean tomorrow when I come over?*

How did she invite Skye over today without it sounding desperate? This stuff was hard. Just another reason why she didn't do relationships.

Bailey: *Sure. Tomorrow. Or if you don't have plans, we could do it today. I'm pretty flexible this weekend. I do yoga, so I'm almost always pretty flexible.* She hit send and then cringed at the yoga comment. Why did she say that? Idiot. She was trying to make a joke to distract from the fact that she didn't have any plans, but Jesus, that sounded dumb or sexual.

Thankfully, Skye didn't make her wait long for a response.

Skye: *Yoga, huh? Sounds intriguing. I'm filing that little nugget away.*

Maybe not as bad as Bailey had originally thought. The little dots kept dancing, so she waited to respond, her fingers tingling in anticipation.

Skye: *I'm pretty flexy this weekend myself. Brunch tomorrow with the fam but am otherwise free. What time do you want me?*

Bailey's clit twitched at the innocent innuendo. Though based on last night, maybe not so innocent. Was right that moment too soon? Once Bailey made a decision, she didn't like to wait. Patience wasn't one of her virtues, as she'd always told her Gammy. At the same time, she was trying to play it cool and didn't want to seem overly eager.

Bailey: *Dinner-ish? five? I'll still cook and can give you a tour.*

Skye: *Perfect. I'll see you then. Don't forget to send me your address.*

Bailey felt like she was walking on air for the rest of that morning. Now the question was, what to make for dinner. Skye was a woman of impeccable taste, after all. It was bizarre to think how much Bailey's opinion of Skye had transformed in the weeks since they'd started working together. Skye wasn't nearly as snobby as she seemed at first. Either way, Bailey wanted to impress her that evening and needed to bring the fire.

❖

Skye double-checked the address on her phone when she rang the doorbell for the second time, and there was still no answer. The front door was open, but the storm door stood closed, and it sounded like there was music playing somewhere in the house, so she wondered if Bailey could even hear her. And if she really was at the right house.

As if on cue, Patsy came charging to the storm door. When she saw Skye standing on the other side, she jumped and hit the handle with her head, hurtling onto the porch.

Skye bent down. "Hi, Patsy. I doubt you're supposed to be out here alone. I wonder if your mommy knows you can do that trick? If she did, I bet she'd lock her storm door."

Patsy kept spinning, licking Skye's arm at every pass. She didn't like the licking, but Patsy was cute and wasn't as wet and drooly as Skye had originally feared, so it wasn't too bad. She couldn't figure out who she was turning into because that didn't sound like her at all. Not even a little bit. But between last night when Patsy had been so well-behaved and how excited she was to see Skye now, Skye felt...warm toward her.

"Well, at least I know I'm at the correct house, right? What do you think I should do, Patsy? Maybe ring the doorbell once more, and if she doesn't answer, let you back in?"

After another unsuccessful doorbell attempt and an unanswered call, Skye opened the door, but when she pointed for her to go in, Patsy sat to wait for her.

Skye was a little early, but where the hell was Bailey? She wasn't *that* early.

Well, shit. She didn't see that she had much choice other than to go in, as Patsy wouldn't go in without her. This was going to be weird, but...she opened Bailey's front door again. "Hello?" she called. "Bailey, it's Skye and Patsy."

Nothing but crickets, though there was definitely music coming from the back of the house somewhere. Skye felt like an intruder as she walked through the house, wanting to both examine everything and look at nothing until Bailey was there. She resisted the urge to snoop and made a beeline for the music.

When she made it into the kitchen, however, she paused while she tried to relocate the oxygen that had vanished from her lungs. Standing at the kitchen island with her back to Skye, Bailey wore booty shorts while cutting up an onion and singing and dancing to Sheryl Crow's "My Favorite Mistake." The sway of her hips and that long expanse of leg below the hem of some *very* short shorts would surely be illegal in all fifty states.

How was Skye supposed to resist that?

She wanted to announce herself but was still ogling Bailey when Bailey spun around during the refrain. She let out a scream, and Skye was relieved that she didn't drop the very large chef's knife on her foot when she jumped. Or lunge at Skye with it.

Bailey grabbed her phone from the counter and turned down the music blaring through a speaker in the kitchen. "Jesus, Skye. And you say I'm like a ninja. Fuck. What are you doing here this early? And how'd you get in?" Her chest heaved with the adrenaline surely surging through her body. "Holy hell."

Skye held her hands up, a mirror of Bailey's posture that evening at Navy Pier, and said, "I'm really sorry. I tried ringing the doorbell and calling several times. Patsy apparently heard me because she let herself onto your porch. Were you aware she can open the door? Also, it isn't safe to leave the front door unlocked." She knew she was rambling, but she was so off-kilter after letting herself into Bailey's house and watching her dance in those short-shorts. God, those shorts.

Hell. There was that temple twitching. How Skye wanted to run her thumb over it until it relaxed. Though...What was stopping her? She took the few steps between them, ran her finger over Bailey's quirking temple. "Sorry. I really didn't mean to startle you."

Bailey's mouth twitched into an almost smile, which Skye took as a win. "What are you doing here this early?"

"I'm only twenty minutes early." She shrugged. "Okay, maybe twenty-five. But that's barely early at all."

"Yeah, I'm not ready. I'm making the guac, and I've still got to get dressed." She used her wrist to push a few strands of hair off her forehead, which had gone adorably red.

Skye made a show of looking her up and down. "This isn't the look you're going for? I don't know why not. It's quite sexy, and I'll admit to feeling a little partial to it. I might be a little overdressed, but I don't mind." She gestured at her own knee-length, A-line dress. "And twenty-five minutes early is late in broker time." Bailey had missed a couple pieces of hair, so Skye swiped the errant ones with her fingertips, lingering for a moment against Bailey's warm skin but managing to resist the urge to run her fingers through her hair.

"Well, in the real world, twenty-five minutes early is *really* early. And thus, I'm not ready." Bailey's tone jumped three octaves as she swirled her finger in the air and pointed to her outfit and the food.

Skye hooked her finger into the one Bailey was waving around and pulled that hand to her hip. "You look ready enough for my purposes." She stepped closer as she stared at Bailey's mouth. A risky maneuver since Bailey was still holding a knife in her other hand, but Skye's hunger compelled her.

Before she could kiss her, however, Bailey took a step back and shook her entire body. "Just stop. Go stand over there so I can finish this guac and go change." She pointed to the other side of the kitchen with the knife.

Skye was reluctant to lose her view. "What if I stand here?" She took two steps back. When Bailey shook her head, Skye took another step back. "Here?" Bailey again shook her head, and Skye took another step until she backed into the refrigerator. "Surely *this* has to be far enough."

"I'd rather you be a little farther, but that's probably okay."

"I can't reach you from all the way over here. What are you worried about?" Skye lifted an arm to illustrate. "See?"

"I'm basically indecent, and the hunger in your eyes…it…well, it feels like touching. So stay over there while I finish over here." She tapped the knife on the cutting board but didn't look away. Skye's heart skipped a beat. Bailey's gaze was locked on hers with such intensity that she could almost feel Bailey's hands on her.

"I want to say I'm sorry, but I wouldn't really mean it, so…" Skye shrugged, grinned.

Bailey shook her head before pointedly going back to dicing her red onion with the hint of a smile playing across her lips. Her hips started swaying again, testing Skye's self-control. She desperately wanted to bring her hands to those hips, press their bodies together, and find the beat as one. To distract herself, she said, "I certainly hope I'm not your favorite mistake."

"What?" Bailey paused to look at her.

"The mistake that Sheryl was singing about and you were dancing to when I first got here."

"That remains to be seen, doesn't it?" Bailey caught the corner of her bottom lip between two teeth. Skye's breath caught at the implication. "Though I think Sheryl is singing about a relationship ending, which isn't really applicable. Certainly not today."

"Oh. Good." Skye breathed out, still staring at Bailey's lips, and desperately hoped that whatever happened today, it would end with their hands on each other and that neither of them would look back on it as a mistake.

Breaking the tension, Bailey grinned. "Safer topic, what were you up to today when I texted? What were you watching and reading?"

"The Monaco Grand Prix qualifying and a smutty book. It's my weekend guilty pleasure."

"There's a lot to unpack there." Bailey chuckled. "Monaco. Grand Prix. Is that like NASCAR but European?"

Skye scoffed. "Not really. But I'm sure if I get into why, you'll call me a snob again, so maybe let's discuss it another time."

"Fair. Then tell me about this smutty book."

"That's a little personal, isn't it?" Skye wasn't embarrassed that she liked to read sapphic romance, but for some reason, the thought of actually talking about it made her blush. She wiped her sweaty fingertips on her dress and laughed. It was annoying as hell that Bailey made her so damn nervous sometimes.

Bailey stopped cutting and stared, eyebrows raised. "I'm literally standing in front of you barely clothed because you broke into my house. Last night, you told me you were going to *take care of yourself* with your favorite shower wand. I *think* we can get a little personal."

Skye's throat went completely dry as she remembered taking care of herself last night to thoughts of Bailey, first in the shower and then with her favorite vibrator after she still couldn't sleep. She cleared her throat but still croaked more than said, "For the record, I didn't break in. Patsy let me in."

"Semantics. Now, tell me about this smut." Bailey's mischievous expression convinced Skye that she wasn't going to let this go.

Skye decided that despite her body's nervous betrayals, she was going to lean into a little flirting. She was going to fake confidence until she felt it. She batted her lashes. "It was just a lesbian romance. A little heavy on the sex. I'm not going to tell you all about it. Though I will let you borrow it once I'm finished."

Bailey pursed her lips. "I wouldn't have pegged you for the romance type."

"Why not?" Skye couldn't decide if she wanted to be offended or proud.

"It's hard to see you going for something mushy. Or getting all misty at a happily ever after."

"Misty? Definitely not. And just because I'm not looking for a happily ever after for myself doesn't mean I don't want to get lost in the romance of fictional women. Plus, sometimes a little erotica can really get you going."

The knife clattered onto the island when Skye said *erotica.* Interesting. She suppressed a smile and wondered if she could use that little tidbit later.

Despite the knife slip, Bailey finished making the guac, covered it in plastic wrap, and put it in the fridge. "I'm going to go change.

Please, help yourself to some wine. That bottle has been breathing for a bit, so it should be good. I meant to offer that to you when you arrived, but…" She shrugged. "You have no one to blame but yourself for my inhospitableness."

"That's an interesting blame shift. But don't worry. I can take care of myself for a few minutes." Skye walked around the island toward the wine, trailing her finger along the edge of the granite while watching Bailey, who oddly hadn't moved even an inch closer to the kitchen doorway.

"Are you sure?" Bailey said softly but with heat blazing throughout every word.

Skye's ribs buzzed in response, and she couldn't recall what they had been saying a breath ago. "About what?"

Bailey hesitated and looked at her feet, then back up. "That you can take care of yourself?"

Holy. Shit. If Skye's underwear hadn't already been wet, they were now. She tried to smile coyly and said, "Well, after you so rudely left me high and dry last night, I certainly was able to take care of myself. First in the shower as promised. And then once more in bed."

Bailey's phone slipped out of her hand and skittered across the kitchen floor until it came to rest against the toe of Skye's shoe. She smiled to herself as she bent to pick it up, happy that despite her edginess earlier, she was able to turn the tables.

Bailey's hand shook as she took the phone. "Thank you," she mumbled. "I'll be right back." She tipped her head ever so slightly and backed out of the kitchen.

Skye watched until she was out of sight and then let out an enormous sigh, trying to ease the pressure threatening to collapse her lungs. Flirting with Bailey was delicious, but the sexual tension radiating when Bailey left the room might suffocate her if they didn't figure out what to do about it. To give her hands something to do, she poured two glasses of wine. Bailey had picked a cab, which was nice as the perfect hint of coolness in the air called for a bold red. It was from a vineyard Skye hadn't heard of, but it was very tasty. The bite helped settle her restlessness too.

Now that she didn't feel like a complete interloper, she took her wine into the living room and looked around at what she'd quickly walked past on her way in. One full wall was taken up with a line of gorgeous mahogany bookshelves. The showcase pieces had glass shelves and were full of photos of Bailey's family and a few odd trinkets. Skye chuckled when she saw that Bailey's Mathlete trophy wasn't on display.

Although she hadn't met them the evening before, she could pick out Bailey's brother and his family, and a cute shot of Gammy showed a man who must have been Bailey's grandfather that had been taken aboard a cruise ship. She wondered if the whole family had gone or if it had been a romantic getaway for the two of them. There was another shot of Bailey, Roxy, and a woman she assumed to be Roxy's twin standing in someone's backyard at a party. The photos were consistent with Skye's impression last night of a close-knit, fun, and loving family.

She felt a pang of jealousy. She loved Mama, Babulya, and Tasha, but they were the extent of her family. No aunts or uncles or cousins, though she knew she was fortunate to still have Babulya.

She shifted from the photos to Bailey's novels and was surprised to see a very eclectic selection ranging from mysteries to biographies to thrillers and even romance. Then she squatted as she noticed a couple of shelves dedicated to lesbian romance and smiled at the hard time Bailey had given her since she was also a clear fan of the genre. She even recognized a few titles that she owned herself.

"Don't mind those," Bailey said as she walked down the stairs. "Just a little light reading from time to time."

Skye stood, still scanning the shelves. "So you give me a hard time for reading a little smut, and you yourself have your own collection? Very interesting, Bailey Kaczma—" But the final syllable died on her tongue as she took in Bailey's new outfit. It should have taken more than jeans and a white shirt to rocket her heart rate up, but the way Bailey's distressed, dark skinny jeans accentuated the length of her perfect legs had her drooling. Skye's fingers were restless as the need to unbutton the half-tucked white button-up—which was only closed up to her bra anyway—vibrated through her.

Bailey came toward her, rolling up her left sleeve to her elbow, and Skye wondered if she'd ever found a woman's forearms so attractive before. Was that really a thing people could be attracted to? She loved watching those muscles flex in all of their sinewy beauty.

Bailey appeared completely oblivious and smiled. "I wasn't picking on the genre. I was surprised that *you* enjoy it. That's all." She stopped right inside Skye's personal space. "Sorry I wasn't ready for you when you arrived. I meant to be dressed and have glasses of wine waiting. How is it?" She gestured toward the glass in Skye's hand. It seemed like putting on clothes had given Bailey armor, so she wasn't as affected by the pull between them, but Skye didn't get the same protection.

Dammit. She tried to check her body's reactions. "It's delicious. I poured you a glass, but it's in the kitchen. Do you want a sip of this one?" She swallowed forcefully around the boulder in her throat as Bailey took the glass, swirled the wine around, and took a sip while watching her over the rim. Skye was self-conscious about the pulse pounding so hard in her throat, she was sure Bailey could see it in their nearness.

"Delicious." It was a near whisper, and Skye leaned in so she could hear better. That brought their mouths closer together, and Bailey capitalized on the nearness to press a soft kiss against Skye's lips. A simple, sweet kiss that belied the intense attraction simmering below the surface that threatened to boil over.

Before Skye could deepen the kiss, Bailey leaned back. "Do you want a tour of the house and garden? I did promise that."

Skye wanted to yell in frustration. She didn't like that Bailey was now holding all the cards, but there wasn't much she could do, so she smiled and said, "Sure. That'd be great."

Bailey grabbed the glass of wine Skye had poured her and gave her a full tour. Skye had no idea how much work went into a garden, and Bailey's was impressive. Bailey seemed excited to detail every plant, and Skye had expected to be a little bored but found herself captivated by Bailey's enthusiasm.

"Unfortunately, other than the arugula in our salads, nothing I made this evening came out of here, but if you come back in a few weeks, I can almost make entire meals out of what I've grown. You won't believe how fresh everything tastes."

Skye had never thought about the freshness of her produce or how far it was trucked in from, but she found herself looking forward to a time when Bailey could cook straight from the garden. Wait, where had that come from? She wasn't a long-term sort of woman. She managed an "Mmm, sounds great," as her heart fluttered at the base of her throat.

They went back inside, and Bailey topped their wine off and grabbed the bowl of guacamole from the refrigerator. "Why don't we eat on the deck? It's a perfect evening for it."

"Sure," Skye managed, still feeling off-balance after her reaction in the garden.

"Are you okay?"

"Sure." Her skin was itchy, and she found herself staring at her shoes.

"I'm not sure I believe you. You don't have a great poker face." Bailey set the bowl down and reached to grab her hand. "You *can* talk to me, you know? About what you're feeling or whatever."

Skye was nodding so much, she felt like a bobblehead on a dashboard, but she had no idea what to say. She couldn't put words to the panic bubbling in her.

Bailey pulled on her hand. "Let's sit down for a sec. Seriously. I don't know where you went, but you're white as a ghost." When Skye sat, Bailey cradled her hand, massaging small circles into her palm. "If you don't want to come back to have a full meal from the garden, that's fine." Skye felt like Bailey was looking into her. There was a warmth there, like a soft blanket, that made her anxiety ratchet down to a manageable level.

"That's not…" Skye huffed and looked away. "Well, I don't know."

"That's a start." Bailey laughed. "Why don't you tell me what it is or what it isn't?"

"I'm just not…" Skye took a huge sip of wine, and her throat burned as she forced it down. "I'm not the kind of woman who thinks about a date a few weeks from now. And certainly not with someone that I work with. I might occasionally have a date or two with someone uninvolved with the real estate scene, but I'm never planning another date after that. And I guess I…panicked. A little." Skye tried to smile but was sure it looked as half-hearted as it felt. She couldn't believe she'd admitted to panicking. That was *not* like her. Hell, she couldn't believe that she had panicked. Even a little.

"That's okay. I'm not that person either. I'm not even sure where that came from. Other than I love my garden and try to share it with as many people as possible." Bailey ran her fingers through her hair, and Skye felt the loss of connection when Bailey had released her hand.

"That's almost worse." She flung both her hands in the air, but Bailey caught them and brought them back to her lap. Her hands were so soft. Deceptively soft for a woman in construction.

"Why?" Bailey said softly.

"Because when I'm with you, I want to be that woman. I want to plan for a few weeks from now. I want to plan for this week." Skye shook her head. "And that's terrifying. And a terrible idea because neither of us wants something serious, and I cannot date someone I work with. And yet I can't get you out of my head."

Bailey took a sip of wine. "What if we plan to not plan?"

"How does that work?"

"Neither of us is looking for anything. And yet here we are, seeing each other and drawn to each other again and again. We're clearly not getting better at resisting, so maybe we accept this for what it is. We hang out. Clearly, we've started to enjoy each other's company." Bailey laughed. "Exclusively hanging out isn't something serious or long-term. We're both too busy for that. But we aren't too busy for fun, right? Keep it away from our working relationship."

Skye started to relax into the idea. Maybe it could work. Bailey *was* a lot of fun. And there was a definite physical attraction, something that could be very fun to explore in their free time. Well away from the Maxwell. "No, not too busy for occasional fun."

"Exactly. It's not like you're going to take me to the annual broker awards gala or something. We'll keep us completely separate from work, and nothing will change there. As my neighbor reminded me this morning, you have to live your life the way you want to and have fun. But—and this is a big but for me—even though we aren't serious, we shouldn't be doing this with anyone else. I don't like that feeling where you have to go get an STD test regularly because you don't know who you've been with secondhand. I've been there." Her voice was full of venom.

Skye never wanted to cause that sort of pain. She squeezed Bailey's hands. "I promise. If we do this, you're the only one I'm hanging out with."

"Okay." God, Bailey was gorgeous when she smiled. "Now that we got that out of the way, are we going to eat this feast I prepared?"

"An even better question is, are there any other options?"

"I made guacamole, tacos, and street corn. Do you not like Mexican?" Her face looked like Skye had just told her there was no Santa Claus.

"No, I love Mexican, and I'm sure what you made is all delicious. I just meant…" Skye scooted closer, placed her hands on Bailey's thighs, and ran her thumbs lightly along the inner seams of her jeans. "I just meant, maybe we defer eating for a little while. I'm a little hungrier for you than I am for food."

Bailey's eyes widened. Skye leaned across the gap between their seats, and when her mouth was less than an inch from Bailey's, she whispered, "Is this an okay detour?"

CHAPTER FIFTEEN

Rather than answer, Bailey pulled Skye's face in and kissed her the way she'd been dreaming of since their aborted make-out session at Navy Pier. She allowed every frustrated moment to fuel the passion in her lips and roaming hands.

Skye squeezed Bailey's thighs, her thumbs rubbing circles along the inseam of her jeans. One finger found its way through a hole to stroke her bare thigh. "Wow," she whispered at the bolt of heat that surged from Skye's fingertips to the apex of her thighs.

"Why don't we go inside? I don't want to embarrass you in front of your neighbors." Skye's cheeks were flushed as she breathed heavily, and it was all Bailey could do not to pull her onto her lap right there on the deck, onlookers be damned.

"You're right. Poor Mrs. Martin might never be the same. Though she went to drunk bingo earlier today, so she might not even notice."

Skye's nostrils flared, and Bailey had to fight the impulse to kiss her again. Instead, she stood and tugged her toward her back door. Once they crossed the threshold, all bets were off. Skye fervently brought her lips to Bailey's, driving her backward into the refrigerator.

Bailey vaguely registered the sweetness of wine lingering on Skye's lips. She'd thought she understood the chemistry between them at the gala, but that had just skimmed the surface. Nothing could have prepared her for the onslaught of sensations from Skye's body flush against hers. The feeling of being sandwiched between the refrigerator and Skye's athletic curves with only a few layers of thin cotton between them was intense. She couldn't remember ever feeling this desperate for someone before.

Skye threaded her fingers through Bailey's hair and scraped her nails down the shorter hair at the nape of her neck. Bailey rolled her hips into Skye's, and vibrations ran from her neck to her toes. She moaned into Skye's mouth and felt the heat of Skye's hips press into hers.

Bailey ran her fingers along Skye's back. Dissatisfied that she couldn't find skin, she lifted Skye onto the kitchen island. Skye gasped and broke their kiss. "You are beyond anything I could have imagined, Bailey." Her voice was barely more than a whisper as she gasped hungrily.

Those words weakened Bailey's knees to the point that she feared she might topple. She steadied herself on Skye's smooth legs. Without breaking eye contact, she began to slide the hem of Skye's dress up. When she reached mid-thigh, Skye moaned, and her eyes fluttered closed.

"Is this okay?"

"Yes." Skye groaned and scratched the muscles of Bailey's shoulders. "Please. More."

Bailey didn't need any more encouragement and slid her hands up until her thumbs were separated from Skye's wet heat by only a thin layer of fabric. She drew her thumbs up and down Skye's labia over the silky underwear. Goose bumps broke out across her arms when Skye moaned and leaned back onto her elbows. Bailey followed and kissed her hungrily again as she shimmied her panties off and tossed them away. She pulled Skye's hips forward until her heat pressed against Bailey's belly. Skye moaned again. Bailey felt her blazing hot wetness through her button-up and shifted to provide Skye with more friction. "Oh God, yes," Skye breathed into her mouth. "Please."

Bailey began a journey south, placing kisses along Skye's jaw and down her neck. When she reached the top of Skye's dress, she nipped at the soft swells exposed above the modest neckline. Skye's skin was so soft and perfect, Bailey could have nuzzled it forever. But Skye's heels pressing into her lower back reminded her how much more skin she hadn't yet seen or touched.

She made a quick stop to kiss each nipple through the fabric of the dress. She grazed her teeth over them until they pebbled in her mouth before dropping to her knees. "You are so beautiful," she said, taking in the exquisiteness of Skye's sex, wet and open before her. She looked up into eyes that were so darkened with lust, they were nearly charcoal. Bailey's clit pulsed with the need to have her.

Skye let out a tiny whimper and knotted her hands in Bailey's hair. "Please, Bailey. I need you."

Bailey couldn't resist that openness and vulnerability and brought her mouth to Skye, holding eye contact until she physically couldn't. If she hadn't already been on her knees, the first taste of Skye would have knocked her to them. Skye's essence was intoxicating, and Bailey ran her tongue through her slippery folds, savoring every inch.

Bailey had never fallen into rhythm so quickly. Skye's heels continued to pull her closer, even as she released Bailey's hair. When Bailey flicked her eyes up, she saw Skye leaning back on one elbow, high enough that she could watch Bailey between her thighs. That sight made Bailey so hot, she struggled to not touch herself to relieve some of the pressure.

Instead, she brought first one and then two fingers to Skye's entrance and slowly slid inside. Skye cried out. Bailey began thrusting in time with the slow cadence of Skye's hips.

In what felt like seconds, Skye yelled, "Yes, yes," and pulled her heels into Bailey's back with bruising force, but she didn't care. She stilled her tongue and fingers when Skye grabbed her head with both hands and squeezed.

"Sorry," she whispered against Skye's sex. It sent a jolt through Skye's body that she wasn't sorry for at all.

Bailey pressed a kiss to the inside of Skye's thighs before standing and leaning over her. "Hi," she said when Skye slowly opened her eyes. She was so gorgeous, reclining on Bailey's kitchen island as if she owned it, her hair mussed and face flushed.

"Hi." Skye levered herself up and kissed her softly, barely a brush of her lips, as though it was all she had the energy for before leaning back on her elbows again. The smile that crept across her face, combined with those hooded gray eyes, took Bailey's breath away. "That was...unexpected," she said.

"Which part?"

Skye laughed. "Which part wasn't?"

"Good point. I mean, this is what I was hoping for when I invited you over, but...I certainly wasn't expecting to barely make it in the patio door. That was so much more than any of my fantasies." Bailey had never been so overcome with need that she'd dropped to her knees in her kitchen rather than making it upstairs to the bedroom.

"I should be saying that, not you. You haven't even come yet."

Bailey leaned in as Skye ran her fingers through her hair and gently massaged her scalp.

"You are adorable," Skye said.

Bailey forced her eyes open. "Adorable? Certainly not." Adorable was about the last thing she wanted to hear. Adorable was for puppies and seals rubbing their noses together.

"The way you were humming from just my rubbing your head. I cannot imagine the sounds you're going to make once I rub your clit. I'm getting wet again thinking about it."

Bailey swallowed hard, fine with the direction Skye had taken the adorable comment, and stood fully. She helped Skye to a seated position, and Skye slid off the counter.

"Let's go to your bedroom," Skye said. "I'm ready for the next course."

"You don't want a snack first?" Bailey prayed the answer was no. She didn't think she could wait much longer to have Skye's hands on her but didn't want to starve Skye, either.

"I am hungry, but I'm looking at the snack I want to devour." She looked Bailey up and down lasciviously. "I don't need anything other than you."

Bailey's breath shuddered. "Right this way, madame." She grabbed Skye's hand and pulled her to the stairs, saying a quick thank-you to the dog gods that Patsy was sleeping peacefully on the couch. As they neared the top step, Skye rubbed her ass. "Stop that," Bailey said.

"Or what?" Skye's smirk was so sexy that Bailey had no choice but to kiss her until it disappeared.

She pushed Skye to the wall and pinned her. "This what." Her mouth was a fraction of an inch away, and all she could do was stare.

Skye pulled her in. Bailey ran her hands up the side of Skye's thighs again, not stopping until she'd gathered Skye's dress just below her breasts and had to nudge Skye's arms up so she could slide it over her head.

Bailey broke their kiss, mesmerized at the sight of her. Skye's dusky pink nipples sat atop her perfectly perky breasts. Her light skin was unblemished save for a few stray freckles. Bailey dipped her head to kiss a freckle below Skye's left collarbone and another between her breasts.

She knelt again and lightly bit the freckle just left of Skye's navel and licked one just above her neatly trimmed curls. "How can you be so beautiful? So flawless?" Bailey said, almost to herself.

"Flawless, huh? Maybe I should add that to my business card next to 'woman of impeccable taste.'" Skye bit her lip as she half smiled down.

"I would give my endorsement, one hundred percent." Bailey stood so she wouldn't knock them down the stairs.

Skye fingered the top button on her shirt. "You're wearing entirely too many clothes."

"Luckily, you're a problem solver. I'm sure you can figure out a way around this one." Bailey ran a thumb along her jaw.

Skye continued to work the buttons, and Bailey shivered when Skye's fingertips grazed her breasts on their way by. She was certain it was not accidental. "Already on it."

"Do you need any help?" Bailey cupped the back of her neck and began to squeeze, massaging the taut muscles.

Skye was already at the fourth button. "Nope. Button undoer extraordinaire here. Don't worry. We'll have you out of this in a jiffy."

"Are you going to put that on your business card as well?"

Skye finished the last button and slid the shirt from Bailey's shoulders. Heat blazed through Bailey's stomach at the intensity of Skye's gaze on her bra-clad breasts. "I just might."

"Do you want me to take this off?" Bailey gestured to her bra.

"Nope." Skye reached around and unclasped the bra one-handed, sliding the straps down Bailey's arms before tossing the bra over the rail of the stairs and down to the floor below. Skye cradled Bailey's breasts, running her thumbs lightly across her nipples.

Bailey's knees softened until she bumped into the rail. "Let's make it up the rest of these stairs. My bed will be much more comfortable. And safer."

Skye simply nodded. Without words, Bailey grabbed one of her hands and led the way down the hall to her room. Rather than flipping on the bright overhead light, she lit two fragrant candles on the windowsills.

When she turned back, she swore at herself for ever having looked away. Skye stood at the foot of her bed like an Amazonian princess. Her hands were planted on her hips, and the posture thrust her breasts forward. Her blond hair was tousled around her face.

"You are stunning." Bailey didn't realize she'd said it aloud until Skye smiled.

"And you're still overdressed. I'm a problem solver, but I can't get those pants off you while you're standing on the other side of the room."

Bailey's heart began to beat in double time as she walked toward

Skye, pulled like metal shavings to a magnet. She sucked in sharply when Skye grabbed the top of her pants and undid the button. Her hands were surprisingly chilly against Bailey's stomach, and her muscles clenched, but the contrast of cool fingers against scorched skin sent another flood of wetness between her thighs. Her muscles quivered as Skye slid her hands down Bailey's legs to push the tight jeans and her panties to the floor.

Bailey braced a hand on Skye's shoulder as she lifted one foot and then the other. When she stood, Skye took a step back and made a show of looking Bailey over. When her gaze reached Bailey's face again, they lunged toward each other. Skye had more momentum and nearly tackled her to the bed.

They landed in a tangle on the soft comforter with Skye's knee lodged perfectly between Bailey's thighs. They scooted up together without disconnecting their mouths or the electric connection of Skye's thigh to Bailey's center.

Skye broke their kiss and licked her lips as she stared down. Bailey would normally have felt self-conscious under the intense appraisal, but the pure yearning in Skye's gaze assuaged her discomfort.

"You are beyond…" Skye paused. "Beyond anything I could have possibly imagined. Beyond even what I fantasized during my special shower last night." The corner of her mouth quirked up.

"I wasn't sure if you were kidding about that." Bailey tickled Skye's side, and she squirmed barely out of reach, but somehow, her knee continued to do amazing things to Bailey's clit.

"I always, always, keep my word, Bailey. If nothing else, I can promise you that." Skye kissed her lightly.

"Is that right? Well, what did you envision us doing last night?"

"Well, first, I imagined us in a very similar position. Kissing you like this." Skye graced Bailey with another brief but searing kiss. She pushed herself up just enough to allow her breasts to sway, and her nipples swept back and forth over Bailey's. "I like to be on top," she said, her voice low and gravelly.

Bailey groaned at both her words and the exquisite contact. She ground her hips up into Skye.

"Not so fast there, killer."

Bailey blinked her eyes open, unsure.

"It's my turn to be in charge." She grabbed Bailey's hands and pulled them over her head.

Bailey got impossibly wetter as she tried to swallow. She was entirely under Skye's spell and would have done anything she asked.

"I let you be the boss first, which goes against every instinct, but it seemed important, and you were *so* sexy doing it." Skye circled her hips on Bailey's pelvis, and they both groaned. She released her hands, but when Bailey started to move, Skye pursed her lips and tsked. "Nope, you leave those there. I won't have you rushing me now that it's my turn to drive."

Bailey nodded. She was so turned on, she thought she might explode if Skye didn't do something soon. "Please, touch me. Please." Bailey tried to keep the whine out of her voice but knew she hadn't succeeded.

Skye's eyes were twinkling more brightly than the North Star on a clear night on Lake Michigan. "Since you asked so nicely."

Bailey strained to keep her hands in place as Skye trailed fiery kisses down her neck, stopping to bite at her collarbone. Though her hands were immobile, Bailey's hips hitched upward, seeking friction.

Skye seemed too busy to notice, lavishing attention on Bailey's nipple after moving on from her collarbone. Bailey's nipples had always been overly sensitive, sometimes unpleasantly so, but Skye had perfected a light sucking motion that, with a softly applied tongue, sent Bailey into orbit.

Bailey's arms shook with the effort of not reaching out and running her fingers through Skye's hair. Skye released one nipple before applying the same treatment to the other. Bailey feared she might have to resort to begging again when Skye began to trace two fingers up and down her very wet slit.

Bailey's throaty groan sounded unfamiliar to her own ears. The sound must have broken some of Skye's resolve to move slowly. She released Bailey's nipple and met her gaze as she slid two fingers inside. Bailey's vision went cloudy, but she wouldn't have been able to stop her hips if she'd tried. Which she absolutely didn't.

The vision of Skye balanced over her, eyes dark with passion, nearly had Bailey coming, so when Skye found the top of her clit, it only took a few well-timed thrusts before the orgasm started in Bailey's fingertips before pulling into her chest, then shattering her into a thousand tiny shards. She clutched the sheet above her head as her heels slid along the mattress, and she milked every ounce of pleasure from Skye's very talented fingers.

"Holy fuck," Bailey said on a long exhale as Skye collapsed on top of her.

"I'm not done yet. As a heads-up. Just taking a tiny breather."

"Yep. Is this okay?" Bailey tangled her fingers in Skye's hair, and although she'd just had one of the best orgasms of her life, she didn't want to assume that Skye's power game was over. But she also craved the feel of Skye under her hands.

"I suppose." Skye sighed, but it didn't sound sad. It sounded full of contentment.

To be certain, Bailey said, "Are you sure? I know this was a little fast. But fuck. That was intense."

"Yeah, it was. But I'm perfect. And as soon as I can move, I'm going to get started on you all over again."

"I like the sound of that." Bailey pulled Skye tighter against her and pressed a kiss to the side of her head. She would've been content to stay like that all night.

CHAPTER SIXTEEN

When Skye awoke, she couldn't tell how long she'd been sleeping, but she was enjoying Bailey's fingers wandering along her back. "Hey, you," Bailey said softly.

"How long did we nap?" Skye cracked her neck from side to side as she lifted her head off Bailey's chest.

"Not long. Maybe forty minutes." Bailey's fingers were heavenly, tracing up and down her spine as though she were playing a piano.

"Mmm." Skye arched her back, feeling like the cat who'd gotten into the cream. The movement had the added benefit of pressing her aching center into Bailey's thigh.

"I think we should take a short pause." Bailey squinted. "As much as it pains me, we should have sustenance. Maybe some of that guac, if it hasn't gone bad already after sitting outside, and check on Patsy. Then back up here. I'm not finished with you tonight." A look of vulnerability flashed across Bailey's face. "Unless you have other plans?"

Skye brushed a short lock of hair off Bailey's forehead. Apparently, it *didn't* stay perfectly upright all the time. That thought made her smile as much as the feel of Bailey's skin against hers. "The only plans I have involve you and this bed until I have to meet my family for brunch tomorrow and maybe shower at some point. If that's okay with you?"

With surprising strength, Bailey hoisted them both into a sitting position, sliding Skye's legs across her lap, and before she knew what was happening, she was standing, completely naked. Bailey grinned in a way Skye had never seen before. It was *almost* unguarded. Skye felt a pang in her heart that she couldn't put a finger on.

"I'm fully in favor of this plan. But I'm starving. For real food.

Let's go get a snack." Bailey bounded away after a light smack on Skye's butt cheek.

"Hey," she cried, "I'm not traipsing around naked for all your neighbors to see!"

Bailey paused in the doorway. "I walk around here naked all the time. I don't think Mrs. Martin is peering in my windows. I doubt she can see that far. Also, if she did, I'm certain she'd be proud of me for luring the famous Skye Kohl into my house and seducing her."

"*You* seduced *me*, huh?" Skye was surprised Bailey was taking all the credit.

"Yeah. I was all ready to wow you with my cooking. Also, I was in booty shorts when you arrived. How could you resist these legs?" She pointed to her left leg and moved it from side to side on her toe, showing off a very defined calf and thigh and making Skye's mouth water.

"All fair points. However, who kissed whom first? Who suggested our meal wait?" Skye said.

"If you recall, I kissed you first." Bailey's self-satisfied smile might have irritated Skye in the past, but in that moment, it was all she could do to keep herself from jumping her.

"Yes, but only because *I* initiated it."

"But I was the one who initiated our kiss at the gala," Bailey said and stepped toward her.

Skye could see the pulse in Bailey's throat beating quicker as she approached. "Nope, I kissed you." Technically, Bailey had been the aggressor that evening, but Skye liked to win, to be the pursuer. She didn't want to concede that neither of them had filled that role entirely in whatever was happening between them.

"Oh, really? I think you cheat, Ms. Kohl." Bailey took another step. She squeezed Skye's hips and pulled her closer.

"I don't appreciate these lies, Ms. Kaczmarek."

"What about last night? If I recall correctly, we met in the middle on that balcony couch of yours. But who ended up on top?" Bailey's face was inches from Skye's. They were breathing the same air, and Bailey's pelvis was pushing against hers. For a moment, she couldn't come up with a retort. All she could think about was capturing Bailey's mouth.

She let out a little huff. But still, no words would come. Had anyone other than Bailey ever made her speechless before? She didn't think so. Yet Bailey did it with nothing more than a heated glance. And this wasn't even the first time.

"Let's call it a draw." Bailey chuckled, but instead of making good on the sexy flirting, she pecked Skye's cheek and grabbed two T-shirts out of the dresser. "Now, I'm saving you from being a streaker and scaring Mrs. Martin, so let's go get a snack."

Bailey wiggled her eyebrows playfully before she skipped toward the stairs. Who knew a little sex would relax her into someone almost… chipper? If Skye had known, perhaps she would have taken this approach from the start. Skye chuckled as she pulled Bailey's shirt on. No, she wouldn't trade the simmering heat that had built to this moment for more immediate satisfaction. That had been half the fun.

Bailey's muted yell from downstairs reminded her that she shouldn't stand staring into space indefinitely. "Are you coming down? This food isn't going to eat itself."

Skye didn't waste any more time before she sprinted after Bailey, in pursuit of happiness she hadn't expected to find.

❖

Skye parallel-parked half a block down from her mom and Babulya's house at 9:58 sharp on Sunday. She'd been surprised by her reluctance to leave Bailey's warm bed, even after Patsy had licked her hand and woke her. Rather gross, but somehow, being held in Bailey's arms, sore in all the right places after a night with not quite enough sleep, was enough to counteract any yuck factor.

She was even more surprised at how much she wanted to invite Bailey to brunch with her family. That was a scary thought. She'd never introduced anyone to her family, and yet, after one mind-blowing afternoon and night with Bailey, she was ready to throw caution to the wind. Although "introducing" her to the family wasn't entirely accurate. Bailey had already met them. But it still felt like too much to bring her this morning.

But she hadn't wanted to say good-bye. At all. Which was not her. At all. After Patsy had woken her up obscenely early, she'd rolled over in Bailey's arms and had watched her sleep longer than she would ever admit to. She couldn't believe Bailey was sleeping so deeply that Skye was able to move around without waking her, but Bailey hadn't fluttered an eye. Either she was an incredibly deep sleeper, or Skye had exhausted her. Either way, it was endearing.

Bailey's face had been entirely relaxed, no furrow between her brows, no tight jaw, no temple twitch. Her breath had come out in little wisps. Skye couldn't help sweeping a few stray hairs from her forehead. Bailey's eyes had slid open ever so slowly, then, and her mouth had curved into a smile that had jump-started palpitations in Skye's chest.

"Hey," Bailey had said, her voice rough with sleep.

"Hey, yourself," Skye had said, the softness in her own voice unrecognizable. Bailey had brought out a side of her that she hadn't realized existed and maybe wasn't ready to accept. Skye had never in her life watched someone sleep. Had never noticed the uneven line of someone's eyelashes. And yet, she'd done those things with Bailey. Someone she would have sworn a month ago that she didn't like at all.

She feared she was getting soft, so despite how badly she'd wanted to stay, how badly she'd wanted to invite Bailey to join her that morning, she didn't do either. Luckily, although they'd lain scattered throughout Bailey's house, her clothes were essentially still clean from the day before since she'd barely worn them. And they would work for brunch since she hadn't had time to run home to change. She'd left Bailey's house with a lingering kiss and a smile.

Now she needed to grill her family about what the hell had happened to them on Friday night that had led to stranding her at Bailey's family's house.

She walked inside without knocking because they hadn't locked the door again. They had classic country blaring, and no one looked up at her standing in the doorway. They were no doubt prepping food, and the music drowned out the door opening. Funny, that had happened to her twice in as many days. Thankfully, however, none of her relatives were wearing booty shorts.

"I could be a mass murderer walking in here, and all three of you would be dead already," Skye shouted over the music.

It would have been comical seeing all three turn toward her if it wasn't so troubling that none of them had noticed her arrival. Natasha was the first to reply. "Jesus, Skye, why do you have to scare the life out of us?"

"If anyone ever locked the damn door, I wouldn't have been able to scare the crap out of you." Skye didn't try to hide her grimace.

Babulya stopped pressing the biscuit dough into a flat sheet and walked to Skye. "Bunny, no one bothers us here." She patted Skye's cheek with a flour-covered hand. "You need to stop worrying."

How could they be so oblivious to the fact that anyone could walk right in? Skye was still clenching her jaw and tried to relax it and release the tension in her fingers as she wiped her face. "I just wish you'd be careful. I worry because I love you."

"We know," her mother said. "But you need to come down from your high horse. You and your self-righteous lectures don't do anyone any good. And like Babulya said, no one bothers us here."

Skye suppressed an eye roll, but it was a real feat. "Fine. What can I do to help?" She stalked into the kitchen, which was too tiny for four grown women, and wedged into a position at the counter.

Mama pulled a bowl of peeled potatoes out of the sink and handed it over, along with a grater. "Because you're the last to arrive, you have to do the worst task."

"Are you sure you don't want to go somewhere for brunch? It would be a lot less work." Skye laughed because she didn't really want to go anywhere. Her mom's potato pancakes were the best, but she didn't relish having to shred all the potatoes and onions by hand.

Mama swatted her with a towel. "You are hotsy-totsy, but I know you don't mean that. IHOP doesn't make potato pancakes like mine. Or onions and eggs. Or your Babulya's biscuits. And don't even start about how much time a food processor could save. You know how I feel about those noisy contraptions. They don't work the same."

Skye wished they had at least tried the food processor she'd bought them before shunning it. Unfortunately, they'd refused, and now Skye had an obscenely expensive Cuisinart food processor with approximately one thousand attachments collecting dust in a cabinet at home. But she'd given up on the technology fight years ago and didn't say, "How can you say they don't work the same if you've never tried them?"

"I know I've lost that fight, Mama. I've thrown in the towel." She picked up the first potato and started shredding as though her life depended on it.

They worked in silence for a few minutes, hips bopping in time with George Strait before Natasha said, "What's going on with you and the very attractive Bailey, Skye?"

Skye glared at her around Mama. They couldn't know how she'd spent last night, but her cheeks heated, and she felt like she was sixteen again and had gotten caught making out with Bette Arnold behind the gym.

"What do you mean? Nothing. And if we're asking questions, what was going on with your stomach, Babulya, that you had to strand me in Jefferson Park at a complete stranger's house?" Even after a day and a half to process it, Skye still couldn't believe they had done that.

"They weren't strangers. We'd spent all evening with them. And nothing was wrong with my stomach *yet*, but I needed to get home to take my pill so it would stay that way."

"Babulya, you *always* take your pills with you. They're a permanent staple in your purse." Skye didn't know what was in those stomach pills, but Babulya always took them right after she ate, and she swore they kept her stomach settled.

"Well, I needed to get home to take them on Friday, bunny. I don't know what else to tell you." She tilted her head from side to side as she sized up her biscuit dough and began folding it into thirds.

Skye might have let it go—Babulya was normally not disingenuous—but Tasha's snicker raised her suspicions. "What are you laughing at, Tasha?" Skye stilled her hands on the potato and grater as she stared at her sister.

"Nothing, dear sister." Natasha turned away and coughed into her shoulder. Skye was pretty sure she was hiding a laugh, and it pissed her off.

"You'd better fess up, or I swear, I'll never drive your ass anywhere again." Her fingers were sore from squeezing the grater too tightly, so she tried to relax her grip, even though she also wanted to throw the potato. At the wall or at Natasha, she wasn't sure.

That stopped Tasha's laughing. Skye was almost her personal chauffeur. To further emphasize her point, she said, "I'm serious, Natasha. You're going to be cut off. Cut. Off."

"Let's not get too hasty." Natasha laughed.

Skye didn't. "Well, tell me what you were laughing about."

"Fine. We all knew you and Bailey were getting a little *friendly* after dinner—"

"What do you mean?" Neither she nor Bailey had behaved in any way that would have given away the tension between them.

"Jesus, Skye, everyone in the room could feel it from the moment she walked in. But…" Tasha trailed off the way she always did when she was reluctant to say something and was looking for a way out. She looked very intently at the cutting board in front of her.

"Stop trying to weasel out of the truth. Just tell me what happened." Skye huffed, and Mama and Babulya guffawed.

"Fine. Roxy went into the kitchen after you disappeared to go to the bathroom, and Bailey disappeared shortly after you. Roxy said she was going to check and make sure everything was okay. She saw you two making out in the kitchen, silently backed out, and told all of us."

"She what? So everyone there—all of you and all her family—knew we'd been kissing in the kitchen?" Her body was hot as embarrassment flooded her at the thought of so many people, many of them strangers, knowing. "You've got to be kidding me." She felt nauseated.

Skye tried to look at them, but all three traitorous relatives were suddenly immersed in cutting or dough. Jesus. She pushed away from the counter and stalked past the tiny kitchen table and into the small living room just beyond.

"I'm a priv—" Skye threw her hands up in the air. "You know I—" She ran her fingers through her hair, scratching at her scalp, forgetting the wet potato starch coating her hands. "I cannot *believe* you all." She continued to prowl, making tiny circles in the miniature space. It might as well be a tiny house. "I'm so embarrassed, I could crawl under a rock and die." Skye valued her privacy more than most probably did. She didn't share much about her personal life with anyone—not that there was much to tell—and knowing a bunch of strangers knew she had been making out in their kitchen was simply too much. She couldn't breathe.

Babulya grabbed her hand and pulled her to the couch, abruptly stopping her pacing. "Sit before we have to pay the landlord to replace the carpet you've destroyed."

Skye stopped resisting and settled in next to Babulya.

"You have no reason for embarrassment. Your family loves you. Bailey's family loves her. We want happiness for you both. We just thought you spending a little more time together would be helpful."

"Oh my God. Everyone was in on us being pushed together." Skye flopped back on the couch, rested her head against the cushion, and draped an arm across her eyes. She didn't think she could ever face Bailey's family again. What a loser they must have thought she was that she needed her mother and grandmother setting her up. "I am so pathetic. And I can't believe you all were in on it."

Natasha and Mama walked over to where she was sitting. "Not pathetic," Natasha said. "Perpetually alone. Like Bailey, according to her family. Loll apparently does this sort of thing all the time."

Skye lifted her head. "This keeps getting worse. So Bailey has a long trail of women she's dated because of her mother? I'm just a number in line?" She dropped her head back again and began massaging her face where her nose met her forehead.

"Not at all. You're the first one she hasn't brushed off," Mama said.

Natasha narrowed her eyes. "So you *are* dating her? What happened after you left that you think you might be 'a *number* in line'? Did you see her yesterday? Were you already dating before Friday?"

"No." Skye sighed. Some of the answers were yes, but if she just answered the last question, maybe she could get away with it.

"Chatty today, huh?" Tasha raised an eyebrow.

"It's too early to talk about…anything. I don't know what we're doing or where we're going. We're hanging out. But we both know getting involved is a terrible idea." Though after last night, Skye hated those words and the truth behind them.

"Why on earth would it be a terrible idea? You like her, she likes you. It sounds like a simple formula to me," Mama said and shrugged.

"Because we work together with one of my most high-profile and lucrative clients. Getting involved with someone at work never ends well, and to make matters worse, we've been butting heads for weeks…" She would never admit this to anyone else, but looking back, the conflicts between them felt more like foreplay than actual fights. She was so screwed. She leaned forward and switched from massaging the bridge of her nose to rubbing her temples with both hands.

"But?" Mama prodded as she rubbed small circles in the center of Skye's back, just as she always had when Skye was a child and was upset. She'd forgotten how soothing it was.

Skye sighed. "But there seems to be something there, and I don't think we can keep denying it."

"Our little Skye is falling for someone."

Skye squirmed in her seat. She wasn't falling for Bailey, was she? No, that would be ridiculous. They just had something physical that they needed to work out. Or burn out. Nothing serious. Neither of them wanted a relationship, and Skye would be damned before she tried to tie someone down who didn't want to be tied. And yet she'd never been drawn to someone the way she was drawn to Bailey, either.

"It's nothing like that, Mama. We're just spending some time together."

"Just keep telling yourself that. Now, let's get back in the kitchen. Brunch isn't going to cook itself." She clapped her hands, and like good soldiers, they all followed.

Despite her family's doubts, Skye was certain this thing with Bailey wasn't going anywhere. It was a little fun for now until they each got it out of their systems. Simple as that.

❖

Bailey liked to process things by working in her garden. After Skye left, she gravitated there on autopilot and started attacking weeds with gusto. Her mind flashed back to the look on Skye's face when she'd slipped off Bailey's bra on the stairs the previous night. The way she'd yelled Bailey's name when she'd come in the shower for the second time that morning before she'd left to meet her family.

The give and take, the struggle for power that went back and forth was more erotic than with any of her previous bedmates. She liked to be in control and always had been in previous relationships, but last night, when Skye had sat on her hips and forced her to hold the headboard instead of running her hands all over Skye's body had been such a turn-on. Bailey didn't think she'd ever enjoyed sex that much since...well, ever. She had certainly never brooded in the garden for this long when reliving a night.

She didn't realize how much she'd pulled until she peeked into her weed bucket, and it was nearly full. She hadn't had time to get out there and weed the way she liked because she'd been so swamped at work. So even though she'd been out there the morning before, the beds had still needed the attention. Bailey only hoped that she hadn't errantly pulled any spinach sprouts in her distraction.

Despite the glowy sex haze she had going on, Bailey felt a niggling panic at what she was doing with Skye. She'd been the one to suggest they keep it light, and yet, she hadn't wanted to let Skye go that morning. She'd been a breath away from asking her to blow off her family and spend the day with Bailey.

She knew that wasn't fair to Skye or her family, but she couldn't picture a better way to pass the day than naked and under the covers with Skye. Those were not her normal instincts, and they frightened her. A lot.

She still had the same reservations about a relationship, but the pull between them made her wonder if she'd be able to keep things light. And if she truly wanted to.

Of course she did. She didn't have time for anything significant between City Beautiful Construction, Patsy, and her family.

What if she did find herself wanting more? She wouldn't, but what if she did? Could Skye even be trusted? That was the big question. Was this newer side of Skye the real her, or was the real Skye the cold, pretentious, manipulative snob that Bailey had dealt with initially? And Skye wasn't even out at work.

The only choice was to make sure things stayed light. That meant no feelings, no seeing each other every day, no attachment.

Bailey was about three-quarters around weeding her planter boxes, her hands covered in soil, when Skye's first text came through: *Your mom sets you up with women all the time, huh?*

Bailey was so shocked, her heart felt like it was taking a ride on a windmill. It was true, but her family must have been very candid with Skye's on Friday night while she and Skye had been walking Patsy. What was wrong with them?

Bailey wanted to respond but didn't want to pick up her phone with dirty hands, so she tried to use Siri, but they had their typical struggles. After three failed attempts to get Siri to respond, Bailey gave up. She wanted to finish weeding, but she also wanted to keep the conversation going, so she went inside to wash and then texted: *Our families must have been very chatty on Friday night.*

Skye responded immediately: *Yep. Your sister apparently saw us kissing and has a big mouth.*

Bailey was going to choke that loudmouth the next time she saw her. *That little shit. You're kidding, right?*

Skye: *I wish I was. But sadly, no.*

Bailey dropped her head back and sighed before she typed again: *Even your family was in on the setup? No stomach issues?*

Skye: *I don't think so. Do you want to come over later and commiserate about our crazy families?*

Bailey typed *yes* on instinct because she really wanted to see Skye but paused before hitting send. Given her resolve only minutes ago to not see Skye every day, to not let this evolve into something beyond light, she should have said she already had plans. She knew it. But she didn't want to.

Her thumb hovered over the blue up arrow. Finally, it dawned on her that she'd already seen Skye today once, so what was the harm in seeing her again? If today was a seeing-Skye day, she might as well take advantage of it. She wouldn't stay the night and thus wouldn't see Skye tomorrow. Problem solved.

She tapped the send button.

Skye: *Bring an overnight bag if you want? And Patsy.*

She was in trouble. Because she did want. A lot. And there was no way she wasn't bringing a bag after that invitation. Shit.

CHAPTER SEVENTEEN

Skye was nervous. Disproportionately nervous. It had been three days since Bailey had spent a blissful night at her house on Sunday. They'd eaten dinner—delivery, of course, since Skye was not a chef—and had enjoyed a few glasses of wine on her balcony looking over the zoo and the lake and had laughed for hours about the antics of their families.

She'd told Bailey about the time that Babulya didn't have any tomato sauce for the spaghetti, so she'd doctored up ketchup with balsamic vinegar, onions, and garlic. It hadn't been terrible. But it also hadn't been good. Bailey had told her about the time Gammy had tried to color her own hair and had accidentally turned it purple.

They also confirmed their chemistry on Saturday night, and Sunday morning hadn't been a fluke, as the sex that night somehow topped the first. Perhaps because some of their insecurities and shyness no longer sat between them.

They'd started on the couch on Skye's balcony again. She felt a rush of heat in her stomach as she thought of the orgasms that they'd both had on that little love seat under a blanket before moving inside, entirely unclothed already. Skye hadn't worried about being seen; there were no tall buildings between her and the lake, and they were too high up for someone on the street to see. It had been so freeing to walk around completely naked. She'd never done that before.

But they hadn't seen each other since. They'd texted quite a few times, but they'd both had busy schedules that week. Today, however, they had a walk-through of the spec suite that CBC was finishing the construction on. Would they be weird with each other? Would everyone know they'd slept together? What if she touched Bailey in a too-familiar way? What if Bailey touched her face or hair?

It was too late to back out once she was standing in front of the Maxwell Building, and the security guard had seen her. She pushed through the revolving door and walked through the lobby, trying to exude a confidence she didn't feel. *Fake it till you make it, right?*

She was, unsurprisingly, the first person to arrive. Brokers ran on their own time that was much earlier than the general population's. She'd accepted it as fact, and it was fine. She always used this time to catch up on emails. She had received the approved lease from Ellie for the attorneys, so she needed to forward that to Rob to send to his clients. She was ecstatic about that win. It was going to be a nice paycheck, and Bailey was going to do the construction since the attorneys were so enamored with the work she'd done on the roof-deck and in the spec suite.

When Skye heard the whir of the revolving door, she looked up to see Bailey walking in. She was dressed in what Skye was beginning to understand was her normal work uniform: dark jeans and a blazer, but today, her blazer was burgundy and paired with a dark gray shirt. The blazer was unbuttoned, and the swell of her breasts at the vee of her shirt made Skye think of how soft the skin there was and how she'd been *very* intimately acquainted with it a mere sixty or so hours before. And prayed to be intimately acquainted with it again soon.

Bailey whistled quietly. "Eyes are up here, tiger. Honestly, it boggles my mind how the entire real estate community doesn't know you're gay." Her voice was so quiet Skye could barely hear, but she felt a rush of prickly embarrassment.

Bailey's lips were quirked in the barest of smiles, her eyes twinkling. Skye cleared her throat. "I, uh, am normally a little more subtle. But you bring something out in me, and I can't help myself." She was, again, a lot more candid than she'd meant to be. She shook her head, laughing at herself.

"I would suggest that you try to help yourself, given that you aren't exactly out at work, and we don't want anyone to know about this, given that we're working together. If Ellie walked in right now, she would see you looking like you want to drag me into that closet behind the security desk and have your wicked way with me." Bailey's expression said she wouldn't mind that one bit.

Skye's face felt impossibly hot, both at being so damn transparent but also at Bailey calling her on it. She tried to recover and stepped closer. Not enough to be improper but closer than she would normally stand to a colleague. "Luckily, Ellie knows about me already."

"Really? You aren't out to anyone other than one of your largest clients?" Bailey's laugh echoed through the cavernous lobby and sounded twice as loud as her original laugh.

"Ellie was a mentor and friend well before she was a client. I met her in my Walter Payton High days, so she knows all my secrets."

Bailey barked another echoing laugh.

"What?" Skye asked, perplexed.

"Just that you were out in high school, but you aren't now. It's a little backward, don't you think?" Bailey put a hand on her chest as she leaned forward and laughed so hard, it sounded like she was gasping for breath.

Skye's hackles went up, but after a breath, she found herself laughing along. Bailey was right. "You make an interesting point, Ms. Kaczmarek." She shrugged. What else could she do? Other than try to stop laughing, as the echoes were no doubt reverberating through the entire building.

"All I'm saying is, you should school your face for the next hour or so unless you want everyone to know. Even if Ellie knows about you, we don't want her to know about us for conflict-of-interest concerns. Though, if you want to look at me that way later, I'm available this evening at home." Bailey cocked her head slightly and grinned.

How could she resist? She'd been longing for Bailey's hands from the moment she and Patsy had left on Monday morning. "I believe I *am* free this evening. Can I bring dinner? What time?"

"Let's plan for six and confirm the exact time around five? I'm a little nervous about when I'll finish up at work."

Skye felt a pang of disappointment at Bailey's prioritizing work over her, though they weren't actually dating. They'd agreed to keep it casual, so what did she expect? "Sure. You want to text me?"

"Hi, ladies," Ellie yelled as she walked into the lobby, interrupting their moment. "Sorry I'm late."

"You're right on time," Ryan said as he walked in behind her. "I am never late." His bookish smile always put Skye at ease.

A sliver of irritation that she and Bailey had been interrupted before they could finalize their plans flickered through Skye, but she squelched it since they *were* here to work. Once pleasantries had been exchanged, she asked Bailey, "Is Jennifer joining us today? Or are we ready to go up?"

Bailey smiled, no doubt at the fact that Skye remembered the intern's name. "She's already upstairs with the superintendent prepping for this punch list walk, and I think Maureen is going to meet us up there, so we're ready to go."

When they walked into the spec office space, Skye was taken aback by how great it looked. "Bailey, I swear, your team and Ryan took the image straight out of my head and brought it to life. It's simply stunning."

Bailey beamed. "I'm so glad you're happy with it."

Ellie also spun around in the lobby, studying the glass wall into the kitchen and break area. "You outdid yourself, Bailey. Amazing design, Ryan, and thanks for the push on this, Skye."

"I'm certain we're going to get it leased within weeks." Skye would have put money on it. The punch list walk went well, and before they knew it, Skye was preparing to head out.

Bailey came up behind her and whispered in a husky voice, "I can't wait to see you later. I'll text you."

Her proximity was intoxicating, and Skye could only nod as she walked away.

"Do you have time before your next meeting, Skye?" Ellie said. "Want to grab a coffee?"

Skye hoped she hadn't seen that intimate moment. "Sure. I'm actually free for the rest of the afternoon other than responding to a few emails."

"Why don't we make it wine, then? It's already three. Once Upon a Wine?" Ellie squeezed her arm. "I don't have any pressing obligations for the rest of the day, and it's already been a week…" She grimaced.

"If my client insists, I certainly cannot turn her down." Skye loved the freedom of being an independent contractor. It had been scary the first few years out of school when she was one hundred percent commission based and wasn't sure if she was going to sign another deal in time to pay her rent, but now that she was established and had a steady pipeline of deals, it was wonderful. She was also a partner at her firm and didn't have to answer to anyone.

Once they were settled and had placed their order, Ellie quickly got to the point of their meeting. "We've talked about it a little bit, but that big redevelopment I mentioned at the gala is going to happen. We have aldermanic approval and officially waived due diligence this week."

Skye was thrilled for Ellie. Her firm would now have significant money that was nonrefundable, and unless something fell through on financing, they would almost certainly close on the property. "Congrats,

Ellie. That's awesome." Skye was genuinely excited as she watched the pride radiate from Ellie. "Cheers," she said, and they clinked glasses. "It's going to be the largest deal of my career, so I'm nervous. Which is why I want you on board ASAP. We have months of construction, but it's going to be a huge undertaking. We need to figure out how to position the property, create catchy marketing, and it's not too early to start preleasing. If we can get one or two more deals at the Maxwell, I can easily slide you over to the new development and let you hand the other Maxwell deals to some of your junior brokers."

"That would be amazing." Skye's brain quickly ran with how much money she could make leasing that property and what it would do for her reputation.

Ellie winced. "If Maxwell leasing slows, I might have to use someone else just to appease the Investment Committee, but we don't even need to think about that since it isn't going to happen. You've been going gangbusters. A few more deals and we're home free."

Skye hated the thought of the new development going to anyone else, but she was confident that it wouldn't be an issue. "I'm certain we can get a few more deals quickly, especially with that spec suite ready to go. Put the thought of hiring anyone else out of your mind." She tried to plaster on her most confident smile despite a little doubt dragon rearing its nasty head.

Ellie lifted her glass. "Here's to our next great success. I know you've got this." They clinked glasses again, and Skye appreciated the bold flavors of the cab. It was the same one she'd shared with Bailey all those weeks ago in this same wine bar, and her heart accelerated thinking of how far they'd come since then. And how far she'd like to go that evening. "Now that we've got that straight, I'm switching from client to friend mode. What's going on with you and Bailey?"

Skye choked when the wine slid down the wrong pipe and somehow also nearly went out her nose. She tried to regain her breath while not gagging as she struggled to breathe through her nose or mouth and feared she might suffocate. Ellie, in a gigantic display of rudeness, just laughed. As Skye continued to cough and took a sip of water, Ellie's laughter became louder and more boisterous.

Skye finally managed to choke out, "Stop laughing, ass. I could die right now."

"Is that any way to talk to your best client?" For a second, Skye thought she was serious…until she started laughing again. "You're not going to die. You thought you were being surreptitious, but I've known both of you for too long. I interrupted something in the lobby, and don't think I missed that little exchange before we left. I could practically see electricity arcing between you." Skye coughed again. "And at some point, before you make the 'Forty Under Forty' list, you should learn to drink appropriately." She was starting to cry she was laughing so hard as Skye continued to gasp for air. This was bullshit.

When Skye regained her breath, she said, "I have no idea what you're talking about." Given that Ellie was already calling her out, she couldn't put a finger on exactly why she was lying.

Ellie looked over her glasses. "Really? That's the way you're going to play this? Especially after that little display?"

"There's nothing to 'play.' We're friends. That's mostly it. I think."

"So the way you stared at her ass was a friendly gesture? Do you check out my ass like that when my back is to you?"

"I wasn't. I don't. Just…fine!" Skye's face felt hot, and she threw her hands in the air. "We aren't dating per se, but we, you know."

"What do I know?" Her eyebrows lifted almost to her hairline.

Skye was apparently going to have to spell it out for her. "We…" She dropped her voice. "Had sex last weekend. A time or two. Or twenty."

Ellie's jaw dropped, and she mouthed, "Twenty?"

Skye thought for a moment. "If you count Saturday night, Sunday morning, Sunday night, and once, no, twice more Monday morning? I didn't keep track, but that sounds about right. Maybe a few more." She shrugged.

Ellie took a large sip of wine and fanned her face with the wine list. "Twenty-plus times? Have you ever had that many orgasms with someone before?"

"Definitely not. Maybe over the course of an entire relationship." She hadn't examined that truth before, but it was there. She hadn't actually spent enough time with any particular woman to have the number of orgasms she'd had with Bailey in thirty-six hours. Not that she hadn't had good sex before, but Bailey was indescribable.

"It's nice to see you finally letting go, Skye."

"I let go plenty. And you aren't worried about any conflict of interest at work?" That question had been weighing heavily on her mind.

"Are *you* worried about one?" Ellie asked.

"We work together, so of course." She couldn't help but worry about what people might assume if they knew.

"Why? She doesn't hire you, and you don't hire her." She paused and took another sip. "I hire you both, and since I'm not dating you, I don't think anything could be seen as inappropriate."

Skye hadn't looked at it that way, but Ellie did have a point. She still wasn't going to advertise anything, but knowing that Ellie wasn't going to fire either of them because of it gave her a small amount of comfort. She nodded rather than saying anything else, absorbing this new angle.

"The next question is...how was it?"

"I had upward of twenty orgasms. How the hell do you think it was?" Skye started laughing so hard, tears sprang to her eyes as well.

"Now you're just being rude," Ellie said. "Rubbing it in."

"Well, what about you? What's going on in your love life?" Ellie had gotten her heart broken a few months ago, but Skye hoped she was at least starting to date again in her search for the elusive "one."

Ellie rolled her eyes. "It gets exhausting always being the person before your girlfriend finds 'the one,' and I'm taking a break. I can't keep trying when I'm emotionally exhausted, and work is about to be completely crazy."

Skye didn't envy Ellie's difficult search for "the one" and was happy she felt no stress about that for herself. She was enjoying what was happening with Bailey, but they both knew it was a temporary arrangement, and therefore, it was essentially a stress-free endeavor. But she was still looking forward to seeing her that evening.

❖

It was nearly seven when Bailey texted, and Skye's stomach was rumbling when she pulled up in front of Bailey's very cute brownstone at seven thirty. She'd swung by her favorite pizza place on the way over for something easy but tasty. And ideally quickly consumed so they could move on to other, more exciting activities.

Patsy greeted her at the door, but unlike Saturday, Bailey opened it before Patsy could. "Hey," Bailey said. She was smiling but stood blocking the door as though unsure what to do.

Skye felt a rush of nerves. She wasn't sure if she should hug Bailey, kiss her, or shake her hand. Okay, the hand shaking idea was dumb, given their weekend festivities, but this was the first time they'd been alone together since Monday morning, and it appeared that Bailey, at least, was unsure where things stood.

Skye didn't want the evening to be awkward and placed her free hand on Bailey's hip. "Hi," she said and kissed her.

The tension seemed to leave Bailey as their lips met.

"Hi," Skye said again as she pulled back.

"Thanks for grabbing dinner." Bailey grabbed her free hand and pulled her inside. "Sorry that was weird for a sec. I'm glad you're here."

"Me too." Skye set the pizza on the kitchen island, a place she had vivid and delicious memories of. "Come here." She pulled Bailey against her and kissed her again, drawing her in with one hand on the small of her back and the other threaded into her hair. Skye pushed her hips into Bailey's, and Bailey's moan sent her stomach fluttering as she deepened their kiss.

Bailey pushed her against her new favorite kitchen island. She could easily get lost in Bailey's embrace, but a loud rumble broke their focus. "Was that your stomach or mine?" Bailey asked, her forehead against Skye's.

"I'm not sure, but I *am* hungry. I picked a one-course meal with speed of consumption in mind."

"I like it. Let me grab plates. Do you want wine?" Bailey gestured toward an open bottle of red on the counter with an empty glass sitting next to it. "I'm already into my first one." She shrugged with a sheepish grin.

"Yes, please, and no judgment. I *might* have had a glass this afternoon with Ellie."

"Oh, really? How'd that go?" Bailey set the plates on the counter and opened the pizza box.

Skye's mouth watered at the smell of cheesy goodness inside. "Great. It was good to catch up. She's got an interesting deal in the hopper. But more interesting, you and I were *not* as clandestine as we'd believed." Skye grabbed the corner triangle and two square edge pieces out of the pizza box. Her favorite pieces were the ones with more crust.

Bailey inhaled sharply and paused with a slice halfway to her mouth. "That's…awkward. Was she disapproving?"

"Not at all." Skye took her first bite. The hot cheese burned the roof of her mouth, but the heavenly mix of crust, tangy sauce, and melty cheese more than made up for it. Chicago knew how to do pizza. Even if they were inclined to cut it into squares. "She was actually supportive. She told me she was proud of me for"—she dropped her pizza slice to make quotes—"letting go. Whatever that's supposed to mean."

Bailey coughed and smirked. "That sounds very similar to a conversation I had with Roxy and Jessica today."

Skye wondered how she'd had time to call both her sisters and had also worked over two hours late. She didn't want to have hurt feelings, but stupidly, she felt them. "Oh?"

Bailey rolled her eyes. "The Bobbsey Twins called while I was in the car to grill me about Friday night. Jessica was very disappointed that she missed it and promised to attend our mothers' next cooking extravaganza. Which is apparently soon. Has your mom called you? Has she tried to press you for more info since you were over there on Sunday?"

"Oh, shit. I missed her call earlier this afternoon, and I totally forgot to call her back."

"You're going to be in trouble." She sang the word "trouble" like a grade-schooler.

"I know. Give me one sec to call her back now. Is that okay?" Skye didn't want to panic at not having called her back, but if she didn't, her mom would try to guilt trip her for at least the next week. Maybe longer.

"Of course. Just don't be too long, or I might eat the rest of this pizza by myself. This is my first meal since my smoothie at seven this morning."

Skye brushed her lips softly across Bailey's and stepped into the living room. Mama's phone rang several times before going to voice mail. Skye apologized and asked her to call when she had a moment. She was secretly relieved that she wouldn't have to evade any questions about what she'd been doing that afternoon or more importantly, where she currently was, even if she felt a little guilty about it.

"No answer." She shrugged as she walked back into the kitchen. "So the family dinner round two is soon?"

"Three weeks. At your house, apparently." Bailey laughed again.

Skye gritted her teeth. Her mother had some nerve. She refused to move to a bigger place or a better neighborhood, but she had no problem inviting a gaggle of people to Skye's house. And yet, Skye couldn't help but laugh too. "It's a good thing I love her. She's...pushy."

"Your mother or Babulya?" Bailey asked.

"I meant my mother, though I suppose Babulya is just as likely a candidate. For some reason, she doesn't frustrate me as much. It doesn't matter, though. I'll give them pretty much whatever they want."

"Really?" Bailey furrowed her brows.

"Why do you say it like that?" Skye was surprised that she didn't get irritated by Bailey's tone when a few weeks ago, she would have assumed it was judgmental.

"Please don't take this the wrong way." Bailey looked nervous. "I just wasn't expecting you to be so…accommodating."

Skye laughed and placed a hand on Bailey's arm. "No offense taken. I'm not accommodating for most people, but the life I have is because of the sacrifices my family made for me and the drive they helped me develop, so there are very few things that I won't do for them. Even when they annoy the life out of me."

Bailey pulled her in for a brief but hot kiss. "Who would've thought you were such a softie." She smiled, and Skye melted. "But you had to get that pushiness from somewhere. I can't say I'm surprised it was them."

This could be trouble. When Bailey gave her that genuine, unguarded smile, Skye felt things she should not be feeling for someone she was only casually hanging out with. She needed to put the kibosh on these pesky feelings now before she set herself up for heartbreak. But unguarded Bailey did something to her that she didn't *want* to stop.

Chapter Eighteen

It had been almost a month since Bailey had first slept with Skye, and she still wasn't sure exactly how she was feeling—or should be feeling—about the ease with which they had fallen into...whatever this was. She'd been trying to not spend every night with Skye despite the internal pull urging her to. Work had certainly helped in that endeavor, and she was pretty sure that if she counted the nights in the past month, they'd spent more nights apart than together. Pretty sure. But for plausible deniability, she wasn't going to tally them up.

Tonight, however, she and Patsy were planning to stay over for the second night in a row. Bailey's family—all three of her siblings and their families, her parents, and Gammy—was descending on Skye's condo for cooking night round two, and Ana and Yulia were going to make Ukrainian holubtsi since Bailey's mom had made golumpki the last time.

The thought that this *thing*, for lack of a better word, with her and Skye was about to be on display for both of their families was terrifying. They'd barely been *hanging out* for a month, but given the ill timing of their second kiss in her parents' kitchen, everyone who was going to be there that evening already knew there was something going on.

Bailey was trying not to be in her head about it, even though it was awkward, and she knew Skye was facing the same discomfort. Given the choice, neither would have chosen to introduce the other to her family right now. *They* weren't defining anything, but their families were certain to try.

Yet despite the stress of the afternoon and evening to come, she was enjoying a delightful cup of coffee while lounging on the love seat on Skye's balcony early Saturday morning with the sun barely creeping above the horizon. "I know you can't cook, but you *can* make one hell of a cup of coffee. You should always be the designated coffee brewer whenever we hang out."

Skye lifted away from Bailey's shoulder where she'd been nestled and looked at her. "That can be arranged, but you are aware that it's not only about how you *make* the coffee, right? It's also about the ingredients and tools. I can't make this at your house."

"Okay?" Bailey said slowly, a little surprised at the impassioned response.

Skye leaned away and stared with her mouth slightly agape. Bailey tried to give a chagrined smile but wasn't sure what she'd said to offend. Skye's affronted face was a delight to look at, though, with her full lips in the shape of an O, eyes glinting.

"You're going to call me a snob again, but a lot of things go into making the perfect cup of coffee."

"What? My coffeepot is standard-issue."

"Oh, honey." Skye patted her hand. "A standard-issue pot is fine if you want standard-issue coffee. If you want superior coffee like mine, you've got to start with exceptional ingredients: properly filtered water heated to the exact right temperature; high quality, fresh, coarsely ground coffee; and a French press so you can extract every ounce of flavor."

Bailey wanted to feel annoyed, but the sexy smirk on Skye's face defused any irritation. "So good coffee cannot come out of a standard pot? Ever?" She had to push sometimes. It was almost a compulsion.

"You can make adequate coffee that some might call good in a standard pot, but I was speaking about superior coffee." She shifted to the other end of the love seat, her eyes locked on Bailey's, and Bailey swallowed hard. Skye took Bailey's cup out of her hands, had a sip, and placed it on the side table. Bailey's empty hands trembled, and she didn't know where to put them. "And when you say I make a hell of a good cup of coffee, I am confident you didn't mean *good* or *adequate* or *standard-issue*. Why settle when you could have superior?" Her voice was low and sexy, and Bailey's sex pulsed in anticipation.

Skye gripped her hips, and her breath caught when Skye pulled her in until she was almost lying on the love seat with one leg on the couch and her other foot on the floor. Skye slid off the couch and settled between Bailey's spread thighs. Bailey thought she might spontaneously combust when Skye grazed her tight nipple with her thumb, only the thin cotton of her T-shirt preventing their skin from touching.

"For example," Skye continued, "we could have *adequate* orgasms alone or with the help of a toy or two."

Bailey managed to nod, but words had packed their bags and headed off to Mexico.

"But…" Skye toyed with the bottom of Bailey's shirt. "What we have here, what we *do* here, isn't simply *adequate*." She slid her hands under Bailey's tee and began to slide them up her body. The damp heat as Skye pressed kisses along the newly exposed skin had goose bumps erupting all along Bailey's arms. "Don't you agree?"

Bailey was too focused on the lips tracing a path up her torso to have any idea what she was agreeing to but managed a "mm-hmm" while hoping that Skye didn't stop.

"I'm interested in your opinion, but I would venture to say…" Skye paused as she pulled Bailey's nipple into her mouth, sucking with the perfect amount of pressure. The cool air that rushed in when Skye breathed through her mouth had Bailey pressing her hips up, seeking some relief for the pounding between her legs, but Skye left her wanting as she lifted out of reach and pulled Bailey's shirt over her head. The chilled morning air was a balm on Bailey's overheated skin. Skye stared at her with an intensity that had her stomach flipping. "I would venture to say *this* is more in the category of superior?"

Bailey tried to say "yeah," but it sounded like a squeak. Skye seemed to understand as she pulled off Bailey's underwear and shorts. Lying on Skye's balcony entirely nude seemed taboo but was so arousing. She wasn't sure if the tingles racing across her skin were from the breeze or the heat of Skye's gaze, but a shudder shook her to the core as Skye sank back onto her heels and pulled Bailey's legs over her shoulders.

"I think you, me, this balcony"—Skye exhaled over Bailey's labia, already spread wide, but didn't provide the touch she was craving—"are exceptional ingredients. Like my exceptional coffee ingredients."

"Oh God," Bailey groaned when Skye licked from her opening to the top of her clit and swirled her tongue around before making the journey back down again and dipping inside. Bailey wrapped her fingers around the couch cushion and tried to anchor herself.

The vibrations when Skye said, "Fuck, you taste so good," had Bailey teetering on the brink.

Bailey squeezed her own nipple and moved her hips against Skye's face. She wrapped a leg around Skye's shoulders to pull her closer. She needed her so close that she couldn't tell where one body ended and the other began. "Oh, oh, oh, fuck."

"Shh. The neighbors are going to know what we're doing if you don't keep it down." Skye's voice was muffled, but Bailey got the message when Skye pressed a hand over her mouth.

Bailey started to move frantically as Skye slipped several fingers inside her, and her orgasm roared through her. She sank her teeth into Skye's hand as she tried to muffle her cry.

Skye held her through her aftershocks, her mouth still against Bailey's center.

"Oh God. Yes, definitely superior. Vasty, vastly superior," Bailey said.

When her trembles finally stopped, Skye pressed a last light kiss against her outer lips and looked up. "The *most* superior, in my experience."

Bailey wouldn't have expected her heart to be able to beat any faster after that orgasm, but Skye saying that their connection was superior had her feeling like a bouquet of hummingbirds had been released in her chest. Was that panic? Was it excitement? Was it happiness? She wasn't sure, but she didn't hate it. Quite the opposite, in fact.

"Come here," Bailey said and pulled Skye closer by her shirt. She climbed on top of Bailey as much as the love seat would allow and gently kissed her. "You are so beautiful. And rather amazing. I was not expecting to end up naked on your balcony again, but this isn't a bad way to start a Saturday. A superior start, I would venture to say."

"I concur. And to have the same superior start at your house, we'll need to get you a French press. And a grinder, an electric kettle, and better coffee beans." Her cheeky smile was…just perfect.

"Oh, it's the coffee that makes this *the most superior*, is it?"

Skye bit the side of her lip, a hint of a smile appearing. "Well, it certainly doesn't hurt."

"Definitely not." Bailey captured her mouth and gripped her hips, but she must have pulled too hard as she started to fall. Bailey caught her, but this damn love seat was too small for proper maneuvering. "Maybe we should move inside, at least to the normal-sized couch. Or the bed. I love this love seat, but there isn't quite enough room for extracurricular activities."

"I'm entirely in favor." Skye stood and reached for her hand.

Bailey allowed herself to be pulled up, eager to fully stretch out with Skye.

"This may seem crazy given the amount of furniture you have already, but have you ever considered getting a full-sized couch or a chaise lounge for your balcony?" Bailey said.

"I've never had a need. You're the first person I've spent so much time out here with. But I'm not opposed."

Bailey's chest warmed. Was she really the first person Skye had ever had naked on that couch? It seemed unlikely, except not really, based on what Skye had said. She so wasn't who Bailey had thought she would be when they'd first met, and Bailey was finding herself more and more enamored with all the layers that made her. Her playful side, her soft spot for her family, her sweetness. Bailey was getting in deeper than she'd bargained for.

She must have stared for too long because Skye asked, "Are you okay? Why are you staring at me like that?"

Bailey shook her head. "Just zoning. Sorry. What time is your family coming over?"

Skye pulled her toward the bedroom. "Not until one thirty."

"Oh good, we've got hours. And I know exactly how to fill them."

Skye giggled and quickened their pace.

❖

Skye caught Bailey's eye from across the kitchen when her family wasn't looking and mouthed, "Are you okay?" Her family had descended on her condo that afternoon like a swarm of bees usurping her hive, and Skye was worried that Bailey might be feeling overwhelmed. Skye was feeling overwhelmed, and they were *her* relatives.

Bailey gave her the most endearing smile and simply nodded while she kept her ear tilted down toward Babulya, who was demonstrating the best way to peel a cabbage. Skye had no idea why that image set a flutter loose in her chest that had her hands shaking, but it was adorable.

She rubbed her thumbs against her fingertips, trying to dry the moisture there and picked up a knife to start cutting the onion she'd abandoned a moment ago. Although small, her family was a lot. A lot. She knew it. And here was Bailey—commitment-phobic Bailey—standing in her kitchen, holding her own, and flirting with Babulya. All after waking up in Skye's arms.

Skye was finding this evolving thing between them less scary than she'd been expecting. The scary part was wondering where Bailey's head was at. She seemed reluctant to spend the night here or have Skye stay at her place, but whenever they did stay together, she appeared to be all in. It was confusing. Bailey had gone through a spectacularly failed engagement, but Skye didn't know the details. She suspected that was the real reason Bailey was reluctant to date versus work, which was what she always claimed.

Skye wasn't sure what she wanted, either, which was also confusing, but she couldn't deny how every moment with Bailey just felt right. How every night spent with Bailey was better than the last. It was wild to think about how much they hadn't liked each other only a few short months ago. She couldn't pinpoint the exact moment they'd begun to give a little grace and a little benefit of the doubt, but that decision had flipped a switch, and everything that had been pushing them apart was now pulling them together. Skye still liked to rile Bailey up, but it was different now. Thoughts of riling Bailey up later started an ill-timed throb between her thighs, and she went back to focusing on her onion.

"Svyatoslava!"

Skye jumped and her chef's knife clattered on the granite counter as it slipped out of her hand. "What, Mama?"

"Why are you mincing those onions? Dice, not mince. We're not making potato pancakes."

Skye looked at the pile of onion pulp in front of her. "Oops," she managed. She'd been so lost in thought that she'd managed to mangle an entire onion. She was lucky she hadn't mangled a finger.

"Just start fresh. That mush won't do." She tossed an onion, and Skye snagged it from the air. "What are you doing with that?" Her mama yelled again as Skye picked up the cutting board and held it over the trash.

"I'm clearing the cutting board so I can start fresh." Skye silently congratulated herself on managing to not roll her eyes.

"So wasteful. You should save it for something you cook later this week." Mama went digging in Skye's cupboards, muttering about finding a container.

Skye tried not to sigh. She was moderately successful. "I don't—"

But before she could get her sentence out, Bailey walked over to the cupboard where her Pyrex was, pulled out a small bowl, and said, "We'll find something to cook them in, Yulia. Don't worry."

"Thank you, Bailey. This daughter of mine can be so wasteful." Mama went back to kneading the ground beef and ground pork together, and Bailey came over and took the cutting board out of Skye's hands. "So wasteful," she said, her voice low enough that only Skye could hear.

Skye's breath caught as Bailey's forearm brushed the side of her breast as she tilted the cutting board over the glass bowl. The gleam in her eye told Skye it wasn't an accident.

"Really?" Skye mouthed and tried to glare to emphasize the point.

Bailey shrugged. "You can't prove anything."

"You are something else, Bailey Kaczmarek." She shook her head and smiled, but her stomach was still flip-flopping from how comfortable Bailey was in her kitchen and because she'd spoken of cooking together that week like it was nothing. Skye tried to swallow, but it took more effort than it should have. She couldn't pull her eyes away from Bailey's.

"Also, who is Svyo...Svya...Svatya..." Bailey's butchered attempts to pronounce Skye's former name got painfully worse with each attempt.

Skye worried that Bailey would judge her for her decision to change her name and didn't want to get into it at all, especially not while her family was there. "I'll tell you later, okay?"

Bailey nodded. "Is everything okay? You're a little pale."

Skye brought the back of her hand to her own face. She was pretty sure she was fine. Perfectly fine. "Yeah, of course. I'm just going to go use the restroom before I start my second attempt to murder an onion."

"Okay." Bailey touched her arm and leaned closer. "Because you did a number on this one. It looks like baby food. I honestly have no idea what I'm going to cook that in."

"Well, I don't think any baby would want to eat it, so you'll have to figure something out now that you promised Mama."

Bailey smirked and kissed her—on the mouth—then seemed to realize what she'd done. Her eyes were huge. "Shit. I'm sorry. I forgot we weren't alone. That's probably weird."

"It's fine. I'll be right back." Skye forced a smile until Bailey returned it, and she could walk away. But she didn't feel fine. She felt panicky. It was rising in her like a pot about to boil over, and she needed to get away before anyone saw it. She liked feeling this intimacy with Bailey. She *liked* having Bailey in her kitchen cooking with Mama,

Babulya, and Natasha. She liked Bailey knowing where her Pyrex was stored. She even liked Patsy sitting in the middle of the kitchen waiting for someone to accidentally on purpose drop something for her.

When she got into the bathroom, Skye splashed some cold water on her face and made eye contact with herself in the mirror. She squeezed the edge of the vanity until her fingertips ached. Why couldn't she breathe? What part of today was making her so uneasy? She loved spending time with her family, and she loved spending time with Bailey.

But them all spending time together was too domestic. When this thing with Bailey ended, as it inevitably would, this was going to make it all a lot more complicated. Her family would know how amazing Bailey was and how Skye must have been the one to mess something up. She knew she could be a little self-absorbed at times and spent a lot of time at work. But was there even something to mess up? Was there a chance for there to be?

Fuck, she was confused. She leaned her forehead against the mirror. She watched her breath fog the mirror and dissipate in time for her to fog it again. It was hypnotic, and she reminded herself to concentrate on the present and stop planning twenty steps down the line. It was what she told her junior brokers all the time. *Stop thinking about the big paycheck you can get or the hundreds of ways a deal can fall apart. Stay in the moment and focus on closing the deal.* Right now, she needed to get back downstairs and focus on making holubtsi with her family. There would be plenty of time to sort the rest out.

All eleven members of Bailey's family arrived at once, and Skye wondered if they had chartered a bus or if they'd caravanned from Jefferson Park. Despite its size, Skye had never had this many people in her house. Ever. But they all were friendly and kind. Loll had baked three cakes because with sixteen people, apparently one or two cakes weren't enough.

Roxy greeted Skye like they were old friends, pulling her into a bear hug before introducing her to her twin and both their husbands, all of whom also hugged Skye too. She met Bailey's brother and his wife, also huggers. It was weird but nice in a way. Skye had been afraid to have twin boys in her house, but apparently, Patsy kept them so busy that they didn't even look for trouble.

"Thank you so much for hosting our little dinner, Skye. It's great to see you again," Loll said as she pulled Skye into yet another hug.

"Likewise. I'm glad you could make it." Skye felt a little surprised at the truth she found in those words. She'd never hosted anything, but despite their quantity, Bailey's family felt *comfortable* there. So weird, but there was no time to obsess about it since she was being overrun.

"Your home is beautiful." Loll gestured around the living area and toward the wall of glass that divided it from the balcony.

Skye's heart jumped at the thought of what she and Bailey had used the balcony for earlier that morning and wanted to steer them all away from it. "Thank you, would you like the full tour?" Again, she expected to feel reluctance to show them around, but she really didn't. It almost felt as though they belonged there.

"That would be wonderful," Loll exclaimed. She clapped to get everyone's attention and said, "Skye is going to give me a full tour if anyone wants to join."

It felt like leading a parade as everyone joined other than Bailey's brother, Brian, and his kids. Even her own family joined, despite having been to her house numerous times, but apparently, Gammy and Babulya didn't want to stop chatting for a breath. The way they had become instant friends with the Kaczmareks was endearing.

They ended the tour on Skye's roof-deck, and while everyone walked around enjoying the view over the lake, Bailey slipped in beside Skye and squeezed her hand. "Hey you," she whispered.

The warmth of Bailey's breath against her ear set off tingles in her chest. "Hey back." She loved the way Bailey's hair shimmered in the afternoon sunlight.

"Is anyone paying attention to us?" Bailey said.

Skye looked around, and everyone seemed absorbed in their own conversations. "Nope."

"Good. I've been dying to do this since forever." She leaned into Skye and kissed her. Pretty thoroughly too, given that their families were only a few feet away.

Skye pulled Bailey's hips against her, missing that connection since they hadn't really touched in the last few hours. "Me too." Reluctantly, she stepped back before someone caught them. "It's weird how comfortable this is, isn't it?"

"Us kissing?" Bailey's eyebrows drew together. "We do that all the time, and it's always lovely."

"No, silly. Having our families together like this. At my house. Getting along like they've known each other since birth." Skye surprised herself with her candidness. Again.

"I hadn't thought about it, but yeah, it's a little odd. I haven't introduced them to a woman since my ex-fiancée. I mean, I haven't dated anyone seriously since then, either. Not that we're…" Bailey waved as she trailed off. "You know."

No, Skye really didn't know anymore. Bailey's words lodged a grapefruit in her throat, and she didn't know what to say or if she could even manage to squeak out a word. She tried to nod.

"Fuck," Bailey said. "Our families think we are, I think. I don't know."

Skye's chest felt tight, but she needed to say something. Something to make it seem like Bailey's words hadn't felt like a punch to the solar plexus. "Does it matter what they think we're doing? We know, right?" *Wrong.* She didn't have a fucking clue. She squeezed Bailey's hand and stepped away.

Bailey reached for her as though to keep her close. "I—" But she was interrupted by her mother.

"Skye, dear, could we eat up here? It's so beautiful, and the weather is perfect to eat al fresco."

Skye was relieved that Loll had walked up before Bailey could make things worse. "Of course. I have this huge table up here that I've eaten at maybe twice." And always alone, but she'd keep that information to herself. "It'll be great to share it with everyone. And you're right. The weather is perfect."

If Loll could tell something was tense between her and Bailey, she didn't let on. "Wonderful. Ana said dinner should almost be ready."

Bailey recruited her siblings, and Skye ran downstairs with them to grab everything. The tension dissipated as they struggled to carry everything up two flights of stairs. Truthfully, the tension might have been completely on Skye's side anyway, as Bailey didn't seem to be affected, but Skye had let it go by the time they sat at her ridiculously-sized teak table. The one that she'd barely used before today.

Skye was talking to Roxy on her right when she felt Bailey's hand rest lightly on her left knee. They touched all the time when they were alone, but Skye was surprised to feel it with their families around. She looked to see if Bailey was trying to get her attention without alerting anyone. She wasn't. She was chatting with her sister-in-law across the table and wasn't looking at Skye at all. Maybe Bailey hadn't even realized she'd done it. Not only was her hand on Skye's knee, but her fingers were tracing little patterns. Skye's stomach clenched.

"I'm sorry, what?" She realized Roxy was staring at her expectantly, but she had completely lost track of the conversation.

"Have you ever thought of putting a garden up here?" Roxy said.

"Oh no. I don't have much of a green thumb, and I'm not home enough to really tend to it." Damn Bailey and her roaming digits and mixed signals. Skye placed a hand on top of Bailey's and interlaced their fingers. She really needed to still them; they were making it very difficult to concentrate. And talk about mixed signals. How did Bailey expect their families to *not* think they were serious when she insisted on touching her in front of them?

Roxy looked around the deck. "Well, it's a shame. You have a great space for it. And you'd get a ton of sun being higher than everything. If you ever change your mind, let me know."

There was absolutely no way that would happen. "I certainly will." She gave Roxy what she hoped was a charming smile to make up for her inattention. What was wrong with her?

By the time their families finally left that evening, Skye was utterly exhausted. Between cooking with her family, entertaining too many people to count, and simply having that many people in her private space, Skye felt like she'd been run over by a Mack truck.

She flopped heavily onto her couch and let out a huge sigh. "That was fun but taxing. Shit."

Bailey chuckled from somewhere behind her. "Yeah, they're a lot."

Skye could hear the plink of ice cubes and the quiet pour of something and wondered what Bailey was making but couldn't be bothered to lift her head from the back of the couch to see. The cushions dipped as Bailey sat, and gravity pulled Skye toward her. When Bailey's fingers combed through Skye's hair, she opened her eyes. "Is that for me?" She pointed at a lowball glass with two fingers of something brown and boozy.

"It is."

"You're a queen. Thank you." Skye traded a light kiss for the drink.

"Happy to serve." Bailey's charming smile sent a shiver of desire down Skye's spine.

She took a sip of scotch and savored the little buzz as it landed in her stomach. "Ah, that takes the edge off. Thank you."

"You said that already."

Skye again rested her head against the back corner of the couch and was momentarily sad when Bailey slid away but gasped when she lifted Skye's feet into her lap and began to massage them. She couldn't stop the groan of pleasure as Bailey dug a thumb into her arch. "That is amazing. The level of my gratitude in this moment is such that thirty thank-yous would be insufficient. Mmm, oh yes, right there." She fell into an abyss of bliss as Bailey found tense nodes in her feet that she hadn't even realized were there and worked them out with the patience of a saint.

"What did I do to deserve these ministrations?" Skye murmured, loving every second of Bailey's hands on her feet and calves.

Bailey chuckled, and it was music to Skye's ears. She had it worse than she'd thought. "You put up with the Kaczmarek clan for hours. You catered to my mother's insistence that we eat on the roof. You didn't run scared when grilled by Roxy or Jess or Brian. And I know that many strangers in your space stresses you out. You looked like you could use a little TLC."

Why was Bailey sending her so many mixed signals? She'd made it clear that she didn't want anything serious with her words, but then she'd held Skye's hand at dinner and was pampering her after a stressful afternoon. What was Skye supposed to make of it all? Part of her wanted to ask a direct question, but she also didn't want Bailey to pull the plug because she was starting to develop pesky feelings. Which she absolutely, unfortunately, seemed to be.

She'd skipped several networking events to spend time with Bailey, and she'd *never* done that before. Not for anyone other than Babulya when she'd been in the hospital. Why was she doing that for someone who wasn't getting as invested as she was?

Bailey found a particularly good spot on her right calf, and Skye remembered. Because she wasn't entirely sure that Bailey wasn't getting invested too. Sometimes, she was so sweet and attentive. But those were often balanced by periods of distance, and Skye felt…confused. Conflicted. Uncertain. None of those emotions were comfortable for her.

She hadn't wanted anything serious, either, but the more time she spent with Bailey, the more time she wanted to spend with her. She didn't want to casually "hang out" anymore. She was starting to *need* more, which was terrifying.

"So." Bailey broke her reverie. "What was the name your mom called you earlier?"

Skye's eyes popped open. She'd forgotten about that entirely. She didn't know why she was afraid to share. It wasn't like she was ashamed. Well, maybe a little bit. But she was worried that Bailey was going to be critical.

Bailey prodded her again. "I know there's a story there, so spill." It stressed her out, but she hoped that with the new trust they had found, Bailey wouldn't jump to judgment. "My birth name is Svyatoslava Kuchytska."

"Wow, that's beautiful. But a mouthful."

"Exactly." Skye let out a little sigh of relief that Bailey maybe understood a little and didn't immediately judge her for flushing her heritage. But she was still a little embarrassed to admit it. She laughed nervously. "Could you imagine that email address? It's twenty letters. It's hard to say, hard to spell. No one has ever heard the name before, and in business, sometimes, the person with a name you can remember— and spell—has the advantage."

"Of course."

"I wasn't trying to pretend I'm not Ukrainian or that I'm not the first generation of my family born here, but I felt like such a complicated name would hold me back. Right or wrong, I changed it in my freshman year of college."

Bailey chuckled. "I get it. Why do you think my email address is BaileyK? I can't believe you didn't mention it before." She tickled the bottom of Skye's foot, and Skye jerked out of her reach.

"Stop!"

Bailey snagged her leg again and squeezed tighter, preventing Skye from pulling away, and she flailed more. Bailey, ornery as she was, didn't let go and said, "What do I get if I stop? I'm going to need something in trade."

Skye tried to push Bailey off with her other foot, but Bailey had surprising strength and managed to grab and hold that leg as well. "I'm not submitting to your extortion."

"Oh no?" Bailey tickled her more, and Skye shrieked as she found herself surprisingly aroused but was tired of being held down.

She struggled for another few seconds before finally shouting, "Fine, fine. Anything you want. Please stop tickling me." Skye was embarrassed at the squeakiness in her tone, but she couldn't take it anymore.

Bailey finally stopped her torture. "Anything I want? Anything at all?" She smirked, and Skye's emotions were at war, but she knew she would give Bailey anything in that moment.

"Anything," she whispered.

"What if I want a kiss?" Bailey's eyes smoldered.

"Do you really think you need to extort me for a kiss? I give those to you for free all the time. I'd give you one right this second if you released my feet."

Bailey looked at the feet in her lap and back up. Was that uncertainty on her face? "What if I want the right to a kiss anywhere, anytime?"

That made Skye pause. Did Bailey mean at a time when Skye would be uncomfortable with it? Did she want a kiss when they were at work? She couldn't imagine that was what Bailey meant. She was a consummate professional and would never behave inappropriately. What, then? Did it matter? Not really. Skye couldn't imagine denying Bailey anything.

"Yes."

"What if I want more than a kiss?" Bailey's face had become serious. Skye wished she could see what was going on in her head. Bailey was trying to get at something, and the uncertainty was tearing Skye's stomach apart.

"What did you have in mind?" Skye finally asked, afraid of what she might say and at the same time, wanting to shake it out of her.

"What if I want a date? A real date."

Skye's heart soared, but she worried she might not be interpreting that correctly. "What do you mean a real date? Haven't we been dating for a few weeks?"

Bailey looked at her hands and resumed the massage. "I don't mean a hang-out date. I mean a real, honest-to-goodness date. Like, I pick you up at your house and leave Patsy with my parents. We go somewhere romantic. Maybe take a walk along the lake and look at the stars. If you have a good time, maybe you invite me back to your place for a nightcap."

Skye's throat felt thick as flurries started in her chest. She heard the words, but after all her weird emotions all day, she struggled to make sense of them. "Like, not casual?"

Bailey cleared her throat and pointedly looked away. "Yes. No. I mean, not if that isn't what you want. Things can stay the same, and I'll collect my kiss sometime here at your place. Or mine. Or whatever." She released Skye's calf as she reached for her glass, and Skye immediately missed the connection.

She laid a hand on Bailey's that was now on the back of the couch instead of on her leg and squeezed. "No, I do. I really, really want that."

Bailey slowly turned back. "Yeah?" she said quietly. The tension melted as her face softened, and her lips quirked upward.

"Yeah." Skye pulled her legs back and climbed to straddle Bailey's hips. "I've been a little broody all day because I thought I was the only one who wanted something more. And it was confusing because your actions didn't match your words, and I didn't know what to think. But every day I spend with you is better than the one before. I'm tired of denying what I want. Which is you. And not casually."

"Me too," Bailey said. She pulled Skye down and began with a light kiss that very quickly morphed into something hotter as her tongue found Skye's.

Skye loved kissing Bailey. They fit together better than anyone she'd ever been with. Bailey's lips were so soft as they moved against Skye's, and there was a casual comfort between them that defied the few weeks that they'd been doing this. She loved every second that they spent exploring each other. She slid her fingers into Bailey's hair and lightly scratched her scalp. Bailey groaned, and Skye broke their kiss. She didn't think Bailey had ever looked more stunning than she did in that moment, with her hair mussed from Skye's fingers and her lips swollen from their kiss. She couldn't help but play with the silky strands of Bailey's hair.

"You are so beautiful, Skye. Truly. I don't think I tell you that enough." Bailey tucked some of Skye's hair behind her ear.

She didn't know how to answer, wasn't used to these mushy feelings. Instead, she rubbed her thumb along Bailey's lower lip and was surprised when Bailey opened her mouth and lightly bit the pad. Even more surprising was the jolt to her lower belly, and she couldn't suppress a growl when Bailey took her thumb and gently sucked on it. She tightened her fingers in Bailey's hair and thrust her hips, looking for friction as Bailey swirled her tongue around the tip of Skye's finger.

That night, for perhaps the first time in her life, Skye was focused entirely on her partner's pleasure rather than her own. Not that she was selfish in the bedroom; she always wanted her partners to enjoy themselves, but it had been more transactional in nature. That night, making sure Bailey felt cherished and taken care of felt like Skye's life mission. She felt like a different person, but in those precious moments, wrapped in Bailey's arms, she didn't feel afraid of the change.

CHAPTER NINETEEN

Bailey stood just off what would eventually become the lobby for the attorneys' suite while the subcontractors wandered the space so they could finalize their bid pricing for her. It wasn't a terribly complicated job, other than the additional restrooms Skye had promised, but even that wasn't insurmountable.

She watched as Jason took measurements for the glass wall and chuckled at the first disagreement she'd had with Skye, when she'd assumed Skye was trying to use her allure to get favors. She knew it was ridiculous, but she was happy it had happened because it had sparked her and Skye's private meetings, which eventually evolved into their current relationship.

It was weird that she was in a relationship. Again. After everything with her ex-fiancée and having sworn off any type of future entanglement. Bailey had been so nervous to ask Skye out on an actual date and had almost chickened out, but it had seemed like Skye had been giving her signals all day that she wanted more than casual, so when the opportunity had presented itself, Bailey had taken the plunge.

And since their first actual date, when Bailey had picked Skye up, taken her to dinner on a rooftop restaurant and, as promised, taken her for a walk along the lake—which had happily ended with Skye inviting her up for a nightcap—Bailey had stopped trying to ration the number of nights that they spent together.

But her job had started doing that for her.

She had been swamped for a few weeks. The replacement she'd hired for Greg was not as good as she'd hoped, so she was back at square one with a new estimator. This estimator wasn't new to the business, but Bailey didn't fully trust her yet and definitely didn't trust her with Ellie's building, given their long friendship and business relationship.

She would have done whatever was necessary to keep Ellie happy regardless, but Ellie had a huge deal in the works to acquire an old building that needed a full renovation to be the class A office she wanted it to be, and Bailey wanted to be the contractor who got that assignment. So she would keep running jobs at Ellie's buildings until she was completely certain that her new estimator was going to cut it. But it was exhausting.

The previous night, she'd had to cancel on Skye because she'd ended up working until midnight, and that was the second time this week she'd canceled because of last-minute emergencies at the office. Sure, the first time, she'd still taken Patsy to Skye's to spend the night, but they were supposed to order takeout, watch Netflix, and have a nice, casual evening. Instead, Bailey had shown up at almost ten and was too exhausted for anything more than a quickie before they both fell asleep.

She hoped Skye didn't think she'd come over just for a quick booty call; she'd genuinely wanted to see her. She'd tried to make it up to her by making her breakfast in bed. But it was hard. Juggling both a relationship with Skye as well as running her company was as hard as she'd known it would be, but she was hopeful too. Since Skye was also a businessperson, she should understand how demanding Bailey's job could be. Especially now that she was shorthanded, which wasn't going to last forever.

But those stolen hours on Saturday mornings when neither of them had anywhere else to be or any work demands to bow to? Those were magical. Drinking fancy French-pressed coffee while watching the sun come up over the lake with Skye in her arms and Patsy at her feet was sublime and reminded Bailey that those charmed moments were *why* she wanted to juggle her crazy obligations.

At the feeling of warm breath against her ear, combined with a whispered "Hey there," a surge of pleasure ran up her spine. She spun, smiling, knowing it was Skye, almost as though she'd conjured her out of thin air.

"Skye Kohl. What would they say if they saw you standing this close to me?" Bailey desperately wanted to reach out and touch her but knew it wouldn't be welcome. Neither was comfortable with PDA at work, but Skye's rules were more stringent. In fact, it was odd that she'd gotten this close on a jobsite at all.

"No one is watching. I checked on my way in." She ran her index finger down Bailey's blazer sleeve until she found her forearm and dipped, just for a moment, beneath the rolled cuff to the sensitive underside of Bailey's arm. The caress was…intimate. Entirely G-rated, but it *felt* anything but. Bailey leaned into the contact, almost kissing her but pulled away at the last moment before she did something she couldn't take back.

Skye also seemed to realize what they were doing and stepped back, dropping her arm to play with the Rolex at her wrist. Bailey understood, but it still pulled at her chest uncomfortably. Skye not being out at work wasn't really a huge deal, but sometimes, it made her wonder how invested Skye could get in their relationship.

But then Skye would smile, and Bailey would melt and remember why she had such a soft spot for the outspoken Skye.

Bailey coughed to find her voice again. "What brings you to this neck of the woods, Ms. Kohl?"

"I had a tour on the fifteenth floor. But I'd heard a rumor this walk-through was today, so I thought I'd pop by to see if I could catch you. I missed you last night." She pursed her lips in a pout. "This was the second time in a week that you canceled. I'm beginning to think you're tiring of me."

Bailey knew the pouty face was mostly an act, but there was an undercurrent of hurt there, and Bailey despised that she was the one to cause it. "I know. I'm really sorry it happened again. I had a last-minute emergency. Another guy got injured late in the day. Not anything serious, but it could have been much more serious than it was. It torpedoed my entire afternoon, and I had several proposals that I needed to get out last night. Please know, I would have much rather been with you." Bailey squeezed her hand for less than a breath, hoping she saw the remorse.

Skye loosed an exaggerated sigh. "I know. But I'm not used to coming second to anything. Neither in my professional nor personal life. It's *very* hard on my ego." She smiled again, but rather than a carefree smile that lifted her entire face, there was a strain at the corners of her eyes, and her lips were thin.

"I'll make it up to you tonight. I promise. I'll bring dinner, and we can have a redo on the Netflix and chill evening we were supposed to have."

Skye chewed on the inside of her lip, and Bailey was captivated. "You promise?"

"I promise."

❖

Skye couldn't believe Bailey had stood her up. Again. Broken her promise. Again. This was seriously getting ridiculous. Sure, it was Saturday, and they were getting together that afternoon, but she only felt confident that she wouldn't get stood up again because they were picking up Mama and Babulya and going to Bailey's family's for dinner, and Bailey wouldn't stand up her own mother. She seemed to only do that to Skye.

What was she supposed to think? Clearly, she was of middling importance in Bailey's life. When Bailey had texted to say she was finished with work and had asked if she should still come over, it was after midnight. Skye had fallen asleep on the couch, and although the buzzing of the phone had woken her up, she'd pretended to be asleep and hadn't texted back until this morning.

She liked sleeping next to Bailey, even if that's all they did, but she didn't want to turn into a whenever, wherever kind of girl. She wasn't willing to be available only at Bailey's convenience. Either Bailey was willing to make time and keep their plans, or she wasn't.

Skye hated the thought of what had to happen if Bailey wasn't, but she had enough self-worth—enough respect for herself—that she wasn't going to pretend to have nothing going on in her life so she could be available whenever Bailey deemed it appropriate. Bailey needed to figure out a way to respect Skye and her time. Skye had just as much going on as Bailey did but somehow managed to make time for them.

But when Bailey knocked on her door around eleven that morning, looking luscious in a maroon polo and jeans, her normal charming smile in place, Skye's resolve faltered. Rather than chastise Bailey for last night's transgression, she grabbed her by the shirt, pulled her into the condo, and kissed her nearly senseless.

When Bailey began to move against her, Skye stepped back, crossed her arms, and gave Bailey her most severe glare. "You have some serious making up to do."

Bailey ran her hands through her hair, pulling at it while staring at their shoes. "I know, I know, I'm sorry," she said so quickly that Skye almost couldn't discern the individual words. Bailey began to toy with the ends of Skye's hair when she finally looked up. "I really am sorry. I hate how busy I've been. I hate having to cancel on you. Work is… well, it's been out of control. I don't want to make excuses. I missed you last night. So much. I really wanted to be here with you." The look on her face was so earnest that Skye couldn't stay angry. She looked like a guilty puppy.

"Just stop with that face." She ran a thumb along Bailey's pouting lower lip. "I can't stay mad at you. Even though I want to. But we need to figure something out. This isn't me, some sad pathetic sack sitting at home and getting stood up. I actually skipped an event last night to be with you, and you ditched me. I don't even recognize myself right now." When she was alone, she didn't understand why she was letting herself become this person, but when Bailey was standing in front of her, looking so delicious and contrite, she felt an inexplicable pull and found herself forgiving anything. She dropped her hand and crossed her arms again. "You need to be respectful of both me and my time."

"I know. I *am* so sorry. As soon as I get someone to fully step into Greg's shoes, particularly at Ellie's buildings, I promise, things will get a lot better." She chewed on her lip. "If you think about it, it's advantageous for me to keep working on Ellie's buildings since you have a vested interest in things going off without a hitch there too."

Skye couldn't stop a laugh at the earnest look on Bailey's face. "You make an interesting point. And I know you're busy. I am too. But I need you to be better at being realistic about when you are going to be available and when you aren't."

Bailey sighed heavily. "I'm just optimistic about finishing, and I want to see you."

"You get that you can't have both, right? That's not fair to me at all." For her own self-respect, Skye really needed a little more self-care and to stop making herself so available when she had other demands on her time.

"I do, and I'm sorry. I don't mean to do it." She grabbed Skye's arms, uncrossed them, and interlaced their fingers.

"How close are you to finding an actual replacement?" Skye asked.

Bailey's thumbs skimmed the backs of her hands and warmth radiated up her arms and into her chest. "Close, I swear. I had someone, but he didn't end up working out, so I've hired two more people, and they both seem pretty good. I think one of them will be ready to fully take over his responsibilities soon. I'm not even supposed to be doing estimating or overseeing jobs." Bailey released Skye's hands and grabbed her hips to pull her closer. The thumbs tracing little circles above her jeans were making it hard to concentrate.

Skye swallowed. "You promise you're close to handing some of this extra work to someone else?"

"I do." Bailey's head bobbed.

"And you'll be more realistic about your availability?"

"I will."

Skye squinted as she tried to decide if Bailey was being completely truthful. Regardless, she committed to stop changing her own plans just in case Bailey was free. It wasn't good for either of them. "Okay," she said, almost a whisper as she leaned closer.

"Okay?" Hopefulness flashed across Bailey's face. "So I'm forgiven?"

"Probably. But I'm sure you could also come up with ways to make it up to me. If you really wanted to get back in my good graces, that is."

"Is that so?" The corner of Bailey's mouth quirked up. "Any suggestions on how I might do that?" She pushed away from the door and started to walk them into Skye's living room. They kissed, and Skye tried to divide her attention between walking backward and kissing, but it wasn't easy.

She broke the kiss, resting her forehead against Bailey's. "I wouldn't want to stifle your creativity by giving you suggestions."

"How long before we have to leave?"

"A few hours."

"Hmm." Bailey released her, took the few steps to the door, and picked up a bag that Skye hadn't even noticed her carrying in. "Why don't I start by making you a delicious brunch, complete with mimosas?" She held up the bag. "Then I can let my creativity run free. Perhaps on your balcony with its too-short love seat but perfect views." She grabbed Skye's hand and tugged her to the kitchen.

"I did skip breakfast, so I am amenable to your plan. But only if your breakfast is superior to all other breakfasts." She smiled to let Bailey know she was kidding. Mostly.

"I'm going to make a frittata with veggies from the garden and extra-sharp cheddar. I promise, it is going to be so good, it will blow your socks off. And maybe even your pants. We'll see."

Bailey's smirk set Skye's heart flitting around in her chest and made her willing to take off her pants right then, but she really wanted to spend some time with Bailey clothed. She loved that Bailey brought over food and wanted to savor the time spent outside the bedroom too. As they laughed over Bailey's food and mimosas, catching up on each other's weeks, Skye thought she could get used to spending Saturdays like this. But preferably with better Friday nights.

CHAPTER TWENTY

Bailey had been trying—really, really trying—to be better. Although she hadn't been able to free up many more evenings, she was getting better at setting realistic expectations. And she was pretty sure her new estimator, Alice, was going to be ready to step into Greg's old role soon. Bailey just wanted to see her run a few more projects, and she'd hand things over to her fully.

This evening, she'd been expecting to work late but had miraculously finished around seven thirty. Skye was meeting with a few of her colleagues that evening but had mentioned she thought they'd wrap up by seven thirty or eight. Bailey was hoping she could grab a drink at the same bar and surreptitiously catch Skye's eye on her way out. It was Friday night, after all, and she'd certainly earned a drink after the week she'd had.

Bailey smiled, thinking of the look of surprise on Skye's face when she saw Bailey sitting at the bar before her expression morphed into that sexy smolder. Bailey loved to see Skye go from business mode to sexy-time mode, as she liked to think of it. Perhaps there could even be a little role-playing fun.

The bar was noisy when Bailey pulled open the door, but there were a surprising number of open seats for a Friday night, so she decided to duck into the restroom before grabbing one and shooting Skye a text to make sure they didn't miss each other. Skye had said she would text on her way out to see when Bailey would be finished, so Bailey felt pretty confident that she was here somewhere.

She scanned the room, both looking for a restroom as well as that telltale lob to make sure Skye didn't see her prematurely, or at least without Bailey planning it out. She saw neither the restroom nor Skye, but there was a corridor to the left of the bar that seemed the most logical place for the restrooms, so she headed that way. As she headed down the hall, lo and behold, she spotted the back of a perfect blond lob sitting at a high-top booth with three men. The musical tone of Skye's laugh as she leaned to the side and shoulder bumped the guy she was sitting next to confirmed that Bailey had found her quarry.

She paused as she decided how to play this. Did she want to forgo the restroom and sit at the bar facing Skye, completely surprising her on her way out? Or should she sneak past now and make eyes at her on the way back to the bar. Although a total surprise was appealing, a little heated glance to make sure Skye knew what was waiting for her when she finished up was infinitely more so.

Before she could keep moving, however, Bailey heard a bit of their conversation.

A scruffy-facial-hair guy who looked like he hadn't shaved in three days yet still could've stepped out of a J.Crew ad laughed loudly enough that everyone likely heard him. "Skye, you can't tell us that you don't have a trail of men crying into their hankies. You're too pretty not to."

The whole table erupted in laughter, and Bailey had to swallow a small amount of bile, but Skye's retort had her laughing too. "Give me a fucking break, Brad. I'm too pretty? The next thing you're going to say is that if I smiled more, I'd get more deals." She threw a paper straw wrapper at him, and Bailey silently cheered her on for calling him out.

The guy next to Skye shook his head and scoffed. "Jesus, Brad. Open mouth, insert foot, douche."

Brad tried to backpedal. "You know what I mean."

"No, Brad, actually, I don't." Bailey could hear the barest trace of venom in Skye's voice but doubted anyone else could.

Brad chuckled nervously, and Bailey almost felt bad for him, facing down what she could only assume was Skye's death stare. However, this guy was clearly an idiot, so she didn't feel too bad. "Uh, well, uh…You're a boss at the office, but at the same time you're really good-looking—"

"Dude," the guy next to Skye tried to get him to stop, but Brad was like a train about to derail, and nothing could stop it.

"How can you be so attractive but not be seeing anyone? You have to be keeping him secret or something." Brad's face was totally red, and he looked like he wished he could crawl into a hole, and yet, he kept digging deeper and deeper.

"Really? I'm attractive, so I have to be seeing someone? Do

you hear yourself? Rob is right, you *are* a douchebag. Firstly, my attractiveness or lack thereof has nothing to do with whether I choose to tie myself to someone. The next thing you're going to say is I'm too attractive to be a broker or a professional. And not that it's any of your business, but no, I'm not seeing anyone. How could I possibly have time? I've done more than twice the amount of leasing as you this year. And when I'm not leasing, I'm forced to reeducate boneheads like you."

Skye laughed, but Bailey felt like she'd been stabbed in the chest. She knew Skye was never going to announce that they were seeing each other, but she also hadn't expected Skye to lie about them, either. Deny Bailey's existence. The existence of their entire relationship. Skye could have easily continued deflecting, but she hadn't. How could that lie roll so easily off her tongue?

Skye might be more like Mary than Bailey had realized. The thought made her sick to her stomach.

She couldn't catch her breath and didn't feel like playing anymore, so she backed out of the hall and headed for the exit. She wasn't sure what she was going to do, but she definitely wasn't waiting around. She needed some space to think.

❖

By the time Skye had made her excuses and escaped, she was exhausted. She'd been playing the guy's guy for what felt like an eternity, and she wanted to get the hell home and catch up with Bailey, though she was beginning to wonder what was going on since Bailey hadn't texted her back yet. Bailey was supposed to be working late, but even when doing so, she always responded to Skye's texts right away.

She was staring at her phone when it started ringing. Her first thought was that maybe Bailey was finally calling, but alas, no. "Hey, Tasha. What's up?"

"Oh, nothing. It feels like forever since I saw you."

That was ridiculous. They'd just seen each other...when? Tasha was supposed to have been at a dinner with Bailey's family the week before, but she hadn't been feeling well, so she'd canceled. Was it the week before that? Shit. Two weeks? She couldn't remember for certain. She normally spoke to Tasha every few days and saw her at least once a week, if not more. "Crap, sorry, I've been busy."

"Doing what? Or should I say, doing whom?" All of Tasha's

neighbors could probably hear her guffaw at her own joke. Which wasn't nearly as funny as she thought it was.

Skye rolled her eyes but laughed with her. "It is an interesting predicament that I have found myself in."

"Is that what you call a relationship these days? A predicament? *Relationship* isn't a dirty word." A flicker of irritation flared in Skye at her patronizing tone.

"I don't know." Skye was walking aimlessly, not really paying attention to her surroundings other than that she was generally heading toward the lake. Bailey had been trying to be more respectful of Skye and not ditching her at the last minute, but relationships were still dicey. And she was still so cautious about her personal life at work. This evening with that idiot Brad was just more evidence that being a lesbian wasn't compatible with her career.

"What don't you know?"

Skye sighed and tried to work out what she wanted to say. "It's…I don't know. Hard."

"Most things worth your time *are* hard."

Skye laughed. "That's probably true. And I love spending time with Bailey, I really do. When we're together, things are nearly perfect, but sometimes, it's like work will always be her number-one priority. And I shouldn't be surprised. She told me from the start that she didn't have time for dating, but I just thought…I don't know." She kicked a paper cup from the sidewalk into the street with the toe of her Valentino caged pump and wondered why she was trying to scuff her shoe on litter. "I just don't know if I'm important enough to her. And I'm tired of lying about her."

"Why are you lying?" Tasha's voice was laced with disbelief. "Who are you lying about her to?"

"Ugh, the idiot bros I deal with at work."

"Why?"

"They don't need to know everything about me and my personal life." Skye tried to release the tension in her jaw at how unfair it all was.

"That may be true, but seriously, Skye. You shouldn't feel like you have to lie to *anyone* about who you are."

"I know, I know. But this is such a man's world, and I'm already seen as an outsider. I don't want to be that dyke bitch broker." That was the piece of it that was so frustrating. It really didn't matter how good she was. If she got blackballed, she'd be ruined.

"Who cares, Skye? They can think what they want as long as you keep getting your job done."

Skye clenched her jaw, annoyed that Tasha didn't get it. "But that's the point. I need to work *with* them in order to close deals. I'm very good, but I need them too."

"Kind of sounds like an excuse because you're scared, but giving you a hard time isn't actually why I called."

Clearly, Natasha didn't understand because she was a writer, not a businessperson. Regardless, Skye was relieved that she was moving on to a new topic. "So you didn't call me to be a pain in my ass? Pray tell, why did you call?"

"To see if you wanted to meet me at SoulCycle in the morning and get brunch after. It's been a while."

Skye's guilt pressed on her chest. If Tasha was calling to go to a class, something that she only ever reluctantly agreed to, she must really be missing her. "Yes, absolutely. Eight a.m.?"

Tasha laughed. "I said brunch after class, not breakfast. Let's do the ten thirty. Don't you have plans tonight? Do you really want to drag yourself out of the arms of a beautiful woman at seven a.m. to meet me?"

Good point. She was *hoping* she would be waking up next to a beautiful woman. Why hadn't Bailey texted yet? "I do have plans. At least, I think I have plans…anyway, fine, you slacker. Can you make the reservations? Front row if they're available."

When Skye hung up, she felt listless. She had walked until she'd hit Michigan Ave. and then back to get her car. She texted Bailey again and stared at her phone, willing Bailey to respond. What the hell was going on? Was Bailey ignoring her? Avoiding her? Bailey was likely still at work, but she never ignored Skye. Could something be wrong?

Maybe she should swing by Bailey's house and make sure everything was fine. If Bailey wasn't there, she would head home, but something felt off, and she couldn't shake it.

There was no parking on the street in front of Bailey's house, though the lights were on inside, so after a brief war with herself, Skye circled around until she found an open spot on the next block. She hated feeling like a little puppy following Bailey around and begging for attention, but she believed in confronting problems head-on and wasn't willing to sit at home and stew over what might be wrong.

Bailey's eyes widened when she opened the door after Skye's

short knock. She stared at her for a brief moment before saying, "Uh, hey."

That was all she got? Bailey had been ghosting her all evening, and she got a hey? Before Skye could say anything, Patsy shoved her nose between Bailey's legging-clad leg and the door and licked Skye's hand. Rather than addressing Bailey, Skye leaned over to pet Patsy. "Hey, sweet Patsy. It's good to see you."

"Do...you...want to come in?" Bailey wiped her palms on her leggings. Why was this so awkward? What was Bailey so nervous about?

Only one way to find out. "Yeah, I'd like that."

Bailey stepped back and let her into the house. It didn't look like Bailey had just gotten home. She had changed out of her work clothes, but there were other subtleties. She had a glass of wine sitting on the coffee table, her laptop was open, and the screen was on. And sitting right next to it was her phone. Bailey had been ignoring her. What the hell?

She knew Bailey could see the thoughts running through her head before she even got a question out. "Let me get you a glass of wine, and then let's talk."

"Okay," Skye whispered. She hated how unsure she felt. She wasn't a tentative person, but this was new territory, this whole relationship thing. And something weird was going on, but she'd just spoken to Bailey that morning, and everything had been fine.

"Here you go." Bailey handed her a glass and squeezed her other hand before sitting on the couch and grabbing her own glass. Skye's hand shook as she sank onto a chair across from the couch.

"How was your day?" That was a pretty safe place to start. Perhaps Bailey's mood had nothing to do with her.

"It was good until the end. Productive. I actually got out a little earlier than I thought."

Ouch. She'd gotten out early, hadn't reached out, and had dodged Skye's calls and texts all evening? That was fucked up. A response escaped Skye entirely, so she took a sip of wine and stared, hoping Bailey would elaborate. Waiting to see what she could possibly say to explain herself.

Bailey looked into her wine, back up at Skye, and then quickly away.

The silence technique seemingly wasn't going to work that night, so Skye said, "So why the complete radio silence?"

"I was...processing."

"Processing what?"

"When I got out of work, I was going to surprise you. Just happen to be sitting at the bar when you finished happy hour and were on your way out. I thought, maybe there could be a little role-play...something fun and spontaneous. I had no intention of intruding."

Skye's stomach started to churn, suspecting what Bailey must have heard, wishing she could go back in time.

"But I went down the hallway toward the restroom and saw the back of your head, so I paused to decide how I wanted to play it, and I overheard you with those guys. I wasn't trying to spy on you or eavesdrop. I only paused for a second and heard..." She pointedly looked away again.

Skye couldn't quite swallow. She'd already felt guilty about what she'd said to her colleagues, but knowing that Bailey had heard it—probably all of it—was worse. Much worse. "I'm sorry. You weren't supposed to hear that."

"That's all you have to say?" Bailey's face grew red, and she shoved off the couch and stalked around the room.

"No, that's not what I..." Skye needed Bailey to look at her as she tried to explain, even though it wasn't easy. She grabbed Bailey's hands. "That's not how I meant it. Those guys are just colleagues. They aren't friends. I'm not obligated to tell them anything, and I don't talk about my personal life at work. It drives them nuts, but I don't do it. It's none of their business."

"I'm not trying to say it *is* their business, but you blatantly lied. You could have evaded, but you actually said, and I quote, 'I'm not seeing anyone.' Do you understand how that feels? To be reduced to no one of importance in your life?" Bailey looked at the floor.

"That's not true. At all." She touched Bailey's chin with her thumb and forefinger and guided her gaze back up. "You are so very important to me. I'm not sure why I lied the way I did. I think I panicked because it scares me just how important you've become to me. You mean so much more to me than I thought you could. I'm sorry I hurt you. I'm sorry I said that, and I'm sorry you heard it. It was shitty. He pissed me off, and I said something stupid, but I didn't mean it. Not at all." She brushed her lips lightly across Bailey's. "I'm so sorry. Please believe me."

"You're better than that. You're an amazing woman, smart, funny, charismatic, you have impeccable taste—"

"I have heard that last one before." Skye chuckled.

"Not just the last one. All of them, and you don't need to hide who you are in order to succeed. I'm not trying to force you to be more open or anything. I hate that you underestimate yourself and your abilities. And I hate feeling like I don't mean anything to you. I'm scared too. This isn't something I do."

Skye's heart cracked knowing how badly she'd hurt Bailey that evening. "I know. I don't do this, either. I feel like I'm fumbling along, trying to figure it all out as we go. But I never want to hurt you. You mean so much to me." She rubbed her thumbs over the back of Bailey's hands. "I promise, I'll try to be more truthful. Maybe not totally open, but no more lying. And never about you. I promise."

The corners of Bailey's mouth lifted, and relief ran through Skye's body like warm honey in her veins. She loved that quarter smile. A little shy, a little smug, a lot sexy. And she knew she'd been forgiven. "You swear?"

"I do." Skye meant it, but she also had to get a little something off her chest as well. If she was going to be open and expose herself completely, she couldn't hold anything back. "Will you promise to not ignore me when you're upset? You had reason to be angry, but I hate that you stonewalled me all evening. It made me feel insignificant too, and I didn't even know what I'd done wrong."

"I promise." She pulled Skye into her arms, and Skye placed her head on Bailey's shoulder as her fingers traced paths up and down Skye's back. "I'm sorry."

It struck her as odd that Bailey was soothing her when she was the one who'd said something stupid. But Skye tightened her arms around Bailey as she realized how lucky she was. Bailey was one of a kind, and all of Skye's tension drained away. What was it about Bailey that soothed her soul?

❖

While Skye lay sleeping upstairs, Bailey sat on the edge of her planter box and grimaced as she pulled weed after weed from around her squash vines. She'd been neglecting her garden again, and it was, unfortunately, showing. The weeds were stealing valuable nutrients from the soil that should be going into her plants, and the vines were suffering as a result. But things had been hectic. She'd been trying to balance the demands of work with her family and with spending time with Skye, but it was hard. And moments like yesterday evening, when Skye had completely denied her existence, made Bailey second-guess herself.

The trouble was that she loved spending time with Skye. She made Bailey laugh like no one else, and when they weren't laughing, there was a comfort level between them that was like being wrapped in a warm hug. They just fit together. It felt like she'd known Skye for years and not a handful of months. She wanted to rearrange her life to spend more time with Skye, but she couldn't. Things at work were... dicey. A lot of people depended on her for their livelihoods.

But, God, Skye. She was beautiful, hilarious, not nearly as stuck-up as Bailey had originally thought, and loved her family in a way Bailey would have never believed if she hadn't been spending so much time with all of them. Bailey slid down her planter box and went to work on the weeds around the base of her tomato plants as she thought back to last night.

After they'd cleared the air and gone to bed, something had felt different from the other times they'd been together. Bailey couldn't quite put her finger on it, but it seemed more intimate. The orgasms had been as fantastic as always, but when they both came at the same time right before they'd fallen asleep, Bailey didn't think she'd ever felt closer to another person in her life. It was like she could feel Skye's orgasm, and it had intensified her own. It sounded woo-woo crazy even as she thought it, but she would have sworn it had happened.

It was as though she was looking over the precipice and could easily slip off the edge and tumble into love with Skye, and that was terrifying. Could she truly make room in her life for Skye full-time? Was Skye committed enough for that? Could she be trusted? Did she want something more too? Or if Bailey let herself go over that ledge, would she hit the bottom all alone?

"Hey, you." Skye's sleepy voice pulled her out of the very unhappy vision of her broken body lying alone at the bottom of a ravine. She'd gone very dark very quickly. Jesus.

Bailey felt an immediate jolt at seeing Skye standing in her backyard, wearing one of her T-shirts as well as the booty shorts that, if she recalled correctly, were the same ones Bailey had been wearing the first time Skye had come to her house unexpectedly early. She certainly had the legs to pull them off. Bailey was surprised she was wearing them outside where the neighbors could see but wasn't going to complain. "Good morning, sleepyhead."

"I wasn't expecting you to sneak out of bed this morning to do yard work." Skye scratched at a spot just above her ear, causing her small but messy bun to shift around on top of her head. Bailey was struck with a strong desire to pull that bun all the way out and run her fingers through those tresses again.

"I wouldn't call it sneaking. I woke up early and wanted to let you sleep. Plus, I figured I could do a little cleanup out here and then get a few things to go in omelets for breakfast." That was nearly true. While Bailey did want a little room to think, which the garden always gave her, she really did plan to make them breakfast as well.

"Oh, shoot, I told Tasha that I would go to SoulCycle with her this morning and then hit brunch, so I can't do breakfast."

Bailey's heart fell. The weekends were when she and Skye were able to spend actual time together rather than just grabbing stolen moments. Then she silently chastised herself for being clingy.

"You could come with us if you want."

"No, I can't do that. You and Natasha haven't seen each other in weeks. You should go have fun. We can catch up later today if you have time and want to."

Skye stepped into the garden and leaned down for a quick kiss. "Oh, I want."

"You taste minty."

"I brushed my teeth before I came out here. I wasn't raised in a barn."

Her devilish smile had Bailey thinking of all the things they could do in a barn. Or in her garage, which they were next to. "I never said you were. Though I am a little surprised at your choice of shorts."

"Do you not like me borrowing your clothes?" Skye's brows furrowed.

"Goodness, not that at all. I love, *love* seeing you in my clothes." Bailey wrapped an arm around Skye's legs. "They might be a little, tiny bit short." She ran her thumb just under the bottom edge of the shorts and was surprised to discover Skye wasn't wearing any underwear. Need flooded Bailey's body. Her mouth ached to taste, her fingers itched to feel, her skin burned to be touched. It was times like this that she wished she lived out in the country and didn't have any neighbors who could see or hear anything.

Skye swatted her hand away. "What are you doing? We're outside."

"I was simply illustrating *why* those shorts were a surprising choice. As is the lack of underwear. Not at all an unpleasant surprise.

You should feel free to wear them like this anytime you like. I think they're perfect."

"Hmm." Skye stared at her with squinty eyes in the morning sun. Even that was gorgeous.

"What time do you have to leave?" Bailey asked, hoping she'd have time for the activities running through her mind.

"Probably an hour."

"Plenty of time."

"For what?" Skye said.

"I think you've asked me that question before, but let's go inside, and I'll show you again. Quickly, before we scandalize Mrs. Martin." Although Bailey had dropped her arm lower when Skye shooed it away, she hadn't let go and was still running her thumb along the back of Skye's thigh.

"You are incorrigible but sexy as hell in your little gardener's outfit." Skye swirled her finger at Bailey's knee-length leggings, tank top, and sun hat. She grabbed both of Bailey's hands and pulled her up.

"It's the sun hat that really gets you hot and bothered, isn't it?"

Skye's tongue darted out, moistening her lower lip. "It really does. You might need to keep that on for what I have in mind."

They both broke out into laughter and raced toward the back door.

CHAPTER TWENTY-ONE

Skye was on top of the world. She'd had drinks the night before with Ellie, who was set to close on her big redevelopment next week. She'd told Skye that after the leasing activity so far, just one more lease at the Maxwell and it was all hers. That assignment was going to be such a feather in Skye's cap, and it was going to give her a very nice cushion in her bank account. At least seven figures if she was as successful as she knew she would be.

Then this morning, she'd closed a deal for another full-floor tenant at the Maxwell, so Skye was looking forward to shifting some of her responsibilities here to a junior team member. And now she was standing in the spec suite with Rob and one of his clients, and it looked like, as icing on the cake, she was going to get another deal today.

The clients were ignoring Rob and Skye as they gushed over everything. They loved the view, they loved the finishes, they loved the layout. And it was lovely for Skye that they were doing all her work for her.

"I keep trying to tell my clients to play it cool. Don't make it seem like you like the space so much. It makes my negotiations much harder when the enemy knows how much they love it," Rob said softly and laughed.

Skye stepped a little closer so they could speak without fear of being overheard. "Oh, Rob, there was no chance of that. These three don't have one poker face between them. If you wanted to keep their love of the space a secret, you shouldn't have invited me," she said, feeling smug.

"You wouldn't let me tour without you, if you recall," he quipped. "But in my defense, I didn't know how much they were going to like this suite."

"Robert, Robert, Robert, why do you think that is?" Skye placed a hand on his arm as she patronized him. "I don't like to miss out on any intel that could give me an advantage. Or put me at a disadvantage." She smiled at him sweetly, batted her eyes a bit, knowing it would irritate the hell out of him.

He rolled his eyes and shook her hand off. "Whatever, Skye. If they lease this space, I win as much as you do, so be as patronizing as you want, but in the end, our goals are aligned. Unless they want to lease somewhere else, in which case, you're out of luck." He flashed his perfect teeth.

"Luckily, that's not these guys." She gave him her cockiest smile because she could feel this deal coming her way in her bones.

"I'm pretty sure you're right, which just makes you annoying as hell, and I don't know why I like you." He shrugged.

"It's because of my winning personality, isn't it?"

"I said you're annoying as hell, and that says winning personality to you?"

She hit him in the shoulder. "Yeah, but I knew you didn't really mean annoying the way you said it."

"You're right. I do like you. Maybe because I actually know you. Speaking of which, God, Brad was being an asshat the other night. I was embarrassed on behalf of my fellow enlightened men at the shit he was saying and offended on your behalf too."

She rolled her eyes but was reminded why she liked Rob so much. "I know, right? What was his problem? I wanted to punch him right in his chauvinistic mouth."

"You and me both. Oh, hey." He stepped closer and dropped his voice further. "After you left, Brad asked if you were a lesbian."

"He what?" She had to fight to keep her voice down in light of her panic.

"It's not a big deal. I know you don't talk about your personal life, so I blew him off and said he was jealous because you'd turned him down half a dozen times before he stopped asking. It seriously doesn't matter to me, obviously, and I'd bet ninety-nine percent of the industry, but I wanted to tell you so you're aware."

It was easy for him to say that it wasn't a big deal. He was married to a lovely woman, and they had two kids and a dog. He fit into the heteronormative world seamlessly. He'd never in his life been made to feel *other*. "Fuck."

"Truly, it's not a big deal. I don't think Brad is going to start anything, and even if he did, no one is going to care. Honestly, the speculation might get you more tours as everyone tries to see if they can tell if you're a lesbian or not."

"Oh my God, Rob, is that supposed to make me feel better? That I'm going to get more tours while everyone comes to gawk at the freak show?" She fought to stay calm even as she could feel hyperventilation building.

"I did *not* say freak show. Just the rumor mill. But come on. It's going to be fine."

"Easy for you to say. Ugh. Why did I tell you about myself anyway?" she said, only half in jest.

"You dated my sister. It's not like you actually *told* me anything."

"Ah, yes. If I'd known you were Andrea's brother, I might have tried being a little more discreet." She didn't actually mean that. It was kind of nice having a few people in the industry know her secret, and Rob was a good guy. "How is Andrea anyway?" Although they'd broken up after a couple of months because Skye had needed to avoid anything serious, she really did like her and wished her only the best.

"She's great. Sharon is expecting again, so that will be number two for them."

"That's excellent," Skye said but was prevented from saying anything else when Rob's clients finally walked back over.

"Oh, we simply love it," one woman said, and Skye felt her excitement build again.

"That's so great to hear," Skye said, suppressing her smile. "I look forward to receiving your RFP."

"Definitely," the same woman said, and Skye was pretty sure she could hear Rob's teeth clenching.

She checked her watch, wondering what was holding Bailey up. She'd texted an hour ago, asking if Bailey wanted to meet for lunch since Skye was unexpectedly at the Maxwell and was pretty sure Bailey was also there for the attorneys' buildout.

❖

Bailey roared away from the Maxwell in disbelief. She'd thought that she and Skye had been making progress. She'd been excited for the impromptu lunch that Skye had suggested, but why on Earth had Skye invited her to meet in the spec suite and had then been groping one of those GQ guys when she got there? It didn't make any sense.

And why did Skye think she needed to behave that way? She was amazing without resorting to flirting or hanging all over guys in order to close deals.

When Bailey had walked up to the glass doors, she'd thought Skye and that guy were standing awkwardly close, but then Skye had put a hand on his arm, batted her eyelashes, and leaned in. And he'd leaned down as well, bringing his ear almost to her mouth.

Rather than walk in, Bailey had turned and headed to her car. Right before she'd pulled away, she'd sent Skye a short text saying she'd been pulled away and couldn't make lunch. She didn't want to freeze Skye out again, but she needed time to figure out if she was overreacting or if her hurt and anger were justified. She felt pretty damn justified in that moment but admitted that she had a little baggage when it came to cheating.

Dammit. Why did she have to walk in on that? Why was Skye flirting with that damn guy? It felt so similar to walking in on Mary with her flavor of the week. She knew the situations were different, but the betrayal felt the same. She slammed her hand against the steering wheel. That felt pretty good, so she did it three more times before the side of her fist got a sore. And she was worried she might hit someone driving in city traffic while banging on the car and not paying enough attention to what was going on in the street.

As she drove, she received a text from Skye that she had the car read: *Sorry we couldn't grab lunch. Are you up for dinner tonight?* "Would you like to respond?"

Bailey didn't really want to respond yet but also didn't want to stonewall Skye again, so she responded with a simple message even Siri couldn't mess up. "Sure. Seven, question mark."

Miraculously, Siri dictated it back perfectly, so Bailey sent it.

At six forty-five, Bailey was still upset and hurt and angry. She wasn't sure how she was going to handle this, but she knew it wasn't going to be a good conversation. She knew she couldn't simply brush it off as though nothing had happened. And yet she hadn't given Skye a heads-up that she was upset or that they needed to talk, so she was sure Skye was going to feel blindsided. But then again, Bailey had been blindsided that afternoon when she'd seen Skye flirting with Mr. GQ broker.

Patsy started whining and spinning in circles at the front door, so she knew she was out of time. Skye was there. She pushed down the nausea and pulled open the door before Skye even had a chance to knock.

Before Bailey could even greet her, Skye swooped Bailey into a hug, spinning her around and said, "I had such a good day today. And yesterday and I can't wait to tell you about…it." Skye's expression fell as her gaze truly fell on Bailey's face. "But you look like your day was the opposite. Do you want to talk about it?"

"Yeah," Bailey said, resigned. "Let me grab a glass of wine. I've got a bottle breathing in the kitchen." She walked into the kitchen as if she had lead weights around her ankles. She did not want to do this, but she couldn't not talk to Skye and still respect herself tomorrow.

When she came back into the living room, Skye was looking at the framed photo on her bookshelf of Bailey and her siblings from about fifteen years ago, when they'd gone on a cruise for their parents' anniversary. "You all look so young here. Happy," she said.

"You think I don't look happy now?" Bailey said.

"Normally? Yes. At this moment, no, and I'm really nervous about it. You look like you're about to face a firing squad. Or like you're going to be on a firing squad, and I'm a little nervous if I'm the one your gun is aimed at." Skye laughed nervously and played with a lock of her hair. A very unusual twitch for her. "But I have no idea what's going on."

"I wouldn't say a firing squad, but I saw you today."

"You saw me today? Where? What happened?"

"In the spec suite with that GQ guy." Bailey didn't think she'd have to spell it out. She hadn't had to after the bar incident.

"Right." Skye drew the word out into three syllables. "Rob and I were chatting while his client toured the space. I think I'm going to get the deal, which is amazing news. I thought you were going to come meet me so we could go to lunch."

Did she really have no idea what she'd done? Apparently, Bailey *had* to spell out every single detail. She ground her teeth to steel herself. "I saw you flirting with him."

"What?"

"I saw you stepping closer, putting your hand on his arm, batting your eyes, practically whispering in his ear." Bailey was trying to keep her voice below a yell, but it was getting harder. Patsy left the room and went to curl up on her bed in the kitchen, guilting Bailey into sitting and keeping her voice at a normal volume.

"Are you kidding me? We were having a quiet conversation because I was making fun of his clients, and I didn't want them to hear. *If* I batted my eyes at him, it was because I was giving him a hard time about not doing his job. I was being patronizing, not flirty."

"That's not what it looked like. You were all over him. He was all over you." Bailey quickly gave up trying to sit and started pacing. "How can you do that? Why do you think you *need* to do that?"

"Oh my God, Bailey, we weren't flirting. I've known Rob forever. I dated his sister briefly in the early days of my career, so he's one of the few colleagues who knows that I'm a lesbian. He's married with two kids. There was no flirting happening."

"Fine, so maybe not today, but you *do* do it, don't you? To get a deal closed." Bailey wasn't sure why she was pushing so hard, but she felt compelled. She had to know, and Skye had to know that it wasn't okay.

"I don't flirt to get my way."

"Are you sure? You never lean in a little close, never bat your eyes just so, are never willing to do anything and everything to sway someone?" To push her point, Bailey batted her lashes.

"No," Skye yelled.

"No?" Bailey couldn't believe she was trying to deny that piece of her skillset when she was pushing to close something. Anything.

"I…" Skye shook her head and took a long sip of wine. "I might occasionally flirt a little, but it doesn't matter. It's not like I mean it. No one takes it seriously. It's a little friendly banter to help close the deal, that's it."

"How is you flirting with guys, or even other women, not a big deal?" Bailey couldn't catch her breath. "Can't you see how hurtful that is?" She paused long enough to take her own large sip of wine. Somehow, she swallowed past the tightness in her throat.

"It doesn't *mean* anything. It's just joking around. And anyway, if you want to talk about hurtful, how about how often you blow me off for work? It's as though I'm in absolute last place behind all your other obligations: work, your family, Patsy…everything comes before I do in your life." She stared at Bailey with her hand on her hip. Bailey could feel the anger seething off her, which was funny since she was the one in the wrong here.

"You can't just change the subject. We're talking about how *you* disregard our relationship whenever being with me is inconvenient.

You lie about us, you blatantly flirt with whomever will get you what you want, as though we don't exist."

"Oh, so you can be hurt when our relationship is disregarded, but I can't be? You can infer something that isn't actually happening and get angry at me, but I'm not allowed to be hurt when you *actually* blow me off? All. The. Time. This goes both ways."

Bailey felt a coldness seep into her bones that she'd never felt before. She'd known for years that she wasn't meant for a long-term relationship, and she'd clearly made a mistake when she'd naively believed that they had a chance to prove her incorrect. "Clearly, we've both been laboring under a misapprehension that we could make this work. That we, two fiercely independent businesswomen, have time for a relationship. Obviously, that was a mistake. I don't have the time, and you don't have the commitment to make something work, so I think we should call this what it is—a mistake—and move on."

"What?" Skye's mouth went slack as she stared, and Bailey felt her lunch churn in her belly.

"I've just realized that this has all been a mistake. We aren't relationship people. Neither of us. We should stop now before either of us gets hurt. Don't you think?" Bailey felt herself completely shut down, and she needed to get Skye out of there before she fell apart.

"You're just giving up?" Skye's voice cracked. "You don't even want to try to make us work? You don't see anything worth trying to save?"

"We tried, but we clearly have different values. Want different things. Think different behaviors are acceptable. We have different moral codes." They obviously weren't compatible, and Skye had confirmed what Bailey had known all along. The person at the helm of City Beautiful Construction wasn't meant to be with someone long-term. First Mary and now Skye. Bailey was too busy to be a good partner, and Skye clearly had other priorities as well. Flirting, manipulating, and gaslighting were only a step away from cheating, and Bailey was never going to end up *there* again.

"Okay, well I thought this was just a fight, but clearly, it isn't. I'll go. Thank you for the education and the wine." She stared as though waiting for Bailey to stop her, but Bailey couldn't. After a moment, Skye said, "I guess I'll see you around."

Skye went over to Patsy in the other room and squatted. It looked like she was saying something to her, but Bailey couldn't hear it. She kissed her on the head and walked out the door without a backward glance.

When the door clicked behind her, Bailey collapsed on the couch and finally let loose the tears she'd been fighting all afternoon, ever since she'd seen Skye with her hands all over Mr. GQ. She cried for what they'd had and lost and what they could've had but now never would. She knew she was making the right decision, but it still felt like she was ripping her own heart out. She'd been falling for Skye, but they were just too different. Their differing opinions on what was acceptable in a relationship was a fundamental stumbling block that would keep them from ever working.

Skye was exactly like Mary.

Patsy walked over and nudged Bailey's hand with her head, and when Bailey didn't start petting her, she licked it. "Come here, girl." When Patsy climbed up on the couch, Bailey buried her face in her neck and truly let go.

CHAPTER TWENTY-TWO

Everything was super. Outstanding. Awesome, even. Skye had closed that deal with Rob's tenants for the spec suite. The spec suite she'd pushed Ellie toward, had helped design, and had ended up leasing for a much higher price than she'd originally predicted. Skye should have felt amazing. She'd also closed another deal for a full-floor tenant and achieved Ellie's leasing goal for the building an entire year early.

She was just great. Perfect, even.

Nothing was wrong. Skye had everything she needed. So why did she feel so…empty? She leaned her head against the cool window of the taxi. She was probably going to get a staph infection or something from it, but holding her head up was too exhausting in the moment, and she couldn't bring herself to do it. She'd always known that a breakup with Bailey had been inevitable.

It had been more than a week, and she hadn't told her family yet. Her mom and Babulya were going to be upset. Though Skye wasn't sure if they were going to be sadder for Skye or madder that they couldn't hang out with the Kaczmareks anymore. Skye hated the thought of being a disappointment. She hated disappointing anyone, but especially her family. Most of her life, she'd tried to make her mom and Babulya proud of her, to make sure they knew that their sacrifices from her childhood had been worth it. She knew that she was knocking it out of the park financially, but otherwise…well, she didn't know if she'd made anyone proud outside of work.

But work…well, work made her feel good. Work gave her self-esteem, self-worth. She got shit done at work. It was why she'd always put work first. She was actually heading to meet with Ellie for lunch and was pretty sure she was going to get that new redevelopment officially. Today was going to be another win.

And thus, everything was super, outstanding, and awesome. Totally perfect. Could not have been better.

She stepped out of her cab right behind Ellie. Perfect timing. Exactly. Everything was totally perfect. She wondered how many times she would have to say that to herself to make it true. Or to at least, make herself almost believe it. At least one more time. Totally perfect.

Nope, still not there yet. Fuck.

Ellie's expression was unbridled excitement when she saw Skye and waved, so Skye tried to match it, even as she thought it quite possible that she was bleeding to death inside. No, that wasn't right. Everything was totally perfect. Yeah.

"Howdy," Ellie said in greeting.

"Howdy, huh? Did you just get back from Texas?" Skye forced a laugh.

"In fact, I did, but I don't think anyone down there actually said howdy. It's a standard American greeting."

"Ah. Standard American greeting back to you, old friend." Skye pulled Ellie into a light hug and kissed her cheek. "You look great, by the way."

"You always say that, but I'm going to believe you this time. You look…" Ellie pursed her lips and studied her with an intensity that made her uncomfortable. "Sad, which I'm not sure I've ever seen. Are you okay?"

"I'm fine, really. Great. As long as this conversation goes the way I think it's going to, I'm perfect." Skye forced a smile she didn't feel, and Ellie just cocked her head. "I promise. I'm fine."

"Okay." She squeezed Skye's upper arm and smiled. "Let's go eat. We have a lot to talk about."

Skye wasn't sure if Ellie believed her assurances of being okay, but she was grateful that she wasn't pushing. Skye wasn't ready to talk about her personal life and would much rather focus on work. Something she was *actually* good at.

Once they were settled and laid the menus back down, Ellie said, "Amazing work in the last seven days at the Maxwell. I asked for one good lease, and you got me three. We've only got a few tiny spaces left in that building, and that's all because of you. I am blown away by your skill, Skye."

"It was a lot of luck and some great decisions on all our parts. Also, that spec suite…" Skye shook her head and couldn't stop her smirk as she thought of how great the suite had turned out. "As I told you, it sold itself."

"Timing and luck always play into everything, but much of luck is being overprepared so you're ready when the opportunity presents itself. You embody that, Skye, and I couldn't be luckier to count you as both a professional ally as well as a friend."

Skye felt her cheeks heat and wished she could stop that physiological reaction that made her embarrassment even worse.

"On that note," Ellie said. "Let's do this redevelopment together."

Skye looked up and drew her lips back into a smile that hopefully looked more genuine than it felt. This was something she'd been working toward for months—something she had been dreaming of—for eons, truthfully, and she knew she should be happy, so she was feigning the happy until she could actually feel it. "Excellent."

"Do you mean that?"

"Absolutely, Ellie. I'm so excited to kick this off."

Ellie smiled big. "Well, okay, do you want to walk the site tomorrow and strategize?"

"I can make that work. Whatever time is good for you, I'll rearrange my schedule." Skye tried to shake herself into excitement. Why couldn't she drum up any enthusiasm for this huge accomplishment? It was the highest profile opportunity of her career. But in truth, she knew the reason—it felt empty not being able to share it with Bailey.

Since that was a hopeless endeavor, she buried it and tried to focus on the exciting new project that she was about to embark on. *Fake it till you feel it.* She could do this.

❖

Patsy harumphed at Bailey's feet under the desk. Bailey knew she was tired of being in the office and was ready to go home and go to bed, but since she'd broken up with Skye, Bailey had been working a lot of hours, trying to keep her mind busy. It was never as successful as she'd hoped as her thoughts again found their way back to Skye. Where they almost always found themselves at this time of night, when her defenses were weak, and the office quiet. Still, better the office than her empty house.

Bailey knew she needed to let Skye go and stop thinking about her all the time. Their breakup had been inevitable. Uncle Chester had four ex-wives, and she had a very near miss with Mary, who'd probably strayed because Bailey had left her alone too often. And there were similarities between Mary and Skye that were hard to unsee once she'd seen them.

Both were a little self-absorbed and were always worried about appearances and status. Both clearly needed a lot of attention—Mary with the women she'd had affairs with and Skye from all the brokers or anyone in her orbit who she wanted something from. Bailey wasn't enough to keep either woman's attention or focus.

Fuck. Bailey rubbed her tired eyes and picked up her phone to check the time. Nine o'clock. Bailey was relieved that she had Patsy with her so she didn't have to ask Mrs. Martin to let her out. Again. Before Bailey set her phone down, however, the picture widget on her home screen caught her eye.

A smiling selfie of her and Skye stared at her. It was from their first real date, when Bailey had taken her to dinner and then for a walk along the lake. It had been a gorgeous night, and that was when she'd really started falling for Skye. Her heart squeezed at how happy they'd been that evening. Bailey had actually been starting to believe that maybe they could have a chance. That night, it had seemed that if she and Skye really wanted to figure out how to make a relationship work despite the obvious hurdles, they could.

Evidently, she was wrong. They'd never had a chance. But she'd been completely happy and fulfilled before she'd met Skye and was confident she could get back there again. Or if not completely happy, at least content. Fulfilled enough. She could definitely find that again.

She ground her teeth at the photo. She opened the app with the intention of deleting it and even tapped her thumb on the trash can, but when the phone asked if she was sure she wanted to do that, she couldn't bring herself to actually delete it. She zoomed in on Skye's face and barely resisted the urge to caress the screen even as Skye's features blurred through tears.

She scoffed at herself and swiped to close everything before laying her phone facedown on her desk. "What do you think, Patsy-girl? Are you ready to head home?"

At the sound of the word "home," Patsy jumped from the floor and stretched. She gave a huge yawn but started walking toward the door. Bailey chuckled at her cuteness. Even when everything else in her life felt like it was going to shit, Patsy always managed to make her smile. She'd done that when Bailey was broken after Mary too.

Bailey picked her phone up again after she put her laptop into her messenger bag and felt the vibration of a new text coming in. Her heart skipped at the thought that maybe it was Skye. Not that she had any idea what she wanted Skye to say since Bailey had been the one to end things.

But thankfully, it was her mother verifying Bailey was going to get out of work early on Friday for dinner. Bailey promised she would even as she dreaded it. She was going to have to fess up to her family about things falling apart with Skye, and she *really* wasn't looking forward to that.

CHAPTER TWENTY-THREE

Skye stepped out of her taxi and took in the grandiose building that was about to become her new baby. It was magnificent. It had been neglected for decades, and getting to play a role in the revitalization of such a beautiful art deco building was exciting. Whoever had let it fall into such disrepair should have been arrested.

Skye's gaze lifted skyward, and she took in the terra-cotta cornices along the rooflines of the lower roofs and the gorgeous, if neglected, spires on the top roof and couldn't help but think of how much Bailey would appreciate this building. She loved restoring something old and repurposing it into something new. And this building had pizzazz. It reminded Skye of that fateful night at Navy Pier when Bailey had pointed out all of the architecture in the grand ballroom.

Skye both hoped and feared that Ellie would be bringing Bailey in on this too. She would hate to deny Bailey this project because she knew how much Bailey would love it. Bailey's company didn't do exterior restoration on this scale, but she very possibly would be the contractor Ellie hired to do the lobby renovation and build out the amenities. Well, Skye would cross that bridge if she came to it. She was confident that she and Bailey were professionals and could work together, even if seeing her every day would feel like her heart was being ripped out and thrown into a vat of salt and lemon juice.

Thankfully, Ellie walked up and pulled Skye out of her inner monologue. "A beauty, isn't she?"

"Oh yes. Don't get me wrong, I love the sleekness of glass and steel buildings, but art deco is my absolute favorite. They have some weird quirks that I sometimes have to do some tap-dancing around to make them sell, but the architecture is breathtaking. Truly."

"I know, I fell in love with this building the moment I saw she was on the market and had to make her mine. Let's go look at the lobby, and I can outline my ideas, and then we can go look at the areas I was considering for amenity spaces."

Skye's breath escaped her again when they walked into the lobby. It was vaulted, about twenty-five feet high. Midway into the space, the light well opened up above the lobby so natural light flooded the space through the geometric-patterned glass. A pair of grand staircases wound around both sides of the lobby to a mezzanine that again reminded Skye of that night on the Navy Pier.

She could still feel the press of Bailey's lips against hers that very first night. She'd had no idea then exactly how well she and Bailey were going to connect on every level. She'd thought she'd been walking away from sizzling chemistry, but in the months since, she'd come to realize how amazing a person Bailey was.

She tried not to admit it, even to herself, but she couldn't deny that she missed Bailey. A lot. She wanted to call her and tell her about this amazing career win. She wanted to subtly encourage Ellie to hire Bailey to do the interior work if that wasn't the way she was leaning, both because Bailey was the best person for the job but also because doing it would bring her so much joy. She wanted to share all of this with her and felt an incredibly deep-seated loss at her inability to do so. This huge win felt hollow. Her chest should have been full with the excitement but instead, it felt like a Costco-sized pill bottle with two aspirin rattling in it.

"Skye? Are you still with me?"

Ellie's voice brought her back to reality. Shit. She so wasn't with her and had no idea what Ellie had been saying.

"Sorry, lost in my thoughts for a second. What were you saying?" Why hadn't Skye said something about being distracted by the space? Dammit.

"What's going on with you? You never space out like that. And you look sad. Sadder than I've ever seen you. And don't tell me it's nothing. I've known you far too long for you to keep lying to me."

Skye smiled and tried to stand up straighter and pull her shoulders back so perhaps her sadness wouldn't be written all over her body.

"It's too late to pretend for me, Skye."

Dammit. "We're on the clock here. I don't want to burden you with my personal problems." Skye wasn't willing to be unprofessional or put any cloud over this project.

Ellie scoffed. "Don't give me that. We are professionals, but we're also friends, and something has you deep down in the dumps. Tell me about it. I care about you." Ellie gasped. "Wait, is everything okay with your mom? Babulya?"

"Yes, they're fine." Skye sighed and resigned herself to tell the truth, if just for expediency. "Bailey and I broke up." Even just *saying* the words was painful. As though she was swallowing glass.

"Oh no, I'm so sorry. I never spent time with the two of you together, but knowing you both pretty well, I thought you were perfect for each other."

"It's for the best, really. We're too different. And we're way too busy. Neither of us has time to commit to a relationship."

Ellie scoffed. "You obviously had time to spend together, as you were seeing each other for weeks, weren't you? Months? What happened that led to the actual breakup? If you don't mind me asking."

Ellie pulled her over to sit on a low marble wall around a planter in the lobby. She leaned back on her hands and closed her eyes, trying to block out the feelings that wanted to overwhelm her. "I don't know…" But she did know. "Bailey saw me chatting with Rob while closing the spec suite deal. She misinterpreted our closeness and thought I was flirting with him to get the deal closed."

"Well, that's absurd," Ellie exclaimed and shook her head. "That's not how you operate."

"It's not," Skye admitted. "And yet, she has some other points. I'm not out in our professional community because I'm afraid it's going to hold me back, and the good ol' boys club won't want to work with me anymore. And I know it's going to sound conceited, but I know I'm attractive, and some of the brokers want to work with me because of it. I make myself into 'one of the guys,' and I'm afraid that if they know I'm dating a woman, they won't accept me anymore and might blackball me."

"That's insane, Skye. I'm out and haven't had any issues. This isn't the same industry of a decade or two ago."

"Yeah, but you're in a different position than I am. You own buildings, and brokers want a chance to get your landlord rep business, and more than that, they want to get paid for whatever deal they can, so they're going to bring deals to you."

"How is that different from you? You represent me as the owner, so if a broker has a client who wants to be in one of my buildings, they're going to bring that client through. They don't care what building their client goes into, as long as it's one that is going to pay them a commission. And we do. Quickly. And the brokers don't want to work with you because you're 'one of the guys' or because you're attractive and flirty. They want to work with you because you're good at your job, you deliver on what you promise, and you work your ass off. You don't cut corners, and you don't waste their time."

"Hmm," Skye said, not committing. She'd always thought Ellie didn't have any issues because as an owner, she was in a position of higher authority, but she supposed it was true that she was essentially an extension of Ellie when she was showing space in her buildings.

"And another thing," Ellie continued. "Being a lesbian would make you more 'one of the guys' than being a straight woman, don't you think? I wouldn't recommend it, but you could talk about women together at the bar, which you can't do right now since you pretend to be straight."

Maybe Skye had been hanging on to this closet for reasons that weren't entirely valid. That was a sickening possibility. It was true that Ellie had always been out. She was pretty femme but had always made it clear when any guys tried to flirt with her, so it had pretty much gone around the real estate community. Skye had always been sure that she was known as the "Bitch Broker" behind her back and had been terrified that "dyke" would be added to that already unflattering nickname if she came out, but maybe none of it was true. "You really don't think I'd be branded that Dyke Bitch Broker?"

Ellie laughed so hard that she snorted and leaned forward. "No, I really don't think so. And so what if you are? Money is a motivating factor for every broker out there, and they aren't going to blackball you to the detriment of their own bank accounts. You rep a lot of amazing buildings, and I'm not only talking about my own. And I have a lot of friends in this industry…the managing brokers at most brokerage houses, a lot of other building owners. If someone tries to hit you below the belt, we'll get him blackballed. Thankfully, that type of thing simply isn't socially acceptable anymore. You have nothing to fear from coming out."

Skye wasn't sure if Ellie was entirely right, but she did have some points that, on the surface, seemed valid. Skye was going to have to sit with them for a bit, but she did feel a little relief knowing that Ellie thought she'd be completely okay if she came out. Maybe if she was out and didn't have to evade questions about her personal life, Bailey would jump to less conclusions.

She needed to steer clear of that line of thinking. She was certain—based on how Bailey had acted like what they'd had was nothing, had never been something—it was too late with her.

"Thank you, Ellie. Knowing you wouldn't fire me if I did come out is a relief." Skye laughed at the ridiculous notion. With Ellie being a lesbian as well, now that she thought about it, she couldn't imagine Ellie firing her. "And also knowing you don't think anything would change for me is a relief too."

After they finished touring the building and discussing ideas for the amenity spaces, Skye didn't feel like going back to the office, so she wandered aimlessly until dusk, when she finally made her way to the lake. She always enjoyed wandering along the Lakefront Trail, listening to the waves gently breaking against the seawall.

She both wanted to believe and yet also feared that Ellie was right. Had she been making this whole professional closet thing much bigger than it needed to be? It was a painful thought. Staying in that closet had ruined her chance at a personal life. A romantic one, anyway. Clearly, it had affected her doomed relationship with Bailey, but it had also hurt every relationship she'd had since college, not that there had been many.

Ever since an encounter early in her career with the first broker she'd ever worked for, she'd believed she needed to keep that side of herself hidden in order to succeed. He'd apparently seen her meeting up with her girlfriend, Andrea, Rob's sister, at the end of a company happy hour. The next morning, he'd pulled her into his office and had told her this industry wasn't ready for "those types of relationships" and probably never would be. He'd also said that if she wanted to be as successful as he knew she could be—if she wanted to live up to the potential he saw in her, the potential that was the reason he'd taken a chance on her right out of college—she'd better keep that part of her life quiet.

He was a dick, but Skye had learned so much from him that she'd always heeded his advice. She'd put a successful career ahead of everything in her life the way he had. He was retired now, but Skye realized that she still lived under the umbrella of his limiting beliefs and bigotry.

She kept walking and eventually found herself in Millennium Park, standing in front of Cloud Gate, also known as the Bean. She'd always loved the cheesy tourist attraction. There was something about the distorted reflection of the city that she found soothing. Looking at the lights in the early evening, the city looked nearly perfect, which it certainly wasn't. The distortion in the curved metal, however, made the perfect image seem more real. A more accurate reflection of a remarkable city that had its share of problems.

She sat on a picnic table and split her attention between the tourists milling about and the reflection in the Bean. She could see herself sitting on the table, even though she was quite a distance away, but she was just a speck, so she walked to the Bean until she could reach out and touch it. It felt as smooth as it looked, but she had a hard time making eye contact with herself.

She'd been reflecting on herself a lot on her walk, and in the distorted reflection, she was afraid she'd see her true self, and she worried about who that was. Was it the person who'd sometimes tried to bully and bulldoze her way through life? She knew she wasn't perfect and would never claim to be, but taking a close look made her realize how she might come off, and she didn't like it at all.

Would she stare back into the eyes of a shameless flirt who sometimes went a little too far when trying to close a deal? She didn't want to admit that, but it was hard to entirely deny. It wasn't like she did that all the time, but it might *occasionally* happen. Perhaps it had been true when she'd been speaking to that subcontractor of Bailey's. She hadn't meant anything by it, but she didn't even know that guy, and yet, she'd leaned into him, touched his arm.

Who was she? Who was she supposed to be? Was she still trying to be that person, or had she decided to ignore the person she wanted to be in her pursuit of the top deals in the market and achieving distinction for herself?

Skye felt nauseated by the person she was sometimes. She knew that the manipulative person who would do whatever it took to get the deal wasn't who she really was at her core, and from that moment on, she would never go back to acting like that. Skye had some amends to make and decided to start with her family and then figure out what she would, or even could, do to get Bailey to talk to her. Although Bailey had completely misinterpreted what she'd seen going on with her and Rob and had jumped to the worst conclusion, she had a point that Skye hadn't been able to see until now.

Skye couldn't fully believe that Bailey wouldn't want to see her. There had always been something about them that didn't make sense and yet made all the sense in the world. She just needed to figure out how to make Bailey understand and give them another chance. One final new beginning.

❖

Skye walked into the apartment without knocking, just as she'd been told to do for years but had so rarely heeded. "Mama, Babulya? Hello, is anyone home?"

"Out here, Bunny," Babulya said from the living room. *Wheel of Fortune* was turned up to a near-blaring level, and Babulya sat in her favorite easy chair with a rocks glass and two fingers of what Skye assumed to be brandy, her favorite, with a few ice cubes. "What are you doing stopping by so late with no warning?"

"It's been a weird day, and I wanted to talk to you and Mama about a few things if you're up for it. Is she here too?"

"She'll be right back. She just walked over to the corner store to get some butter pecan ice cream."

"Of course she did." Skye chuckled and kept her stress remark about how her mom shouldn't walk to the grocery store this late in her head. And truthfully, the neighborhood *was* much safer than it had been when she'd grown up. She really needed to let go of her bias from twenty-plus years ago. They were happy here, she reminded herself.

"A private guided tour," Babulya yelled. But the contestant asked for an "F" and lost his turn. "Dummy," Babulya muttered.

Skye loved watching Babulya watch *Wheel of Fortune.* "Why didn't you ever try to get on this show, Babulya? You would've kicked everyone's ass."

"You have to go to LA for the show, and we never had money for it." Babulya shrugged, and Skye remembered exactly how many sacrifices Babulya and Mama had made to make sure she and Tasha were able to chase their dreams.

Remembering her new resolve, instead of trying to push her into going now, she said, "If you ever get a hankering to do it, we could all go together. You, me, Mama, Tash. No worries about money. Just crossing something off your bucket list."

"You're sweet, Bunny, but I'm too old for that sort of thing. Plus, what would I do with all that money once I took *Wheel of Fortune* to the cleaners? I've got everything I need here." She smiled and swept her hand around the living room.

The door opened, and Mama walked in carrying two bags. Skye jumped up to help her. "Skye, I thought that looked like your car on the street, but I couldn't imagine you coming over unannounced so late. Are you okay?"

"Of course. I wanted to talk about a few things and was in the area. Sort of."

"Okay, then. Do you want some ice cream?"

Skye rarely indulged in ice cream but decided it would be good for her soul in that moment. "Sure, Mama, that would be great. Can I help?"

By the time Skye and Mama got the ice cream scooped into bowls and had settled on the couch, *Wheel of Fortune* had just gone off. "Okay, Bunny, tell us what's on your mind," Babulya said.

Here goes, Skye thought. "I wanted to apologize."

"Apologize? Whatever for?" Mama cocked her head to the left as she took a bite of ice cream.

Skye swallowed and jumped in with both feet. "I know I can be a *bit* of a freight train at times. I want you both to have the best of things. Anything you could possibly want. Anything that could make your lives easier because you sacrificed so much for me and Natasha. But where I've realized that I go wrong is that I make myself the judge of all the things you must have to be happier. And I know that I don't listen to you when you tell me what you actually want or need. So I'm sorry for being that way in the past, and I want you to know that I'm here for you if you need anything—anything at all—but I'm going to let you tell me what you need rather than trying to force you to need something that you don't. Starting with your apartment. Everything I have today is because of the two of you, so what's mine is yours. All you have to do is ask. Or hint. I'm sorry. I love you both so much." Skye let out a long breath when she finished her big speech and felt a weight, one she hadn't noticed she'd been hefting around for years, float off her shoulders.

Mama reached out and laid her hand on Skye's. "Thank you. We love you too. More than anything." Skye sat her ice cream down and placed her other hand on top of Mama's and blinked, ignoring a pesky stinging in her eyes.

"We know your heart is always in the right place, Bunny. Even if you are a pain in the ass sometimes." All three of them laughed at Babulya, even as Skye acknowledged the truth in her statement, and she smiled, looking between them.

"What brought this on, Skye?" Mama asked.

"Looking back, I realized I'm not always happy with my behavior, and that started at home, with you two, and spiraled out from there." Skye sighed loudly as her skin prickled with embarrassment at her sometimes egotistical, self-centered actions.

"Is that all?" said Mama, her eyes solemn.

Skye closed her eyes, and a picture of Bailey laughing flashed in her mind. "Yes and no. It's all the same thing, but I made a mess of things with Bailey too." She struggled to take a breath when thinking about everything she'd done to mess things up with Bailey—not that she was alone in the messing things up department. Bailey had overreacted to an innocuous interaction, but Skye couldn't deny her past behavior had laid the foundation for the misinterpretation, and the pressure behind her eyes intensified, so she squeezed her eyes tighter.

"Oh, Bunny," Babulya said.

Skye squeezed her mom's hand and continued. "I'm not really out in the professional world, and I made her feel like a dirty little secret. Then she saw me and a colleague joking around, and she thought I was flirting with him to close a deal, but that wasn't it at all. But...I...I don't know. Sometimes, I do maybe cross the line when trying to close a deal. I'd never do anything truly inappropriate, but...she could have a point, even though what she saw wasn't what she thought she saw. I tried to explain, but she kicked me out." The tears Skye had been fighting did start to fall, then, much to Skye's chagrin. She was *not* a crier. She dropped her head onto the back of the couch, trying to use gravity to stop the flow.

"Have you tried talking to her?" Mama asked softly.

"No," Skye tried to say, but it came out more of a sob than a word. "I don't think she wants to see me, and I'm not sure how to get her to listen."

"I think you should try to see her now that both of your emotions have had time to settle down," Mama said. "I'm sure she'll see how sorry you are about everything in your face, your demeanor, just as I do. When you look at me, that is."

Skye lifted her head at that. "You really think?"

"Of course, Bunny. And if she doesn't, she isn't nearly as smart as she seemed," Babulya said.

"Thank you, Babulya." Skye rose and leaned over to give her a hug.

Skye couldn't make eye contact with either of them as she asked,

"Are you disappointed in me for being less than what I could be? And for ruining things with Bailey?"

"Of course not. You are a strong, fierce, independent woman. We are so, so proud of you, and you could *never* disappoint us. Ever," Mama said and stood to pull Skye into a hug. "Never ever." She squeezed even tighter before releasing to look at Skye. "And whether or not things are ruined beyond repair remains to be seen. I know you to be quite persuasive when you put your mind to something. Now, let's eat this ice cream before I have to go back to the store because it's completely melted."

Skye sat and enjoyed the butter pecan with Mama and Babulya while they watched some procedural police show Skye wasn't familiar with. Which was fine as she couldn't stop thinking about Bailey and how she could convince Bailey to give her another chance.

CHAPTER TWENTY-FOUR

Despite it being only eight thirty, it had been an exhausting day. It seemed like everything in Bailey's office that could go wrong, did. One of her best site superintendents put in his notice, a property manager pulled the plug on a huge deal that had been awarded to Bailey the day before, a truck delivering lumber to one of her sites had gotten into an accident and was going to put the job behind by five weeks while they waited for another shipment, and she just didn't think she could take any more for one day. She should still be at the office, but she hadn't taken Patsy in with her that day and didn't want to leave her home alone too late. She could admit that it also gave her a good excuse for a mental break so she didn't work until midnight. At least, not at the office.

As Bailey drove past the front of her house, heading to the alley, she saw someone sitting on her front porch. She couldn't tell who it was as she'd forgotten to leave her porch light on, but that was odd. Rather than continue around back to park in her garage, Bailey parallel-parked a few houses down and hopped out, her pepper spray in hand.

As she approached her steps, however, her heart leapt into her throat and made it nearly impossible to breathe. Skye sat on her front porch swing holding a bouquet of gerbera daisies, Bailey's favorite, with a sheepish smile. "Hey, Bailey," she said. "Sorry, I know I should've called first, but I thought you might not answer, and even if you did, I was afraid you'd tell me not to come."

"So you decided to just show up and stalk me on my front porch?" Bailey injected extra anger in her voice to cover up the jolt she felt at seeing Skye again. She wasn't prepared for her body's reaction. Damn traitor.

"I...did. I'm sorry, but can we talk? For even a few minutes?"

Skye bit her lip as she looked at the flowers. "I think there are things that should be said. Things I want—no, need—to say to you."

As much as Bailey wanted to deny her, her heart objected to that course of action, and she finally said, "Fine. Wait here. Let me put my truck in the garage, and I'll let you in."

Bailey stomped away, frustration coursing through her at Skye just showing up on her doorstep. The *nerve* of that woman. She was right. Bailey wouldn't have answered if Skye had called, but still. A woman's home was her sanctuary, and she shouldn't be expected to have unannounced people showing up. Especially the one person who still made her heart pound harder than it did the first time she'd ever seen her. Dammit.

Between the moment that Bailey walked away to the moment she nearly yanked her front door off its hinges, her emotions went through a roller coaster of hell. She was angry that Skye had just shown up, excited to see her, frustrated that she hadn't had time to prepare, angry again that she couldn't snuggle with Patsy as she'd wanted to and go to sleep, and angry that seeing Skye had started that familiar burn in her lower belly, and she was, in fact, a little turned on. She tried not to snarl as she flatly said, "Come on in. Patsy is out back."

Skye looked nervous, which Bailey had never seen before. "Thank you for letting me in. I…I wasn't sure if you would, but I had to try." She thrust the flowers forward. "These are for you. I didn't know what I should bring, but I know these are your favorites. Even if you threw me out, I thought you could at least have something pretty on your kitchen island for a few days."

Feeling very awkward, Bailey reached out and took them. Cleared her throat. "Thank you. I've got a vase in the kitchen." Bailey headed to the back, not sure if she wanted Skye to follow her or not.

Skye did follow—that was probably better—but silently, as if she didn't know what to say. Maybe she didn't. What was there to say? Their relationship had been doomed from the start because neither one of them was capable of a real relationship for a multitude of reasons. It was better that they'd called it quits before either of them had gotten in any deeper.

Bailey tended to the flowers, her back to Skye, and then turned and leaned against the counter, taking in Skye for the first time in full light. She still looked amazing, but there was a sallowness to her face that was unfamiliar. She also looked a little thinner than the last time Bailey had seen her. Sorrow welled in Bailey at the sight before she shoved it back down. "So?" she asked, hoping to get to the bottom of Skye's visit sooner rather than later. As much as she was conflicted about Skye's appearance at her home, and as much as she wanted to pull Skye into her arms, she knew that was the wrong choice and needed to get through this as quickly as possible. Before her treacherous heart made her do something colossally stupid.

"I...I'm sorry. I've missed you. A lot. I had a whole speech planned out with bullet points, but now that I'm standing here in front of you, I'm having a hard time remembering anything."

Bailey scoffed. "I find that very hard to believe. Skye Kohl is never without words."

"Well, believe it. I should've brought note cards." Skye rubbed her thumb against her index and middle fingers in a show of nerves that Bailey only recognized because she'd been studying her for months. She doubted if anyone else would recognize the tell. Skye cleared her throat. "I wanted to tell you that you were right."

"I was right?" Bailey couldn't believe those words had come from Skye's perfect lips. "Oh, that we were destined to fail? I know. But you didn't need to come all the way over here to say that."

"No, not about that. I vehemently disagree with your reasoning there, but we'll get to that shortly. You were right about being my dirty little secret. I hate that I did that to you, and I'm embarrassed. My first boss told me that if I wanted to be successful in this industry, I would need to remain hidden because I would never be accepted. I've realized in the last two weeks that he was a homophobic bastard, and that my sexuality isn't a big deal. At all. Ellie helped me a little there, but I also opened my eyes and realized that the paradigm I'd believed to be true was all bullshit. I haven't taken an ad out in the paper or anything, but I'm done lying. I'm done hiding. I would be lucky to be able to yell from the rooftops that you're my girlfriend. I'd be lucky if you were on my arm when I went to the NAIOP awards ceremony next month or the charity gala next year." Skye reached out as if to grab Bailey's hand, and instinctively, Bailey sidestepped and moved to the refrigerator.

She pulled out a beer for herself and lifted one to Skye as well. That was rude, as she'd picked beer because she knew Skye didn't like it unless she was at a baseball game and wouldn't accept. But she wasn't feeling hospitable.

"No, thank you." Skye cleared her throat again and fiddled with her watch. "Also, although I think you already know that what you saw between Rob and me that day wasn't at all what you thought—he's my friend, and we are sometimes going to have conversations that require us to stand close so we aren't overheard—I've realized I sometimes, maybe, do cross a line when trying to close a difficult deal. I've never, and would never, do something truly inappropriate, but you're right. I maybe occasionally lean a little close and bat my eyelashes a little bit. And it's stupid. I don't need to do that. It doesn't actually do anything for me."

"You're amazing at what you do, and that manipulative shit is beneath you. It cheapens you." Bailey felt a little guilty when the color drained from Skye's face at that last barb, but she didn't take it back. Even as she felt a little sick saying it. She maintained icy eye contact even as she unsuccessfully tried to wash the bad taste away with a swig of beer.

"I probably deserve that. I hate that I didn't even see that I was doing it before, but I can assure you that Skye Kohl is turning over a new leaf. She will use only her superior verbal skills of persuasion to close any and all deals. Which is important since she's going to be leasing Ellie's two-million-square-foot redevelopment. That's a lot of deals to close."

Bailey's throat was tight. She couldn't believe Skye had said she'd been right about all of that. Seeing Skye standing in her kitchen, opening herself so fully, admitting to her flaws, had Bailey taking a step toward her before she caught herself and pretended she was casually going for a glass to pour her beer into. She wondered if Skye noticed, but it didn't seem so. Thankfully.

Bailey slowly poured her beer, tilting it and pouring along the side to prevent too much head. "I don't really know what to say to all this. I'm sorry."

"I'm hoping you'll say you forgive me, but I hope, at least, you'll think we might have something worth saving. Something worth fighting for."

Every cell in Bailey's body urged her to scream "yes" because they did have something. But she couldn't do it. Terror seized her, squeezed her windpipe so tightly that instead of saying all the things her heart wanted her to say, she said, "I can't. I'm sorry. I thought I could make time for a relationship, but this business takes up all my time. You're someone special, but it's not enough."

"I'm not enough?" Skye whispered, a quiver in her voice.

"Not that you aren't enough. You are enough. You will make someone very happy, I'm sure. But I can't commit. I wish I was that person, but I can't be. I tried it once before, and I drove the woman I loved into the arms of countless other women because of my focus on my work. My uncle who owned CBC before me had the same problem. This job is too all-consuming to be able to have a relationship with someone. I don't have the time. I'm sorry."

The last two weeks had been painful but manageable. Bailey knew that if they got back together, she would still end up driving Skye away again, and the next time, maybe she would be well and truly in love with her and didn't want to let herself get in any deeper before the inevitable heartbreak came again.

"But you made time in the beginning. And you said that as soon as you had another estimator trained, you could back down your hours. Is that not true anymore?"

"No. There's no way. I was being naively optimistic." Bailey kept her voice flat. Emotionless. She wasn't sure how she was pulling that off but was grateful she was able to.

"And there's no way I can get you to reconsider?" Skye's eyes were starting to glimmer with the beginnings of tears. "At all?"

The last was nearly a whimper, but Bailey shoved all her emotions into a tiny box in her chest, never to be opened again. Maybe she could light it on fire just to be safe. "No. I'm sorry. There isn't."

"What if I told you I loved you? What if I told you I'd do whatever we needed to make this work? Would that be enough? What if I took out a plane banner at the Bears' home opener that said, 'Skye Kohl loves Bailey K'?"

Bailey's lips were fused together; she couldn't make her mouth spit out a single word. Her head was spinning in excitement, but overpowering the excitement was the terror. Even if Skye loved her, she'd eventually find solace in the arms of another woman when Bailey wasn't there for her. Just like Mary. Just like Uncle Chester's wives. She so badly wanted to sweep Skye into her arms and tell her she loved her too, but she refused. Since her lips still weren't working, she managed a shake of her head no and tried to clear her throat.

Skye grabbed a napkin from the counter and dabbed at her eyes. "I guess that's that, then." Bailey stood frozen in place. Skye reached out as if to touch her temple, which had to be spasming as Bailey clenched her jaw so tightly, she thought she might crack a tooth, but Skye dropped her hand. "Guess I don't have the right to do that anymore." She licked the corner of her lips and sniffed. "I'll see myself out. Give Patsy a kiss for me since she's still outside."

When Bailey heard the click of her front door closing, she slowly lowered herself onto the stool at her island, dropped her head onto the countertop, and cried every tear she'd been repressing the entire time Skye had been there. She cried for the love she felt for Skye but was afraid to express. She cried for the future that they could have had. And even more, she cried for the futility of the situation because she knew in her bones that there was no hope.

❖

Bailey still felt raw two days later when she arrived at her mom's house for a family dinner. She still knew that she'd made the right decision by sending Skye away, but, God, it hurt so much more than she had thought it would. Even so, she understood that sometimes, the right choice, even if painful now, would save her in the long run.

She clipped Patsy's leash on her collar and let her out of the truck. "Let's go see Grandma, sweetheart."

The smell of chicken baking had Bailey's mouth watering the instant she walked in the front door. "It smells amazing in here, Mother." Patsy seemed to have the same thought, as she made a beeline to the kitchen as soon as Bailey took her leash off.

"Where's Skye?" Jessica asked as she walked into the living room drying her hands on a kitchen towel.

"Uh…" Bailey *really* should have prepared for this question. She'd forgotten Skye was supposed to be at this dinner. All the men in her immediate family had gone to some fishing thing, so it was a ladies' dinner that evening. Of course they were going to ask about where Skye was. Shit. "She…couldn't make it."

Before Bailey could come up with a better cover, Jessica yelled, "Mother, Gammy, Roxy. Please come here. Something's up with Bailey and Skye."

"What?" her mother said as she walked into the room. "Where's Skye?"

Bailey still hadn't come up with a better diversion, which would have been futile anyway. She sighed and admitted, "We broke up."

"You what?" Roxy said, never one to be left out.

"We weren't right for each other," Bailey said. "So it was the only thing that made sense."

"Let's everyone sit down." Gammy was always the voice of

reason, thankfully. "It's always easier to be relaxed when we start an inquisition." Maybe not so reasonable, after all.

Once they were seated and Jessica had made them all a cocktail, Bailey's mom spoke first. "What happened, Bailey? Are you okay?"

"I'm trying to be okay." She recognized that was the truest thing she could have said. She'd had such a sadness lying over her for the last two weeks. Everything was gray and drab, and all of her favorite things weren't enjoyable. Every step on her runs was pure misery. She tried to enjoy a glass of wine, and it tasted bland. She tried to go for a walk on her lunch, but all she could think about was the walk she'd taken with Skye along the lake on their first date. She wasn't okay, but she really was trying to be. Somehow.

"So tell us what happened? Did she break your heart?" Gammy said.

And although Bailey hadn't intended to tell them anything that evening, she found herself telling them the full story. From Skye denying her existence to flirting with colleagues, and even her visit from a couple of nights before. By the end of the story, everyone's mouths were gaping.

"So after all of that, her admitting you were right, starting to come out, and committing to be different, you still turned her away?" Roxy said. Her voice held a judgmental tone Bailey didn't appreciate at all.

"Well, yes, but you don't understand. All of this just made me realize that our relationship was doomed from the start. We shouldn't have even started down this path."

"What?" everyone else said in unison.

"I don't think I was meant for a relationship. I don't have time. Just like Uncle Chester before me, this is a hard business to run. It requires a lot of hands-on time. I can't simply set it and forget it. We were going to break up eventually, anyway, once she got tired of my long hours and sought comfort elsewhere. Breaking up before either of us got in any deeper was the only logical choice." Bailey hoped that, as she continued to say it, the message would also be received by her heart.

"Please. Bailey, why do you tell yourself such lies?" It was Jessica's turn to give her a hard time.

"They aren't lies. History doesn't lie. Look at Mary. She was great until she cheated. All of Uncle Chester's wives? Cheater after cheater after cheater."

"No one liked Mary at all. Our hearts broke for you when you caught her, but honestly, Bailey, we all let out a sigh of relief too," Gammy said.

Bailey was taken aback. Gammy never spoke ill of anyone, and to now say they were all relieved when Bailey's heart had been broken? "What do you mean?"

"Mary was a beautiful woman, and she *could* be kind, but her nature wasn't kind. In the years that you were together, she never snuck into the kitchen to do the dishes. She happily let either your mother or me, who had cooked every time, do them when you both came over. She never once hosted us in her home. She didn't have a close relationship with her own parents.

"Skye might not have actually invited us, but she went along with her mother's invitation for us to all come over and couldn't have been more gracious or generous the whole time we were there. You could see in her every interaction that there was nothing she wouldn't do for her family. Mary couldn't even spare an hour a month for hers. And I'm not sure if you noticed, but you spent a lot less time here when you were with her. I always assumed that was from her pressure."

Gammy's words hit Bailey like a punch in the solar plexus. She knew that Mary was a little self-absorbed, but she'd never truly compared Skye and Mary. She'd thought their self-involvement made them similar, but the truth was, they were nothing alike. Although Skye came off as self-involved, she really did put her family first, and Bailey too. That stung, as Bailey had to admit she hadn't offered her the same respect nearly as often.

But—the big but—was that Bailey still didn't think that the company allowed for a relationship. "But that doesn't change Uncle Chester's and my track record with cheaters. The necessary commitment to keep the company thriving makes a relationship impossible."

Her mother sighed. "Bailey, no offense, but millions of people in this country run small businesses and are married. You can *find* the time. Make the time. It's not like you're so strapped for cash that you can't hire more help. And furthermore, regarding Uncle Chester, his wives wouldn't have cheated on him if he hadn't been cheating on them first. He had a wandering eye. He cheated on every single one. I think the only reason he sticks with one woman at a time now is because he can't keep them straight if he doesn't." The whole room broke into laughter. "If he had time to have as many affairs as he did, I'm sure *you* can find time to have an honest relationship with a good woman and still run the company. It's not like it's always been a curse. Your grandfather certainly didn't run around on Gammy."

"You're damn right. I would've cut him if he had, and he always knew it," Gammy said with a mischievous glint in her eye. She was a little crazy, and Bailey loved it.

But Bailey wasn't as certain as her mother was. Mary might not have been perfect, but she still didn't think Mary would've cheated if Bailey hadn't pushed her into it. Even if Uncle Chester's wives had all cheated because he did, he clearly didn't have to spend as much time at the office as Bailey did. Since she'd bought him out, she'd grown the business significantly. That required more oversight. More hours. Some people just weren't meant for relationships, and Bailey was certain she was one of them. Her marriage had to be to City Beautiful Construction and the employees whose livelihoods depended on her. No matter how much she wished it otherwise.

CHAPTER TWENTY-FIVE

The next morning, Bailey found herself in her garden, her favorite thinking location, weeding again. The rest of dinner with her family had been a struggle. Once Gammy had talked about threatening Pop KZ with a knife the one time he'd been tempted to stray, they'd moved on to other topics, but her mind had been on Skye and her heartfelt pleas in Bailey's kitchen a few nights before.

Then, right before she'd left, when her mom was saying good night, she'd squeezed Bailey tight and said, "Please think about giving a relationship with Skye another chance. I hate thinking of you alone, and Skye isn't Mary or any of Uncle Chester's wives. I really like her, and her willingness to bare her soul to you the other night despite how coldly you rebuffed her proves how much she isn't like any of them. And remember, you aren't Uncle Chester. You are so much more like your father and Pop KZ. I love my brother-in-law, but he's a cad and couldn't be less like his father or brother when it comes to being a good partner. I love you and want you to be happy. Just think about it, okay?"

Bailey had barely squeaked out an "okay." She'd given her mom one final squeeze and a kiss on the cheek before she'd left.

Bailey had barely slept that night as her mind had continued to replay Skye's confession and her pleas for Bailey to change her mind. She still couldn't think of much other than those tense moments and her mom's reminder that Skye wasn't Mary and that she wasn't Uncle Chester.

She stood from weeding and surveyed her garden. She had enough produce to cook a meal for Skye with food exclusively from her garden, just like she'd promised, and her throat clenched painfully. That was before they'd even started seeing each other, but she'd meant the offer. She would have loved to cook for Skye.

To distract herself, she switched to tending her tomato plants, which were nearing the top of their six-foot cages. She added a few strategic ties to help the plants continue growing.

And had an epiphany.

Tomato plants could only grow as large as their supports allowed them to. If her plants had flimsy three-foot cages, the tomato plants would be much smaller and produce a lot less fruit. Because she had huge cages, her plants were basically growing into trees.

Could the same be true in life and love? Would she have room in her life for work and love if she had the support of a partner who wanted to cultivate both with her? If she could get past her fear and trust Skye to support her, maybe she'd be able to find the strength and room in her life for everything.

Bailey sat back on the edge of her planter box and stared at her hands. Had she gotten everything all wrong? Was she throwing away her first real chance at happiness because of an unfounded fear?

"Are you okay, Bailey?"

She lifted her gaze to see Mrs. Martin standing at the fence. "Yes, of course. Why?"

"You've been staring off into space for some time, dear. I could see you from my kitchen window."

Bailey had no idea that she'd been spacing out that long.

"Also, it took me saying your name a few times before you looked up. That's not like you at all."

Sheesh. "Sorry. Nothing's wrong. Just deep in concentration."

"Does this have to do with that beautiful woman who hasn't been around in a few weeks? I haven't had a chance to mention it to you, but I spoke with her for a few minutes the other evening when she was sitting on your front porch waiting for you."

"Oh really?" Bailey was surprised. She didn't think Skye and Mrs. Martin had ever really spoken.

"Yes, she helped me carry in some groceries I was struggling with. She's a kind girl."

"She's a lot kinder than I thought she was when I first met her." Bailey smiled and remembered all of the small kindnesses she'd found in Skye. Sneaking away to wash the dishes so her mom wouldn't have to, putting up with Bailey's entire family invading her home, kissing Patsy on the head before she left the house, actually putting up a fight for Bailey herself...

"I almost didn't end up marrying Mr. Martin."

That was an abrupt subject change, but Bailey tried to keep up. "Really? I didn't know that."

"His mother didn't like me very much, and I was afraid I'd never be accepted into his world. But he begged me to marry him and told me I'd given him the strength to stand up to his mother. He told me we'd both regret it for the rest of our lives if we turned away from our love. He was right. I don't regret a second of the time we spent together. In fact, the only regret I have is that I waited so long to marry him. Every day wasn't perfect, but that kind of love doesn't come around every day. If you find it and you're smart, you'll do whatever it takes to hold on to it.

"Just food for thought. Speaking of food, I'm looking forward to some of those tomatoes. I'll see you later, dear. Off to boozy brunch with the ladies. Glad to hear you're doing okay, but don't forget that love is the champagne in the mimosa of life. Without it, you just have orange juice, which is fine, but boring." She shrugged and continued toward her garage.

"See you, Mrs. Martin." Bailey stood to get back to her tomatoes and saw a text from her mother asking about dinner that night. She apparently wanted to go to some place in Wicker Park, which seemed bizarre, but it was owned by a friend of Roxy's or something. Bailey didn't have other plans. She felt like she knew what she needed to do about Skye, but she needed more time to sit with it. And brood. Let it marinate. She couldn't make another mistake. If she went to Skye, she wanted to be sure that she didn't have a single doubt, and in that moment, she was doubting everything. Was terrified of everything.

She texted her mom back and said she'd meet them that evening at six.

❖

Skye parallel-parked on the street and wondered where Tasha's car was. And why on earth she'd been willing to drive Mama and Babulya to the restaurant. Them needing to shop sounded very suspicious. Especially given how much Tasha didn't like to drive. Ever.

She pulled off her sunglasses and tucked them into the front of her shirt when she walked into the restaurant, letting her eyes adjust. Could that be…

Someone bumped into her from behind. "Excuse me," he said and squeezed around, but she couldn't be bothered to acknowledge him. She was gripped by the person on the other side of the room.

Standing less than fifteen feet away, looking down at her phone, was none other than Bailey. Skye's heart stumbled over itself, not believing what her eyes were seeing. Could life be that cruel that both their families were eating in this restaurant that evening? Her stomach felt like it was falling straight into a quivering mass on the floor. Could that happen? Someone might need to call 9-1-1.

Bailey was focused on her phone, and Skye could see her little temple twitch. Bailey closed her eyes, and Skye watched her shoulders move as she took a deep breath. Perhaps feeling Skye's eyes on her, Bailey looked up and made eye contact. Was that a hint of a grimace on her face? Fuck. Bailey started to walk toward her.

Her pulse increased from elevated to frantic, and it felt like all the moisture left her mouth and found its way to her palms, which were instantly slick with sweat. Bailey looked really good, her long legs emphasized by dark-washed jeans.

"Skye," Bailey said.

"Bailey. Small world, huh?" she said, a small tremble in her voice. The pain of her embarrassment from Bailey's harsh rebuff after she'd exposed her soul still burned in her throat and at the backs of her eyes.

Bailey's face looked so blank. "Not as small as you might think. It would seem that we've been played."

"Huh?"

"I forgot, you aren't as used to this subterfuge from your closest relatives. Apparently, our mothers and grandmothers got together and planned this. But rather than it being for our entire families, it's just us. No one else is coming."

"Oh God. It makes so much more sense why Tasha said she was driving. It was because they weren't ever coming. I feel so stupid, I'm sorry."

"What are you sorry about?"

"Well, this is pretty awkward, isn't it? I just stood in your kitchen begging you to love me a few nights ago, and now, here we are. Me drowning in my embarrassment for throwing myself at you. Actually, you know what?" Skye said, remembering that she'd done nothing wrong. She'd put her heart out there and had nothing to regret. If anyone should feel regretful, it was Bailey for throwing away everything that they could have had. "I'm not sorry. But I *am* going to get out of here before I make an even bigger fool out of myself. Good night, Bailey."

"Wait. Please?" Bailey lightly grabbed her arm. At the touch, Skye's shoes seemed to grow roots into the polished concrete floor. She looked back and waited for Bailey to continue. "I…I don't have anything planned to say, but do you want to sit and have a drink? I've been doing a lot of thinking. And I think there's more to say. At least, I have more to say. If you have time. If you don't mind spending a little more time with me, that is."

Skye wanted to run, but the pleading in Bailey's eyes had her reconsidering. Bailey had told her the other night that her love wasn't enough. What else could she add? But a little piece of Skye sensed that this might be their last chance. If she walked away now, she didn't think she'd ever have another stolen moment with Bailey. Even as she feared for the safety of her heart, she wasn't ready to say good-bye forever, so she gestured for Bailey to lead the way, either to a table or to the bar.

Her knees went weak as Bailey intertwined their fingers and pulled her toward a quiet corner in the lounge area. Bailey dropped her hand to allow her to slide into one side of the booth, and Skye missed the physical connection, but they both picked up drink menus. Neither spoke until they ordered, and Skye waited for Bailey to start. She had already said everything the other night and wasn't keen to rip that bandage off again.

"Thank you for staying, Skye. Even though this was a stupid setup by our mothers, I wanted to see you. I needed to see you, but I didn't know how. Not after I'd shut you down the other night. Not after I'd been so aloof and callous. Cruel. I was trying to figure out how I could reach out to you without you rejecting me on the spot when you miraculously walked into this restaurant."

"Oh?" That was a surprise. Bailey had been cold as an iceberg earlier in the week—hell, even when she'd first seen Skye in the front of the restaurant—but Skye's heart began to beat a drumline of hope.

"Yes. I've believed this whole time that we were condemned from the start because I can't sustain a relationship with my work burden. I was hurt when you denied our relationship, and I was unsure of where I stood, but more than that, I was afraid. I was afraid that neither of us could or would do what it takes to make this work. I saw an innocent exchange between you and a friend and used it as an excuse. I told myself you weren't the person I thought you were and reminded myself we never had a chance anyway, so it was better to walk away then."

"I know it was that interaction with your sub all those months ago that planted the idea that I sometimes manipulate people with my looks, and I've realized that you weren't entirely off base. I refuse to be that person anymore, but you have to understand that what you saw with Rob a few weeks ago was completely innocent. We are friends, even though I want to punch him sometimes, and we were bantering—"

"I know. I'm so sorry about that. I swear, I'm not a jealous person. I saw you, and I was already worried about us and still raw over you having denied the existence of us a few days before, and I just used it as an excuse. It *became* the reason that we didn't make sense, and it reaffirmed that we would never work. It was stupid. I was stupid. I was scared, and I ran." Bailey's eyes were so wide. Her nostrils flared, and it looked like she was holding back tears.

The server brought their drinks, interrupting the tense moment, and Skye took a long sip of her smoky old-fashioned, appreciating the burn almost as much as she appreciated watching Bailey take a sip of her vodka tonic. She watched the long column of Bailey's neck as she swallowed and the peek of her tongue getting a drop left on her lip when she pulled the glass away. The world was a cruel place.

She continued to sit silently, waiting Bailey out. Her favorite negotiation tactic didn't fail her. It rarely did.

"My mom reminded me that you aren't my cheating ex, nor are you Uncle Chester's wives, all of whom cheated on him. Also, I am not a cad, apparently, like my uncle is. I'm not sure why I struggled with that for so long. You have a few superficial traits that seem similar to my ex-fiancée, but you are nothing like her in all the ways that matter." Bailey grabbed her hand. Skye leaned into the touch, loving the feel of Bailey's skin against her own again. "And I make my own choices, which will never be the same as my uncle's."

Hearing that she reminded Bailey of her cheating ex was a bit disconcerting. "You never told me I'm similar to your ex."

"It's not something I was conscious of right away. But the thing is, you aren't that much like her at all. I think I was a little afraid that you were, but you've shown me time and again that you aren't. Mrs. Martin told me this morning that you helped her with her groceries the other night."

Skye smiled. "She's such a sweet woman. She told me she'd be happy to give me a tip. When I was able to stop laughing, I told her I appreciated the sentiment, but I was fine. Then she showed me some pictures of her husband. She hugged me and wished me luck when I left. I don't think she really knew why I was waiting."

"Mrs. Martin is something else. She told me that she almost didn't marry Mr. Martin, but he convinced her that their love could conquer anything and that when you found your great love, it was worth fighting for. Then I got to thinking about my tomatoes."

"That's a weird hop," Skye said. "True love to tomatoes?" She rubbed at her earlobe, confused.

"Technically, it was the reverse order, but it's all going to make sense, I promise. I hope, anyway. Are you aware tomatoes will grow as tall as the support cages around them will allow them to? Most plants stay small because they only have a small cage, but with a six-foot cage, my plants grow into veritable trees because they have the support to keep going up and up. I think that's what my problem was. I've never had someone to help support me, so I was afraid, and I never had a reason to try to make room for love to grow. Do you see what I mean?"

Skye was starting to but was still afraid to believe what she thought Bailey was trying to say. "Maybe," she said, hedging her bets.

"I love you. I'm sorry I didn't say that the other night. I was too afraid that we were going to hurt each other in the end. But I do think—I know—that our love is enough. We can figure out all the rest."

Skye squeezed her hand but wasn't ready to let her off the hook yet. She took another sip of her drink. "That running thing has to stop. I know you talked to me after the second incident, but you really didn't even let me explain. You just shoved me away and gave up on us. When you're hurt or upset or worried, you have to talk to me."

"I know. I have this tiny tendency," she held her index finger and thumb a millimeter apart, "to run away when I'm afraid or hurt. I promise you…" Bailey squeezed Skye's hand until she looked at her. "I promise you, I won't ever do that again. We're a team, and we need to figure out our problems together."

"What about your lack of time? Can you really find time to be with me?" Skye was so close to throwing herself—and so desperately wanted to throw herself—across the small table, but Bailey had been so damn adamant about not having enough time for anything real. If they were going to do this, she wanted to make sure they were both all in. She couldn't give her heart fully unless she was confident Bailey was going to do the same.

"I've already started handing off a lot to Alice. We're doing well enough that I can hire another full-time person to take more off my plate too. I was reluctant to let go of some of the reins, but I've realized I can't control everything. I have to be able to trust my employees, which means giving Alice more freedom, and I'm sure you and Ellie will tell me if anything starts to go amiss. Though I'm confident that she's going to be great."

"Really?"

"Really. I love you, and I can't imagine a future without you anymore. Every time I try, it's monochrome and drab and lonely. So what do you think? Will you be my tomato cage? Except, my living tomato cage so we can grow together. Can we make this our last new beginning?"

Skye laughed. "Being a tomato cage seems bizarre, but I like the sound of the rest. And I want to be whatever support you need, so if it's a tomato cage, count me in. I love you too." She leaned across the table to capture Bailey's lips as best as she could. She'd missed the perfect feel of them. The smell of Bailey. Her entire body gravitated toward her, but the edge of the table pressed into her stomach and kept her from kissing Bailey the way she needed to.

Bailey must have felt the same way. She slid into the booth next to Skye until their knees touched. "That's better," she said softly.

Skye nodded and ran her thumb along Bailey's cheek; her skin was so soft. "I've missed you so much. I was so afraid I would never get to touch you like this again. Talk to you like this again."

"Me too." Bailey held Skye's hand to her cheek and turned her head to tenderly kiss Skye's palm and then each of her fingertips. Bailey's warm, wet breath sent a shiver through Skye, and she leaned closer, squeezing Bailey's thigh with her other hand to keep her balance when she started to swoon.

"What you do to me, Bailey, I swear." Skye slid as close as she could and found Bailey's warm mouth. It started as a gentle brushing of lips, but the feel of Bailey nipping her bottom lip sent an electric current through her body, and she opened her mouth. The lavender and vanilla scent that Skye always associated with Bailey surrounded her and pulled her in, welcoming her home like an old friend. Skye's head was light as Bailey's tongue quickly found hers. She moaned softly and tried to pull Bailey closer.

Bailey leaned away and murmured, "Perhaps we should take this somewhere else? Somewhere a little more private?"

Skye didn't want to stop kissing, but she feared wolf whistles might break out around them if they didn't, so she acquiesced. "You read my mind." But as Bailey went to stand, Skye held her in place.

"Aren't you ready to go?"

"Almost, but I can't live another moment without telling you how much I love you, and I don't care who knows it. I might take out an ad in the *Chicago Business Magazine* just to make sure everyone does."

"You're something else, Ms. Kohl. I love you more than I love to breathe." Bailey stood and took her hand. She helped Skye up, and as they walked together to the exit, Skye couldn't help but feel like they were walking hand in hand toward the rest of their lives together.

About the Author

Krystina Rivers has been a lover of romance novels since she was probably too young to read them and developed an affinity for sapphic romance after she found her first one on a shelf in a used bookstore in 2001. Despite a lifelong desire, she never made the time to write her own until the COVID-19 pandemic struck, and she had extra time with no daily commute or work travel.

Krystina grew up in Florida but, after spending six years in the military, finds herself now calling Chicago home—though she frequently travels so often for work that she forgets what city she's in. She works in real estate and lives with her wife and their two pit bulls and two cats. When not working, traveling, or writing, Krystina can be found reading with a glass of wine in hand, doing yoga (occasionally with a glass of wine in hand), snuggling with her fur-babies, or trying to convince herself that it's not too cold to go for a jog outside.

Books Available From Bold Strokes Books

Catch by Kris Bryant. Convincing the wife of the star quarterback to walk away from her family was never in offensive coordinator Sutton McCoy's game plan. But standing on the sidelines when a second chance at true love comes her way proves all but impossible. (978-1-63679-276-7)

Hearts in the Wind by MJ Williamz. Beth and Evelyn seem destined to remain mortal enemies but are about to discover that in matters of the heart, sometimes you must cast your fortunes to the wind. (978-1-63679-288-0)

Hero Complex by Jesse J. Thoma. Bronte, Athena, and their unlikely friends must work together to defeat Bronte's archnemesis. The fate of love, humanity, and the world might depend on it. No pressure. (978-1-63679-280-4)

Hotel Fantasy by Piper Jordan. Molly Taylor has a fantasy in mind that only Lexi can fulfill. However, convincing her to participate could prove challenging. (978-1-63679-207-1)

Last New Beginning by Krystina Rivers. Can commercial broker Skye Kohl and contractor Bailey Kaczmarek overcome their pride and work together while the tension between them boils over into a love that could soothe both of their hearts? (978-1-63679-261-3)

Love and Lattes by Karis Walsh. Cat café owner Bonnie and wedding planner Taryn join forces to get rescue cats into forever homes—discovering their own forever along the way. (978-1-63679-290-3)

Repatriate by Jaime Maddox. Ally Hamilton's new job as a home health aide takes an unexpected twist when she discovers a fortune in stolen artwork and must repatriate the masterpieces and avoid the wrath of the violent man who stole them. (978-1-63679-303-0)

The Hues of Me and You by Morgan Lee Miller. Arlette Adair and Brooke Dawson almost fell in love in college. Years later, they unexpectedly run into each other and come face-to-face with their unresolved past. (978-1-63679-229-3)

A Haven for the Wanderer by Jenny Frame. When Griffin Harris comes to Rosebrook village, the love she finds with Bronte de Lacey creates a safe haven and she finally finds her place in the world. But will she run again when their love is tested? (978-1-63679-291-0)

A Spark in the Air by Dena Blake. Internet executive Crystal Tucker is sure Wi-Fi could really help small-town residents, even if it means putting an internet café out of business, but her instant attraction to the owner's daughter, Janie Elliott, makes moving ahead with her plans complicated. (978-1-63679-293-4)

Between Takes by CJ Birch. Simone Lavoie is convinced her new job as an intimacy coordinator will give her a fresh perspective. Instead, problems on set and her growing attraction to actress Evelyn Harper only add to her worries. (978-1-63679-309-2)

Camp Lost and Found by Georgia Beers. Nobody knows better than Cassidy and Frankie that life doesn't always give you what you want. But sometimes, if you're lucky, life gives you exactly what you need. (978-1-63679-263-7)

Fire, Water, and Rock by Alaina Erdell. As Jess and Clare reveal more about themselves, and their hot summer fling tips over into true love, they must confront their pasts before they can contemplate a future together. (978-1-63679-274-3)

Lines of Love by Brey Willows. When even the Muse of Love doesn't believe in forever, we're all in trouble. (978-1-63555-458-8)

Only This Summer by Radclyffe. A fling with Lily promises to be exactly what Chase is looking for—short-term, hot as a forest fire, and one Chase can extinguish whenever she wants. After all, it's only one summer. (978-1-63679-390-0)

Picture-Perfect Christmas by Charlotte Greene. Two former rivals compete to capture the essence of their small mountain town at Christmas, all the while fighting old and new feelings. (978-1-63679-311-5)

Playing Love's Refrain by Lesley Davis. Drew Dawes had shied away from the world of music until Wren Banderas gave her a reason to play their love's refrain. (978-1-63679-286-6)